FREDERIK POHL

MARS PLUS

THOMAS T. THOMAS

BAEN

MARS PLUS

This is a work of fiction. All the characters and events portrayed in this book are fictional, and any resemblance to real people or incidents is purely coincidental.

A Baen Books Original

Baen Publishing Enterprises
P.O. Box 1403
Riverdale, NY 10471

ISBN: 0-671-87605-8

First printing, June 1994

Distributed by Paramount Publishing
1230 Avenue of the Americas
New York, NY 10020

Library of Congress Cataloging-in-Publication Data

Pohl, Frederik
  Mars plus / Frederik Pohl, Thomas T. Thomas
  p. cm.
  ISBN 0-671-87605-8 : $20.00
  I. Thomas, Thomas T. II. Title
PS3566.O36M37 1994   93-44782
813'.54-dc20   CIP

Printed in the United States of America

For Lester del Rey
Most helpful of editors,
Most loyal of friends

Prologue

Among the Ochre Dunes

The ochre-colored grains of fine sand ground under Roger Torraway's feet. He heard the sound of crunching like a cricket song in the thin Martian air rather than felt the grinding through his ankles. Not many human nerves connected to the steel shanks and hard plastic wedges that comprised his feet.

He glanced down at the tracks that he and his companion, Fetya Mikhailovna Shtev, were leaving on the windward face of this dune. A newcomer to Mars might worry that they were scarring the landscape for a millennium, so feeble must be the winds under an atmospheric pressure of something less than one percent of Earth average.

But what the air lacked in pressure it made up in mass, being ninety-five percent heavy molecules of carbon dioxide. Also, because this feeble atmosphere could not effectively spread the heat load that solar radiation pounded into the Martian landscape, weather systems tended to be global in scale: single wind cells circulated across the equator from the summer hemisphere to the winter latitudes, and thermal tides flowed from the warm dayside to the chilly night. Those winds racked up huge speeds as they went. A

1

long-time resident like Roger had personally seen how, when the surface velocity exceeded 100 meters per second, large sand grains and small stones literally skipped over the face of the dunes, scattering tinier grains and sending up clouds of dust that would hang in the atmosphere for months, like smoke.

His and Fetya's tracks would vanish with the next storm—which was about thirty-six hours away now, according to Torraway's weather sense. That prediction was based partly on his own on-site observations of temperature and pressure, partly on his latest download from the planetwide cyber grid which reported satellite data and issued hourly forecasts for the major human colonies at Schiaparelli, Solis Planum, and Tharsis Montes. These were places he rarely visited anymore, but from their weather reports he could easily triangulate and interpolate the conditions he was likely to meet anywhere in a wide band across Mars's surface.

Roger Torraway, U.S. Air Force colonel (retired— but then so was his branch of the service, along with most of the country it had belonged to), had seen a lot of Mars in his forty-odd years of exploration. He had traveled around his adopted planet at least six times, from Olympus Mons to Hellas Planitia, and skirted the edges of the dry-ice fields at both north and south poles. He had even visited the infamous Face of Mars in the Elysium region. As his world's number-one citizen, Roger felt he should investigate for himself this phenomenon, which had so fascinated and inspired the masses of humans left behind on Earth.

Feature writers in the Sunday supplements had debated the Face's probable origins ever since the Viking 1 orbiter had relayed the first photographs of the enigmatic, faintly smiling formation in 1976. Many people wistfully believed it was a purpose-built artifact aimed at the sky, like the Nazca pictographs in the Peruvian desert. But Torraway had established with digital scans returned from his own faceted eyes that the staring Face was indeed just an illusion of the camera. It was totally invisible at ground level. Roger had found none of the distinctive planes and shadows that had aroused such intense simian curiosity, nothing but a small saddleback hill littered with boulders. He was not even sure he had identified both of the ashpits that, from far overhead, had resolved so clearly into eye sockets.

In his life on Mars, Roger Torraway was often alone but never lonely. From time to time he met up with one of the thirty or so true Cyborgs who lived a free and natural existence under the Martian sky. Since each of them was designed to be a self-contained unit, independent of the dug-in human colonies as far as rations and energy supplies, routine repairs, tools, weapons, and grid links went, the members of the Cyborg population had nothing to share with each other except personal histories and observations in rare, fleeting companionships.

Some of these human-machine constructs were more self-contained than others. For example, the Cyborg Fetya Mikhailovna Shtev. She had to be the second oldest Earth-born creature on Mars. Fetya had much larger solar arrays than the ones in Roger's design. On Torraway's shoulders, those elegantly structured webs of photovoltaic film folded or extended themselves as neatly as a bat's wings. Shtev's panels, on the other hand, formed a broad standing canopy above her head like a potentate's parasol—ugly, but it meant she could rely entirely on Mars's relatively feeble ration of solar energy. So, unlike Roger, Fetya did not have to return at regular intervals to the path of the microwave footprint laid down by the orbiting fusion generator lodged in a crater on Deimos. Roger did. He needed that extra boost to charge the batteries powering his backpack computer, which monitored his auxiliary sensory systems.

Still, whenever Shtev met him under the tingling energy shower, he noticed that she tended to walk more slowly and seemed to glow with relaxed health. She even smiled a bit.

The differences between the two of them went deeper than their energy capacity. For example, Fetya was the product of the late Russian Republic's Cyborg program, also aimed at Mars, which had operated in parallel with, but secret from, the program at the U.S. National Laboratory at Tonka, Oklahoma—now the sovereign state of Texahoma in the North American Free Trade Partners—which had created Roger. With their typically Slavic approach to problem solving, Fetya's doctors had surgically removed all physical traces of her femininity, sparing only whatever kernel of identity lived in the cybernetic convolutions of what remained of her mind. (But why then, Roger wondered, had she retained the female-gendered names, the *imya* and *otchestvo* of a Great Russian, instead of adopting a serial number as the other Cyborgs of her line had done?)

Maybe that had been innate survival instinct, Fetya sensing it was necessary to keep alive something from her human past. Maybe it had worked, too. She still functioned, while the rest of her compatriots were long dead, having given out well before any unrecoverable systems failure or metals fatigue should have claimed them.

Another difference in the Russian Cyborgs was their skin. Roger's glistening, midnight black covering—his "bat suit" somebody had called it once, back on Earth—had been turning a deep, bruised purple over the years of exposure to Mars's high levels of ultraviolet radiation, unblocked by any ozone layer because the planet's atmosphere had never had enough free oxygen to create one. Fetya's skin was a dull green. With her overall heavier build and tentlike solar array, she resembled a cross between one of Rodin's larger bronzes left to tarnish in the rain and an old U.S. Army truck with a layer of grime on its olive-drab paint job.

As the two of them walked west, Fetya pointed her right index finger at a spire of rock that stood out from the gray cliffs that obscured the horizon. When her forearm reached full extension, her hand dropped at the wrist, reflexing in an impossible 110-degree angle. The movement opened a dark cavity through her metacarpals, exposing the blunt end of a blackened 9mm barrel.

"Bang!" her voice said in Roger's head.

"Do you still have ammunition for that thing?" He had not heard its discharge in the thin air. He had seen no muzzle flash, nor any wisp of expanding gas. And, even at extreme long-range viewing, he could detect no flying chips or spray of stone dust on or about the spire.

"Yup." Her hand snapped back, becoming just a hand again.

"With you?"

"Not anymore—too heavy. Nothing to shoot here, anyway. But I got it cached where I can reach it real quick—both nine-mil, and double-aught for the scatter tube in my left arm."

"But then . . . why bother going through the motions?"

"Practice. Keeps the circuits limber," Shtev explained. "Target acquisition and ranging, parallax correction, muscle alignment and tensing . . . these subroutines can get stale. Bit tables pick up holes. Have to keep them combed out."

"Did you hit anything?" he pressed, trying to see the outcrop through her very different senses.

"Yup."

"How would you know?" Roger was curious about all his friends whose systems were differently wired than his own.

"Retinal imaging says so." Shtev shrugged. "Point-nine-nine probability, anyway."

"Does that account for windage and parabolic dropoff?"

"Yup. Calibrated for Mars light gravity, even. . . . Or used to be, before that module decayed to fifty-percent reliability and terminated. . . ."

Torraway knew about deteriorating datastreams from first-hand experience. Despite the triple redundancy built into his cyber systems and the constant checksums they took with backup units orbiting overhead, Roger's computer-controlled senses had become subject to intermittent failures. "Microseizures" he called them, when his world went black for two or three whole seconds while the backpack computer reset itself and then rebuilt his mechanical sensorium from the raw signals.

Roger understood that he was just getting old. But what the actual design-life expectancy on his mechanical and cybernetic systems was, not even the humans who had built them could say. Alexander Bradley and the rest of the interface team back in Tonka had been shooting for a uniform fifty-year mean time between failures. That would have allowed Roger to live out at least the normal human span of three score and ten.

As if he were normal anymore. Or, for that matter, human.

Still, the discoloration of his skin and the increasing frequency of those microseizures gave him cause to worry. Was it possible that Brad and the other designers had slipped up? Were there other miscalculations buried in his near-perfect Mars-adapted body, ticking away like some kind of viral logic bomb?

Torraway looked down at his own legs. Even apart from the discolorations, he was beginning to worry about his skin's surface integrity. Over the years, despite his preternaturally accurate sense of balance and Mars's helpfully low gravity, Torraway had taken his share of tumbles and scrapes. He still had a supply of patches and quicksealer, of course, but there comes a time in the life of any garment, skin included, when the mass of patches will no longer hold together; it lacks the tensile strength of the whole cloth. The covering on Roger's lower body was approaching that moment. Worse yet, he feared the incessant radiation was doing more than changing his color: that his glossy, impervious hide might suddenly become . . . brittle.

Roger's biggest concern of all, however, lived outside his body.

The fusion generator on Deimos was subject to implicit design limitations—namely, its fifty-year fuel supply. Once, back when Roger had first walked on Mars, that span had seemed like a lifetime. But now those years had almost all ticked away. Torraway still felt no older, or not in the human terms of aches and pains, aside from the random glitches associated with his computer-aided senses. In fact, the excruciating surgeries that had made him Cyborg seemed to have gifted him with eternal vigor and stamina. But someday, soon, someone had better do something about the old magnetohydrodynamic reaction horn up in orbit.

He must have mentioned this worry to Fetya—or had she been listening in to the echo of his thoughts as they cycled through his backpack cyber and leached out to the computer grid?

"You know," she said, "colonials are all time building more orbital power stations. Maybe they spare you some juice?"

"Wouldn't work," Torraway replied. Each of those stations was up in geosynchronous orbit, locked in over one point on the surface and beaming its power down to a single colony complex. "If I depended on their generosity," he said aloud, "I'd be trapped within a hundred-kilometer radius of one tunnel city or another—like an Indian at a U.S. Cavalry fort."

"Which means what?"

"Uhh . . . You'd say I was like a Jew in the Czar's *shtetl*."

"Ah!"

"I don't want to be tied down."

"So, is simple. You must go back among humans. See to the refueling. Demand your rights as Mars first citizen."

"It's not that simple, Fetya. . . . That's an old-style fusion device up there, running on deuterium and tritium. The builders extracted its original fuel from Earth's oceans, but there's no setup on Mars to reprocess our limited water supplies like that. So the replacement fuel would have to come up from Earth. And that means one of the colonies would have to trade for it. In turn, they'd have to give up something the human colonists wanted more. My status as 'first citizen' just doesn't swing that much weight. Besides, I don't know the situation on Earth anymore. Nor, to be truthful, much about current Martian politics. I suspect the tension over Earth's claims to Martian territory would make peaceful trading rather difficult, especially in a contraband item like fusion fuel."

"Don't know until you ask."

"But that's the humiliating part—asking."

"Humiliation? So you feel human emotions still? After so much time away?" Shtev grunted in his head. "How long since you went under pressure and talked to human people with air-driven voice?"

"Not since Sulie died. . . . Oh, and I did go back for Don Kayman's funeral, but I just stayed behind a rock and watched the burial."

"Otherwise, just monitor computer grid when suits you?"

"Yeah, I listen in, sometimes."

"So? Listen in harder. Find out what colonials need. Help them get it. Humans suck up for gratitude."

"I don't know. . . ."

"She's right, Roger!"

The voice came from his left. He turned around to see the outline of his first wife, Dorrie. She was walking lightly along beside him on the crest of a dune. Instead of a pressure suit, she wore a tiny pair of shorts and a halter, with her dark hair flying free on the feeble Martian wind. It was a bit-image that Torraway sometimes wished would decay faster than the other random dropouts in his backpack computer.

"You really should go back and talk to the administrators about your fusion generator," Dorrie's silvery voice warned. "Time on fuel supply is growing short. . . . Only eight hundred and thirty-two Martian days left! Do something about it!"

"All right, Dorrie, I'll talk to them," he agreed—if only to turn the warning image off.

"What?" Shtev asked, from his right side.

"I said I'll see to it."

"Good. Preserve us all."

Roger nodded. After a few more paces, he glanced over to his left again but Dorrie was gone. She had not even left phantom footprints in the ochre sands.

Chapter I

She'll Be Coming Down the Fountain When She Comes

Tharsis Montes Space Fountain, June 7, 2043

Demeter Coghlan plunged toward Mars in a blaze of glory.

The tiny passenger pod attached to the space fountain fell at an acceleration of 3.72 meters per second squared, at a rate equal to the pull of Mars's gravity. At this stage of her eight-hour descent from geosynchronous—or was that *areo*synchronous?—orbit down to the planet's surface, the dynamic braking of the car's magnetic couplings restrained her hardly at all. No more, really, than a shuttle rocket in reentry mode.

Coghlan's understanding of the underlying physics of the Hyde Industries, Inc. fountain technology was sketchy at best. Somewhere along the equator near a place called Tharsis Montes, a linear accelerator stood upright at the bottom of a well dug deep under the Martian surface. The accelerator shot a series of ferrite hoops, each a meter in diameter and weighing almost a kilogram apiece, straight up into the sky. Moving at some tens of kilometers per second, this fountain of objects created a tremendous kinetic energy. At the upper end of their flight, the hoop-stream entered an electromagnetic torus that functioned like the pulley

11

wheel in a sheave block: bending the stream back on itself to descend at gravitationally increasing speeds toward the planet's surface. There the stream entered another torus which passed it across to the accelerator again, completing a closed loop of flying rings.

The system resembled a chainsaw held together by the forces of inertia and magnetism.

The impact of a gazillion of these iron rings against the magnetic field of the top block had originally boosted it—and the freight-transfer station built around it—high into the Martian sky. The top of the fountain extended from the well at Tharsis Montes almost up to synchronous orbit. As the top station had sailed aloft during the initial stages of construction, the engineers fabricated and attached a series of collapsible shells to its lower perimeter, enclosing the ever-lengthening stream against random winds at ground level and providing spaced magnetic deflectors that nudged the higher segments eastward to counteract the planet's Coriolis forces.

In those early stages, bringing the hoop-stream up to speed had consumed nine-tenths of the system's energy. The flying rings had consumed whole quads of electricity, enough to drive the industrial sector of a fair-sized moon. That initial input had come from a cloverleaf of solar farms and fission piles constructed on the planet's surface for this purpose. Once the operation was balanced, however, it required only minor additions of maintenance energy to stabilize the stream and the structures it supported against the pull of Mars's gravity. The power plants could then be diverted to serve other needs in the local economy.

The fountain only required small inputs to replace the minuscule amounts of kinetic energy that the freight handlers bled off in the form of electricity. They used this current to pass cargo and passenger pods to and from the interplanetary ships that crossed above the tower in intersecting orbits. The electricity also worked mass drivers, which pushed goods and people up and down the exterior tower shell between the top station and the surface.

Although the system had cost billions of Neumarks to build and power up, it now saved as much or more every year in the costs of rocket propellant and hull ablation—not to mention the occasional pyrotechnic tragedies—associated with orbital shuttles. Being wholly electric in operation, the Tharsis Montes Space Fountain was as quiet, non-polluting, and safe to ride as a trolley. In principle and structure this system copied the Earth-based fountains operated by the U.N. at Porto Santana, Brazil; Kismayu, Somalia; and Bukittingi, Indonesia. Like Tharsis Montes, these were all on the planet's equator and served geostationary transit points, although the technology worked at all altitudes and at any latitude; the small fountain at Tsiolkovskii, for example, was nowhere near the Moon's equator.

Although the Mars fountain's supporting stream of flying rings was silent and vibrationless in operation, their iron composition did induce momentary currents in the tower's metallic superstructure. These showed up as ionization along its outer surfaces. Against the star-filled blacks of space surrounding the tower's upper segments, Demeter sensed an aura of plum-colored light at the periphery of her vision. But as she neared the planet's surface and entered what remained of Mars's indigenous atmosphere, the blacks faded to salmon pink and the glow dimmed to a patina of lilac over the gray of finished steel.

Her mother's colors.

Despite the massive energies involved in erecting and maintaining the space fountain, at this point in her trip Demeter Coghlan was still essentially in freefall, after seven months of microgravity on the transport ship coming up from Earth. Looking out the viewport past the purple mists of atmospheric ionization, she was barely conscious that she floated on her stomach with her heels higher than her head. Demeter didn't at all mind a few more hours of swimming weightlessness; she was just glad she could finally give up those mandatory three hours of osteopathic exercise per ship's day. Demeter hated jogging on the wheel with her arms and legs strapped into spring-weights—even if the workout had taken off thirteen pounds of cellulite that she really could afford to lose.

Craning her neck, and pressing her cheek against the cold glass—or whatever clear laminate they used for pressure windows here—she tried to look down and see the base of the fountain. The column of violet light seemed to touch the ground in the wide caldera of a shallow lava cone. Coghlan thought this was Olympus Mons itself but decided to query that fact with her personal chrono, which tied into the local computer grid whenever it could. Certainly the fountain's transit pod would have an RF antenna in the walls or something for the convenience of passengers and their cyber servants.

"Hey, Sugar!" Demeter whispered into the titanium bauble on her bracelet. "What's that-there volcano I'm looking at?"

"Could y'all be a tad more specific, Dem?" came back the pearly voice with the Annie Oakley twang she'd programmed into its microchips.

"Well, I'm riding the space fountain on Mars, y'see, and we're just about at the bottom. There's this big crater right below us—I thought maybe Olympus Mons, you know? Looks like it could be, oh, sixty or eighty klicks in diameter, with an ash cone maybe five or six times that wide. So, is this an important piece of real estate or what?"

"Please wait." The lag must have been mere microseconds, because Sugar spoke again almost at once. "Regretfully, I can establish no interconnect with network resources. Electromagnetic interference inherent to the operation of Hyde Industries' space elevators must be blocking my radio signals. However, knowing that we were going to Mars, I did pack some general history and geography into spare memory. Want to hear it?"

"Go on ahead."

"Olympus Mons—with a diameter of six hundred kilometers and an elevation of twenty-six, the Solar System's largest volcano—is located at twenty degrees north latitude. That would be almost twelve hundred kilometers from your present position. I doubt even the southern shield of the Olympus traprock would be visible from your current elevation on the fountain's lower structure. On the other hand, the transaction coil for the Mars elevator is based at one-hundred-twelve degrees west longitude, zero degrees latitude, adjacent to the population center known as Tharsis Montes. That is the second-largest tunnel complex built by Earth's colonists to date."

"I already know that, Sugar."

"Ahh, right. . . . So, the nearest natural feature of any prominence is Pavonis Mons, with a height of twenty-one kilometers. This is one of the largest calderas of the Tharsis Ridge. After accounting for variables like pod elevation, atmospheric density, and probable dust-storm activity, I deduce this to be the cone you-all are describing, Dem. Chance of error is less than twenty percent."

Coghlan summed up. "Okay, so Tharsis Montes is the name for the colony—"

"And this whole volcanic plateau," Sugar put in.

"—while Pavonis is the big crater. Got you. Thanks, Sugar."

"No never mind, Dem."

Ever since her accident, Demeter Coghlan had placed certain operating restrictions on her chrono. For one thing, she had voice-programmed it with a persistent courtesy, rendered in such null phrases as "please" and "never mind." That didn't make Sugar any more human, but Coghlan found it easier to relate to a machine that talked like one. For another, she had limited the unit's on-line access to the planetwide computer grid. Consequently, Sugar had to announce where she was getting her data from and the probability for error in any calculation—something most cybers omitted in talking to humans these days. As a third precaution, whenever Coghlan went to bed she put Sugar and her charm bracelet in a drawer or under a water glass. That way, the device wouldn't pick up anything she might say in her sleep and report it back to the grid. Probably paranoid behavior on her part, but all the same it made Coghlan feel better.

Demeter now had little to do but watch the crater rise out of the Martian plain, coming up like an ancient puckered mouth to kiss the descending pod. She had the vehicle practically to herself, having boarded it between the rush of docking transports. Aside from several containers marked FRAGILE, which could not withstand the forced drop of a freight pod, there were only two other passengers.

One was a dark-skinned gentleman in a sea-green turban and knotted beard who spoke no English, strapped himself tightly into one of the contour seats against the suspension of microgravity, and haughtily immersed himself in the shimmering holos of a news-board. Occasionally he grimaced and grunted over the stories. Looking across the pod and reading in reverse through the projected page, Demeter could make out the masthead as *The New Delhi Deliverancer*, with an angry lion worked into the Old English lettering. All the rest was in some cursive script she thought might be Hindi.

The other passenger was a woman, fair-skinned with streaky blond hair, who wore a slinky metallic sarong that reminded Demeter of the South Seas. It had an embroidered slit up the right side that bared one pale and pimply hip; the loose fabric fluttered in the weightlessness and drafts from the cabin's ventilation system. The woman's only ornaments were a round, garnet-colored scar above her sparse brows and a large blue tear tattooed at the outside corner of each eye. Early on, Demeter had tried to engage her in conversation, but none of the languages Coghlan had practiced at school—Diplomatic English, Universalniy Russkovo, Mex-Tecan Spanish, or Classical Arabic— seemed to work. The blonde just shrugged and smiled a lot, in between tucking her sarong tighter around her knees against the Sikh's covert glances.

Demeter kept on her solitary sightseeing with the crater growing larger below her all the time. Just when it seemed about to swallow the pod whole, the rim's outside edge shot up past the viewport. Coghlan was left staring at a long slope of weathered, gray rocks.

A few seconds later the floor began rising under her. First her toes, then her knees dropped to the carpeted surface, then her outstretched hand settled in among the seat cushions. After months of free-floating ease, she suddenly had to support her own weight against gravity. The pressure grew heavier as the pod's descent slowed—although even Demeter knew without Sugar's telling her that the surface gravity would never reach much more than a third of Earth normal.

With a bump that threw her down on one elbow, the pod touched down on Mars.

The window showed a curved face of machine-smoothed rock, illuminated by work lights set at odd angles. Immediately she heard and felt the *click!* and *clatter!* of grapples locking onto and stabilizing the pod, of power leads connecting to its batteries, and the airlock mating with its exit port. After a few seconds, the door slid upward. Demeter's ears popped with the difference in pressure, the tunnel complex being maintained at a slightly lower ambient.

Coghlan glanced at her two fellow passengers, but they were busy gathering themselves for departure. She straightened her one-piece, wine-colored jumper, draped her nysilk scarf artfully over her shoulders, and plucked her two pieces of luggage from under the restraining straps—noting how light the bulky, soft-plastic carryalls felt in point-three-eight gee—and marched out ahead of them.

In the narrow, steel-paneled passageway outside there was no one to meet or direct her. Officially, Demeter was on vacation. Grandaddy Coghlan had thought she needed something new and exciting—certainly not more course work in dry subjects like

Practical Negotiation, Boolean Economics, or Cultural Apperception and Assimilation—not after she had just finished nine months of physical and psychological therapy, learning to use her brand-new, vat-grown, rebuilt brains. "Go to Mars, why don't you?" he had urged. "See the frontier, ride a proxy, shoot a wild thorax or whatever." G'dad Coghlan could easily arrange the transit fees and residence permits, too, being Vice President of the Sovereign State of Texahoma. And so Demeter had done just that, taken a vacation . . . with a few strings attached.

It was because of those strings that she expected someone to meet her discreetly at the fountain stop and at least carry her bags.

Down at the far end of the corridor—where it teed into a wider tunnel, this one faced with white tiles— she saw someone moving away.

"Hey there! Y'all got any—"

She came up short and dropped her luggage. Her voice, even to her own ears as modulated by masses of throat muscle and cubic centimeters of sinus cavity, had come out high and squeaky. Something like "Hee thir! Y'eel get eeeny—" Minnie Mouse skyrocketing on amphetamines.

Demeter grabbed her left wrist and ducked her head to put the titanium bangle close to her lips. "Sugar! What's happening to me?" she husked—and it still sounded like a screech. "I'm hyperventilating or something—"

"Wait one," the cyber said impassively. "Pulse normal, considering your elevated stress level. Respiration normal, ditto. Blood sugar and electrolytes all check out. O-two content is slightly high, though. Why do you think you're in trouble, Dem?"

"Listen to my voice!" Coghlan squealed.

"Wait one. . . . The Mars grid informs me that the inhabited tunnels are normally pressurized with twenty percent diatomic oxygen, seventy-nine percent diatomic helium, and traces of carbon dioxide, water vapor, hydrogen sulfide, formaldehyde, and other organic compounds residual to human respiration and industrial pollution."

"Why the high content of helium?" Demeter asked, curious.

"This inert gas replaces the proportion represented by nitrogen in Earth's atmosphere. Nitrogen is only marginally present on Mars, either in the atmosphere—two-point-seven percent—or bound up in the lithosphere. All recovered amounts are required to be introduced into the soil for improved crop yields. Consequently, the colonists supplement their habitat pressure with helium, which they draw off as a by-product of methane collection from deep wells. . . . I have four-point-two megabytes of supplementary data on the planet's gas industry and eight gigabytes of introductory material on tunnel ecology and the algorithms governing environmental balance. Do you want to hear them?"

"Some other time."

"Never no mind, Dem."

Demeter Coghlan drew a deep breath, calmed down, and decided that the air tasted like any of the canned stuff she'd been inhaling since she got up to low Earth orbit. It would pass for breathable, but it sure wasn't a Texas alfalfa field on a June morning.

By now the man at the end of the corridor was long gone. Demeter was vaguely aware that sometime during Sugar's dissertation on atmosphere composition the Sikh and the South Seas girl had pushed past her. She would have to hurry and get herself processed before the next wave of tourists arrived down the fountain.

At the tee junction she found another Martian, several of them in fact, all striding purposefully about their business.

"Excuse me," she wheezed. "Where do I check in?" . . . *Cheek een?*

One of them turned and pointed to a sign. "Anywhere," the man whistled. *Eeneeweer. . . .*

The sign said: ARRIVING CASUALS (NON-RESIDENT ALIENS) PLEASE ANNOUNCE YOURSELF TO THE GRID FOR FURTHER INSTRUCTIONS.

Demeter raised the silvery patinaed bead to her lips again. "Sugar, get me in touch with the local grid, will you? It seems I need to clear my passport or something."

"Sorry, Dem, no can do," the chrono replied after a millisecond's hesitation. "The grid wants you on one of its wired-in terminals. Something about giving them a thumbprint."

"Okay . . . which way?"

"Should be a terminal in the wall to your left."

Demeter looked, saw only a dozen meters of white tile. "Nothing there, Shoogs."

"Oh, sorry! Thought we were facing south. Your *other* left, then."

Coghlan turned around and found, about five meters down, a shelf with a keyboard and screen. The screen was blinking an empty moiré pattern. "Got it."

Demeter went up to the public terminal and studied the layout. On the shelf to the right of the board was a trackball; to the left was a contact pad for taking and BIOSing neural patches; and below was a two-handed glovebox. Theoretically, she could control a limited virtual reality from this spot—if the cybers would let her. She stepped up to the shelf, evidently breaking a proximity line somewhere.

The screen changed to: PLEASE ENTER YOUR FULL NAME OR CITIZEN CODE, AND THUMBPRINT in six different languages. The top line, she noted, was in Diplomatic English.

She typed in her name and laid her thumb on the pad.

"Welcome to Mars, Ms. Coghlan," the cyber said in colloquial Texahoman English—but pitched to the high squeak of a human voice on helium. Meanwhile the screen displayed tourist stills of the Martian landscape and tunnel habitat that vaguely matched the ensuing monologue. "Your visa is approved for a four-week residency. Accommodations for your use have been reserved at the Golden Lotus, Level Four, Tunnel Twenty-One, Bays Seven through Eighteen. Please regard this as your home away from . . . Austin, Texas.

"An account with credit in the amount of forty thousand Neumarks has been established in your name with Marsbank Pty. Limited. Statements will be sent on a six-month delay at the then-current exchange rate to your home bank . . . the Double Eagle Bank N.A. of Austin.

"While your tourist visa includes no travel restrictions among Mars's various complexes, please be aware that many communities enforce multicultural sensitivity awareness. Also, you may not engage in any form of employment for either salary or wages, actual or deferred, while you are a registered guest of Mars.

"Mars quarantine laws require you submit to examination by a registered medical practitioner to ensure against the spread of communicable diseases. An appointment for this purpose has been made in your name with Dr. Wally Shin, Level Two, Tunnel Nine,

Bay Six, at fourteen hundred hours today. Please be prompt and do limit your contact with others until after this examination.

"Thank you and have a good day," the voice concluded.

"Excuse me, but—"

The screen flashed its original message, in six languages.

Demeter checked her chrono. "Hey, Sugar! What's local time?"

"Thirteen hours, forty-seven minutes, Dem."

"Yikes, I'm going to be late to this Dr. Shin's!"

Coghlan gathered her two bags and headed down to the end of the corridor—the only end that seemed to make connection with the rest of the complex. She hoped to find, real soon, some tunnel numbers and maybe a static wall map with a big you-are-here sticker. Going back and asking directions of the computer grid sounded like a jackass idea, and Sugar's inertial compass was getting too easily turned around in this maze.

Demeter had made about seven left turns, all the time moving into wider and more crowded corridors as she went. Around her the air was filled with the treble whistlings of people in casual conversation.

Most of the tunnels in the Tharsis Montes complex were raw rock cut in smoothly arched tubes between tiny, hexagonal chambers. Side entrances from these little foyers led into the residential or commercial suites that made up the community. The rock surface, gray with red and sometimes black streaks, was sealed off inside with clear epoxy. The residents could never forget they were living underground—and under strange ground, too—instead of wandering through sterile internal corridors of white or beige tile.

As Demeter passed from one hexcube to the next, someone came up fast behind her and caught at her elbow.

"Excuse me, ma'am?"

She turned. A young man, curly brown hair and an Oriental cast to his eyes, was wearing a determined frown. He didn't let go of her elbow. She noticed he had a blue armband stamped with CITIZEN'S MILITIA in white letters, both in English and in some *kanji* characters.

"Yes?" Despite the rough handling, she tried to keep her voice level in John Law's presence.

He leaned in close to her ear and took a hearty sniff of her trademark perfume, Odalisque.

"Like it?" Demeter asked as coldly as possible.

"I'm going to have to cite you for a scent violation, ma'am. Mars's privacy code is very strict when it comes to infringing the sensory space of other citizens." He handed her a pink card with exposed gold contact pins across one end.

"What do I do with this?"

"You redeem it for the amount of the fine within five days' time. Any local terminal will handle the transaction for you."

"And if I don't?"

"Then the card will emit an RF alert that locks you out of your place of residence, forfeits your transport rights, and forestalls any commercial transactions—such as food purchases—until you pay up."

"I see. And suppose I just throw the card away?"

"It's now keyed to your body temperature, ma'am.

The minute you discard it, the circuits will emit a siren that usually draws an immediate—and armed—response. . . . You'll notice the surface already has your fingerprints?"

Demeter looked at the citation more closely. Where her fingers had first touched it, her whorls were now outlined in purple and green. They didn't fade when she held the card by its edges.

"I suggest you pay the fine quickly," the militiaman said pleasantly. "Have a nice day . . . and, ma'am? Please wash off that stink as soon as you can."

Coghlan nodded blankly and hurried off down the corridor, clutching the card between the knuckles of the hand that held the shoulder straps from her bags. An arrow in the wall directed her to a broad ramp for Level 2. She walked down it, tripping occasionally in the weak gravity.

In a few more minutes Demeter found Tunnel 9 and Bay 6, but no Dr. Shin. There was a doctor's office on the right-hand side of the hexcube, but it belonged to a Dr. Wa. The scrolling light sign—in three languages, only one of which used the Roman alphabet—proclaimed: DR. WA LIXIN, MD, PSYD, DDS . . . INTERNIST AND GENERAL PRACTICE FOR ALL FAMILY AILMENTS . . . PSYCHOTHERAPY, DEEP REGRESSION, AND LAYERED SYNDROME COUNSELING . . . HERBALIST AND ACUPUNCTURIST, SPECIALIZING IN THE HARMONIOUS WAH. . . .

Surely, that last word was a typo. "Way," Demeter corrected to herself.

TEETH EXTRACTED WHILE YOU WAIT. The sign flickered and went through its loop again.

"And a humorist, too," Coghlan said. Well, if nothing else, this Dr. Wa could give her directions to the absent Dr. Shin. Probably a screwup in the physician's directory, or the Chamber of Commerce's referral service, or something.

Demeter pressed the button next to the door.

Tharsis Montes, Commercial Unit 2/9/6, June 7

Dr. Wa Lixin was playing *go* against his desktop medical diagnostic computer—and winning. That bothered him because Dr. Lee, as everyone in the colony knew him, was simply a terrible strategist. So, when the grid let him win, he could only conclude it was buttering him up for something.

Everyone understood that the Autochthonous Grid—both the network here on Mars and the parent system back on Earth—was full of bugs and prone to error. Sometimes the cyber you were working on crashed its system through no traceable fault in the coding. Sometimes the system worked but your application crashed. Sometimes the application worked flawlessly but skewed your data with obvious—and unreproducible—results. Sometimes a Tenth Dan–level program dribbled away its stones in nonstrategic *ataris* and lost to a *go*-playing fool.

Some people said this was because the grid was infected with the mother of all viruses. If so, it was one so insidious that nobody had ever seen it, so rabbit-fast at replication that nobody had ever cornered it, and so mean that nobody would ever kill it. To actually kill the virus, they said, humankind everywhere in the Solar System that shared grid resources and datastreams— the wide nodes all over Earth, the local networks dug in on the Moon and Mars, the new nexus under Europan ice, and the freeloading terminals of the L-point colonies—every one of them would have to shut down their connected cybers simultaneously. Then they would all have to follow a prescribed set of debugging procedures and start up again using fresh-out-of-the-box system software and applications. Oh, and with all new data, preferably entered by hand from a penpoint or keyboard, or voice-op with a fresh sound-bit package.

And *that* just was not going to happen, folks.

Hard facts about what was actually wrong with the grid were difficult to come by, but Dr. Lee had heard plenty of rumors. The subject was the focus of a popular culture all its own.

One theory held that the grid was alive, that the virus infecting it was simple sentience. These people took it as an article of faith that a naturally occurring heuristic algorithm arose anytime you linked up a billion or so cyber units; each one acted like the node on a gigantic neural net. This argument made sense when you considered that most of those independent cybers were already operating in the teraflop range and could, with the proper programming, compose Elizabethan sonnets while beating any three geniuses at chess, checkers, and double acrostics. What the argument lacked was any scientifically verifiable underpinnings. Its adherents, however, had only to point to the grid itself and say, *"Ecce logo!"*

Some people maintained that the grid was God, pure and simple. This was the Gaea Principle written in silicon: any system that grew big enough and complex enough would begin casting random errors that *looked* like a sensible pattern. They said that God—or gods, or "the old ones," or some species of elves, sprites, or leprechauns—had once lived in rocks and trees, in the local babbling brook, or in a skin-covered ark somewhere. And now He or She or They lived in the sightlines and dwelt in the House of Number.

Still others said that the government had transmuted the grid as a means of spying on and controlling
its citizens. In this scenario, every cyber malfunction or
error was actually a fingerprint of the universal com-
puting conspiracy. The grid itself wasn't watching you
and hexing your data; some faceless bureaucrat was at
the other end of the fiberoptic, manipulating it for his
or her own purposes. How this belief system squared
with the fact that no single government, on Earth or
anywhere else, was big enough to encompass the grid
and all its multiplex activities, these conspiracy theo-
rists did not bother to explain.

Yet another group insisted that the grid was actually
the Devil, the Christians' fallen Lucifer, Archfiend
and Destroyer. They insisted that many people—not
they themselves, of course, but a "friend of a
friend"—had already sold their souls to the
machine. All you had to do, they said, was walk up to
a common terminal connected anywhere into the
grid and type in the command "MFSTO:". Then,
depending on your identity and billing code, your
background and status in society, and what the grid
thought you had to offer, you might get an interesting response. The demon, popularly called
"Mephisto," would propose to make a deal for something you wanted. Were you manifestly flunking a
course at school? Mephisto could change your test
scores and grade. Would you benefit from the
futures price of kilowatt-hours or whole-kernel corn
going up or down next September? Mephisto could
arrange it. And what you had to give in return, that
would depend . . . but it usually involved anything a
human being could do or know or influence, and a
machine could not. The Devil had a lot of resources,

these believers said, because he controlled so very many willing hands and minds.

So, while everyone knew the grid was spooked, no two people could agree on just how it was done. They only knew that the problems were unpredictable, irreproducible, and bigger than any one human being and his or her personal concerns. The scale of error was probably also unimportant. Once the grid and its cybers had crunched your numbers, you tended to accept them. The data might have defects and shadings—but so what? The answers the grid gave were still a thousand times more reliable than if you took off your shoes and tried to do the long division on your toes. And, after all, the results just *might* be accurate. You paid your buck and you took your chance, the same as with anything else in life.

Dr. Wa Lixin placed a black stone on the nineteen-by-nineteen lattice that the screen displayed. The computer responded by placing one of its white stones at random, then filling up the board with black stones and conceding the game with profuse compliments on Dr. Lee's skill.

Then again, maybe the machine was just broken. . . .

"You have a patient, Doctor," the screen announced. "Shall I open?"

"Go ahead," he said, turning toward the entrance to the waiting room. The door beyond, into the corridor, slid back on a plump young woman in a purple jumpsuit, her shoulders weighted down with luggage.

Dr. Lee perceived at once that she was more interesting to look at than the *go* board. She was high-breasted and narrow-waisted, with generous hips that promised good carriage and easy delivery. She had long, wavy brown hair, pulled back from her ears in a loose braid.

Her jade-green eyes were eerily clear and far-seeing; they looked like nothing so much as openings into another physical dimension. The coloring went well with her pale skin, which was dusted with the pigment splotches that the Caucasians dismissed as "freckles" and everyone else knew as a benign melanin irregularity. She was decidedly cute—if you liked Round Eyes.

"Yes? Can I help you?" he called.

"I'm looking for a Dr. Shin?" the woman said with a rising inflection. "The computer grid told me I had an appointment—"

"Are you Demeter Coghlan?"

"Yes, but—"

"Then I'm your assigned doctor, Wa Lixin. Everyone calls me Lee, though."

"Oh . . . Wah-Lee-Shin. I get it." She slid the bags off her shoulders onto the banquette beside the door and came through into the examination room. Her right hand still clutched something—a pink card, a fine from the local militia.

"You can put that down with your things," Dr. Lee said.

"But it'll go off, the patrolman said. And then the Marines or something—"

"Oh, piffle! They only mean to scare you, being a foreigner and all." He sniffed. "Odalisque? Nice scent, but a bit pervasive. We usually cut that brand here with three-eighths isopropyl alcohol. That'll get you past the gas sensors."

"Okay, thanks."

"Give me the card."

She hesitated. "What are you going to do?"

"I'll pay it out from my terminal. Then you don't have to worry about fending off the Marines."

"You'd do that for me?"

"And tack it onto your bill, of course." He checked the card's denomination. "It's only for ten Neumarks. Your money all comes from the same account, doesn't it?"

"Yeah, I guess. . . . Say, do you really have that much surveillance here? I mean, just coming down from the fountain, I've seen swivel lenses, motion sensors, and earjacks in every corridor. Now you're telling me about gas sniffers, too. I didn't expect—"

"Expect what? Civilization? Modern technology?" Dr. Lee grinned. "Our grid gives us an interconnect level about equal to any medium-size Earth city. This isn't the frontier, you know. We don't have drunken cowboys and cattle rustlers—or whatever you were expecting."

"But I thought Mars would be a bit less . . . supervised."

"If you're looking for wide-open spaces, Miss Coghlan, go on to Europa. They're still chipping out the first public dome up there. But here on Mars we've got hot water already, plus a five-star hotel, a sushi bar—though I'd stay away from the fungus under glass—and a whole library of virtual-interactive entertainments. We even, sometimes, have the rule of law."

"I get you," she said with an answering grin. "I just thought maybe I'd for once gotten away from the more oppressive aspects of society."

"Not likely. Not with three thousand people crammed into less than twenty thousand cubic meters of holding pressure. That's only in Tharsis Montes, of course. Some of the outlying tunnel complexes are even more crowded. . . . So, are you here on business?"

"No, just playing the tourist."

"This is a long way to come for a vacation."

"It was an early graduation present from my grandfather."

"I see. Well, hop up on the table." Dr. Lee tapped the lightly padded surface.

The woman hesitated again. "Do you want me to take my clothes off?"

"My, you really do think we hunt buffaloes out here. No, just lie back and center your head, hands, and feet along the yellow lines." Dr. Lee helped adjust her arms. "This will only take a minute or two."

As she sank into the table's depressions, he reached into the lower cabinet and took out the transdermal air gun. He chafed her right forearm and then shot her with a full spectrum of telemites. While the diagnostic terminal probed her bones and soft tissues with ultrasonics, the beads would spread out in her bloodstream to examine her body chemistry, inventory her antibodies, and report on a dozen other organic functions. Each bead contained an array of technologies for medical analysis: gas chromatography and barometry, carbohydrate reagency, ion streaming, DNA combing—along with the telemetry to broadcast their findings back to the table's receptors. Each of these nanomachines was inscribed on a friable silicon wafer held together by a soluble substrate. Twenty-four hours after Dr. Lee had finished examining Miss Coghlan, her kidneys would sweep up and dispose of the shards of his most sophisticated diagnostic equipment, which he bought by the thousand from an off-planet catalog service.

"Ow!" she said, rubbing her arm.

"Too late." He grinned. "Now, just lie still for one more minute." He studied the terminal's screen as it built up the template display of a small female skeleton in three-dimensional outlines, coded beige. The bones enclosed various pulsing, squirming sacks—her organs and connective tissues—that were shown in standardized colors, mostly in the pastel range. The small gold ring on her third finger right hand, the silver bracelet with the communications charm on her left wrist, the metal snaps down the front of her garment—all came up as hard, white gleams on the screen, as would any other foreign objects or prostheses about or within her person.

"I don't see why you-all have to put me through this," Coghlan declared, her jaw and throat muscles blurring on the screen as she spoke.

"You must hold still," he chided. Then Dr. Lee quickly brought his cursors up to the routine query points.

"But I've been in the equivalent of quarantine on that transport ship, for months and months," she said. "Surely any bug in my body would have died out by now."

"Of course," Wa Lixin agreed. "Still, we don't know what you might have picked up from the crew or other passengers, do we? Martian society cannot regulate interplanetary travel, you see, but we can prescribe for the citizens and casuals who actually touch down on our planet. So it's the law that everyone coming under our pressure be surveyed for communicable diseases, as well as for preexisting conditions that could create a liability situation."

"Oh."

"Now, *don't move!*"

He rushed to complete the examination, taking the telemetered data and making his reference comparisons.

"You're clear," he said finally. "No abnormalities whatsoever. And quite healthy." Perhaps a little too healthy, considering the way she was stretching that jumpsuit.

"How's that?" the woman asked, turning her head quickly, so that the upper part of the screen blurred again. "You got no traces of my accident?"

"Umm." It was Dr. Lee's turn to hesitate. "What exactly should I be looking for?"

"Well, 'head trauma' is the term they used back in Austin. You see, about a year ago I was having my hair done in an autocoif—that's an automated shampoo-curl-and-cut contraption?" she explained when he gave her a blank look. "Anyway, the machine kind of seized up. Seems the solenoids all burned out along one side of the helmet, or so the techs said later. It drove the point of the scissors right through the side of my head. Did it with such force that—"

Wa Lixin put up a restraining hand and stared hard at the scan on his screen. He zoomed and rotated the image to the approximate site of the injury she described. As he did so, curls and ridges of scar tissue—bone that had healed from an indented star fracture—built up around the outside of her skull. A smooth plastic insert gleamed whitely in the triangular hole that pierced her parietal plate just above the lower suture. The distorted tissue completed forming as he watched.

"Must be a lag in the processing," Dr. Lee murmured to himself. "All right, Miss Coghlan, I can see it now. Um . . . do you have any recurring symptoms?"

"No, nothing serious. Just sometimes, off and on, I have trouble concentrating."

"Enough to bother you?"

"I cope," his patient said bravely—perhaps even defiantly. "Look, this has all been fun, but can I go now?"

"By all means. And welcome to Mars."

The woman nodded curtly, slid off the table, and moved quickly out into the waiting room. She gathered up her bags and approached the outer door, which opened for her automatically. Only then did she half-turn and give him a wave of farewell before stepping into the corridor. Then she was gone.

Dr. Lee tapped keys that stored her somatic image and biomedical history in the grid's archives. That done, he settled in for another quick *go* game, before his next patient arrived.

Chapter 2

We'll All Go Out to Meet Her
When She Comes

Golden Lotus, Residential Unit 4/21/9, June 7

Demeter Coghlan's accommodations at the Golden Lotus were best described as a closet within a closet. Once she had dropped her bags on the floor she found herself walking in half-circles to keep from stepping on them. The bed swung down sideways on straps, just like in a Houston Judiciary Department detention cell—except the straps were clean and not too frayed. The screen and keyboard of the room's terminal wedged into a recess in the native rock, which had been dusted with gold flecks to make it look like the Mother Lode back on Earth. The communal bathroom was down the hall and metered.

But the room was a place to cache her change of clothing unwrinkled. It also gave her a sense, at least, of privacy.

Coghlan eyed the terminal. If she pulled down the bed, after hanging up her clothes, she could sit almost facing the screen. She tapped a key and waited for the screen to come up. It printed: HOW MAY I HELP YOU, MS. COGHLAN?

DO YOU TAKE VIO? she entered, two-fingered.

"Yes, this terminal is so equipped," a neutral male

voice, still three octaves too high, answered from a speaker somewhere in the rig.

"I could have told you that," Sugar piped up. "Just ask, Dem."

"Thanks, but I'll handle this," Demeter told her. "Um, Grid . . . How do I get out to Valles Marineris?"

"The Canyonlands Development Limited Pty. of North Zealand has this area currently under development for a residential and food-processing complex expected to accommodate fifteen hundred people in the first phase," the terminal replied, sounding like a canned spiel. "Named for the nineteen-hundred-kilometer-long gorge system and its many tributaries, which were apparently shaped by streamflows at an unknown previous time when Mars is presumed to have possessed quantities of free-flowing surface water, this district includes some of the lowest elevations yet charted in the planet's surface."

As the grid talked, still photos of the project came and went on the screen in almost random order.

"Construction activity on the tunnel complex is continuously monitored by my Library Function, Channel Thirty-nine, for the interest and entertainment of guests of the Golden Lotus. A virtual-reality tour of the finished complex model is available on Channel Forty-three, for those terminals equipped with interactive V/R capability. Applications to be considered for future residential or commercial status will be accepted through this unit by requesting—"

"Maybe later, guy," Demeter interrupted. "Look, I just want to get out there and *see* the place. How do I get hold of a U-Drive-It, or something? And which direction do I head out in?"

The terminal paused for what seemed like a whole

bunch of nanoseconds. "Personal transport on the Martian surface must be requisitioned from the Dockmaster, Tharsis Montes. Accommodation is usually assigned on a priority basis. As the Canyonlands Complex in the Valles Marineris District is some two thousand six hundred fifty-two kilometers from this location, you should plan on at least fourteen days of travel time." The screen showed her something like a silver-and-red Travelways bus galumphing along on eight articulated stilts. "The approximate cost of mounting such an expedition is—"

"Skip it. You're telling me at least three reasons—but in the nicest way possible—why I can't get thar from here, aren't you?"

Another excruciating pause. "Personal travel on the Martian surface is extremely difficult for nonadapted humans," the grid admitted.

"Well then, how do we 'nonadapted' types get around?"

"By proxy."

"How so?"

"Proxy . . . a person or device equipped with recording and telemetry functions to act on the request of, or in place of, another person."

The screen displayed, first, a human person under a helmet that was ringed with lenses and antennae. The person was also wearing what looked like a manplifier suit with detachable waldos. Next the terminal showed a metal ball of indeterminate size knobbed with similar pickups. The ball walked on feathery spider legs and sported two nearly human arms—which gave Demeter a queasy feeling.

"Right." Coghlan bit her lip. Something was not getting said here; she sensed she needed badly to know what that something was.

"Um, how do I get in touch with a proxy?" she asked.

"Through an interactive V/R terminal."

"Are *you* that kind of terminal?"

"This unit is not so equipped."

"Then how do I access?"

"Many public terminals, and those for short-term lease in some private establishments, are equipped with full sight-sound-touch reality interaction. Some of these units also provide patches for the inner ear, thereby stimulating the sense of balance, and to the rhinal cortex, stimulating the senses of smell and taste. Such features are usually provided at additional charge—"

"Thanks, I already know what Mars smells like." Burned rock and used gym socks, she guessed, with the sting of a vodka martini heavy on the vermouth. "How do I *find* a terminal that can handle virtual reality?"

"The Golden Lotus provides a full-feature simulation parlor for your relaxation and entertainment. In the public corridors, look for any device marked with the red V-slash-R symbol." And the screen showed her a picture of one.

"Thanks, I'll go out now and—"

"It is strongly recommended," the grid interrupted her, which was something new, "that first-time visitors be accompanied by an experienced guide. This is for your protection, so that you do not become spatially disoriented, and to protect the colony's equipment, which in the case of your incapacitation might become damaged or lost."

"I see. And where do I get a guide?"

"Many citizens will agree to escort casuals for a small fee, which may be paid directly—"

"Right. Now find me one, will you?"

"We will arrange for an appropriate person to contact you," the grid presence said stiffly. Then it went silent. As if to make its point, the screen pattern blinked off. End of conversation.

"How about that?" Demeter said to herself. "I finally managed to insult a machine."

"You do it all the time, Dem," Sugar observed from her wrist. "Why, the things you say to *me*—"

"Shut up, Shoogs."

"Never no mind, Dem."

Suddenly the gold-flecked walls seemed to be pressing in on her. The air in her room felt all used up. Demeter stood, letting the bed swing back into its recess. After making sure that the doorlock was properly keyed to her thumbprint, she went out into the hallway, turned left for the main tunnel, and went on an unsupervised meander.

Tharsis Montes, Agricultural Lot 39, June 7

Jory den Ostreicher pulled the plastic sheet tight over the seedbed and tacked it with a nailgun. To avoid ripping the material, he put his spike through a grommet molded into the rolled seam.

Tending the new crops—this one was low-hydro carrots, by the tag stitched into the seam—was just part of his outside duties. Every citizen of Mars had three or four jobs, all assigned according to his or her skills and adaptations. Putting in carrots, or any other plantform, was a communal effort.

To begin with, an injection crew shot a perimeter wall all around the plot, going down to bedrock or permafrost, whichever came first; this formed an impermeable barrier against the Martian atmosphere. Next, someone with a rototiller had to prepare the soil, which meant breaking it up and raking it smooth. Then someone else spread the necessary mix of chemicals, including a healthy dose of nitrogen-fixers. Finally, Jory came around with his rolls of film and tacked them across the top of the barrier dike.

The double-layer film was made by someone else, probably a home-factory cooperative working with methane feedstocks from the gas wells. They sealed the edges, adding the anchoring grommets and inlet tubes for pumped air and water. Another cooperative sprouted the seedlings under blotting paper and studded the film with them. They left the finished rolls in a compartment lock for Jory to pick up and spread. It was a real community effort in the best Martian tradition, and everybody got a share of the harvest.

Jory's special skill wasn't any green thumb—he personally couldn't make hair grow. Instead it was his adaptation for working outside in the natural Martian atmosphere. Jory was a Creole, halfway between the old-line Cyborgs and the nonadapted humans. In the cold and partial pressure, the average colonist would last about fifteen seconds before his feet would freeze and his lungs collapse; with the ultraviolet bombardment his skin would go melanomic and flay off within days of his return to a protected environment—if he ever got that far. The Cyborgs, on the other hand, were an import. They had to be gutted out and retrofitted on Earth because of the complex surgeries that adapted them to indefinite, self-contained, and unprotected living on the surface. But after that, they were more machine than human.

Creoles were the perfect compromise. The surgery that it took to make a Jory, brutal and vast in scale as it was, was well within the capabilities of the Martian medical system. A Creole had the best of both worlds.

Unlike the Cyborgs, the Creole looked quite human. He could move easily, almost inconspicuously, among his nonadapted friends and relatives. Yet he could also work and play out on the surface, unprotected, for up to three hours at a time without distress. If there was one thing you wanted to be on Mars, it was Creole. Not the least of the advantages was the bonus pay he got for light-duty, bonehead jobs like tacking down a sheet of carrots.

"Jory den Ostreicher . . ." the grid said in his ear. Among his other adaptations was a neural implant that put Jory in continuous contact with the colony's main cyber network, both sight and sound.

"Yes, what is it?" he replied, more thinking the words than saying them with his throat.

"We have an escort assignment for you. It is a newly landed casual from the Earthly state of Texahoma."

"Well, yeah, but you can see I'm busy right now."

"The contract is flexible. You may finish your outside duties first."

"Does this casual have a name?"

"Demeter Coghlan." His visual cortex flashed a sixteen-bit sketch of a chubby little face and dark hair drawn back into a ponytail.

"A girl! Aww-right!"

"Ms. Coghlan is twenty-eight years old and is well connected to the Texahoma political establishment," the grid droned, tipping a data dump from a file somewhere. It often did that of its own volition. "Ms. Coghlan studied three-and-a-half years at the University of Texas, Austin, in the School of Diplomatic Relations, but failed to take a degree. Other than her family resources, she has no visible means of support, yet her expense account is reckoned at . . . data-not-available. Ms. Coghlan's stated purpose for visiting Mars is personal tourism, but we suspect other reasons and are presently researching this with our contacts on Earth."

"A *rich* girl." Jory whistled under his breath. "I'm liking this better all the time."

"We advise caution in your dealings with this person, Jory den Ostreicher."

"Oh, sure! I'll be careful. . . . Did she say how much she would pay for my services?"

"You may ask any reasonable figure. The Government of Mars will supplement to meet your price."

"Great! Where can I find her?"

"Ms. Coghlan has been assigned space at the Golden Lotus, but she is now moving about the complex in a pattern that has not yet been analyzed. When you have completed your tasks at . . . Agricultural Lot 39, you will be given directions to her current location."

"Great!"

"We thought you would be pleased." In a blink, the voice was gone from his head and Jory was alone.

The quality of Jory den Ostreicher's work in tacking down the remainder of the seedling sheet was even more boneheaded than usual.

Red Queen Bar, Commercial Unit 2/4/7, June 7

Looking for some human company, Demeter Coghlan wandered into a bar called the Red Queen on the second level. It was hardly more than a largish cube off the corridor hex, crammed with half a dozen stand-up tables, no stools or chairs, and no human bartender, either.

Instead, there was a Mr. Mixology™ wall unit, ubiquitous throughout the human-occupied Solar System. Demeter wondered if she ordered a Texahoma-style margarita, would the machine do a better job of salting the glass than the last one she'd tangled with? Better, she decided, to simply order a beer and discover what new definition the Mixology Corporation's R&D Department had come up with for "draft."

Most of the tables were full, but a discreet peek showed her that only about half the room's occupants had legs and feet. The rest were holograms from a swing-out projector mounted under the table's scalloped edge. So, the humans who were actually here were enjoying a quiet drink and a chat with a friend or loved one who was somewhere else—on another level or in another colony half the planet away. And vice versa, of course.

None of the humans was unengaged and thus likely to want to meet a "casual"—for that's what the grid kept calling her—fresh up from Earth. And it didn't look like anyone would stay around long enough to begin a friendship, either. From the size of the room to the chest-high configuration of the tables, the Red Queen was saying, "Take your drink, enjoy it, and then get on with whatever you were doing." Even with the low gravity, you didn't want to stand around hanging by your elbows for long. This was a real worker's culture.

Demeter stood off, watching the quiet action, sipping her beer with progressively larger sips, and decided she really didn't want to interface with a hologram as soon as a table came free, aside from the fact that she didn't know anyone on Mars, except that Dr. Lee. . . . When the suds were gone, she tossed her mug into the cycler and went out cruising.

One level up, she came to a sign directing her still higher, to "Dome City." She decided that might be interesting. Demeter wasn't at all sleepy, despite the fact she had been awake for going on twenty-three hours now. The problem was the time difference: moving from the interplanetary transport's Zulu or Universal Time, in synch with every other ship and orbiting station, to Mars's own rotational time—which included a day thirty-seven minutes longer than Earth's. Add in the fact that the tunnels here were evenly lighted at all hours, and Coghlan quickly felt like she was floating in a bubble of unalloyed frenetic energy. Maybe going up to the surface and seeing what the sun was doing would help her adjust.

The first indication that she was leaving the underground corridor system was a landing in the upward-slanting ramp where it went through an airlock. Both sets of lock doors were open at the time, but she noticed that each was poised to swing closed at the first sign of pressure loss. Swing, that is, with the encouragement of explosive bolts whose arming sequence carried three warning signs pasted on the tunnel wall on either side of the door. From what she could see of them, the doors looked to be made of plate armor.

Evidently, the Tharsis Monteans—Tharsisians? Tharsissies? Monties? Montaignards?—suspected that explosive decompression might well be accompanied by a nuclear attack.

Above the airlock, the quality of the ambient pressure changed. Coghlan's ears popped, and she was suddenly aware of a . . . well, *surging* quality to the atmosphere. It was like being in a suit, where each beat of the induction pumps thudded against your ears and rebounded from the fabric of your neckseal.

Layers of fiberglass and steel sheathing concealed the actual juncture between Martian rock and the human-constructed domes. After a dozen steps,

Demeter was conscious of translucent plastic over her head. The material billowed gently: not enough to flap, but just enough to say that internal air pressure was the only thing holding its shape—and that there was a steady wind on the other side. She was positive the designers would have included more than one layer of ripstop between her breathable air and the attenuated carbon dioxide whistling across the Martian surface, but Demeter was suddenly aware that those fast-acting lock doors had a real purpose.

Judging from the quality of light coming through the UV-yellowed plastic, the sun had gone considerably nearer the horizon than it had been when she came down the space fountain. She started looking around for a window to check this.

The first dome was about fifty meters across and twenty meters high at the center. The space was walled off with head-high partitions. A second and even third level extended into the upper reaches of the enclosed space with pipework scaffolding that looked none too steady. Demeter noted that the cubicles directly under the platforms were tented over for modesty. Otherwise, the living or working units—or whatever else they were—enjoyed the bland sky of the dome's fabric.

Coghlan wandered around this collection of split-level huts, looking for the perimeter wall and a view of the planet's actual surface at ground level. During her search, she glanced through the doorway of one cubicle, which was incompletely covered with a hanging cloth. Inside, she saw a modularized office: a half-desk, V/R terminal, string chair, disk rack, and what looked like an old-style drafter's board—but with a couple of mice and an interactive surface. The sign outside the door said, CIVIL ENGINEERING, D2, WATER RESOURCES.

Clearly, whatever passed for government services in Tharsis Montes got second pick of the available office space. If there was ever a meteor strike against this bubble's fabric that didn't at once seal itself, it would be a bunch of low-level Civil Service bureaucrats who would be the first to go toes up. That thought did not surprise Demeter, who knew from experience that that was how governments usually worked.

This dome didn't seem to have any outside windows. She strolled through the igloo tunnel into the next one, which seemed to be some kind of garage. A large fiberglass pressure lock was set into the far side of the wall area. Under the bubble were a collection of walkers, sized according to the number of pairs of legs they had, like insects. Demeter had read somewhere that articulated footpads were the preferred method of travel on light-gravity planets such as Mars. It wasn't just because of the rough terrain, where practically every journey was offroad, since there were no roads. Wheels themselves were not Mars-friendly. They relied too much on traction to work. When the load to be hauled massed the same as on Earth, but actually weighed less than the coefficient of friction between the wheel and the underlying sand, then you could sit and spin for a long time without going anywhere. Left foot, right foot was the only sure way to get around.

The walkers inside the garage all had their hatches open and their access panels up. People and autonomous machines all had their heads under the panels, working on the innards. So, Demeter guessed, this wasn't just a storage area but a repair shop of some kind.

Not until the third dome did Demeter Coghlan find a window on the world.

This turned out to be some kind of low-gravity gymnasium area, with vaults, bungees, trampolines, and a pool of blue water for swimming and diving. The height of the fabric overhead made most of these activities practical, where they wouldn't have been in an underground tunnel. As soon as she walked through the strip door, Demeter felt her jumpsuit begin to wilt with dampness from the pool. Chlorine stung her nose. The room was almost deserted; she guessed everyone else was at work somewhere, looking forward to playtime.

Broad patches of the far wall had been left clear with a view to the east and south, and blowing dust hadn't yet scratched the window's outside surface too badly. Demeter walked up to the opening and looked for the nest of peaks guarding the Valles Marineris District— where she so longed to go. They were not visible over the curve of the horizon.

She turned and walked across the dome to the west side, to look at the sunset. On Earth, a heavier atmosphere buffered the sun at dawn and dusk, so that a person might stare directly at the swollen, reddened orb. Mars's minimal blanket of air could not create that effect, but the plastic window had a fader circuit— something she hadn't expected to find—and Demeter tuned it to the darkest setting. With that protection she could look directly at the silvery expanse of the photosphere, which was about half the diameter of the apparent disk as seen from Earth.

It was descending more slowly than the minute hand of an old-fashioned analog clock, right into the shoulder of the large crater she had seen during her descent, Pavonis Mons. The sun's low-angle rays picked orange and red flashes out of the cone's dark lava and cinders. In the foreground was the lower superstructure of the space fountain, already bathing the shadows with its own spectral violet light.

"Miz Coghlan?" a male voice said behind her. It was a high-pitched voice, even after accounting for the helium atmosphere.

"Yes?" She turned and saw a young man with bronzed skin stretched over a very handsome set of pectorals and a flat stomach ridged with smooth lines of muscle. His thighs were bunched and corded like Michelangelo's *David*, with that cute inward cant to the left knee. Demeter guessed he had a nice, tight set of buns, too.

"I'm Jory den Ostreicher. They told me you needed a guide?" He was naked except for a pair of gray leather shorts and a utility belt or harness that buttoned to them like a pair of *lederhosen*. His feet, she saw, wore only a pair of light slippers, also of the same gray material. The boy, this Jory, was hairless, with a head as smooth as the bottom of a copper pot, except at the back. There some kind of dark, braided tassels hung down his neck and dangled between his shoulder blades, like a Chinese mandarin's queue in an old-time woodcut. When he turned his head, she saw they were cables tipped with jumper plugs.

"Yes, they did. . . . I mean, I do," she replied falteringly.

He had some kind of beard, too, she thought at first, or at least a mustache and a little goatee. But a closer look showed this was not hair. There was some sort of dark pouching of his skin. The folds on either side of his mouth concealed Velcro tabs for hooking up a breathing mask.

His ears were long and cupped, like a German shepherd's or a bat's, and stood away from the side of his head. The focus of the lobes' curves was not ear canals but small buttons of transparent skin, like miniature timpani. They were perfect for hearing in a fractional atmosphere yet could function under normal pressure as well.

"Unh . . . what *are* you?" she asked after an awkward pause.

"I'm a Creole." He grinned. "Adapted for work on the surface."

"Oh, a Cyborg, you mean."

"Nah, they're nothing but wires and pistons, with a computer where their brains used to be. But I'm fully human, except for some enhancements."

"I see. So, you'd be my . . . proxy? I'd look through your eyes to—"

"No, *I* don't prox for nobody. Underneath this skin I'm a person, just like you. But I'll go along with you when you take out a unit. With my knowledge of the territory around here, you won't get lost."

"Do you know the Valles Marineris District?"

"Sure, been there a thousand times."

"Can we go now?"

Jory's face froze. His eyes took on a faraway look and his head tilted slowly to one side. The seizure, if that's what it was, lasted for about ten seconds. Demeter started toward the boy, afraid he would fall and hurt himself.

"Not today," he said finally, his eyes coming back into focus. "All the proxies within walking distance of the Valles are currently booked. But I've reserved a pair for us tomorrow."

"A pair?" Demeter said, stepping back into her usual conversational space. "Do you use virtual reality, then?"

"Hell yes, lady! I mean, I *could* walk there, but it's a hell of . . . a long ways to go. Mars gets real cold at night, too, if you know what I mean."

With that last comment he gave Demeter a look that—despite the nictitating membrane that involuntarily wiped across his eyeball in the moist, chemical-laden air—could only be described as a leer.

"I understand, Mr. den Ostreicher," Demeter said coolly. And she hoped *he* would understand, too.

Mars Reference 0° 2' S, III° 7.5' E, June 7, 2043

From the rattling and gurgling that assaulted her audio pickup, Sugar deduced that Demeter Coghlan had once again worn her comm bead in the shower. Yes, the focused roar of the hot-air jets, along with a marked rise in internal temperature, proved it. Oh well, Sugar was guaranteed waterproof.

From the readout of her inertial guidance system, Sugar estimated that they had returned to Demeter's room at the Golden Lotus, and from there to the bathroom. Now, from the aural imaging of doors opening and closing, and from the *clank!* as the charm bracelet to which she was attached hit some flat surface—with, by the sound of it, one-point-two cubic meters of storage space underlying a layer of compressed fibers that might or might not be plaited polystyrene—Sugar knew her mistress was bedding down for the night. Time for Sugar herself to suspend function and recharge her batteries from the grid's broadcast wave.

Then the chrono heard a distinctive rattle: the keys depressing on the room's terminal board.

"Communications!" Demeter's voice spoke softly.

"Yes, Dem?" Sugar replied instantly.

"Not you, Shoogs. I want the room's terminal."

"Never no mind, Dem."

"Yes, Ms. Coghlan?" the terminal said—in what Sugar judged to be a slowed and octave-adjusted synthetic female voice trying to pass for nonaggressive male.

"Take a letter," Coghlan directed. "Digitize and compress for Earth transmission with the next signal alignment. . . ."

Sugar countermanded her own SUSPEND order. Any correspondence the boss initiated, she would probably want to call up and discuss later. Sugar decided to listen in and at least find out the file number for grid reference.

"Recording," said that fakey voice.

"To Gregor Weiss, Survey Director, Texahoma Martian Development Corporation, Dallas—and look the rest up in your Earth directory—Dear Greg . . ."

Demeter's voice paused for many nanoseconds.

"Umm, I've arrived on Mars, place called Tharsis Montes, where the elevator is, without incident—ah, Terminal?"

"Yes, miss?"

"You might put a few prepositions in there for me— whatever sounds good—and a few less commas. You don't need to register every breath I take, hey?"

"Very good."

"Text resumes. I'm passing the cover story you and Gee-dad worked up, about my needing a long vacation, and so far nobody's interested. Nobody even knows I'm here, except maybe the computer system, and it doesn't seem to care, either. They made me get a physical, looking out for contagious diseases, they say, and that's about all.

"Paragraph. I've already established that the Zealanders are pushing ahead with the Valles Marineris area. Them or their agents here on Mars, that is. I didn't get any maps, yet, but from the pix the grid was showing me, the site of their development seems to be right in the area we're claiming. At least, the erosion layers look enough like the aerial survey analysis you made me memorize.

"Paragraph. The development, which they call quote Canyonlands unquote—Terminal, use punctuation marks there, will you, not the words themselves—claims to be for residential and food processing. And it looks as if they're digging in, just like every other colony complex on this dustball. So, Greg, I would guess they *haven't* figured out yet that the Marineris District is at a deep enough elevation for air pressure to build up faster than anywhere else on the surface. And open water, if and when, will collect there soonest, too. I don't know if the Zealanders can be brought around to our terraforming scheme. And you might get me a care package of better intelligence a sap—no, Terminal, that's one word, all caps . . . Jesus! you're a dumb machine!—but, anyway, I guess they'd be almighty unhappy if they were to finish digging out a honeycomb of tunnels below bedrock just about the time we flood out the area with a lake or inland sea or something.

"Paragraph. Anyway, I've got a date tomorrow with one of the locals to go vee-are with a piece of the construction equipment or something. That'll get me a sight of the area, and we can begin figuring how big an ouch the Zealanders will start registering when we file our project. I'll have more when I get back.

"Paragraph. On other topics—yee-ee-hew!—no, that was a yawn, so don't print it—I said, back up and erase that—no, not the whole—shit!

"Paragraph. On other topics, tell Gee-dad I'm in great

shape and think I'm fully recovered from the accident. And no, there are *no* little third-generation Coghlans on the horizon. This is a working trip, not some kind of shipboard romance. Though, I tell you, Greg, if I were tempted to rattle the old fuddy's chain, there's this sexy little bunch I met today with the slickest skin, about medium chocolate, if you know what I—"

Thunk!

Sugar knew that sound, too. It was some kind of cap or cover coming down over the charm bracelet, blocking out all distinct sounds.

Demeter had this thing about even talking sex in front of computers, let alone doing it. But, of course, what did she think was taking her dictation right then? Anyway, Sugar's eavesdropping was over for the evening. Time to get some juice.

SUSPEND. . . .

Chapter 3

Teaching Your Grandfather
to Suck Eggs

Golden Lotus, June 8

After a morning shower that was both metered and timed—allowing her only twenty-five seconds to shampoo and rinse her long tangle of hair—Demeter Coghlan went for breakfast in the hotel's cafeteria-style dining room. The scrambled eggs (if that's what they were), sausage, and vegetables were served chopstick-style, with enough sauce to bind them for first-timers in the low gravity. Demeter broke down and asked for a spoon, got something that resembled a high-sided rowboat with a long prow, and ended up popping down the biggest pieces with her fingers. Different cultures, different manners.

She still had about an hour before her date to go touring with that gorgeous guide, Jory Whatsisname. Demeter decided to use it improving her intelligence.

Normally Coghlan would prefer to go snooping with Sugar's help, because the little comm unit could be amazingly discreet if she was told to be. But for this job Demeter wanted visuals, full-motion if available, and binaural audio as well as pure voice-only data. So, back in her room, she called up the terminal.

"Umm. . . ." Demeter hesitated, trying to frame her

questions casually. "I'd like some information on some other people who might be visiting Mars about now."

"Casuals are listed in Directory Four," the machine told her.

"Oh!" So Coghlan wouldn't have to get personal with the grid after all. Her two fingers glided across the trackball, pulling down the correct directories and constructing her search pattern. What she wanted was a feeling for the opposition. The index showed a total of five North Zealanders and two United Koreans on-planet. Demeter called for dossiers—or whatever the local courtesy term was—with pix if possible.

The five Zealanders looked to be duds: two married pairs and a single, all with ages above fifty.

One of the pairs—the Bradens, William and Jane— had formally applied for colonial status. The other two—Peter Wendall and his wife Genevieve—were shown as visiting the Bradens in their new farming community on the edge of Elysium.

Further analysis showed that these four people were actually related: Jane Braden being Peter's sister. Demeter didn't have a detailed picture of the North Zealand Economic Development Agency, known as "N-ZED" in the business, but she didn't think their operating budget extended to paying passage on four people and colonial-placement fees on two more just to place one spy. Besides, Elysium was half a world away from Valles Marineris—not very convenient for keeping subtle tabs on the locals' progress with their Canyon-lands development, even with telepresent capability.

The terminal screen showed her in succession four alert faces, all with strong chins and heavy brows, all with white skins kept tanned and taut by clean living, hard work, and lots of exercise under expensive lamps.

Pioneer types with first-rate educations, they would probably bring a whole arsenal of physics formulas to the job of fixing a water pump, but Demeter had no doubt they'd get it fixed.

The unmarried Zealander, Alfred Mann, was no relation to this family grouping, and his reason for visiting Mars was shown as "astronomical interests," which was vague enough to be suspicious. But Demeter determined that he had touched down at Tharsis Montes just long enough to get a shuttle ride up to Phobos, where he'd spent the last six months at the observatory. So he could be eliminated as a factor.

The two Koreans caught her eye. They were traveling together, officially as master and servant—an odd listing for functionaries from one of Asia's nominally most democratic nations. Although, actually, United Korea controlled just the enclave around Seoul, from Kaesong in the north to Inchon in the south, hardly a nation in itself. More like a city-state.

The dominant member of this pair was one Sun Il Suk, whose profession was simply "playboy." That meant some kind of family money, withdrawn from one of the *chaebols*. The servant was a Chang Qwok-Do, whose employment status was shown as "retainer to the Sun family."

The screen showed her two sallow Asian faces, one fat, one thin, both in their twenties, both with the sort of eyes that were used to squinting down the sights of a rifle when the game went on two legs instead of four. Either or both of these might well be agents of the U.K. Ministry for Foreign Investments.

As Demeter was snooping around in the visitors' database, a new entry fitting her search parameters came up on the screen: Nancy Cuneo, nationality North

Zealand, registered for casual status within the past
twenty-four hours and due to arrive on the transport
Spacewinds during the next thirty-six. Her bio showed
her leaving Earth from the Sumatra Space Fountain,
which might or might not be the most direct route
from her home in Auckland. Traveling in a hurry, was
she? Cuneo's destination was listed as Tharsis Montes,
which was as far as Demeter herself had gotten. The
woman's reason for visiting Mars was listed as "commercial representative," but with the company
affiliation left blank.

Demeter's senses screamed, "Spy!"

The only trouble was the passport photo, which
showed a woman in her late middle life, with an official
age of forty-two. The hair—straight and black in a
modish helmet cut—showed no gray at all. The eyes
were lively and young. But the raster scan had picked
up a webwork of wrinkles at the corners of her eyes
and scallops of hard smile-lines around her mouth.
Even a good basecoat of pancake and a dusting of pow-
der couldn't hide the loss of skin elasticity worked by
gravity and time. Cuneo was sixty-two if she was a day
—that was Demeter's professional opinion.

Well, not all spies had to be young and beautiful.

Coghlan memorized the face and hair and the
sketchy details from Nancy Cuneo's biography . . . one
old dame she would watch out for!

By the time she was through with the terminal,
Demeter was already ten minutes late for her tourist
session with Jory.

Ingot Collection Point 4, East of Tharsis Montes, June 8

Jory den Ostreicher walked down the trail into the
lowlands valley and approached the squirming pile of

von Neumann processors. A good crop had come in, better than last time he did this job. About twenty-five percent better.

"That is according to yield projections," the grid told him.

"Yeah, but it always amazes me when the real world fits its curve," Jory explained.

He reached for the nearest processor. It was still moving, trying to climb the pile to reach the exact center of the homing ground. With his pincers clamp and striker bar—tools adapted for this particular job—he cracked its top shell along the bifurcation line. Instantly, the von Neumann stopped moving, just like it had been programmed to.

"Connect me to the public terminal outside the Red Queen Bar," he said to the grid.

"Do you have the link number?" that disembodied voice asked.

"No, just trace it, will you?" And subvocally, as barely a conscious afterthought, he added, "Earn your keep, why don't you?"

"We heard that! . . . Connection is made, you may proceed voice only."

Red Queen Bar, June 8

When Demeter got to their agreed-upon rendez-vous, the Red Queen, there was no Jory. She could have asked him to pick her up at the hotel, but that situation had implications she was not ready to explore. It just felt safer to establish a neutral territory.

Except, he hadn't shown. Demeter consulted Sugar and learned it was only eleven minutes after their appointed meeting time. She thought the boy was being unreasonable, not to wait *that* long. After all, she was paying him, wasn't she?

Coghlan walked over to the nearby wall terminal, about to register a formal complaint with the computer grid that seemed to run visitor functions here on Mars. As she put out her hand, the screen lit up with a picture of Jory den Ostreicher, smiling carelessly into the lens. From the quality of the image, and the raw state of the surgery around his mouth and eyes, she guessed this was an identity pic of the newly created Creole, drawn from some disk archive.

"Hello, Demeter?" the speaker said, loud enough to be heard across the corridor.

"Jory? Where are you?"

"At work. Look, I didn't forget we had a date, but we'll have to call it off. I couldn't get any proxies for the Valles area. The two guys who had the tourist models have extended their booking, and all the utility machines are scheduled out. Maybe we can go tomorrow."

"Oh, damn, that blows the whole morning."

"Hey! Hey! Not really. You have to get checked out on the controls anyway, so why not take a spin around this area? And while you're at it, you can watch me as I do a job necessary for colony maintenance."

"Well . . . all right. How do I get into the V/R circuits?"

"That terminal is enabled," Jory said as if he knew. "Under the keyboard shelf is a closed cabinet."

Demeter checked. "It's locked!"

Click! "Not anymore. . . . Now take out the helmet and gloves. Put them on."

Coghlan did so, adjusting the bone-induction microphone against the mastoid behind her ear. "Now what?"

"Now I link you into the nearest proxy . . . which is about four kilometers away."

The pupil-focus of her goggles went from that bland image of Jory's bruised face to a flaring, full-color display of some black rocks lying on pink sand under an Arctic-pale blue sky. Demeter jerked at the transition, and the motion sensor inside her helmet transmitted the move to the proxy, whose sensor head immediately jerked upward. That left the binocular cameras looking directly at the faraway sun, and a pair of polarizing filters stopped the scene down to nighttime lumen levels. Demeter slowly dropped her gaze; the proxy lowered its viewpoint to match; and the display went to daylight normal.

It had been six or seven months since Demeter Coghlan had worked with virtual reality. This system seemed less responsive, more telemetry-delayed, than she expected. The rig would take getting used to.

"You got some place to sit here?" she asked.

A stool-arm swung out of the wall and bumped gently at the back of her knees. Demeter squatted, now totally absorbed in the proxy's mechanical processes.

"How do I make it walk?" she asked Jory, or the grid . . . whoever.

"With your elbows. The manipulators attached to your gloves don't have any that you'd recognize. So, if you just do a one-two forward crawl, like infantry going under barbed wire—the gauntlets will pick up the motion—you'll set the proxy to walking. Dig in with your left elbow or right to turn the machine. Its internal controls will take care of details like traction, braking, slant angle, inertial balance, and all that."

Demeter made the requisite swimming motions, and the proxy began striding forward over the stony ground. She glanced down and got a shock to see a pair of human hands—well, human in the same way that

Frankenstein's monster was human—jutting out before her. Beyond them, churning softly in the dust, were the front pairs of the machine's spidery legs. These were long, curved whips of steel, furred with sensory hairs. Very . . . buglike.

"How do I tell it to find you, Jory? I don't even have a map!"

"It's all set. I've given your proxy a homing point. See you in about ten minutes. Enjoy the ride."

"But what about—?"

From the sudden curious deadness in her earphones, she knew he had gone offline, back to whatever task he had been doing. Demeter wanted to know what would happen if she stalled the machine, or walked it off a cliff, or something.

A few minutes later, she got a short demonstration. The machine approached the top of a steep slope. The angle would be enough to put the proxy's center of gravity ahead of and outside the circle of balance defined by its leg radius. If it tried walking down, either forward or backward, or sideways for that matter, it would tumble head over—over whatever bulbous body part was following its sensory apparatus.

Instead of proceeding, the proxy stiffened in place. Demeter glanced down to see the legs folding into a springy, six-sided cage of bowed steel. With one limb, the machine pushed off, going over the edge.

Demeter's viewpoint spun end-for-end and side-for-side. Her breakfast made a quick surge in her throat and then settled down. The proxy glanced off a boulder and was briefly airborne, bouncing farther down the slope. The background sound in her ears was like a shopping cart rolling over rocks. The rollover slowed finally and stopped most of the way to upside down.

With methodical slowness, the legs unfolded and righted the body, taking Demeter's perceptions along with it. The machine seemed to shake itself, the arms came away from their reflexive clutch against the belly, and the proxy continued on its way.

After another few minutes of fast walking, it brought her to a shallow valley among the ridges somewhere east of the tunnel complex.

Demeter drew in her breath.

The valley was crawling with horseshoe crabs. Dark, humped-over bodies—that blind forward curve, the articulated back section, the wicked spike of a tail—stumbled over the nearby hills and clawed their way into a pulsing pile. Demeter was reminded of an arachnid mating ritual. A gang-bang out of the Paleozoic Era. Trilobite City!

Demeter had heard that Mars had some native life-forms, mostly one-celled colonies under mushroom caps of silicate. And there were reports of certain hardy Earth forms that had gone feral—one was a kind of gerbil that had been bioengineered for minimal respiration and cold-adaptation, locally known as the "pack rat." But she never expected these living marine fossils to come crawling out of the desert landscape.

"What are those things?" she asked. Demeter had spotted the Creole standing at the edge of the slowly pulsating pile. He was actually doing something to one of the little horrors, taking its eggs or something. With Jory for scale, she guessed each crab's carapace was about a meter across.

"Johnnies," he replied, turning around to spot her proxy. "That's what we call them, anyway. 'Von Neumann processor' is the formal name."

"It's an animal?" she asked.

"Of course not. It's just a machine, but a pretty clever one."

He explained their function, which was part exploration, part minerals processing. Powered by photovoltaic circuits imprinted in the pattern of its shell, the mechanical trilobite crept along. Aside from chip-coordinated navigation and recording gear, and a roving command structure similar to that animating her proxy, the von Neumann consisted mostly of mouth and guts.

The mouth was a chemical analysis unit—based on the same kind of nanotech gas chromatography circuits that Dr. Lee had shot into her bloodstream—attached to a grinder and shovel. The guts were a series of tiny separators and smelters. As the machine walked over the Martian surface, its mouth sampled the soil and any likely outcroppings of rock that the cluster eyes noticed. When the parameters matched variables inscribed on its microprocessor brain, the von Neumann sat down and began to feed.

The first crop of alloys, silicates, and organic strings was passed to a third system inside the shell. This was the hatchery, where two—count 'em, two—new and full-sized von Neumanns were cast in pieces. The parent extruded them under a leveraged lift with its tail and then assembled them with a pair of micromanipulators folded under the front edge of its shell.

Once these replicas were launched and walked away to a life of wandering, sampling, recording, and eating, the mother machine settled down to really stuffing itself. Its taste and diet shifted to pure metals and crystals, stored in the half-domes under the carapace and eventually loaded into spaces formerly occupied by the replication equipment, which was similarly digested.

As soon as every spare cubic centimeter under the shell was packed with refined mineral products, the machine turned around and homed on a designated spot—this valley was one of them. "Send out one von Neumann, and eventually it comes back," Jory finished his lecture. "Then two more. Then four. Then eight. And so on, practically forever."

He picked up one of the machines, broke its back open with a wrench-thing in his hands, and extracted two copper-colored disks, a sausage that looked to be made of pure glass, and several loops of spaghetti-like fiber. These he put in bags hung around his utility harness.

"Each one is bursting with usable stuff," he explained. "Not to mention the shell itself, which is mostly soft iron with some strengthening fibers."

"Why put a shell on them at all?" Demeter asked, curious.

"Sandstorms. We get some really fast winds here, without any heat sinks like Earth's oceans, to modify the thermal absorption. The poles regulate the temperature, mostly, and they're a long way away."

"The shell keeps out blowing sand?"

"Well, no. It keeps the beast upright and moving. Aerodynamics, really." Jory spoke offhandedly, while his fingers dug and probed. "The harder the wind blows, the more stable the von Neumann becomes. Wind actually helps it dig into the ground. Otherwise it would blow around and lose its sense of direction. Then these things might never come back for collection."

"What about the proxies?" Demeter described the way her apparatus had balled up and rolled down that rocky slope. "These things stay outside all the time, right? So how come they don't blow around like tumbleweeds and get lost in the process?"

Jory shrugged. "They're smarter than a von Neumann, even without a human driver. They know how to report into the grid, which tracks them with RF beacons—most of the time. But, hell, losing the proxies occasionally is the only excitement we get around here. You'd be surprised the new territory you find that way."

Demeter seemed to remember the grid's being a little less cavalier about the prospect of abandoned equipment. But the thought passed.

Jory examined the most recently gutted machine's curved shell for, apparently, breaks and scrapes. He worked its legs back and forth, and noted a broken tip on one claw. Finally, he fingered a notch in the spiked tail. With a shake of his head, Jory dismembered the von Neumann into other collection bags about his person. Then his fingers popped a tiny slab out of the last piece of shell he was holding. This item he dropped carefully into a pocket of his shorts.

"What's that?"

"Its brain. Carries an imprint of where the von Neumann went and what it saw. We'll feed that into the grid, and some cyber somewhere will add its data to our topographic mapping program. Little by little we're coming up with a really detailed survey of Mars."

After watching him tear apart three of the critters, Demeter finally asked, "Can I help?"

"Sure! It's easy!"

He showed her how to snap open the carapace, which parts were product and which process, and how to spot a damaged machine. Her manipulators worked just like normal hands, although she needed some getting used to their odd spatial orientation and the nonhuman range from eye to fingertip. Jory gave her a set of the shell-cracking tools and the sorting bags, which he hung from the knee-joints of her proxy within easy reach of her hands.

"What do I do with a carcass that *isn't* damaged?" she asked, finally finding one. No cuts, no nicks, and all joints working with soft clicks.

"Give it here."

From a case on the ground at his feet, Jory took a mechanism that seemed to be made of crystal and steel. Demeter glanced into the case and saw a dozen more just like it, nestled in foam cutouts. His deft fingers snapped the gadget into the embrasure under the shell where the defunct smelter had been. The new unit had the same kind of grinding mouth and chemical sensors as the old one. When he was done, Jory set the machine down.

It lay there for a moment, absorbing sunlight. Then the legs began to churn, the shovel curve of the carapace pushed forward against the sand, and the von Neumann wandered off—away from the pile of its fellows.

"What is it?" Demeter asked.

"Second generation. It has the same basic command structure of its earlier form: go forth and multiply, twice. Except, this one will never return. This Johnny's now a Johnny Appleseed."

She must have looked perplexed; he grinned. "From the old Earth story," he explained. "You don't know it? Doesn't matter; anyway, it's got a biological package it didn't have before, and a new program. After it has reproduced itself, new biological package and all, that Johnny is now programmed to wander at random over the planet's surface until something actually kills it. And as it goes, the thing will eat sand and manufacture glass capsules that it will fill with its payload of tailored protozoans."

"And what are they? What do they do?"

Jory looked around, as if he had been saying too much. But if that were the case, he should never have brought her out here.

"There are two cultures, basically. One a kind of blue-green algae, the other a bacteria. Both have been genetically altered until they practically *can't* die. The bacteria are supposed to be from a strain that microbiologists found in Antarctica, which gets almost as cold as Mars and can be just as dry.

"Together, these cultures will form something similar to a lichen, which the von Neumann encapsulates and seeds in protected areas on the surface. The algae use sunlight to turn carbon dioxide into oxygen and carbon compounds, while the bacteria extract latent moisture from the air and the permafrost layer. This creature also helps prepare the ground with its waste products, turning it into organic soil."

"And you'll eat this stuff?" Demeter asked.

"Oh, no! Not even if it tasted good!" The Creole appeared profoundly shocked. "This is work for the future. We're trying to change the planet. By adding to the atmosphere's reserves of free oxygen, we hope one day to grow our plants out in the open. And by darkening the soil with organics, we not only raise its yield potential but also increase the amount of solar heat it will retain.

"Our calculations show that if we can get the average ground temperature at the equator—here, that is—up to about 270° Kelvin, we can have liquid water."

"You're going to bring back *rivers*? On Mars?"

"Why not? After all, parts of this planet get as warm as that for about one-eighth part of the year. It's not an impossible goal."

"And what about atmospheric pressure?" Demeter objected. "Won't your free oxygen and water vapor just leak off into space?"

"Sure, some of it will," Jory said with a frown. "Still, the lower elevations will build up a favorable balance eventually. It's going to take a long time; these von Neumanns work real slowly. But our calculations show it *can* happen."

"Ayuh!" Demeter said aloud.

She went back to the work of stripping out the Stage 1 von Neumanns and looking for Stage 2 candidates.

Jory obviously believed what he was saying, although Demeter's briefing with the Texahoma Martian Development Corporation had stressed that most Martian colonists were skeptical of terraforming in principle. Just another Earth-crazy boondoggle, they said, designed to let the politicians back home claim they were actually making something of this new frontier that had taken big chunks of taxpayer money to open up.

The average Martian, G'dad Coghlan had told her, was a lazy sort. The colonials were content to plant their paltry crops under plastic bubblepack, hack out a few more cubic meters of rock for themselves each year, and play V/R games all the livelong day. Long-term planning, coordinated action, and perseverance were not in their foolish natures.

But here was evidence—out in plain sight and openly shared with a casual from Earth—that the Martians had their own plan for making over the surface of their world. It wasn't going to be as quick or impressive as the Texahoman strategy, which included crashing a few stony asteroids and carbonaceous chondrites into the southern highlands to create a global dust cloud that would heat up the atmosphere. That in turn would encourage massive outgassing of water vapor from the permafrost layer. The computers in Dallas estimated it would rain for half a year—half a Martian year, that is—after just two such episodes. . . .

Demeter wondered who was this "we" that Jory spoke about. "Our calculations," indeed! She hadn't seen enough government here on Mars—aside from the busy-bodies who ran around tagging you for wearing perfume and stole from your bank account doing a medical exam you really didn't need—to pack a decent-sized church social, let alone plan for long-term weather modification and soil transformation on a planetary scale.

After the two of them had shucked seventy or so of the von Neumanns, reducing the pile by about a third, and released maybe a dozen of the Stage 2's, Jory put aside his collection bags, stretched, and sank down on the sand, sitting cross-legged. Demeter consulted the clock function built into her V/R gear and found that the morning had gone.

"Ever tried V/R sex?" the Creole asked with elaborate casualness.

"Huh? With you?" Demeter tried to maintain her composure. "Are we talking hump-the-terminal here? Or something with electronic bodysuits? Just what are you suggesting?"

"It's done with skin electrodes—there should be a pair back in your hotel room," he explained. "Everything happens inside your head, of course. Just like in real sex. Except you can be anything you want, do it any way you fancy. You can even be the guy, if that suits you. I'm flexible. . . ."

"Are you making a pass at me?"

"Not—well—just—with electrodes . . . you know?"

"Jory, are you blushing?" Demeter cranked the head of her proxy around to get a tight focus on his face. The ultraviolet-barrier in the boy's artificial skin made sensitivity analysis almost impossible. That didn't stop Demeter Coghlan, though. "I believe you *are!*"

"Forget I said anything," he grated.

"No, Jory, that's one thing I won't do. . . . Well, three things I won't do, actually. First, I don't do it with machines. Second, I definitely want to play the girl's part. And third—you started it!"

The Creole glanced up at her proxy's lenses from under his bony, slick-skinned eyebrow ridges. He was grinning at her. Suddenly, Demeter was glad that, physically, Jory was several kilometers away and on the wrong side of an airlock; he looked randy enough to mount the proxy itself. She had places to go and things to do today. But Demeter was going to have a lot to tell her diary tonight.

Chapter 4

Making New Friends and Influencing People

Office of the Civil Administrator, Solis Planum, June 9

The room had upholstered chairs, finished with a brown organic plastic that was molded and stitched to look like real leather. Somebody had paid good money to import the dyes that could work this effect on vat-grown fibers. The two-square-meter desktop was cast out of a yellowish resin grained with coal-black stripes. The grain appeared to go remarkably deep into the surface. . . .

It took Roger Torraway a full minute to realize he was looking at a hunk of real wood, not an optical simulation. That was impressive. Every stick of wood on Mars had to be brought up as freehold cargo—that is, imported at personal expense.

Of course, with the Civil Administrator, it might be hard to tell what was freehold and what government requisition. Technically, Bogan Dimelovich Ostrov was a personal employee of the mayor of Solis Planum, capable of being hired and fired at leisure. He was supposed to be something more than a secretary and less than a deputy. But Roger figured that mayors might come and go with each election—the current officeholder was a woman, Ludmilla Petrovna Sar-something—while the Civil Service went on forever.

"Frankly, Colonel Torraway, I don't think you understand the magnitude of the request you are making." Ostrov smiled broadly, meaning to take away any sting his comments might leave. "Importing fifteen hundred kilograms of refined deuterium-tritium is well beyond the means of this administration."

"Cost about as much as that desk of yours," Torraway commented internally. Then, guiltily, he checked to see that his backpack's link with the grid was currently inactive.

"I understand the costs involved," Roger said aloud, forcing his thin lips into a return smile. "But, of course, I'm not seeking charity. In exchange for Solis Planum's grant of an Earthside purchase order and import license, I'm prepared to offer exclusive rights to my memoirs as Mars's first citizen. That would include survey notes for areas of the planet that human colonists have not—"

"We have no interest in publishing, Colonel." The administrator grimaced. "Martians don't read. They don't buy books, not even to look at the pictures. Everyone's too busy."

"Then I would be . . . willing to . . ." Roger spoke slowly, fully understanding the implications of his next offer. ". . . to turn my recorded sensorium into a virtual-reality experience. That way your citizens could get a feel, full sound and visuals, of what it meant to be the first man to walk on the surface of—"

"We already have that record, of course." Ostrov shrugged. "I've played the Torraway Game a time or two myself. My personal favorite is the module 'Outwit the Mad Computer.' Right up there with 'Survival on the Polar Frost.' Very exciting stuff. But the market is saturated with bootleg versions by now, all of them more exciting than you could ever produce from your own life experience. Can you imagine Colonel Lindbergh's first transatlantic flight—the cold, the boredom, the anxiety—trying to compete with the thrills of an aerial dogfight? Which would *you* rather play?"

"All right then," Torraway said, imagining how his teeth would be gritting by now—if he still had any in his titanium-wired jaw. "You people in the colonies seem to be beset with competing territorial claims from Earth-based states. I still have some stature with those governments. After all, they paid billions to put me here. As your representative, I could—"

Ostrov was shaking his head again, that smile still fixed on his wide, rubbery lips. "Colonel Torraway, it's obvious to all of us that you served your purpose—served it with distinction, I might add—but that was fifty years in the past. With the situation now—"

"But if you would just let me contact the National Aeronautics and Space—"

"Isn't anymore."

"Then the successor agency! Which state would that be? Let's see, our lab was in Oklahoma but NASA was originally based out of . . . Houston. So that would be in Texahoma either way," Roger concluded. "The Space Administration must have some continuing legal function, if only on a regional—"

"The Texahoma Martian Development Corporation, yes." Ostrov looked sour. "They are one of our biggest headaches. But there's nothing that you can do for us in that regard, Colonel. The TMDC assumed all of NASA's residual claims anywhere in the Solar System about half an hour after they foreclosed on the Space Center in Houston. Now I'm not a legal expert, but I would guess that you, your body, your equipment, and your recorded experiences are included in those claims. As an investment worth a couple of billion prewar—'dollars' is the term?—your ass is simply not yours to sell, sir. If we tried to play you back Earthside as some kind of ambassador or negotiator, they'd slap a lien on you so fast, you'd think your backpack there had shorted out."

"I see. . . ." Roger Torraway sat upright in the lavishly upholstered chair and fixed Ostrov with his mildest stare. The Cyborg smiled to himself, although not a muscle of his face moved.

If the Civil Administrator enjoyed playing simulated games, then let him try the Statues Game, especially the module called "Will Somebody Please Get the Cyborg Colonel Out of My Office?" Roger could sit rigid for hours, for whole days at a time. In fact, not a muscle in his body except for his lips, jaw, and mechanical larynx had moved in the past ten minutes. If Ostrov called in a pair of roustabouts to come and try to lift Torraway out of the chair—aside from the fact that Roger's modified body weighed almost one hundred and thirty kilograms—they would have to sweat and strain with a package that was all locked knees and elbows angled into elaborately awkward positions.

So the Cyborg just sat there, fixing Ostrov with his ruby-red glare, all flecks and glints, without a shred of humanity in the softly glowing facets of his eyes. His trump card of last resort: becoming an indignant paperweight.

"This isn't going to help anything, Roger," Dorrie

said. She was sitting in the chair next to his and put her warm, moist palm on the back of his hand. He could feel it through the impervious skin layers.

"This man can't do anything for you—even if he wanted to," she went on. "He has already talked with his superiors. They have already heard about your fusion generator. It is they who have forbidden him to help you."

"Who are *they?*" Torraway asked inside his head. "The mayor? The other colonies? The Texahoma people?"

Dorrie looked troubled. Her signal started to break up, sending jags of interference across her pretty face. "I can't . . . don't know, Roger." Her signal cleared momentarily. "Just that becoming petulant with this *little* man won't get you anywhere. . . ." And then she was gone without even a carrier hum.

Torraway relaxed, unbent his knees, and shuffled his feet, as if preparing to rise. "I understand, Mr. Ostrov. The matter is out of your hands."

A look of pure relief flooded the Civil Administrator's face. "I assure you, Colonel, the people of Solis Planum have the greatest admiration for you. Anytime you want to tap into our mains—"

"I'll be sure to take you up on a generous offer like that."

Without moving to shake hands, Roger turned and walked toward the door, any door, that would take him out of this oppressive atmosphere and back to the clean, cold near-vacuum of his adopted world.

Hoplite Bar & Grill, Commercial Unit I/7/7, June 9

"You ought to meet some friends of mine," Jory said, suddenly dodging left into a commercial foyer.

Demeter guessed that Jory had only that moment

spotted his friends. Like everything else with the young Creole, the thought of introducing her had just occurred to him.

Sitting at one of the tables—this establishment provided chairs for its patrons, as well as real-human service—were a man and a woman. He was fair-skinned and tall. Nearly two meters, Demeter estimated, from the way his shoulders, elbows, and knees overhung the edges of the chair. He was slouching on his tailbone and looking out on the world from under a thick set of blond eyebrows. As he sipped his small, pale-brown drink and eyed the doorway, he reminded Demeter Coghlan of a three-card monte shark in a Galveston saloon on payday.

The woman was slender and dark, almost as tall as he was. She had long, black hair that went across her shoulders, down her back, and tucked under her rump. Her hair glistened in the subdued lighting every time she turned her head. The woman's features showed the exquisite curves of a Polynesian or other Pacific Islander, with the sun-browned skin coloring to match.

"Lole! Ellen!" the Creole called from the entry arch. The two of them looked over. "Boy, am I glad I caught you!" Jory pushed his way between the tables, Demeter trailing behind him.

"Demeter Coghlan, I'd like you to meet Lole Mitsuno and Ellen Sorbel. They're hydrologists with the complex's Resources Department. Sometimes I help them out with surface assignments."

"Hi there," from the woman.

"Howdy, ma'am," from the man.

Coghlan figured he must be the "Lolly" of the pair, because he sure didn't look like any "Ellen."

"Demeter is a tourist up from Earth," Jory explained. "From Texahoma State, to be exact," he added with a meaningful glance at Mitsuno.

"What exactly does a 'hydrologist' do?" Demeter asked conversationally, sitting down at one of the free chairs. The Creole rotated one around from a nearby table and squatted on it in reverse, crossing his arms over the back.

"We find water," Sorbel replied.

"Well, shucks," the man said. "Ellen here *finds* it. I just go and dig it out."

"And I help them, sometimes," Jory repeated.

"Are you really from Texas?" Mitsuno asked, his grin tightening with unexpected interest.

"Texahoma, actually."

"You know any cowboys?" He made a twirling motion with his right index finger above his head.

"Lole is very interested in the Old West," Sorbel explained.

"Well, I know a couple of rig drivers, work out of El Paso. They sometimes carry a load of frozen myolite."

The tall man knitted his brows.

"Processed protein product?" Demeter suggested. "But like as not they're carrying rockcandy silicon or liquid propane, you know. Or anything break-bulk."

"They ever do rodeo?" Mitsuno asked hopefully.

"Not since the Animal Rights Act of ninety-six."

"Then I guess you don't have shootouts or—"

"Not since my grandfather's been in office."

"Oh."

"Sorry."

The conversation entered a barometric decline, with everyone staring at the tabletop. Demeter wondered what she wanted to drink at ten o'clock in the morning, local time.

Jory suddenly looked up and stared at the far wall. He seemed to be receiving messages from beyond it. "Hey! Gotta go!" the Creole announced. "I'm late for the duty roster." He unhooked his legs from the chair rungs and dashed out.

After he was gone, Demeter and her two new friends resettled themselves in silence. Coghlan glanced at the pair across from her, sensing an easiness about them as if, sitting three feet apart, they still touched at several points. She wondered if they were lovers.

"So . . ." Demeter began again. "What kind of name is 'Mitsuno'? I'd have said Japanese, but you look a long way from—"

"Finn," Lole supplied. "My ancestors came from above the Arctic Circle. I guess that's why someone thought I'd be good at finding ice."

"Gosh, do you still speak Finnish at home?" Coghlan asked.

"Nobody speaks Finnish here anymore." He shrugged loosely. "Russian's easier to pronounce, and English's got simpler spelling rules."

"I see. . . ." She turned her attention to the young woman. "So, how do you find water? Go out in the hills with a witch-stick, or what?"

"I am a cyber ghost," Sorbel replied. "After Lole fires a string of sonic charges and brings up a field of data, I sniff around to see if anything looks possible."

Demeter sort of followed what Ellen was saying. She knew enough about tele-operators to know that ghosts worked in virtual realities which most of the rest of the human race wouldn't find particularly "real." Inside molecular structures, say. Or wedged into the laminar flows of a plumbing complex. Or, as here, looking at rocks and soil from the inside out.

Cyber ghosts went beyond the simple-minded rotas of expert systems. They did things that computers in the grid could not do. The computer mind might be able to tabulate sonic echoes and gravimetric survey data into matrices and layers, but it lacked the essential human element—"intuition" was the only word for it—that let an Ellen Sorbel enter the datastream, "sniff around," and then decide whether that particular formation was worth drilling for ice. In simplest terms, humans could exercise creativity and imagination, while computers just processed numbers.

"And then I go back out in a walker and put down a bore hole wherever she says to," Lole Mitsuno finished up. "In a way, it's a lot like wildcatting—if you know what *that* means."

"Sure. We're not so far from our roots, down in Austin," Demeter acknowledged.

"Well, good!" He gave her a big grin, making Coghlan feel she had just passed some kind of test. "Now, if you'll excuse me, I have to go make a contribution to the aquifer."

"Huh?"

"He means to 'take a leak,'" Ellen supplied, as Mitsuno unfolded himself and made his way between tables to the convenience.

With just the two of them left, facing each other now, Demeter decided to make a stab at girl-talk. She'd gotten rusty, living so much of her recent life out of a suitcase.

"So . . . are you and Lole engaged or anything?"

"Define 'anything,'" the woman returned her volley.

"Well, in love, in lust, into aggressive hand-holding . . . *you* know."

"You mean, is he free?"

"Yeah . . ."

Sorbel considered. "Lole's about the freest man on Mars—which isn't to say he's not expensive. We used to be real tight, working practically inside each other's minds all day long. The mental just led to the physical 'n' all that—and it was good. But now we're more . . . Well, I don't mind you making a move on him, because he is an upright piece of manhood. But if you hurt him, Dem, I will arrange to have you killed."

"Uh, point taken." Demeter tried to smile.

"Just so we understand each other. . . . How much of Mars have you seen already?" Sorbel asked, changing the subject.

"Only what you can glimpse from a window, actually. Coming down the Fountain—that was great. And I did get out in a proxy."

"Where did you go?" Lole asked brightly, rejoining the table.

"Just over the next valley or so. I helped Jory shuck crabs."

"Von Neumanns." Ellen nodded.

"That as far as he would take you?" from Lole.

"We did have a kind of excursion planned, out to the Valles area, but all the proxies on site there were taken. Maybe tomorrow. . . ."

"Oh, the proxies are all right," he conceded. "You get as much feel for the land as a well-done travel sim, I guess. But you really have to walk on the surface and wiggle your toes in the sand if you want to know Mars."

"You put your *toes*—?"

"Your boots, anyway."

"I was told about the safaris," Demeter said. "They sound expensive."

"They can be, sure. Unless you go as supercargo with a work party. Look, I'm checking out a walker tomorrow to go eyeball some new formations that Ellen likes. If you want to come along, I can sign you on to guard the sandwiches and such."

"Sure!"

"Let me just confirm it with our department and get you assigned your own air bottle. . . . Wyatt, do you copy?" he asked, turning his face to the nearest surveillance lens.

"Confirm," said a neutral voice, emanating from an air duct overhead. "One to accompany your June-ten-slash-eleven-fifteen out time, person of Demeter Coghlan, tourist from Earth."

"Who was *that*?" Demeter asked.

"Wyatt, the cyber that thinks it runs our department," Ellen replied.

"Why do you call it 'Wyatt'?"

"Short for 'Y-4 Administrative Terminal.'"

"Is not!" Lole said flatly. "Short for Wyatt Earp, 'cause he kind of lays down the law around our office."

"How did you get access without turning it on?" Demeter asked. She remembered having to key the terminal in her hotel room.

" 'Turn it on'? Why, Dem, the machines are *always* 'on.' All you have to do is get their attention, so the grid will access you correctly."

"Always on?" Demeter was surprised. "What a novel concept!"

Of course, she silently corrected herself, Sugar was *always on*, but she was no bigger than a pumpkin seed, was usually discreet, and only tied into the local grid when Demeter told her to. The idea of having the whole machine network of the planet looking over your shoulder, waiting for you to crook a finger—as Lole had done—and listening for any word it might-could interpret as a command, doubtless recording everything else on the off-chance the communication might turn up something useful . . . She found the idea unsettling.

Of course, Demeter told herself the next minute, many of Earth's cities were almost as interconnected. Between personal chronos and civic terminals, plus the ever-present Committees of Public Safety in some of the newer cultures, a human being might well feel monitored all the time. But on Earth you could always go outdoors, walk off into the middle of a field some-where, hike into the mountains, row out into a lake. Then you could know that you were alone except for any little cyber you brought with you. Here on Mars, on the other hand, everything was indoors. You were always inside these tunnels, with the grid's monitors everywhere. You couldn't go outdoors unless you wore a pressure suit or traveled in a walker or visited through a proxy—and each of these tied into the grid for safety reasons. So you were never really out of touch.

Coghlan could feel her chest tightening at the thought of being always under surveillance. Super-vised. Scrutinized . . . *Watched.*

"Yes, isn't it convenient?" Ellen replied. The smile she gave Demeter certainly seemed sincere.

Chapter 5

Shadows Beneath the Surface

Valles Marineris, by Proxy, June 9

When Demeter Coghlan wired into the proxy that was waiting for her in the Valles Marineris District, she found herself looking at a pattern of horizontal lines.

What the goggles showed her were even layers of fine-grained material, brownish-red over reddish-brown, looking, more than anything else, like a Chocolate Decadence with raspberry sauce. Then Demeter noticed that the machine's lenses were focused at the MACRO setting. She reset them for normal viewing and backed the proxy away from whatever it had pushed its nose into. The image resolved into the sidewall of a canyon, layers of iron-stained clays and sands deposited in strata, pressure-welded into hard stone, and then carved away by the force of wind and, perhaps, water.

"Humph," Demeter grunted. She had teleported her head 2,600 kilometers to gaze at a rock wall.

Earlier that afternoon, Jory den Ostreicher had come to Demeter's hotel room—although she didn't remember giving him either the Golden Lotus's name or her room number—and announced he had finally gotten that pair of proxies released. The machines were supposed to be some distance away from the actual

Canyonlands development site; so he and Demeter would have to walk them back. He led her into the hotel's simulation parlor to take over the proxies.

Demeter was about to pull the machine's sensor head away from the canyon wall, to turn and get a wider view of the terrain, when something caught her eye. It was a lump of glassy material, half-buried in the strata.

She knew about the glass-capped plant life that the earliest human colony on Mars had discovered. Could this be a fossil of an earlier form, only now emerging from between the layers? Well . . . no. For one thing, these sedimentary rocks showed that Mars had once possessed abundant free water. That implied a thicker atmosphere, and the silica shell of the modern flora was generally agreed to be a late adaptation to thinner air that permitted lethal amounts of ultraviolet radiation to reach the surface. So, it was unlikely the glass cap had any counterpart in primitive forms.

Could this be an animal, then? Some kind of hard-shelled marine life?

Demeter cranked in the MACRO setting again. The object exhibited none of the symmetries—bilateral, radial, pentahedral—that one associated with life. It was a lump, nothing more. An almond of milky substance deposited in the layer-cake of the region's geology. But before Coghlan turned away from the anomaly, she did a fast scan of the wall.

Other almonds leaped out at her. All of them lay in the same line of strata, more or less, as if deposited there but not above or below. As if, sometime in the distant past, a shotgun blast had peppered the surface of the mudflats with nuggets of . . . of whatever.

Demeter scratched the vertical surface of the outcropping with the clawed whip of her machine's No. 1

right walking leg. This was a touring proxy, lacking either the handlike manipulators or saddle pouches of the working models. In six centimeters of downstroke, she covered a hundred thousand years of layered sediment. One of the stones popped loose.

"What are you doing?" Jory asked in her earphones.

"Looking for fossils . . . ?" Demeter replied meekly.

"Right! Sure! Our people have been digging around in this valley for ten years, every one of them hoping to turn up a crustacean or a clamshell or something. And you think you're going to walk up to a blank wall, kick it once, and make the discovery of the age! You've got balls, Demeter!"

"All right. It was just a notion." And it was the perfect touristy thing to do, Coghlan thought, congratulating herself. Already she felt like a spy.

"Just like a little kid . . ." the Creole steamed.

Before Demeter turned away, she tried to memorize the shape and texture of the loose stone—it would be too conspicuous if she were to put the V/R helmet in RECORD mode just then. The object was translucent, almost clear, with a ridge of gray matrix still clinging to it. Bigger than her thumb, too. Coghlan was no geologist, but she knew something of a planet's power to form deposits. This nugget was no part of an igneous vein, which was how quartz beds formed. The stone had been created by intense pressures, deep in the mantle, then shot out of a vertical well in a single gout of magma.

The word "kimberlite" crossed her mind and stuck.

But that was all the prospecting she had time for, although she vowed to remember the site and come back to it if she could. With a pang, she suddenly realized that the last person to use this proxy—the one who had abandoned it with his guide in this part of the Valles—must have been looking at this wall of amygdaloid nuggets. Had he also seen the anomaly and investigated? If so, did he understand the implications? She had no way of finding out.

Consumed by these thoughts, Demeter turned the proxy away from her find, raised its lenses, and clicked to ZOOM. The valley floor came into focus. Her and Jory's machines stood on a slight elevation near the North Wall. The far side of the Valles rose up and up in an escarpment of runneled passages and sheer bluffs.

The Marineris system was deeper and longer than the Grand Canyon on Earth, which Demeter had visited through V/R simulation before taking on this assignment. But where the Grand Canyon was a network of tiny, narrow gorges twisting and recurving through a tableland of etched buttes, the Valles Marineris was a broad, flat-bottomed valley, like California's Yosemite or Hetch Hetchy. Except, for their size, the bastions and knobs and domes here outranked even El Capitan.

"Which way to the development?" she asked Jory.

"To the left and down. It's about two kilometers."

"Have Lole and Ellen done any exploration out this way?"

"I don't think so. Why?"

"There was water here once. That's obvious."

"Water was in a lot of places—once," he said. "That doesn't mean any of it stayed."

"Oh. . . . Well, let's go down and see the construction works."

"Sure thing!" And they started walking their six-legged mechanical steeds downhill toward a glint of reflected light in the valley.

Canyonlands Complex, by Proxy, June 9

Jory led Demeter down toward the construction area in the center of the valley. For now, from this distance, it was just a jumble of brightly painted equipment, in colors of phosphorus yellow and neon green that had never before been seen in the Martian wilderness. The big machines were walking about and chewing up the soil among tumbled drifts of broken stone from the pits and rocks fallen from the canyon walls. An occasional flash of sunlight off a windshield or porthole told him that the crews were on shift and toiling away.

Jory den Ostreicher knew a couple of the people who had signed on with the Zealanders to build their new township. A few were Creoles like himself, the rest contract tunnelers and construction hands from Tharsis Montes and Solis Planum, the nearest large settlements. It wouldn't do, of course, for Jory to butt in during shift, asking questions and showing off for Demeter. Not when he was traveling by tourist proxy and couldn't lend a hand himself, as was proper.

Instead, they came up to the edge of the spill line and observed the closed rigs at work.

The walkers were megasize, bigger than anything except a full-blown excursion bus, self-contained as to atmosphere, with their own airlocks and carrying food, water, and breathable air for fourteen days. The operators even had beds and a pair of simulation hoods for passing their off-duty hours. The machines picked up shovels of red dirt and stone here, put them down over there, in a pattern that only made sense after a few minutes of watching. The dirtmovers were ladling the tunnel spoils over oblong bubbles of clear film, each about ten meters on its long axis. Another machine on the far side of the field was blowing the bubbles out of fast-setting epoxy and extruding them onto pads of leveled sand.

"Why are they burying those domes?" Demeter asked. Even though she was sitting right next to him in the gaming parlor of her hotel back in Tharsis Montes, her voice came to him over the dedicated radio frequency between their two proxies.

"Protection," he explained, groping for a reason. "Sometimes we get meteors, you know? Or from the hard ultraviolet sunlight. Putting the Quonsets underground is easier than patching them up later."

"I don't understand. Are there going to be people living in them? And if so, why do you still have exposed domes at Tharsis Montes? Don't meteors come down here, too? I'd think that, as an older settlement, and a more important one—"

"Hey, look! I don't know!" Jory protested, unconsciously waving his proxy's front legs in the air. "This Canyonlands deal isn't a regular Martian project. The Zealanders are in charge, see, and they've got their own ideas about how to do things. . . . Okay?"

"All right," she said stiffly. "Anyway, I guess I could check it out in the project specs or something. I just thought you were an expert guide."

"I've been out here a time or two, that's all."

"Can we get down inside the tunnels?"

"Not in these units. We'd be underfoot with the work crews."

"Oh, poop!"

"Hey, that doesn't mean we can't see what's going on! They must have the tunnel borer on a monitor channel. We can leach off its signal and watch along with the operator."

"Isn't that sort of thing—um—restricted?"

"What? Watching someone else work isn't popular on Earth?"

"Sidewalk superintending," she said cryptically. "Yeah, I guess so."

"What's a 'sidewalk'?" Jory asked.

Golden Lotus, June 9

Jory showed Demeter how to switch her helmet over to the tunneling machine's monitor signal. Before she did, however, he had her check out the proxy's command circuits and then put the silver spider in standby mode so it wouldn't wander off and get into trouble.

Taking virtual-reality sim-feed from the borer was an exhilarating experience. She didn't have the controls to guide the equipment, and the channel was one-way only, but she still got a tactile response as the drill jumbos cut into the face of hard, dark stone. Through the neuro-inducer, it felt like her own teeth were twirling in their sockets while her shoulders and elbows pushed back against the tunnel walls. Then, when the blast holes had been cut and the tampers were pushing forward their package charges, it felt like her own fingers were thrusting into the rock channels. Relays clicked in her head as the machine checked out its firing circuits, and the bulk of the borer withdrew on articulated treads to the far end of the tunnel, around a protective corner.

Boom! The helmet seemed to rattle on Demeter's skull and the inducer pushed an overpressure up against her diaphragm.

"Very impressive," she commented, as the goggles showed her the formal plan of the underground complex, with another bite visibly extending one of the horizontal adits.

"Yeah!" Jory replied. She could hear him undoing his helmet's chinstrap and peeling off the neural gloves.

"That's about all there is to see." He spoke, not over the earphones, but through the air from the terminal next to hers. His voice had a quaver in it. Clearly, all that neural stimulation was getting to him.

Truth to tell, she found it pretty exciting herself.

Demeter was not surprised to feel a delicate finger-touch brush against her shoulder, slide tippy-tap across her back. Something soft and warm caressed the short hairs at the nape of her exposed neck. She felt her body begin to stiffen, then remembered in a flash the sight of his hairless, glistening deltoids, his sculpted pectorals. Demeter wondered what the Creole's perfect, bronzed skin would look like, stretched over his gluteals.

"Is there someplace we can go?" he asked huskily.

"My room," she answered, scrabbling at the strap under her chin.

Once there, she did a fast scan of the cubicle. The blank eye of the terminal caught her attention. "Always on," Lole Mitsuno had said. Demeter went to the cupboard and retrieved her jacket, something she would have worn against the weather "outside" on Earth. On Mars, in the balanced environment of the tunnel complex, it was a useless garment—with one saving feature. It was thick-lined and opaque. She draped it over the video pickup and tucked a dragging sleeve around the audio. Then she shucked off the charm bracelet that held Sugar and upended a water glass over it.

Demeter turned and bent over to let down the bed. Suddenly she felt his hands snake around her from behind. They traveled up the length of her body, from knees to breasts, cupping and probing as they went. His lips were on her neck again, hot and slick. His weight—like a boy's in the partial gravity—was bearing her down onto the bedspread. Too fast. Too fast.

She heard a *rip!* as Jory's strong hands shredded the collar of her jumpsuit and began to pull its back seam apart.

Demeter gasped. "Unh, wait a minute!"

She bent her knees—first the right and then left—and reached down with a blind hand to slide out of the hotel's courtesy slippers and her socks. Then she opened the front snaps of her coverall and pushed its remains off her shoulders, down to her ankles, and kicked them off, freeing her legs. She turned to face him in his loose embrace and rolled down her briefs, kicking them off, too.

Somewhere in all these contortions, Jory's *lederhosen* and utility harness had disappeared. He was standing naked between her legs. His domed, pink member slid up toward her face as she sank back on the bed with the points of her shoulders against the padding that had rucked up against the wall. She spread her thighs and arched her spine—and stopped thinking.

She stopped feeling with her head. She just let her skin take over, let the muscles deep in her gut go to work with the *thrust, thrust . . . thrust* that became the geometric center of her universe. She rode wave after wave of the heat that flooded her. She closed her eyes and . . . absorbed.

After a time she could not count, Jory's hips stopped pumping. The arch of his pelvis stopped thudding into hers. His shoulders sagged, and the skin of his abdomen relaxed slickly against hers. He was not heavy at all, more like a child who had crept into her arms for a motherly cuddle.

They hung like that, suspended from her shoulders and neck wedged up against the wall, supported by her hips where they jammed into the bed's thin mattress. His breathing eased to a gentle, damp puff against her skin. After a few moments, he lifted his head and began to nuzzle her slackened breasts again.

"Hey! No more," she protested, but her voice came out a whisper.

"Didn't you like it?"

"Of course I did. But once is enough."

"Once is never enough," he murmured. His lips began to snail-walk toward her right nipple.

"I mean it." She struggled up on one elbow, rolling him gently off on his side.

Jory curled into a loose fetal position. His hand casually passed down between his legs and . . . Demeter stared. His glans and testicles had disappeared. His lower belly was as smooth as a girl's. She could see daylight through his crotch. He had not simply pushed his male equipment back between his legs. It had completely disappeared.

"How did you do that?"

"Do what?" He roused, seeming perplexed.

"That thing with your cock and . . ."

"Oh, that!" He laughed. "One of the advantages of being a Creole. We can put the jewels out of harm's way." He slid a finger down there, and she heard a sound like parting Velcro. A tip of pink skin peeked out of a slit that was placed far too low on his body for a fly. It looked disturbingly like a vagina's lips.

"Airtight seal, too," he commented idly.

Demeter fought off a wave of *otherness* that threatened to change him from a simple, carefree young male to something alien and lizardlike.

"Why did you put a—a shirt, is it?—over the computer terminal?" he asked suddenly.

"I don't like anybody watching when I . . . do it. That kind of breaks the mood for me."

"Who would be watching?"

"Well, the computer link was on, wasn't it? It's on all the time."

"So? Who would be watching?" he insisted.

"The grid. The machines."

"Yeah, but no*body* is watching. They're *computers*, Demeter. Don't you have them in Texas?"

"Not in our bedrooms. And we can turn them off if we want."

Jory chuckled. "Maybe you *think* you turn them off. . . . Anyway, they don't care about things like that."

"How do you know they don't?"

"They don't have any reason to. Why would they?"

"I don't know what reasons a computer might have. Neither do you," she added.

"All right," he agreed. "So, next time, I'll tell them to blank the optics in this room."

"You're taking a lot for granted, aren't you?" Demeter was thinking about his casual use of "next time," but decided not to make an issue of it. After all, the sex really had been good. "I mean, you're dealing with an intelligent system," she pointed out.

"That's still to be proven."

"Okay then, a 'self-programming system that exhibits a high degree of volition.' Either way, could you trust it to do what you told it? And how could you prove it had obeyed you? I mean, it might just switch off the ready light and go on watching."

"Well, you wouldn't know, I guess." He had a thoughtful look, which seemed strange on him. "But, again, what difference does it make? The grid won't go whispering to your friends about it. You'll never know the difference."

"I'll know."

He sighed. "You're a complicated person, Demeter. More complicated than anybody else I know."

"We're like that, we—" She paused. Coghlan had been about to say "we humans," which would have been a direct insult. That sense of *other* overwhelmed her again. "—Earth people," she finished lamely.

"Must be your culture," he said. "Older and more, um . . . *devious.*"

Demeter let the word slide.

"Say, that reminds me." Jory brightened. "Do you want to go back to the Valles tomorrow? If so, we'd better get another reservation in. The men who were using those proxies will probably be wanting them again. They're supposed to be traveling—I mean, in the flesh this time—but the grid shows them due back in Tharsis Montes tomorrow."

"Oh, Jory! I can't! I've got a date—an appointment with your friend Lole. We're going out to hunt some water. . . . But who are they, these people?" Demeter asked casually. Beneath her surface composure, her senses were coming alert. She remembered those strange pebbles she had found in the Valles geologic formation when she first wired into the touring machine.

"It's a Mr. Suk, up here from United Korea. He took a proxy for himself and one for his servant, too. . . . Very big of him."

Coghlan's flesh went suddenly cold. She could feel

little nervous bumps rise along the skin of her arms.

"You mean 'Sun,' " she corrected him without any particular emphasis. "The man's name is Sun."

"Oh. You know him?"

"No, no. But, like most New Asians, the Koreans put the family name first. That's all."

"I didn't know that," Jory said. "Kinda neat . . . Mister Sun. Lucky ol' Sun."

In a moment, the boy was asleep.

Chapter 6

Shadows on the Horizon

Airlock Control, Tharsis Montes, June 10

Unlike the inflated plastic domes that Demeter Coghlan had walked through on her last visit to the colony's surface structures, the lock complex was a solid building. It was erected out of composite panels that keyed into I-beam frames with lattice buttressing from the outside. The raised floor felt solid underfoot. The walls looked as if they would even stand up under a pressure loss.

Demeter was not feeling particularly good about herself this morning. Her tryst with Jory the afternoon before—and she had *not* asked him to stay the night—had left a surprisingly sour taste in her mouth. Sure, she liked sex. It was one of the great pastimes, especially good for making new friends and influencing people. But not with children. Not even with muscular man-boys like the Creole. What the two of them had shared, struggled through . . . endured . . . had not been love. It was not even good, healthy sex. More like a fumbling rape that had gone uncontested.

It was not clear to Demeter which of them was the rapist. The trouble with playing among the chronologically challenged, like Jory, was all that groping, grasping, hurry-hurry-or-I'll-wet-my-pants stuff. Aside

97

from being over too soon for Demeter's taste, it lacked the necessary control and self-discipline that kept the . . . encounter from becoming demanding and potentially turning violent. Grasping could too easily become hitting if she didn't rise fast enough.

Demeter liked a firm hand with her sex—not a whip hand.

Still, at the defining moment, she herself had been eager enough. Demeter supposed it was because both of them had been taking neural induction from that tunnel-boring machine. All those concrete sensations pouring into nervous systems that were not quite ready for them. The operators who guided those machines must be either eunuchs or brain cases. Or maybe both.

The previous afternoon had left her physically and emotionally drained. So much so, that Demeter had fallen asleep in the middle of filing her evening report with the Texahoma Martian Development Corporation. Not that she had too much to report. She remembered discussing the expedition she would be taking this morning and her excitement about actually getting out on the surface. Not that she would learn much about the Valles Marineris today . . .

There was something else she was supposed to report, or had reported . . . or at least had thought might be important. Something about geology—or did she merely dream that? Oh, well . . . The key item was that today she would get some valuable local experience by going out in a walker with Lole Mitsuno.

Coghlan looked around the airlock terminal. It reminded her of the elevator lobby of a Dallas mega-highrise. A long, open corridor slanted up from the underground complex and ended in this six-sided bay with a sealed door in each wall. They were very impressive doors, each operated by either servomotor or handcrank, with a readout panel to the right having both needle gauges and a digital display. There was a painted, red-bordered sign in seven languages across each set of paired panels. In the floor before the threshold was a steel trip plate. Each door was numbered, beginning clockwise from the left-hand side of the entry ramp. The lighting there in the lobby was day-bright, even though the tubes were baffled and recessed. Somebody was trying to prepare tunnel-sensitized eyes for the glare of sunlight on sand.

People came and went while she waited for Mitsuno. Whenever one of the doors opened, Demeter tried to peek past it into whatever lay beyond. Trouble was, that involved staring directly at whoever was coming out, which was the worst possible manners. Instead, she watched the backs of the people going in, and that gave her mixed clues. Sometimes the space on the other side of the door was a simple lock, no bigger than a commercial elevator, fitted with pressure suits and survival gear. But once or twice Demeter glimpsed whole rooms that were furnished with chairs upholstered in luxurious fabrics and the glow of electronics with LEDs and colorfully patterned screens.

She wondered about those pressure suits. Demeter had never worn one, although she'd traveled almost 280 million kilometers through interplanetary vacuum to breathe Mars's particular species of canned air. So she had questions. For instance, could she wear the suit over her own street—or tunnel—clothes? Demeter fingered the lapel of her jumper. If not, would she have to strip down in Mitsuno's presence? And if so, how far would she have to go? To the skin? Or was underwear allowed? . . . What was the etiquette of nudity in a strange society?

In the groups of strange faces coming and going on the ramp from the lower levels, she suddenly glimpsed the hydrologist. The outline of his golden hair, rugged jawline, and squinting eyes rode above the foreshortened tangle of heads as he strode up the corridor. Suddenly Lole was standing beside Demeter and she had to crook her neck to look up at him.

"Just how tall *are* you?"

"Two hundred ten cents," he answered. "About . . . eighty-three inches. Is 'inches' the correct unit for cowboy talk?"

"Feet," Demeter supplied. "You stand six foot ten, pardner."

"Ah, so many *foot*."

Demeter shook her head. "You must have had skyscrapers for parents."

"Sky—? Oh, buildings. No, I'm just first generation. My parents were both émigrés, no taller than you," he said appraisingly. Demeter stood five-nine in her stockings and, as a teenager, had been considered gawky. "It's the lower gravity, you see," he explained. "We Mars-born just shoot up, or so my mother always said."

"Then what happened to Jory?" Demeter burst out. It was an unfortunate personal remark, and she hoped Mitsuno wouldn't take offense for his friend.

"Jory is Creole. He was Mars-born, too, and of course fully human. But soon after puberty they did things to his body. Some you can see, like the impermeable skin. A lot you can't, like his entire endocrine system."

"Oh, right." She hurried to change the subject: "Where are we going today?"

"Headed for a place called Harmonia Mundi, Mars Survey Reference CQ-6981. Wyatt's reserved a medium-sized walker for us. Door number five."

Mitsuno led her over to the airlock as he talked, where Demeter read the digital display: RESERVED T.M. RESOURCES DEPARTMENT OFFICIAL BUSINESS. Her guide spoke into the recessed mike: "Okay, Wyatt. Let's get this show on the road."

"May I have your thumbprint, please?" the panel replied coolly. A small square lit up white.

"Voiceprint me and open."

Without further comment, the door's servo-operated dogs unsealed themselves and the panel split and slid apart.

Beyond it was one of the elevator-sized varieties of interior space. When Mitsuno stepped aside for her, Demeter walked in and reached for the neck ring of the first pressure suit that came to hand.

"What are you doing?" he asked.

"Isn't this an airlock? Don't we have to get dre—?"

Mitsuno keyed a wallpad, and an internal door folded back. Demeter was looking into a truck cockpit, but one finished in steel and plastic instead of nice fabrics and simulated woods. Closest to the door was a utility space with facing benches and a pull-down table. Farther along was a driver's console with a minimum of instrumentation. Windows on either side and across the front showed red desert with various of the complex's buildings in the foreground.

"We'll use suits when we get to the worksite," he explained. "Until then, we travel in style."

Mitsuno secured the door behind them, waved her to a seat on one of the benches, and sat down at the console. He studied the board for a second, hit three keys, then swiveled around, away from the windshield.

"What do you think of Mars so far?" he asked casually.

"Big on the outside, small on the inside," she replied, thinking of lives that seemed to be lived mostly underground.

"Yeah, people up here go in for virtual simulations. Gives our brains room to breathe, anyway."

Demeter noticed that scenery was passing the window ahead of the driver's console without him paying the slightest attention. "Shouldn't you look where you're driving?" She gestured toward the front—bow? nose?—of the vehicle.

"No need. Wyatt knows the coordinates of the Mundi reserve better than I do, and this car's pattern buffers do a better job of keeping out of collisions than either of us."

The ground out in front did look hilly, with tall projections of gray rock that floated on past the side ports. Demeter craned her neck forward: the machine was following no road she could see. She sat back and sensed the ride with her butt. It felt like pneumatic tires on laser-aligned ferrocrete. Better even. Although the terrain outside was definitely shaping up into foothills, the vehicle's floor remained dead level.

"This buggy sure rolls along smoothly."

"Inertial compensators," Mitsuno replied, "built into the leg circuitry. From the outside, this thing moves like a spider doing ballet."

"You've actually *seen* a spider?" Demeter wondered. "I mean, they somehow got past your quarantine rules?"

"No, we raise 'em. It's the only way to keep down the flies."

The floor took a reeling step—a sudden lurch forward and a long circle back, like a camel with the staggers.

"Whoops!" Mitsuno grinned. "Spoke too soon. Wyatt, what the hell was that?"

"Sorry, Lole." The machine voice didn't sound at all contrite. "That was a chuckhole."

"Don't tell me you have gophers here on Mars!" Demeter broke in.

"No, Miz Coghlan-Demeter-Cerise," Wyatt replied with her full name. "'Chuckhole' is a colloquial human reference. The correct term is 'nonventing paleogeological fumarole.'"

"Chuckhole will do," she said evenly. There it was again: geology . . . something to do with . . . whatever.

"Next time we'll take a blimp," Mitsuno grumbled.

"Department funding does not permit excursions by lighter-than-air transportation over distances less than four thousand klicks," the computer node said primly.

"I'm *kidding*, Wyatt."

Silence. Demeter fancied the machine was sulking.

"What do you do when you're at home?" Lole asked after they had gone a few more kilometers.

"I was a student, studying for foreign service."

"Is that some kind of military outfit?"

"Oh, not at all! We help to maintain peaceful relations all across the planet. You see," she explained, "Earth has so many nations and regional trading alliances and ecological defense blocs and economic shield treaties that maintaining the world's diplomatic balance is a full-time business. Foreign service is a good career, too. If I complete my coursework, and with the pull my grandfather can generate, I'll have my pick of an embassy or consulate job in just about any country Texahoma exchanges relations with."

"*If* you complete your courses." Mitsuno accurately picked up her inflection. "Why did you stop?"

"I . . . Well, I had an accident."

"Oh. And where would you like to be assigned?" He politely declined to follow up on her personal difficulties.

"Haven't decided yet. I might like to get away from all these machines for a while. That would mean taking a post in some society that's gone Professed Primitive—like Seychelles, Montana, or the Republic of Hawaii—but sometimes the Pee-Pees can be a little too orthodox about their stature. As an alternative, I might just go to some developmentally challenged state like Dakota or del Fuego. Life there can be pretty desperate, of course, but I'd draw diplomatic privileges such as immunity and escort service. I'd also get to buy in special stores, go to the head of any queues, and park in reserved spaces."

"Park?" the Martian asked.

"Uh . . . temporarily store my car?"

"Ah! I've heard about cars. Do you actually own one?"

"G'dad does—he's my grandfather. And when I make ambassador rank, I'll be entitled to one, too."

"You could come to Mars," Lole offered. "We're about as foreign as you can get. And not nearly so primitive. Or desperate."

"You're a little *too* foreign. None of the Mars colonies has established diplomatic relations with Earth yet. In fact, your governments—or what I can see of them, at least—actively resent intrusions from the mother planet."

"Yeah, you got that right," he agreed. "Besides, we

don't have much room for embassies here on Mars. How many nations do you people have now?"

"Thirteen hundred and some. The count changes every couple of days."

"That's a lot of tunnel space. And most Martians would get ornery about giving special privileges to social parasites. . . . No offense intended," he added quickly. "I'm sure your Earth governments really value what you diplomats can do."

"Most of the Martians I've met have been down-right friendly."

"That's because *you're* a paying guest."

"Oh, right." Demeter had almost forgotten her nominal role on this visit.

"Although . . ." Mitsuno went on slowly, "when somebody says 'diplomat,' I usually hear 'spy.'"

Demeter saw him grin to take the sting out of his words.

"Why, whatever would there be worth spying on up here?" she asked innocently. The real answer, of course, was other Earth spies. Everyone came to Mars to scope out the territory and defend the old claims. "A million square miles of blasted rock, is all," she concluded aloud.

"And water," he pointed out. "Mineral rights, too."

Minerals . . . geology . . . something. The thought went out of her head immediately.

Demeter noticed that the walker had stopped moving. The vista out the front window had stabilized on a valley floor of lemon-colored sand littered with black rocks. She started to gesture when the robot voice cut in.

"You have arrived, Lole."

"Let's stretch our legs," Mitsuno said to Demeter, heading for the airlock at the back of the vehicle.

He showed her how to put on the pressure suits. They were sensible garments, cut on the one-size-fits-most pattern. On Demeter, that left plenty of room for her street clothes as well as freedom of movement. The suit offered no plumbing. It would keep her alive on the Martian surface, or even in low orbit, but not for longer than her bladder could hold out. The helmet was big and rested on a well-padded neck ring, which she appreciated. She did not have to carry its weight on her skull and push the bobby pins into her scalp.

Before Demeter pulled on the gauntlets, she took off her charm bracelet and tucked Sugar into an inside zippered pocket. No sense in letting delicate electronics get caught in the snapseals.

Then she and Lole crowded into the airlock, and he flushed its atmosphere back into the vehicle's holding tanks. When the outside door opened, Coghlan expected they'd have to climb down a ladder. After all, the view from the windows had shown the walker carrying itself a good three meters off the ground. But the lock rim was a gentle step off the valley's sandy floor. Demeter glanced back and saw that the machine had assumed a low crouch, with its knee joints flexed above the cabin roof.

"What's on the program for today?" she asked, once she'd figured out the suit's radio channels.

"I'm prospecting for water or ice, and you're helping me."

Mitsuno went over to the side of the walker's belly and opened a compartment hatch in the smooth space between two leg swivels. He took out various aluminum cases, laid them on the sand, and unsealed their lids. Inside, inset into foam cutouts, were gray melon-shapes with little black bracing feet on either side and a data panel on top.

"What're those?"

"Transponders."

"What are you going to do with them?"

"You're going to take one and walk about three hundred meters out *that* way." Mitsuno pointed to the east. "Then you take another and go the same distance in the opposite direction. And when that's done, you'll put out two more, going north and south this time."

"And what will you be doing?"

"Watching you." Lole grinned up through his helmet bubble and handed her the first of the recording devices. It was solid-feeling, but not all that heavy.

She moved around the walker's outstretched foot-pads and started off toward the horizon. None of the stones that lay on top of the desert floor was big enough to make her alter course. She just stepped over them, keeping to as straight a line as possible. Soon Demeter had crossed a small rise and walked into a shallow pit. She looked over her shoulder and noticed that the walker had all but disappeared.

"Lole?"

"Yeah?"

"I can't see you," she said. "Does line of sight matter to these widgets?"

"Naw, they read ground motion and compare with their own inertials."

"Okay."

When she had counted off something like three hundred paces—each one close enough to a meter for this kind of work—Demeter set the transponder down, cocked its legs as Lole had shown her, and turned it on. When she straightened up, she noticed a group of silhouettes on the far horizon. They were dancing figures in inky leotards, with what looked like fluttering capes or demon wings on their shoulders. All except one. It was bright green. It looked, more than anything else, like a jade carving of the Laughing Buddha. It was holding up an aerialist's parasol.

Coghlan wished the helmet visor was fitted with zoom optics. As it was, she could get no more definition than naked-eye. The entities looked like mirages or possibly dust devils, and she might have dismissed them as such—except for that lone, green figure.

When she got back to the walker, she mentioned the apparition to Mitsuno.

"How many were there, would you say?"

"Three or four. All alike enough to be some kind of heat distortion. Oh, but one was larger than the rest and green—looked like the Michelin Man with a sunshade."

"Wait a minute." Mitsuno clicked off her frequency. Demeter could see his mouth moving inside the bubble, carrying on an extended conversation.

"Okay, we're done for the day here. Go and bring back that transponder, would you?"

"What's wrong? Aren't we hunting water?"

"No need. They say this is a dry valley."

"They? *Who?*" Demeter felt her neck hairs rise with the finality in his voice.

"The Cyborgs you saw."

"Those were Cyborgs? I didn't know there were any of 'em left."

"Why not? Each one is essentially immortal."

"And omniscient?" she asked.

"When it comes to things Martian—yes, usually."

"So we're just going to pack up and go home? How about we walk over and meet them?"

"That's . . . not a good idea. Old hands find it smart to give Cyborgs a wide berth, unless they ask for your company. And this bunch sounded real short."

"Are they dangerous? They looked pretty skinny to me. Most of them did, anyway."

"Those guys don't have meat for muscles, Dem. They're all servos and solenoids, with tempers to match. You catch them wrong, they could pop your suit before you got turned around to run. Remember, they can breathe out here and you can't."

"I see. So we make like shadows."

"Damn straight."

"Don't know if I want to go back for that transponder now."

"Just keep your head down and mind your business."

"You go," she insisted.

"I wouldn't recognize the spot where you left it," Mitsuno said reasonably.

So Demeter trudged back over the rise. When she got to where the sensor was and retrieved it, she glanced up at the horizon.

The dancing shadows were gone.

Hoplite Bar & Grill, June IO

When Ellen Sorbel arrived at the Hoplite, it was clear from the rackup of empties on their table that Lole and Demeter had been there for an hour or two. Probably since they docked.

Of course Ellen had heard about the bust at Harmonia Mundi. Wyatt had informed her even before Lole locked back inside the walker and turned it for home. The administrative cyber was too pleased with his big chance to say "I told you so." All along, as Ellen had struggled to analyze the new orbital survey data, Wyatt kept mentioning some old ground report—no, he couldn't cite a reference—which he *thought* showed a total lack of any anomalies hydrologic, seismic, or otherwise under the Mundi area. Ellen wondered if the Cyborgs had known about that report; they were usually were even worse at recordkeeping than Wyatt.

"Hey, guys!" Ellen said cheerfully as Mitsuno looked up.

"Ellen!" Demeter turned and seemed genuinely glad to see her.

"Sorry about the site—" Lole began.

"No need. We all strike rocks once in a while. But why were your Cyborgs so sure there was no water? Have they been digging—?"

"Roger says it's the wrong kind of formation."

"And he would know, I suppose," Ellen grumped. She had spent most of her life plugging her head into geological core samples, infrared survey data, and acoustic interferometry matrices—and she still didn't know half as much about Martian substructures as Roger Torraway had squirreled away in that cybernetic backpack of his. "What was he doing out there?"

"'Cyborg business,' he told me," Lole replied. "As in 'Please kindly butt out.' Torraway seemed to be holding some sort of caucus with his friends—including the Russian girl, Shtev."

"One of those Cyborgs was *Torraway?*" Demeter asked, suddenly looking up. "Colonel Roger Torraway?"

"Sure," Lole said. "Why?"

"He came from Texahoma. I've been to the place where he was made. I should have gone over today and said hello, greet a fellow countryman."

"Demeter is a diplomat-in-training," Lole explained to Ellen. "Thinks she's got to make contact with the local nationals." He turned to Coghlan. "Torraway is *not* Texahoman, Demeter. He's one hundred percent Martian. And anyway, when they made him, your country—the Oklahoma part, that is—was still joined to the United States of America. Torraway was an official in its Air Force, which I guess means he ran a blimp or something. But he became the first true Martian when they brought him here."

"Now you're telling me Earth's history?" Demeter had a smile on her face.

"Our history, too," Ellen put in. "Every Martian schoolchild learns about the age of colonization."

"What I never understood," Lole went on, "is why, if those scientists in the United States and Russia wanted to create a race of native Martians, they didn't let them breed. Why make them surgical eunuchs?"

"That's obvious, Lole." Coghlan shrugged. "The human parts could breed, sure, but they couldn't adapt their babies with all the hardware needed to survive."

"Why not? The von Neumanns do it."

"But those're machines! They were designed to—"

"So are the Cyborgs, machines," he said reasonably.

"It's different," Demeter insisted.

"What *I* never could figure out," Ellen interrupted, "is why your country—the old country, whatever—went to the expense of building Cyborgs in the first place. The cost just about broke your economy. And it certainly helped sink the Russians."

"Why, so they could explore Mars," Demeter explained.

"Ordinary people can explore Mars," Lole pointed out. "You did this morning."

"Well, I guess, it was before they had settlements like this for growing food and stockpiling tanked air and such. It was just easier getting around as a self-contained Cyborg."

"But they brought up nonadapted humans on that

first mission to accompany Torraway. One of them was his doctor, along to make repairs. *They* managed just fine, growing food in domes and compressing the air."

"I'm sure there was a good reason for the Cyborg programs. The scientists must have checked it out, made computer models—"

Lole was grinning now. "They made computer models."

"What you mean," Ellen said, "is the *computers* made computer models."

"And the computers made them the way they wanted them, to achieve the goals *they* had in mind," Lole finished up.

"Are we talking fairy tales here?" Demeter asked with a stiffly superior air. "I've heard all those stories, too, you know. The grid is self-aware. The grid is God. The grid is the next stage in human-machine evolution. . . . Right, guys! Look, the good Lord knows I have reason enough to distrust the machines. But I don't anthropomorphize them. I don't *demonize* them. Sure, I talk to my charm bracelet. And you two talk to thin air and think of it as this 'Wyatt' character. But it's still all just a machine. Just a bunch of really *fast* silicon platelets running self-branching response loops."

The woman stopped, her chest heaving now, and glared from Lole to Ellen.

"Are you so sure?" Sorbel said quietly, after a pause. "Jory tells me you don't even like to *talk* about sex if they're listening."

"Jory has a big mouth," Demeter said dryly. "And yes, he's right. But I also don't like doing it in front of my cat. That doesn't make Bitsy part of a feline cabal that's supposed to dominate human affairs."

"Still, you have to admit," Lole said, "the Earth

scientists went and did something really stupid—on the advice of all those computer projections."

"But it came out all right in the long run, didn't it?" Demeter insisted. "Look at yourself today. All geared up to run your seismic tests, and then this ghost voice from out of the wilderness says, 'Don't bother.' So you tug your forelock and back out of there quick enough. Those so-called biased computer projections have given you a council of elders, the voice of tribal wisdom, and a free-floating resource of inherited knowledge. The Cyborgs help make this planet a little more approachable, a little more friendly. *That's* what those computer projections from the last century knew you'd need to survive here."

"Maybe you're right," Lole agreed, but he looked uncertain.

"Of course I'm right. I never said the grid and its nodes weren't smart, or subtle. Devious, even. But they just aren't . . . human."

"Is anybody else thirsty?" Ellen asked, to change the subject. "I sure am."

Golden Lotus, June 10

When Demeter was really tired, or had a few drinks in her—or both, as now—she couldn't focus enough to compose an intelligible report. So, instead of trying to gather her own thoughts, she put the hotel room's terminal in interrogation mode. The machine would ask her what she had seen and done during the day's safari, then it would prepare a draft report taking cues from her previous conversational style. In the morning she could review and edit the final version before sending it off.

Concept-processing was a function Coghlan had long ago installed in Sugar. Hell, Sugar could probably

write up the day from her own aural recordings—
except for the time she'd spent tucked in a pocket.
Relying on machines like this would eventually turn
Demeter into a moron, she knew, unable to think
sequentially or remember more than two ideas at one
sitting. But tonight the program was a godsend.

"Where did you go?" the terminal asked.

"Some place called Har-something Monday, map
reference . . . well, look it up yourself. We were going
to do geolog—no, *hydro*logical exploration, looking for
possible subsurface water." Demeter's jaw quivered as
she stifled a yawn.

"What did you find?"

"Nothing. We met—or rather, saw in the distance—
some Cyborgs who warned us off. Lole says they were
having a coffee klatsch of some kind. I didn't talk to
them. . . . *Yee-heww!*" She yawned again, opening her
mouth until the top of her head was like to fall off.

"What did Lole Mitsuno say about the Cyborgs?"

"That they were dangerous . . . difficult, short-
tempered. Strong, too."

"We know all that. But later, when he was talking
about their origins—?"

"Oh . . . that making them was some kind of mistake,
that the computers on Earth had screwed up the projections." Demeter could hardly keep her eyes open.
This was going to be one garbled report, despite the
terminal's best efforts. "A lot of old wives' stuff . . .
actually."

She yawned again. Rather than try to sit up, Demeter lay down on the bed and crawled toward her pillow.

"Now listen very closely . . ." the machine suggested.

Demeter was already asleep and snoring.

That didn't matter.

Chapter 7

Cries and Whispers

120 Kilometers East of Harmonia Mundi, June 11

"Revolution is not in their programming, Roger."

Fetya hadn't spoken in more than three hours. She had simply kept pace with him as Roger Torraway put long distance between himself and that embarrassing confrontation. Together their clublike feet stamped over the wind-packed sand.

"I wasn't talking about 'revolution,'" he objected. "Just some kind of concerted action. A protest march. A demonstration of strength. After all, they benefit from the Deimos generator, too."

"Protest implies power shifting."

"That's deep!" He could hear the bitterness in his own voice, slopping over onto the closed signal that carried between them. He detested the feelings that were now bubbling up in him: of dependence and obligation.

"Is true!" the other Cyborg said. "We were made for exploration. For observation. For description. We serve human needs on Mars, in support of colonizing efforts. Our purpose is not dictating terms to human settlements. Now you want we should damage colonials."

"Not damage! Just . . . withhold our counsel and advice. We have to show the burgomasters how

115

much they need us. How they need us as free and independent beings. Show them how scary and hostile a place this planet can potentially be without us."

"Implies somebody has to die first, yes?"

"Well . . ."

"Tell me story of omelets and eggs again, Roger." She let out a grating chuckle.

"Damn it, this is serious!" He stamped the ground in midstride.

"Serious to you means obvious to everybody else?"

"What is *that* supposed to mean?"

"You figure out. . . ."

The pair plodded along in silence for another hour, good for an additional eight kilometers. With Roger's compressed time-sense, it passed inside a few gliding seconds. Only the scenery was different: steeper hills, more exposed bedrock, the beginnings of erosion gullies.

"Make their problems your problem," Fetya said at last. "Not other way around."

"How do I do that?"

"Find out what humans need."

"I've already tried that. They just weren't buying any."

"No, Roger. You made offer to sell what you had, not what they need. Is difference."

"But I offered to sell myself, my innermost—"

"Still not what they *need*."

"Yeah."

Fetya was right, of course. But what the hell did the humans on Mars need? Something that only he, or one of the other Cyborgs, could supply. And, of course, something they weren't already supplying, according to their "programming."

That was the stumper.

The Russian Tearoom, Commercial Unit 2/0/1, June 11

Sometime during the previous afternoon as the conversation wandered from this to that, Ellen Sorbel had mentioned another Earth-based casual who was interested in hydrology and the workings of the Resources Department—a Mr. Sun from United Korea.

Demeter was resigned to finally having to meet the man in the flesh. So she had asked Sorbel to arrange an introduction. Demeter supposed she could always share her experiences at Harmonia Mundi as an ice-breaker.

The hydrologist met Demeter at the Golden Lotus and walked her up two levels and across the complex to brunch at Tharsis Montes's most fashionable tearoom.

"They actually do serve tea there," Sorbel explained. "Thick brown stuff they've been bubbling for a week or more in a genuine Russian samovar, imported from Petrograd, solid silver and *heavy*. Then they dilute it with vodka, whiskey, lemon juice, or whatever you want. It's really disgusting."

"Why does anyone go there?" Demeter asked, curious.

"Because it's . . ." Ellen shrugged. "Where you can be seen, I guess. The tourists all love it."

"I've never heard of the place."

"Their little cakes are famous. Very crumbly, mostly sugar and butter—well, sorghum extract and some kind of saturated lipid, but you get the idea." Ellen gave a wicked grin.

"You sure know how to whet my appetite."

"That reminds me. . . . If you're getting tired of tooting around the Martian surface, you really ought to take a tour of the orbital power satellites. Especially the new one they've got under construction over Schiaparelli. Taking a V/R of microgravity can be a real kick. I can arrange a hookup for you, if you want."

Demeter paused before replying. *What* would remind Ellen of such a thing? Had Demeter said something about it yesterday? Why should Sorbel be so interested in feeding her this new experience? Maybe . . . Demeter's head whirled. It was culture-lag or time-shock or something. It was making her suspicious of the simplest friendly overtures. Or possibly she was just keyed up about meeting up her first foreign-national spy.

The Russian Tearoom's decor was all white cloth and porcelain, bright silver and chiming crystal. The walls had been whitewashed and then painted in stark black lines that were supposed to be barren trees in a Russian winter—from the perspective of an artist who had never seen a living tree. Somewhere in the background a recording of violins played *Zigeunerweisen*—Gypsy music for a Czarist setting. Oh, well, it could easily have been a chorus of Cossack voices. Next, Demeter expected to find waiters dressed in black jodhpurs, waist sashes, and red-silk blouses. Fortunately, however, the service was both automated and unobtrusive.

Ellen walked past the seating chart and into the main room, towing Demeter in her wake. She went right up to a center table where sat a fat young man in a conservative gray suit. Demeter recognized the face from her snooping in the directory of casuals three days ago. The eyes were more deeply buried in their folds of fat than the pixel dump of Sun Il Suk's travel holo had suggested. His skin was much yellower, less healthy-looking. She glanced around surreptitiously for the servant, Chang Qwok-Do, but found no one fitting his image. Probably back in the kitchen, arranging to barbecue a dog or something.

"Sukie, I'd like you to meet a friend of mine," Ellen was saying. "This is Demeter Coghlan, who's also up from Earth. Demeter, Sun Il Suk is a distinguished visitor from United Korea."

The young man shifted his bulk from its tight wedge against the table and flexed his knees. The movement passed for a polite effort to rise. He then raised his hand to her and tilted his head, the eyes narrowed in line with his outstretched fingers and cocked thumb, as if aiming a pistol.

Demeter grasped the hand—it was soft and damp—and pumped it.

"Won't you ladies join me?" he wheezed.

Ellen Sorbel begged off with the claim of pressing duties and quickly departed the tearoom. That left Demeter and the grimly smiling Oriental. She accepted the chair opposite him.

"I understand, Miz Coghlan, that we are both interested in this planet's natural resources. We two have visited many of the same places. . . . Valles Marineris, for one."

"Mine is a purely academic interest, I assure you."

"Ah, yes. Academics. The databases tell me you have studied for your country's foreign service. Perhaps you are planning to add exogeology to your curriculum vitae, then?"

"That's a thought."

"But you already have the credits required to take your degree," Sun pointed out.

"Not quite enough," she corrected.

"Sufficient, apparently, to know your business. That is, if you have accepted this assignment."

"What 'assignment' would that be?"

"Why, to come here and investigate the Zealanders' development in areas currently claimed by your own Texahoma. . . . And by United Korea, of course."

"You have an active imagination, sir."

"Oh? Then Texahoma does *not* claim—?"

"No—about my being on assignment. I wish someone *would* pay me to take vacations and play the tourist. As it is . . ."

"As it is, Miz Coghlan, your grandfather pays you to do exactly that. And to 'keep your eyes peeled.' Or 'get the wax out of your ears.' Or whatever colorful Americanism the old man uses with his favorite granddaughter."

"And why would he tell me that?" Demeter asked demurely.

"Come, my dear!" Sun Il Suk laid a confiding hand on her forearm. "Do not play the naive with me! Your august 'Gee-dad,' as you call him, is a political power in your country. Officially, at least, Alvin Bertrand Coghlan is next in line for the Big Chair in Austin. Unofficially, he already steers the party apparatus of the Inde-Goddam-Pendents, where the real authority exists."

"Well . . ."

"Do I lie?" His smile was full of white teeth.

"No, but we Texahomans don't like to talk so openly about a man's prospects. It puts the kibosh on him, we say."

"'Puts the kai—?'"

"Another colorful Americanism." Demeter showed her own teeth. Damn, but she was beginning to enjoy this! "For your collection."

"Let's be straight with each other, my dear. That's

the correct phrase, is it not? You and I are here for the same purpose—to find out what the Zealanders are up to and, if possible, throw a few logs in front of their wheels. Not—" He held up a hand before she could respond. "—that it will matter in any practical way until long after both of us are mere dust blowing on the wind. No effort to terraform this planet will come to anything in less than a hundred years. Two hundred. But since we are all on Earth—or in Mars—for so dismally short a time, we two might as well make common cause and hay while the sun shines. Yes?"

"Are you telling me you are a paid spy, Mr. Sun?" Demeter made her eyes go wide.

"But of course! And United Korea pays well for my humble efforts. Does not yours?"

Coghlan was reminded of a quip by one of her professors, Simonson, who taught Industrial Espionage and Economic Theory: "Beware of geeks when baring grifts." He must have had Sun Il Suk in mind.

"Now," Sun continued, "which of the current crop of North Zealand visitors do you favor? The farmers out at Elysium? The stargazer up on Phobos? Or the new one, the Cuneo woman?"

"Well, for my money—"

"Cuneo, of course. She *does* care for the future, especially in the Valles Marineris District. And yes, she knows all about the Texahomans' secret plans for mutating the Martian atmosphere. If she were to discover our true purposes, yours and mine, she would do anything to inconvenience us. Probably even agitate to have us removed from this planet. Either back up the fountain or . . . out into the desert somewhere. That woman is capable of anything."

"Aren't you being a little dramatic? Even if she—"

"See for yourself! Tell me those aren't the eyes of a fanatic!" Sun Il Suk gestured to a table just beyond the one next to them.

A lone woman sat there. The face *might* be the same one Demeter had scanned in her hotel room three days ago. In person the features were . . . blockier, somehow. The body was stockier than Demeter had imagined from the passport description. But the hair was entirely different: red and curly and cut full to the collar of her jacket, not the severe black helmet the grid had shown earlier. Of course, it could be a wig, one way or the other.

And Sun's information was so good in other respects, why would he make a stupid mistake now?

"If that's really her," Demeter began, "and she really is the dangerous person you believe her to be, then is it safe to be talking about her so openly?"

The Korean pointed to a small white box sitting on the table linen, lost among the sugar and cream and the obligatory bud vase with a paper flower. It sat against the edge of the table between them and Cuneo. Demeter had noticed the box and thought it was a pillbox with some kind of medicine for Sun.

"Phase inverter," he announced. "The device has the gift of turning any sound made within a circle of—oh, a meter and a half across—on its head. Feeds it right back into the air as pure gibberish. I'm surprised, Demeter, that your government hasn't provided you with something similar." He lifted one finger and raised his voice. "Personally, I think all North Zealanders smell like the breath of thousand-year-old eggs."

Cuneo's head shifted with a cup halfway to her lips. She looked over at Sun and Coghlan—but it was the distracted glance of a lone diner in a crowded place.

There was no recognition, let alone sense of insult.

"See?" he said in a more normal voice. "Just white noise."

Demeter noted in passing that any device so tiny yet powerful had to be cybernetically controlled—probably using sophisticated processing algorithms supplied through the local grid. And she would bet Texahoma dollars to the Russian Tearoom's greasy little donuts that any conversation going into the white box got stuck somewhere in the grid's capacious datastreams.

"You do like to live dangerously, Mr. Sun," she said.

"No, my dear, I like to *live*. Period. Full stop. And you can put that on my gravestone. . . . But please, do call me 'Sukie.' You'll do that now, won't you?"

Despite her every instinct, Demeter liked him.

Chapter 8

Hidden Meanings

Jory waited nearly two hours in the corridor outside the Golden Lotus. To avoid questions, he busied himself with tools from his harness, a logic probe and beadlight, to take apart a motion sensor that nobody had actually reported broken. People didn't make Creoles feel unwelcome or awkward inside the Tharsis Montes complex, but loiterers anywhere—human or modified—could arouse a certain level of apprehension. Jory didn't want to answer questions from any of the Citizen's Militia.

It was true he had no assigned tasks, not for the whole day. He was supposed to be resting and correcting an electrolyte imbalance specified by his renal filters. But that, like the wall sensor he was pretending to fix, was a polite fiction.

In reality, he wanted to see Demeter Coghlan again; yet he couldn't *appear* to want to see her. So instead he waited outside her hotel room, busy with something important yet unobtrusive. That way, when she came out, he would happen to meet her accidentally. For Jory, it was a clever plan.

The door to Unit 9 opened behind him. The Creole, halfway up the wall and hanging by one hand from an open socket, turned with an eager look on his face.

"Why, Jory!" Demeter cried. "What are you doing here?"

He dropped to the floor on cat feet. "Uh . . . fixing a . . . uh . . ." He pointed back up the wall. "Sensor."

"Right outside my door?" Demeter glanced up and down the corridor. "What a coincidence."

"I . . . did want to see you again." Jory stared at his toes.

It had never bothered him before that the impenetrable skin he wore was thickened and ridged across his soles, that his toes were both webbed and spring-tensioned for rebounding equally well off powdery sands and unyielding rock. Shoes were not only unnecessary but impossible for him. Now his feet seemed naked: wide and ugly—unlike hers, which leather pumps smoothed and tapered into delicate pieces of sculpture. Like a gazelle's slender hoofs.

"That's not a good idea, Jory."

"But I thought—!"

What did he think? That he and this exotic creature from another planet could actually . . . *be* together? That her rich and important family back on Earth wouldn't come hunting for her? That the two of them could set up housekeeping at Tharsis Montes on his stipend as a Grade 6 Maintenance Helper? That she would one day bear his children and then allow them, in their twelfth year, to be taken up, skinned and gutted, and transformed into Creoles like their father? Was that what he really thought?

"I thought you liked me," he said simply.

"Oh, Jory!" Her face clouded up. "I *do* like you. You've been a good friend to me. But today I've got a schedule to keep and—"

"I have a surprise for you," he blurted out.

Nothing was going as he'd planned.

"A surprise? But—"

"Come on!" He took her arm, gripping just above the wrist in a practiced lock, and pulled her forward, just enough to bring her off balance. "I'll show you."

"Couldn't you just tell me?"

"Then it wouldn't be a surprise."

She was already in motion, putting one foot out to catch her balance, when he steered her left down the corridor and started walking and talking—*fast*.

"I remember how you said you didn't like the computers watching you when you—when you had personal functions to perform—so I tried to think of a place where they couldn't see—and it came to me that there's places like that all over the complex. You just have to think ahead and do a little preparation. So I decided to see if I couldn't set something up for you— and me, too, if that's how you like it."

He was babbling badly, something his mother had always warned him against. "Better to be thought a fool," she would say, "than to open your mouth and remove all doubt." But Jory sensed that Demeter Coghlan, a human addicted to words and explanations, would plaster her own interpretations over any unvarnished setting he presented her with. So Jory had to crowd her out with a flow of chatter, however feeble it might be.

As he talked, he took her down two levels and across the wide avenue, twice as broad and high as the average tunnel, that had been planned into the complex's development. This strip would be called the Arcade when it was finished. It would feature commercial booths having their own walls and ceilings, erected under the arch of rock. Here Jory and Demeter were moving beyond the comfortable, pleasantly rounded-out districts of Tharsis Montes as it was, a pleasant village built around a transfer station. They were entering the harder geometric outlines of the larger Tharsis Montes that would eventually grow up under the volcanic slopes: a great trading center and perhaps even the hub of mercantile civilization on Mars.

Twenty paces farther, and the pair moved from orderly tunnels with finished floors and smooth walls, with electrical and service connections, with light and air and fiberoptic, to a cold steel door anchored by four oblong steel dogs.

"Is that an airlock?" she asked.

"Not really."

Bracing his fingers like the jaws of a wrench, Jory twisted the bolt caps in quarter turns until the dogs hung loose against the seal rim. Then he curled his fist around the vertical bar, levered his weight away from the door, and hauled it open against the pressure difference. A thin sighing, like the winds of Mars, sounded in the crack between door and frame.

Jory took her wrist again and stepped through.

"Wait a minute!" Demeter pulled back. "You may be able to breathe in there, but I can't!"

"Sure you can! It's good air, just not quite up to a full nine hundred millibars."

Jory felt around at the base of the door behind the hinge, found the flashlight he'd left there, and clicked it on. The wide-angled beam showed up scarred walls of gray stone that still reflected occasional lines of scoring, parallel with the floor, where the drill jumbos had cut into the rock but the blasting mixture had failed to penetrate and completely cave the matrix. This tunnel was in a hand-drilled area, so near to the populated levels; there was no room to bring in a big borer—like the machine he and Demeter had watched working in the Valles—and make a clean sweep.

"It's cold in here!" Her breath smoked.

"Sorry. . . . You'll warm up in a minute."

He took her down twenty meters of openwork, around a left turn, and through another door, this one closed with a simple bar latch. Beyond it was a dead end, an irregular cavern with only a single entrance and not even a service duct cut into the walls yet.

"Here we are," he announced with a grin.

"This is your surprise?" she asked cautiously.

Jory shone the light down on the roll of high-gee packing and the emergency blanket he'd laid over it. With a little imagination, it looked like a bed and was certainly just as soft.

"See? No video or aural pickups installed yet." He swung the beam up one wall and across the low ceiling. "Not even motion sensors or sniffers—nothing to move in here, and no gas pockets to seep in."

"All right . . . why?"

"Well, you said the computer grid listening and watching all the time bothered you. So, here's a place they can't see or hear."

"A love nest?"

She said the words with no particular enthusiasm, but it didn't stop Jory. He took them as a signal to make his move. He slid his left hand forward, touching her hip, finger-walking around her waist, drawing her body toward him, until the curve of her belly was brushing the front of his shorts.

"Jory. . . ."

His mouth pressed over hers. The mask flaps that

grew from his cheeks like a leathery beard tenderly brushed the lower part of her face.

His left hand dropped to her buttock, pulling forward so that her groin dug into his. When her weight shifted, he lifted her right leg up around his hip, and his right hand moved between them, working on the snaps that closed the front seam of her clothing. Where his nails—composed of a fused aramid fiber and periodically replaceable—were too thick to insert between the snap's baseplate and gripper, he just pinched the whole mechanism free of the surrounding cloth.

"No . . . wait!" she said breathlessly, trying to talk around the pressure of his lips and tongue. "I'm not in the moo—"

Jory released his grip a fraction and raised his head.

"Oh, yeah, I forgot," he said, taking up her left hand. The silver charm bracelet swayed around her wrist. Jory pulled it off, bunched it in his palm, tugged open the hook-and-eye closure on her jumper's breast pocket with a *brrrip!*, and poured the bracelet in. He sealed the tab with a circular motion of his thumb that widened until it took in the firmness of her nipple.

Then Jory pulled Demeter's body even closer, working his hips up and down, pressing the bony arch of his pelvis into her convenient hollowness. Something let go inside her. She began moaning at the back of her throat as Jory reached down to the pouch between his legs and released his expanding member.

Demeter pulled back. But she only meant to peer down at it, rising between them in the dim light.

"This time don't tear my clothing," she warned.

Golden Lotus, June 12

Demeter Coghlan was still bemused by the time she returned to her room at the hotel. Her plans for the day had gotten sidetracked in the cavern somewhere under the city.

That morning she had decided not to see the smooth-skinned little Creole again, but after five minutes with him, she could think only of rutting until her brains exploded.

Demeter decided she really had to take a firm hand in calling off this—dalliance? This whatever-it-was. Nothing could come of the two of them—and if anything did happen to come of the affair, then G'dad would be purely furious.

Which, come to think of it, might not be *all* bad.

Even though Demeter had spent most of the afternoon on a mattress, all she wanted to do was climb into bed, pull the covers over her head, and sleep for a week. She made a minimal toilet, set out a water glass, and started to unfasten the bracelet at her wrist.

Oh, right.

She fumbled in her top pocket for the silver bead.

"Now what was *that* all about?" Sugar asked as Demeter brought her out into the light. "I heard some mighty interesting *rustling* going on there. Lasted quite a while, too."

"Shut up, Sugar," Demeter said tonelessly as she laid the charm on the shelf and began to turn the glass over.

"Never no mi—yi . . . ah, wait one, Dem."

"What is it?"

"Message coming in for you. From Earth. Code red."

"Coming on this terminal?"

"Yes," the chrono said. "But Dum-Dum there can't interpret the code. I can. Shall I divert? It's just text."

"Go ahead." Demeter sat down on the edge of the bed.

"'Weiss to Coghlan, eyes only,'" Sugar began dictating. "I guess that doesn't include *me*, huh?"

"Just read."

"'Reliable agents in Oakland report and said dispatch of commercial contingent with full consular status sometime late October stop. Given orbital transit times should be coming down on your head any day now stop. Sorry for late warning but this departure held extreme hush and defended most violently endit.' . . . What's that all supposed to mean, Dem?"

"Shut up and let me think."

"Never no mind."

Where in the hell was "Oakland"? And why would Gregor Weiss have agents there? And if he did, why should it matter to her? Demeter Coghlan was puzzled. "Violently defended" hinted at terrible things: maybe some people dying to get this message back to Dallas and so forwarded on to her. But she didn't know how to interpret it!

Then something occurred to Demeter.

"Sugar, spell 'Oakland.'"

"A-U-C-K-L-A-N-D, Dem. Just like it sounds."

Now *that* was beginning to make sense. Auckland was the North Zealand capital. So the delegation *might* be something to do with the Valles Marineris project, which was under the auspices of the North Zealand Economic Development Agency. If so, granting the newcomers diplomatic status could give them the negotiating clout to pull the disputed territory right out from under her.

Still, Weiss's message did not confirm this interpretation.

"Read the whole thing again, Sugar."

The chrono did so, with exactly the same inflections.

The message was, of course, in Weiss's nineteenth-century, secret-agent telegraph slang. But for all that, Gregor was still a meticulous bureaucrat. That grammatical fault in the first code group—"report and said"—simply did not sound like him.

Report and said.

Report *and said.*

Report . . . N-ZED!

"Sugar, does the character group N-hyphen-Z-E-D appear anywhere in the text?"

"Of course, Dem. In the first sentence. Just like I read it."

"I've got to get your speech chip fixed, dear."

"Ain't no flies on me, Dem. You're the one ought to get her ears fixed."

Chapter 9

Head Trips

Golden Lotus, June 13

Demeter woke up the next morning with a panicky rush that closed her throat and made her heart pound. The situation here on Mars was rapidly getting away from her. Weiss's message implied that the North Zealanders were about to make some kind of political move on the Valles Marineris District . . . and all Demeter had done so far was take a couple of sightseeing trips and introduce herself to a few of the locals.

Well, what else could she do?

Demeter was officially on planet as a simple tourist, with no diplomatic status. In fact, from what she'd observed so far, Mars didn't seem to *have* any formal government structure—nothing that she could apply to for accreditation, in any capacity. The upward limits of Martian organization appeared to be a series of local, municipal bureaucracies. The highest official Demeter had ever heard of was a mayor in Solis Planum. The business of government was communications, record-keeping, taxation, commercial exchange, infrastructure maintenance—and all of it was carried on by an overlay of cyber functions in the ever-present grid.

How the party of Zealander bigshots proposed to establish diplomatic relations with *that* was beyond her.

There was one thing Demeter herself might try. She could use those informal contacts to make whatever government there was begin working for her.

That was the spark Demeter needed. She shot up from the bed, let it slam against the wall, and climbed into her metered, one-minute shower. With her hair wrapped in a turban and drying slowly, she ordered coffee and a yogurt for breakfast. The hotel offered its yogurt in just two flavors, Dutch chocolate or lemon. She had already found the lemon reminiscent of battery acid; now she discovered that the chocolate tasted like chalk and diesel fuel. It had to be something wrong with the mother culture.

As she brushed her hair, Demeter set out to find her friends. Like all searches on Earth or Mars, this one began with the grid. Demeter faced her room terminal, switched it to PRIVACY mode, and said: "Um, let me speak to the entity known as 'Wyatt,' please."

"Yes, Miz Coghlan-Demeter-Cerise?" replied a cool voice. It was somehow a different inflection from the terminal's usual tone: superior, more self-satisfied, less eager to please. In one move, she had reached Wyatt in the flesh—or the electron.

"I need to locate Ellen Sorbel. She's probably not at work yet, but—"

"Miz Sorbel is fully occupied."

"*Where* is she?"

"Hydrology Lab, Dome Two, but this is not a good time to—"

"Thanks, I'll be right there." Demeter was never one to take hints from a machine, especially one attached to a large bureaucracy. "Um, how do I find Dome Two?"

"Take Lift Four to the surface levels, follow Tube Y-Nine to the west, the rest is signed. But you really should—"

Demeter blanked the terminal, pulled on her coveralls, grabbed up a handful of pins for her hair, and went streaming out into the corridor.

Hydrology Lab, June 13

Ellen Sorbel slid through the interstices of the matrix, following the line of least resistance. The granules she passed were rugged, globular shapes floating above or below her awareness. Each one represented a particle of fine sand, barely a millimeter in diameter, so tiny that in life it might disappear beneath one of her fingernails. Yet, at this scale, her mind swam and dove past the bits like a seal cresting the spires of a rocky headland.

She was a water droplet.

Ellen drifted lower, finding her own level. She was seeking a clay substrate reported to underlie the Desert of Agnus Dei, some two hundred kilometers southwest of Tharsis Montes. She slid forward across one crowning mass of glittering quartz and feldspar. Sorbel somersaulted down its leading edge and clung to the underside—clung not with her hands but with the adhesion of surface tension. There her back brushed against another jagged particle below it. She oozed away from the upper surface; her awareness flipped over, righting itself against the pull of gravity. She flowed onto the lower footing and began heading for its outer perimeter.

Another tumble, and Ellen found herself at some kind of boundary layer. No longer loose chunks with space between them, but a hardpan of aluminum and magnesium silicates that formed lozenges only two or three microns in diameter. There was even less space between them. Her awareness flattened out, spreading and diffusing like pancake batter. There would be no more joyous tumbling. This certainly felt like the clay—

"What are you doing?"

The voice came from somewhere off to her left in the void.

Ellen turned with eyes that were not eyes and saw nothing.

"Who's there?"

"It's me! Demeter!"

"Oh, hello . . ."

"Am I disturbing you?"

Yes! Ellen wanted to shout.

"Not really. . . . Um, how did you get here?"

"One of your technicians lent me a headset and gloves," Demeter replied. "He said you were here in the . . . where is this place? It's like an asteroid field!"

"We're in a bit of desert, about fifty meters below the surface. Or, anyway, this is what the computer *says* should be below the surface."

"Wyatt says?"

"No, a much bigger boy."

"What are you looking for?"

"I'm trying to discover where the water would have gone . . . if it ever existed here," Sorbel explained. "I think I've found a lens of clay which—"

"Where?" Demeter demanded.

"Somewhere below you, I guess. You're probably still up in the sandy layer."

"Is that so? How do I get down?"

"You don't—unless you know how to use your gloves to, well, *flow.*"

"I can't," Demeter said after a minute. "Couldn't you come up to me? I can't *see* you."

"Eyesight isn't important down here. Why don't we

just talk?" Ellen made herself limp and flattened out even more against the clay substrate. "What do you want?"

"Well, unh, this is difficult. . . . Can anyone overhear us?"

"You mean, aside from the cyber that created this geological simulation and is now monitoring it?"

"Yeah."

"Not really. Your headset is hushed."

"Then what I want is your help as a programmer. I need to hack a few terminals that're attached to the grid. I want a download of anything they send or receive over the next few days."

"Which terminals?" Ellen was merely curious.

"One is in the quarters of a North Zealand woman named Cuneo, first name Nancy. She's a casual on Mars like me. The others are wherever our Korean friend Sukie is staying—one terminal in his private room, the other with his manservant Chang Qwok-Do."

Sorbel considered the request for a passing moment. Then: "Lole was right about you, wasn't he? You're a spy."

"Ellen . . . we're *all* spies. Sun Il Suk admitted as much as to me when you introduced us. He knows about the Cuneo woman, too, but I'd picked her out long before that. Either or both of them probably has a tap going on my room already. . . . I just want some insurance to hold against payback time."

"And you thought I could—"

"You're the most computer-friendly person I know here. Hell, everyone on Mars practically lives in the machines' hip pocket. But you're the first person I've met who actually puts her head inside one for a living."

"We're not inside a *computer*, Dem. This is a geological simulation that's wired into a V/R sensory setup.

It's not all that different from the ones you use for role-playing or proxy touring."

"Whatever. I still figure if anyone has the smarts to help me, you do."

"I might have the smarts. Don't count on my willingness. Sukie is my friend. And I don't know what this Nancy Cuneo has done against me and mine . . . although I don't like the idea of anyone spying on Mars."

"We're not spying on *you*, Ellen. We're watching each other. It all goes back to the political situation on Earth. We three just happen to be on Mars right now. That's all."

One of the talents Sorbel's job had developed and strengthened in her was pattern analysis. She was adept at piecing together tiny clues to form an outline of what was really going on. From the nuances in Demeter's voice, Ellen understood one thing: she was lying. Demeter's story was too complicated and involved; the truth would be much simpler. This was unfortunate, because Ellen really liked the Earth woman. She was saddened to think they couldn't be honest with each other.

"You and your friends can play hide-and-seek all you want," Sorbel said finally, "but please don't ask me to do anything that will surely get us both in trouble with the Militia."

"You can't stay neutral forever, Ellen."

"What's *that* supposed to mean?"

"The situation is going to change fast now. In a few days it's probably going to boil over. I can't give you details yet, because I don't have them. But this conflict is going to have a massive effect on the geol—no, the meteorol—the hydrology—shit! *That's* not right! I mean the envi-vi-ron-mental b-b-balance of this p-p-planet. It could change everything about the way you and everyone else on Mars lives."

"Change for the better?" Sorbel asked hopelessly.

"Clearly not."

"I see. And you're the only one who can keep this mysterious something from happening?"

"I think so."

Ellen Sorbel reflected for another long minute. "You're my friend, Demeter. But you are also telling me that other of my friends are not what they seem. In that case, I really don't know *who* to trust. You see my position?"

"Perfectly."

"Then I will . . . consider what you're asking me to do."

"Thank you."

Ellen didn't feel the loss of connection, but suddenly she knew Demeter Coghlan had withdrawn from the simulation.

Solar Power Station Four, by Proxy, June 13

The power satellite that provided the community of Tharsis Montes and its various machinery, including the space fountain, with 7,000 megawatts of electric energy rode in areosynchronous orbit some 500 kilometers east of the settlement. That was as close as it could get. As the simulation's artificially intelligent host explained, it was unsafe to position the satellite any closer because of the necessity of providing clearance with the elevator's upper transfer station. Neither object was ever likely to shift in orbit, to be sure. Still, the fountain required a broad fairway for the passage of ships entering and leaving its domain. The solar collector duly compensated for this eastward offset by angling its microwave beam westward; the rectenna field that was its target was somewhat closer to the tunnel complex.

Demeter Coghlan found herself nodding, closing her eyes briefly inside the goggles as she tried to absorb all these dry mechanics. They were an inescapable part of the simulation's introductory narration. The visuals the AI presented during its speech were the builder's original schematics, and not at all layman-friendly. They were littered with dotted lines to show the relevant angles and vectors of orbit, dimensions scaled in with arrows and numbers, and color coding that indicated energy flows, structural stresses, and thermal buildup—all quite overwhelming. The tour had obviously been set up for engineers.

After putting her proposition before Ellen Sorbel, Demeter had the rest of the morning free. She had decided to take the programmer up on her earlier suggestion to visit the offworld satellites. Ellen probably found all this technical stuff fascinating. Demeter didn't, but she listened gamely as, in the course of the next fifteen minutes, the machine's pedantic voice explained that, at Mars's greater distance from the sun, the solar cells had to be roughly twice the size of those circling Earth to provide the same energy output. To achieve Station Four's 7.58 gigawatts, average over the daily orbit, the station's area of exposed semiconductor totaled some 210 square kilometers. Magnetic thrusters kept this vast expanse of polymorphic silicon aligned on the sun with a deviance of only one-half second of arc. The diode net of the microwave-receiving station on the Martian surface spread over an area of one hundred and thirty kilometers, with power conditioners spaced every—

"Um, excuse me?" Demeter spoke up.

"Yes?" the AI replied after a pause.

"Could we skip the electronics lesson and go *see* this thing?"

"Your understanding of the scale of the station would not be complete without—"

"I know all that. But I'd really like to take in the sights before I have to put in another quarter."

"'Put in a . . . quarter?'" the machine repeated, mystified. "There is no such unit—"

"Just wire me into the nearest proxy and keep your database to yourself, hear?"

"As you wish."

The black background inside her goggles, representing the void surrounding the computerized construct of the station in abstract, suddenly glittered with stars. On the periphery of her vision, sand-colored Phobos tumbled slowly past.

Demeter looked down. Her hands were no longer bone-and-blood hands in the V/R gloves. They had become what passed for manipulators with this proxy, and they were methodically walking up a ladder. Instead of fingers, the hands used parallel gripping surfaces which opened and closed with a barrel-screw drive, like an old-style Crescent wrench. These keyed into square holes bisected by a bar of sturdy metal. The holes—the rungs of the ladder—were aligned along the outside of a tube about two meters in diameter. Demeter let her gaze rise from this near view of continuous, repetitive motion up the tube . . . and up . . . and . . .

She almost lost her balance—at least, part of her did, the part that was sitting in the flesh on her chair in the Golden Lotus's simulation parlor. The proxy never swerved from its obstinate, mechanical climb. The tube it climbed seemed to stretch to infinity, sloping away from her like the curve of the horizon, leaving her with an endless number of steps to negotiate, ascending forever.

Demeter took a stern hold on her stomach and looked away for some relief.

Off to her left, a field of gold blossomed in her goggles. The image flared with reflected light, then dimmed as the proxy's video chips bumped the signal down a few steps. When her goggles had stabilized, Demeter could see that the field was an array of solar cells, as blue as Earth's upper atmosphere. The glare came from their spiderwork of wire cathodes momentarily catching the distant sun.

The solar cells appeared to be massive hexagons, each perhaps a kilometer from point to point. It was hard to tell, exactly, because Demeter was seeing them almost edge on, from a totally flattened perspective. She could only approximate their outline from the angle of the various borders that stretched away from her single point of view, dark blue against the black of space. The AI narration would probably have something to say about hexagons being the simplest shape for tiling such a large area.

Demeter looked back up the tube: more infinity, with stars.

She looked off toward the right, and saw more flattened hexagons.

She tried looking down, toward wherever the proxy had come from in its climb, but the sensor head would not swivel that far.

After another fifty steps or so—each with its complicated slot-grip-and-pull gait—Demeter decided this was boring.

"Um, Narrator?"

"Yes, Miz Coghlan?"

"What is this proxy used for when it's not piggybacking tourists?"

"This unit is a maintenance robot. It is assigned to walk the satellite's support spars and inspect for meteor damage to the cell's visible surfaces. It performs this function by interpolation of the—"

"*Thank* you. Now, do you have any proxies that, oh, fly around and fix things? Is there anything interesting like that for me to see?"

"Maintenance operations are carried out only in the event that actual damage is detected. Of course, we do have an interesting presentation, which—"

"*No*, thank you. Um . . . this is a completed and fully functioning power satellite, isn't it?"

"Solar Power Station Four went into pre-startup operation on December 19, 2039. It attained full power on—"

"All right, all right. But you've got a station still under construction, don't you?" Demeter remembered something else Sorbel had told her. "Over Schiaparelli, isn't it?"

"That would be Station Six."

"Do you have any proxies there I could look in on? It would be interesting to see your orbital construction techniques."

"No tourist proxies are currently installed on that project."

"Well, could you plug me into a worker robot? I'll accept visual signals only. I wouldn't want to mess up its routines."

"I will see what feeds are available," the AI said primly.

The image in her goggles clicked through a brief spurt of static, and Demeter found herself at the center of a bouquet of arms. They were all jointed in two or more places, waving up around her sensor head like the stamens of a flower. Some had gripper claws holding pieces of irregularly shaped metal and moving them into position; others ended in tools like arc-welding probes and pop-riveting rams, which sequentially zipped and hammered the panels into the wall two meters in front of Demeter's face.

This scene didn't look anything like the vast planes of the other power station, filled with darkly glimmering hexagonal cells crisscrossed by silvery wires. The metal pieces here were all bluntly curved and—from what she saw when one was being turned away from her— all several centimeters thick. Plate steel, Demeter guessed, but the color where the arc touched it was strange, purplish. Maybe some kind of alloy?

She wished she could see more. She had no control over the sensor head, of course; that was reserved for the program directing this machine's work. But from the views she snatched as the robot glanced here to gather one piece, there to align another, she figured out that this particular segment of the construction work was taking place inside a large, hollow cylinder some tens of meters in diameter. The space was already enclosed, the scene illuminated by high-intensity worklights. The robot seemed to be adding a second, interior wall to the one that defined the canister.

What kind of a double-walled bottle would be needed on a solar power station? Demeter understood from the earlier narration that these satellites were fully automatic and so required no human habitations. And the nacelles for the transformers and microwave horns were small things, weren't they? Three or four meters in any dimension, tops.

Putting up two layers of thick metal might serve to protect critical components from asteroid strikes, especially this close to the Belt. But that didn't seem to be the pattern of Martian orbital construction, at least as far as she'd seen it. The solar satellites apparently relied on redundant function and constant, mobile maintenance. Building bunkers in the sky just didn't fit the established profile.

"Narrator? What am I looking at? Is this some kind of hybrid station, maybe, with a reactor pressure vessel supplementing the—?"

The goggles went dead black. No stars, no wire guides, no compass pattern. Demeter's head filled with nothing. Her gloves clenched once, spasmodically, and went limp. The phone beads in her ears generated a steady, low hum.

After thirty seconds—or perhaps thirty minutes, thirty hours—of this induced sensory deprivation, the voice of the AI narration returned.

"I am sorry. You were plugged into an incorrect data feed."

"Oh. Then that *wasn't* Solar Power Station Six?"

"It was . . . not. What do you think of the geology of Mars so far, Miz Coghlan?"

"The geol—?" For just a moment, her tongue clung to the roof of her mouth. It took an act of will to unstick it. "What the hell are you talking about?"

"Nothing. . . . This concludes your simulated tour of the Mars power stations. Have a nice day."

The low humming in her ears stopped. The goggles clicked once and turned themselves off without going through the closing logos and date-time sequence she had come to expect with these things.

Shaking her head, Demeter pulled off the V/R helmet and stripped off the gloves. Suddenly, she didn't feel very well.

Commercial Unit 2/9/6, June 13

Dr. Wa Lixin was surprised when the grid warned that he would have to take an afternoon appointment out of rotation. It wasn't the disruption to his schedule that surprised him, but the fact that he could not identify the patient as one of his own.

"Coghlan? Demeter?" he asked, searching his memory. "Do I know him?"

"She is a transient casual," the disembodied voice replied. "You gave her a preliminary examination last week as part of your reimbursed civic practice. Now she claims to have symptoms and wants to see you again."

"Oh, all right." Wa Lixin sighed and closed the journal file he had been reading. He sat up straight in his office chair and sent the screen into a neutral moiré pattern. "Send her in."

As the young woman stepped through the door, he recognized her. The plump Caucasian girl with the supposed cranial accident. "Hello, Miss Coghlan. Nice to see you again—I hope?"

"Hi, Dr. Lee. . . ." She perched on the edge of his examination table, rather than taking the chair facing him across the desk. "I wanted to . . . um, that is . . ."

"Yes?"

"When I was here last time did I mention, well, *mental* problems?"

"Let me see." Wa turned to the screen and pulled up her file from the archives. It was fragmentary but did include his comment about intermittent complaints of "inability to integrate," which she appeared to have fully compensated.

"You said you had occasional trouble concentrating."

"Yeah. I fall asleep at odd times, too. And, just since

I got here, I've had the hardest time, well, *sticking* to things. Like, personal decisions I just made."

"Since you got here?" He picked up the verbal clue right away. "But not before?"

"I don't remember it coming up before. Maybe I'm all turned around by the cultural differences, meeting new people, that sort of thing. But I feel I've been acting, well, *weird*."

"For example?"

"Well, twice now I've had sex with a man whom I find totally immature. Even a little repulsive. In an alien kind of way."

"Is he . . . not of your race?" Wa Lixin had heard that most continental Americans, Texahomans especially, were closet xenophobes.

"He's a—what you call a Creole."

"Ah? Yes, I see. You would find such a person exotic."

"Well, at first. Now he's just crude and boring."

Dr. Lee smiled. "You are not the first person to be seduced by a foreigner, Miss Coghlan. Or by a Cyborg."

"All right, I guess I needed to hear that. But what about the other? The drowsiness—"

"We have a longer day here."

"—and the zoniness."

"Pardon?"

"My head's up in the clouds half the time," she said. "I say one thing and something else seems to come out—the wrong word, or sometimes even a completely different thought. It's like my head's stuffed with cotton wool."

The doctor tried to imagine such a substance and failed. "These are the same symptoms as before?" he asked. "Having to do with your concentration problems?"

"Yeah, I guess."

"And, after the accident, did your doctors or therapists prescribe anything for it?"

"Cocanol."

It was the brand name for a synthetic alkaloid, derivative of cocaine, that enhanced the action of neurotransmitters in the brain by delaying the enzymic breakdown of acetylcholine at the point of synapse. Cocanol was supposed to be nonaddictive, but Wa Lixin had his doubts. Any patient who came in complaining of vague symptoms but pronouncing a ready affinity for the drug aroused his suspicions.

"I see." He kept his face an unreadable blank.

"Cocanol seemed to help, back on Earth. At least, I could think of something for longer than ninety seconds at a time."

Patients who took Cocanol in clinical tests reported having "a mind like a laser" and being able to "see through a brick wall." Or that was their perception, anyway. Then Wa Lixin decided to relax and give the woman what she wanted—so long as a check with Earth's grid nexus confirmed her previous prescription. After all, Demeter Coghlan wasn't really his patient.

"As your locally assigned physician, I can prescribe for you," he told her. "I'll make sure the grid issues you a supply. It will be waiting at your hotel."

"Thank you, Dr. Lee." With a brief, reflex grin she jumped down from the table. "That's all?"

"Subject to the usual billing. I still have your account number."

"Ta, then." And, once again, she passed through his waiting room and out of his life.

Golden Lotus, June 13

The doctor was as good as his word: when Demeter put her thumbprint to the touchplate that protected entry to the Golden Lotus's suite, the doorkeeper announced that a package was waiting for her at the front desk.

She took the parcel back to her room and opened it. A month's supply of patches spilled out on the bed. Demeter peeled one and slapped it against the skin behind her left ear. The darkened flesh tone of the disk's outer covering blended with the short hairs at the nape of her neck, concealing her use of it.

Almost instantly, the familiar licorice flavor filled the back of her throat, the sign that her bloodstream was receiving the medication. In a minute or two, Demeter could feel her head clearing, her thoughts untangling, her brain coming alive.

"You have a visitor," the room announced.

"Oh? Who?"

"Lole Mitsuno, hydrologist with the—"

"Let him in."

The door slid back on the tall, blond man. He gave her a nice smile, but she could read just a hint of worry at the edges. It was the way the corners of his lips turned down. That, and the slight defensive position of his hands, cupped at his thighs, as he stood there.

"Lole!" Demeter came forward with her hands outstretched, palms down, willing him to take her in his arms for a friendly hug. Or something more. Anything more would do.

He grasped her fingers, like a trapeze artist who had nearly missed a flying catch. He held her practically at arm's length, and the worry lines stayed with his smile.

"Glad I found you," he said. "Did you . . . have an interesting day?"

"Why, yes. Um—" Demeter glanced back into the room, which really had nowhere for them to sit but on the bed. "Let's go to the lounge where we can talk."

"Sure."

As she led him down the corridor to the hotel's public rooms, Demeter was sure he would grill her about that foolish request she'd made of Ellen Sorbel. Lole had once practically accused her of being an Earth spy when they had gone out hunting water; then this morning she had admitted as much to his closest coworker. Mitsuno would want to examine her motives—and the secret information she'd hinted at with Ellen—before either of them offered to help.

Not that Demeter particularly needed Sorbel's programming skills now. With the Cocanol at work, fluffing and combing her brains, Demeter could think of at least a dozen other ways of getting access to the messages sent by her opponents. Probably the simplest would be to turn Sugar loose on a badger hunt in the grid's databases to dig out the archivals of all interplanetary communications. Any quasi-governmental system would routinely keep offline copies, if only to indemnify itself against damage claims from garbles and lost transmissions.

So, all Demeter had to do now was convince Lole that Ellen must have misunderstood her. As a fallback, Demeter might even claim that she never entered the Agnus Dei geological data at all—that Ellen must have been hallucinating, or encountering a cybernetic hiccup, or something.

Hey! Demeter had finally said it—or thought it, anyway. "Geological," the word that had been playing on her mind and tangling her tongue for days now. She

congratulated herself on finally going to the doctor and
getting the medicine she needed.

In the lounge, Demeter steered him to one of the
armchairs. Then she positioned herself on the settee
next to it, curling one leg attractively underneath her
and twisting her body to offer her best profile. "What
did *you* do today?" she began brightly.

"The usual—walked the pipelines, looking for wind
erosion around the support brackets and pebbling of
the conduit surface."

"You went outside again?"

"No, we use satellite surveillance. I do my patrol
through a pair of goggles and gloves."

"Seems like everyone works that way," Demeter
commented.

"You went up to the power satellites, didn't you?"

"Ah . . . yes. How'd you know?"

"The system logs in all visitors. Ellen told me."

"She did."

"What do you think of our orbital construction
program?"

"Well, I didn't see much of it. What there was
looked pretty boring. Miles and miles of blue sheet silicon, all etched with little silver wires. After you get
your mind around the sheer size of the thing, it seems
fairly uncomplicated."

"Did you get to see the new station?"

"Which one's that?" Demeter had to think for a minute.

"The one that's still under construction."

"I don't believe so. Does the logbook say I did?"

"No."

"Then I guess not. The touring software showed me
something. . . ." Demeter tried to sort out her memories—they were still a little hazy—from the time before

she took her medicine. "But it wasn't anything to do with solar power. I'm not even sure it was in orbit. The signals got crossed up somehow. Typical cyber foulup."

Lole Mitsuno was looking at her thoughtfully.

"What?" Demeter said after a long pause. Maybe twenty seconds.

"You really don't like computers, do you?"

"I use computers like everyone else. I don't have to *like* them. And I don't get sentimental about them."

He pointed to the charm bracelet on her wrist.

"She's just a machine, Lole. A tool."

"'She'? Does this person have a name?"

"Well, I call her 'Sugar.' But that's just easier to say than 'cellular activating wrist chronograph and tran-scribing stenographer.'" Demeter shrugged.

"I see." Mitsuno was giving her that peculiar smile again.

Well, whatever for? Did he think she was hiding some kind of secret life as a cyber-witch? There were stories of humans who sold their souls to MFSTO: and then reaped unfair advantage in business and politics, love and war. Come to think of it, that was another way Demeter might try getting into Sun's or Cuneo's mes-sage files. She could just go to a nearby keyboard and make a midnight deal with the grid's *daemon*. Sure! And then it would report her attempted invasion of privacy back to the referenced clients, just like the E-mail protocols specified. Not very smart!

Suddenly, Demeter wanted this handsome man to think well of her. He was fully human, integrated into his community, good at his work, admiring of her supposed cowboy origins. And he was currently unattached—she had that straight from the woman who ought to know.

"Look, I had a problem with a cybernetic device, once," Demeter explained, deciding to play the sympathy card. "I got punched in the head by one—malfunction in a hairdressing unit that burned out and cut me. So I don't expect our 'silicon friends' to always function perfectly. And . . . that's part of the reason I'm up here. I needed a little rest and relaxation while I recuperate."

"Oh! Does it—?" Lole looked properly compassionate.

"Hurt? No, I'm fine. Really."

"Good. . . . You hungry? How about some dinner?"

Demeter held her breath, to see if he would mention bringing Sorbel along.

He didn't. "The Hoplite grills up a mean steak and beans," Mitsuno offered.

"Real meat?" Her mouth was watering.

He shrugged with one shoulder. "Coloring's right."

"You're on." She unwound herself from the end of the couch. "Give me a minute to change."

Chapter 10

End Games

Mars-U-Copia, Commercial Unit 1/5/9, June 14

After the engagements and excitements of her first week on Mars, Demeter rewarded herself with a day off to go shopping. The best place for that in Tharsis Montes was the Mars-U-Copia, a combination Moroccan bazaar and duty-free shop on the upper levels.

Most of the merchandise was junk: last year's recycled fashions from Milan, but cobbled together out of chintzy, synthetic fabrics; evening-wear jumpers designed on a mock-spacesuit theme, with corrugated rubber inserts in all the wrong places; framed, amateur watercolors of the Martian landscape, two shades redder than the real thing; and a . . . wait a minute!

Demeter fingered the necklace that was lying out, unattended on the jewelry counter. It was either the real thing or an awfully good copy.

She picked it up. The necklace was strung with *fleurs de vitrine*, the hardy Martian groundwort that grew a silicon shell for protection against ultraviolet radiation. The hollowed-out beads had been sorted by size from tiny, button-shaped, two-millimeter caps to the big, flattened, centimeter-wide lenses. The artist had assembled only the rare, red-tinged shells, so much more delicate than the common blues and grays.

With slightly trembling fingers, Demeter turned over the price chip. Glassflower jewelry was a rarity on Earth, outrageously expensive, even by Tiffany's standards. The numbers engraved on the chip came into focus. Demeter squinted away the phantom zeros that her fears and a momentary tearing of her eyes had added to the price.

Two thousand Neu.

It was a steal.

"It's a copy," said a voice at her elbow.

Coghlan glanced down. The woman was incredibly short, not much over 140 centimeters. She wore a plain suit of good, gray worsted wool and real leather hightop shoes. The woman's hair was a naturally curly blond, cut short and combed with a rake. Still, she had the same square, flat face of a farmer's wife, with wind-etched lines and a natural sunburn. It was the face Demeter had studied at odd moments in various settings over the past week. The hair must be a wig: nobody could bleach, dye, and rinse that often and get away with it.

"Why do you say?" Demeter asked, holding the necklace fractionally closer to her body.

Nancy Cuneo reached for it. Their fingers brushed as she took the artifact, and Demeter felt the hard edge of calluses. Probably from weapons practice. The Zealander turned the jewelry over, exposing the backs of the shells, where the tiny gold wires went through.

"See these radial creases?" A blunt, yellowed fingernail traced folds in the red-stained silicate. "That's where the glass was crimped when the blower was rolling it out. Instead of lines, a real shell has rings here, just like on a tree. They, too, are a sign of seasonal growth."

"I see."

"It's a pretty thing, but not worth the price." The woman smiled up at her. Those obsidian-black eyes were harder than the glass beads looped over her fingers.

"Thank you," Demeter said coldly, taking the necklace back and dropping it carelessly on the counter.

"You are Demeter Coghlan, aren't you? From Texahoma State?"

Demeter was too intelligent to consider denying it or evading notice for even a moment. Cuneo would have access to the same grid resources and had probably been studying her as assiduously as she had been studying Cuneo.

"Yes, I am. And you are . . . ?" Demeter allowed herself a last, tiny bit of subterfuge.

"Nancy Cuneo . . . but then, you knew that already." The woman gave her a knife-edged smile. "I thought it would be nice for us to meet on neutral ground, as it were." She waved a hand around at the hangings of the bazaar.

"Yes?" She couldn't think of much more to say.

"I know why you're here, of course," the older woman went on, still smiling. "Your people in Texahoma are nervous about what we may be planning to do with the Valles Marineris. They sent you to check us out."

"Why would you think that?"

"Then you are *not* concerned?"

"Well, sure, I'm *concerned.* What citizen wouldn't be? After all, we have territorial claims going back to the first time Captain William Schorer of Houston, Texas, set foot in the valley. He set up a flag and everything."

"You saw that in your schoolbooks, did you?"

"Yes, of course," Demeter said stoutly.

"The flag of the United States of America—which is hardly congruous with the current state of Texahoma."

"We cleave to the Texas part of the legend, ma'am."

"But, of course, your concern is in no way *official*, is it?"

"No, ma'am. I mean, how could it be?"

"You're very young, dear." Cuneo put out a hand, touching her wrist. Only later did Demeter guess this one touch might be as good as a polygraph.

"I don't see what that has to do with anything."

"What can Alvin Bertrand Coghlan have been thinking?" the older woman asked, mostly to herself. "To send his *grand*daughter on a mission like this. . . . You are what we call an ingenue, dear, a dilettante in the great game. Let me give you a word of advice for the next time you choose to dabble. You do not have to answer every question, nor meet every sally with a riposte. It makes you seem far too eager to prove your story, which in itself is damning."

"I—!" Demeter wisely closed her mouth.

"Let's lay our cards on the table, shall we?"

Coghlan thought about this offer for an instant. "My G'dad used to say that's when all the aces get swept up somebody's sleeve."

Cuneo laughed at the joke. "A wise man, old Alvin Bertrand. But seriously, Demeter, we should join forces. All those historic claims are hopelessly tangled, and you know it. North Zealand traces its ownership through the Potanter Trek, when the party camped out in the Valles for six months."

"Before they perished in the mountains to the east of there," Demeter reminded her. "And they never filed a formal interest."

"Parry and riposte, again?"

Demeter Coghlan clamped her jaw shut on a response.

"Anyway, a piece of paper laid before the U.N. Commission on Mars is not the clincher you seem to believe. Our friend from United Korea would argue strenuously that they are entitled to the district for reasons of population pressure alone, regardless of the astronomical expense of relocating their people. Heavens, he *does* argue that point. Endlessly. And Korean claims are tied by the slender thread of a ten-percent interest in one unmanned Chinese rocket that made landfall on Mars, half a planet away from the Valles."

"Is there a point to this history lesson?" Demeter asked sweetly enough.

"Merely that it would be a mistake to treat any of this minuet too earnestly. Even with N-ZED providing full financial backing for development work in the Canyonlands—isn't that a charming name for the district, too?—we North Zealanders are hardly cementing our claim. And I'll tell you something even your Alvin Bertrand doesn't know: that our agency is behind the new power station a-building in orbit. That's part of the overall package. But what does it matter, in the end?"

Cuneo looked at Demeter, as if expecting a response. Demeter did not give her the satisfaction.

"Nothing. Nothing at all!" the woman went on. "We'll all be dead and dust before the Valles complex is worth more than a handful of paper credits. So why should we fight? There will be plenty of time to work out some kind of joint tenancy—if that's what your grandfather is angling for?"

The pause drew out in uncomfortable silence.

"I'm sure I don't know his mind," Demeter said at last.

"No, of course. But then, Texahoma has much better claims down south, near the polar cap. That area is much more hospitable—better supplied with water, for instance."

"But aren't the caps predominantly dry ice?"

"Well, of course, but I'm talking about the permanent frost layer, the undercoating to the CO_2 crust." The woman waved the issue aside with one hand. "At any rate, a trade delegation is about to arrive from North Zealand. They're reasonable people. I'm sure you'll get along with them. There is no reason why our two nations should not cooperate—or at least agree to defer further dispute until we have something *concrete* to fight about."

"I'm sure your traders are lovely people," Demeter agreed. "But I still don't see what that has to do with me. I'm just a college girl on vacation, recovering from a terrible accident, taking in the sights—and about to buy some native artifacts." She touched the necklace once more, wistfully, then left it alone for good. "Until you offered to help me, that is."

"An accident, did you say?"

"Certainly. You can check my records, if you want." Demeter shrugged, convinced the woman already had. "Deep cover" is what G'dad chucklingly called it. "I had a run-in with an autocoif during my senior year. Deep lacerations all along one side of my head. My hair covers the scar now. But it was like to kill me."

"You poor thing!"

Demeter preened in the satisfaction of having successfully defended her story.

"You want to take much better care of yourself, while you're on Mars," Cuneo went on pleasantly.

"There are so many more opportunities for getting yourself killed up here. . . . And maybe taking one of us along with you." The woman's saccharine smile did not extend to her eyes, which bored into Demeter like twin nine-millimeter gun barrels.

Demeter had to take an involuntary step backward.

"I won't," she promised.

Hoplite Bar & Grill, June 14

Ellen Sorbel was running late on the morning's workload. She decided to take an early lunch break before the afternoon came around and crushed her. So she dashed into the Hoplite for a seafood handwich and mug of nonalcoholic ale—wet enough to wash down the krill cakes but with nothing to cloud her head. She found Demeter Coghlan at one of the tables near the back, picking at what looked like a salad but could have included some kind of farina noodles.

"Hey, Demeter!"

"Ellen! . . . Good to see you." The Earth woman looked pleased, set aside her fork, and pushed the plate away. Sorbel settled into the free chair.

"Look, unh, about your request yesterday—"

"Oh, that! Forget it, please. It just never happened."

"I'm grateful because, you know, I could lose my job if anything happened. Especially if someone complained. And honest work is hard to come by if you're a cyber ghost."

"I said, forget it ever happened."

Ellen glanced over to see if Demeter was angry. The grin playing around the corners of her mouth said she wasn't. Sorbel was relieved.

"Are you still seeing Jory?" Ellen asked, to change the subject.

"Not if I can help it."

"Oh? I didn't know you had a problem there."

"Not really, he's just— I'm sorry, he's your friend and all."

"An acquaintance, actually. Lole and I kind of took him under our wing, once, when he had some trouble with the Department."

"All right then. You know what I'm talking about. He can be so immature and . . . well, demanding. Like he's still fourteen years old."

"In many ways he is," Ellen said judiciously. "The process that makes a Creole does strange things to the hormones, not to mention the nervous system."

"Yeah, but he can be fairly sensitive, too. Do you know, when he found out I don't like doing it in front of the computers, he took me to this cave he had pre-pared. It's not even connected to power and water yet, let alone cyber services."

"Oh . . . !" Sorbel sagged against the chair's arms. She was thinking furiously. How had Jory found out about the . . . ? Or wait! *Had* he found out? "Where was all this?" she asked cautiously.

"I didn't really make a map."

"But in general terms—inside the complex? Out-side? Up slope or down? Did you have to suit up?"

"Inside, and down a couple of levels. We crossed a big promenade that looked like a shopping mall."

"A . . . 'mall'?"

"Sure, an indoor arcade, usually full of boutiques and eateries, with an anchor store or a hotel. Except this one was empty, still getting built."

"Okay, and his hideaway was nearby?"

"Fifty meters away, more or less. It was where some kind of expansion work had been closed off—tempo-rarily, at least."

Then it *wasn't* the site Ellen was thinking of. Thank Heaven, or that other place, for small favors.

"But, Demeter, he actually told you the computers couldn't see or hear in there?" Suddenly the humor of it overtook her. Ellen tried to keep from laughing.

"Sure, no cables, no fiberoptic. The place was bare rock. Perfectly clean."

"Yeah, but *Jory* was in there with you."

"What do you mean?"

"He's hardwired for communications. The grid can monitor him on a private radio channel, twenty-four hours a day, waking and dreaming."

"So he could—!"

Ellen nodded. "He not only could, he does. Automatically. All the time, and with stereo sound and full-motion video—better than your charm bracelet there."

"That little creep! Does he know he does that?"

"He has to. It's part of the price of cyberhood."

"Damn him!"

"He only looks like a child, Demeter. Under that slick skin and elfin face, he's actually quite intelligent. Just not . . . socially adept, if you take my meaning."

"Perfectly." Demeter picked up her fork, made a halfhearted pass at the noodle salad, then flung both fork and food at the far wall. The utensil went *ting!* against cold rock.

Boy, was she mad! Ellen made a private note against ever getting on this woman's bad side.

Residential Unit 2/6/34, Apartment C, June 14

Kemil Ergun always returned home at the middle of the day. He had done this every working day of his life, as his father had before him, his father and his father's father, too, going back to the Old Country. Ergun's routine was always the same: a light meal, maybe a spinach salad and shashlik—or, within the culinary limits of this strange new world, hydroponic cress and braised lizard strips; one glass of homemade retsina; one hand-rolled, black-sobranie cigarette—and be damned to the air-filtration edicts; followed by a brief and feverish encounter with his wife Gloria; and finally a short nap. Only then could he go back to his work as a ballistics engineer with the space fountain, refreshed and relaxed. In civilized places, they called this ritual the "siesta."

This day, however, Kemil Ergun found nothing relaxing at home.

The hummus salad his wife served was lumpy, with bits of bean husk still floating on unabsorbed oil. The retsina was a new batch and sour. And, crowning indignity, she had let the household supply of sobranie run out and made no effort to tell him so he could acquire more through his special sources.

When Ergun questioned her on this, all she would say was: "It's contraband." Meaning: "I don't want it in the house."

Gloria Chan was not a proper wife. Respectful enough, yes, when his face was toward her. Compliant in bed, to be sure. But like all Chinese she had a willful streak. Deep down, she thought she was better than her husband. Better than any non-Chinese.

Actually, she was quite ignorant. She knew very little about the proper seasoning of his food. Nearly nothing about winemaking. And nothing at all about the secondary businesses in which Kemil Ergun engaged, with contacts on the space fountain's cargo dock, that allowed them a houseful of little luxuries. Her family was huge and raucous. They seemed to spread over half this level of the complex and had a finger in every other pie, none of which they would trust with a Turk. They thought he could afford everything the two of them had on an engineer's salary. More fool they!

"The smoking is my pleasure," he said today. Quite reasonably, he thought.

"It's dirty. You stink up the house."

"What good is it to *have* a house," he said with a shrug, "if a man cannot stink it up occasionally?"

"I have to live here too!"

"One cigarette? It never bothered you before."

"It bothered me. I just never said anything."

"Well . . . there then!" Kemil struggled for advantage on this slippery rhetorical slope. "This is no time to start complaining."

"I can complain if I want to. My hair and clothing always smelling like burning tar. Every day the Citizen's Militia come sniffing around, making rude eyes at me. My food tastes bad—"

"*Your* food always tastes bad!"

"You pig! You filthy Turkish *pig!*"

The encounter, no longer likely to be brief, quickly passed through the feverish stage as Gloria hefted the unfinished plate of hummus and slung it at his head.

Ergun ducked and heard the crockery smash against the wall behind him.

"You'll just have to clean that up." He shrugged again.

"I'll clean *you* up!" She snatched a knife, holding it pointed toward his midsection, a meter and a half away with the table between them.

It was a dull blade, the one he used for spreading the garbanzo bean paste. It could do him no conceivable harm. Not in her hands, anyway. Ergun grinned at her.

"Eeee-yi-heeee!" she shrieked. In frustration, he thought.

Gloria Chan made a feint around the table. Then, in one smooth move, she flipped the knife expertly in her fingers, drew her hand back, and threw. Aiming low.

Ergun ducked again, but the blade caught him between the shoulder and chest. It could not penetrate very deeply, but it made him pause and blink in surprise. He felt a cold wetness against his skin. The residue of oily, yellow-brown paste on the blade would surely stain his shirt. Now he would have to change it before going back to work. His eyes squinted in fury, Ergun came around the table fast, charging at his wife.

Gloria turned and fled down the hall, headed for the outer door, the public corridor beyond, and a total scandal.

She was still shrieking. "Help! Murder!"

That was exactly what Kemil Ergun had in mind.

Level Two, Tunnel Six, June 14

Demeter Coghlan was crossing between one ramp and another on Tharsis Montes's second level, heading back down to her hotel after lunch, when the shouting caught her attention.

"Help! Murder!"

Demeter was still so steamed over Jory's two-faced treatment of her that she wasn't thinking straight. Prudence, in a 21st-century urban setting, said you moved *away* from a cry of murder. Instead, Demeter was drawn to it: the voice was a woman's.

The corridors were narrower here than elsewhere in the complex—one sign, she had come to understand, of a private residential zone. The hex cubes were laid out with their connecting tunnels branching off at opposing angles, so that the eye was not oppressed by long vistas of drab, dull rock. Demeter threaded her way from one cut chamber to the next, seeking the origin of that shout.

On either side of the corridor, doors were opening and heads popping out. Martians might value their privacy above all else, Demeter reflected, but that didn't mean they couldn't enjoy a ruckus when one presented itself. Most of the faces seemed to be some blend of Earth's Asian populations.

Demeter had gone perhaps fifty paces down the tunnel when a young woman came around a corner and ran full-tilt into her. Demeter held on to the other's arms as the two of them went down.

"Let me go!" The young woman struggled. From her severely styled hair, Demeter guessed she was ethnic Chinese. "He's going to kill me!"

By the time Demeter had untangled herself and risen to one knee, other people were around to keep the woman from flying off.

"What's happening?"

"Who's been killed?"

"Isn't that Gloria Chan?"

"Help! Murder!" the Chinese woman shrieked again and pushed her way through the crowd.

The source of her terror appeared one second later. A man stumbled out of the cube she had just left. He wore dark slacks and a white shirt, blotched with blood. The handle of a knife stuck out of the shirt at a high angle. His dark face, crossed with a black and bristling mustache, was purple with rage. His eyes certainly sparked murder.

"Stop him!"

"It's the Turk!"

"He'll kill her!"

"Killer!"

The man passed by Demeter at a stiff-legged run, going after the woman, whose name appeared to be Gloria Chan. The people on all sides tried to grapple with him, but the sight of the knife handle put them off. One man fell, shrieking, and pulled down another. In two seconds more, neighbor had struck neighbor and a brawl was under way, everyone screaming in high-pitched gabble that bore no relation to English.

Demeter, still down on one knee, shrank against the tunnel wall and tried to keep out of the flight path of fists and feet. She raised the charm bracelet to the vicinity of her mouth.

"Sugar, call the police or whoever."

"Never no mi-ii—"

A hand reached down and clawed at Demeter's arm. The bangle was torn away and flew across the corridor. A silvery wink among dark and bobbling heads was the last Coghlan saw of her personal chrono.

She pressed into the one of the hex corners, made herself small in the junction between walls and floor, and waited for a break in the action so she might crawl into a doorway.

Demeter was still waiting when the corridor flooded with gas. Even with a fold of sleeve pressed over her nose and mouth, she felt its effects after a moment. Then she felt nothing at all.

Municipal Lockup, June 14

Ellen Sorbel's head had been deep in the geological strata, feeling her way across a layer of broken schist, when Wyatt's voice came for her.

"You are wanted in jail," he said smugly.

"What? Now?" Ellen never brought her senses out

of the datastream, just spoke as one disembodied voice to another. "Why?"

"A casual has been picked up in a public disturbance. She gives your name as a reference. Shall I say you are otherwise occupied?"

"Who is it? Oh, let me guess. Demeter Coghlan, right?"

"The woman can give no clear account of herself. She seems to have lost both her identity cards and her chrono. But Coghlan is the name she used."

"Tell them I'll be down directly."

Wyatt paused before responding. "Really, Miz Sorbel, your work for this department is much more important than looking after a . . . a *barfly*."

"Where did you get a term like that?" Ellen wondered aloud. "Demeter is a friend. Now unhook me . . . and pass my message, will you?"

"Very well," the machine said stiffly.

Ellen had to appear at the cells in person to make the identification, now that Demeter had lost her electronic persona. When Sorbel arrived at the secure area, obvious from its uniform gray paint and its location down at the complex's lowest finished level, she found a dozen pallets laid out in the open corridors. Each one held a sleeping body, covered to the chin by a white sheet. Some of the sheets were spotted with blood. Here and there a medic attempted to bind a scalp wound or pressure-cuff a broken bone. It looked like the aftermath of a tong war; every exposed face was Chinese or Central Asian. This disturbed Ellen, because the Pacific Rim community was one of Tharsis Montes's most peaceful enclaves.

"Where is the Earth casual?" Sorbel asked the first militiaman she encountered.

"That way." He inclined his head down the tunnel.

She passed five cells, all large communal blocks three meters on a side. They were filled with drooping, listless people of mixed race, again with Chinese predominant. Some of the prisoners stared back; one or two smiled at Sorbel's own Pacific Rim face and coloring. None of these looked at all like Demeter. But from the sixth cell she heard: "Ellen! Over here!"

Demeter's Anglo features shone out like a beacon.

"Demeter, how did you get in there?"

"Some kind of riot. I just walked into it, minding my own business."

Ellen sensed this was not the entire truth. "I'll see if I can get you out," she promised.

Sorbel went back and found the militiaman. She offered her chips for verification and got Demeter released into her custody. Before he would let the Earth woman go, however, the man outlined Ellen's responsibilities in detail.

"I have to accompany you in court, personally, if there's to be a hearing," she explained to Coghlan as the two walked past the gray-painted walls, through a door made up of steel bars, and into the public corridors.

"Will they call me as a witness?"

"No, as a defendant. In cases like this, the presumption is that you went out of your zone and gave someone cause to take insult."

Demeter gasped. "But . . . I was trying to *help*! This woman was crying out in terror, so I went over to help her."

"And sparked a racial incident."

"No, that was the man with the mustache. And the knife. He was a Turk, they said."

"You *saw* such a man?"

"He went right past me, close enough to touch. He was trying to kill the woman."

"Kill her with the knife?"

"No, it was sticking out of him. Here." Demeter jabbed fingertips at an angle above her own left breast.

"Sounds like a family dispute that got out of hand. Then there probably *won't* be a court of inquiry. Not if enough people tell the same story."

"Does this sort of thing happen every day?" Demeter asked.

"Well . . . more often than we'd like. Living so close together, and underground most of the time, people get tense. Tempers flare up."

"What will happen to the couple that started it?"

"They will be counseled, then each made to wear homing bracelets for a while."

"Homing—?"

"Don't you have them on Earth? They allow the grid to track your whereabouts at all times. You can go to your place of employment during your normal work hours, then you go straight home. Show up anywhere else and you provoke an armed response from the Citizen's Militia."

"Charming. How long does this leper treatment usually last?"

"Some weeks. Long enough to make an impression and achieve a measure of behavior modification. If drugs or alcohol are found to be contributing factors, they will be forbidden for the duration of the homing period."

"How do you achieve that?" Demeter smiled. "A stiff warning?"

"Slivers of Antabuse, surgically inserted along with the bracelet. Take a drink or pop a lid with that under your skin, and you'll think you died. You'll certainly puke enough *to* die, though the homer helps by monitoring your vital signs. Nobody's actually gone out while under therapy—not in the last ten years or so, anyway."

"You people know a thing or two about crowd control, don't you?"

"We have to." Ellen shrugged. "Think what would happen if a full-scale riot boiled over to the surface levels and somebody punched out a door. That is not a docile climate out there, like you have in Texas."

"I suppose not." Demeter didn't sound happy. "This place isn't a *thing* like Texas."

Golden Lotus, June 14

Demeter Coghlan missed Sugar—even if the titanium bangle was just a machine. She missed the routine of putting her to bed under a water glass, pretending that the chrono might hear Demeter talk in her sleep and report the details to someone, something, somewhere.

That way, at least, Demeter could imagine that *some-body* cared about her. As it was, she had to make her report to Gregor Weiss alone that night, just her and the room's dumb terminal. It was not a happy report.

"I'm blown, Greg. That's the long and short of it."

Demeter leaned back against the pillows, keeping her head turned toward the microphone. Although, in this small room, how much could directionals matter?

"The Korean agent knows all about me. Even a lightweight like him spotted me within five minutes. And the Zealander woman blew my cover even before that. Today she was actually giving me pointers on how to be a better spy, for future reference. This place is just a sieve. Every time you turn around, someone's poking you in the shoulder, telling you how to mind your own business. Half the time, they aren't even human. Just some mechanical presence, always pushing you around."

Demeter thought about that for a moment. She decided to let the sentiment go out as spoken.

"Paragraph. I've tried to get out to the Valles Marineris for evaluation. That's a bust, too. I've seen about as much as you can by walking over the ground inside an animated tripod with a three-dee sensor head. I've also taken feed from the dirtmovers on site. But getting there in the flesh . . . well, it's just not going to happen. Not unless I mount a full-blown overland safari, with native bearers and elephants—or their mechanical equivalent. You got a budget of a million Neu for this gig? I thought not.

"Paragraph. The bottom line, Greg, is I want to come home. Mars is not a happy place. Too many people living in too small a cubbyhole. Even the air is stale. I can't breathe most of the time. So, book passage for me, will you? Next available transport. I'll take anything you can arrange. Ore boat on a long traverse to the Kirkwood Gap, if you can get it. Just remove me from this sufferin' anthill!"

Demeter tried to think of anything else to say. There was nothing.

"Endit. Code and send. . . . And, Terminal?"

"Yes, Miz Coghlan?"

"Turn off the lights, please."

She was too tired to move, and her eyes were too wet and blurry to find the wall switch.

"Of course, Miz Coghlan." After a moment's pause, long enough for her to punch up the pillows behind her head, the room went dark.

Chapter 11

A Visit with the Elders

Golden Lotus, June 15

The new day brought Demeter Coghlan out of bed with a much better mental attitude. With luck, this was going to be her last day on Mars. Or, anyway, the last before she got a positive commitment to bring her home, which was almost as good.

That being the case, she wanted one final stab at reconnoitering the Valles Marineris District, pulling out all the stops and giving it her very best effort. To do this, Demeter decided, she had to overcome a load of cultural taboos and talk directly to Roger Torraway, Mars's unofficial first citizen and *Guinness Guide* title-holder as eldest Cyborg. He ought to know something about the Valles, if anyone did.

Demeter walked into the hotel's simulation parlor, plugged herself into the nearest booth, and called up the resident menu. There was no entry for people, even famous ones, just the usual packaged tours.

"Terminal . . ."

"Yes, Miz Coghlan?"

"Patch me through to Roger Torraway."

"Colonel Torraway is not a token holder on this network."

"Huh? I thought all Cyborgs were hard-wired into the grid."

"That is true: packet radio communications are not optional for recent human-Cyborg conversions. However, Colonel Torraway's processors precede the fabrication of this nexus."

"All right, then," Demeter said reasonably. "Find out his present location, and slot me into the nearest proxy."

"There are no tourist proxies within one hundred kilometers of Colonel Torraway's present location."

"Then I'll take a working machine and pay the surcharge."

"There are no proxies of any kind within that radius."

"Well, hell, then I'll *walk*. Put me inside the nearest device at any distance. Supply it with a detailed map and a good-guess ETA."

"Colonel Torraway will not allow an uninvited mechanism to approach him. This is his expressed desire, and his speed over the ground permits him to enforce the prohibition by running away."

"Damn, damn, damn it," Demeter said without particular emphasis. "Put an emergency override on his comm system," she directed.

"That is not the routine procedure. Does your situation constitute an emergency?"

"Mephisto . . . I *order* you to connect me with Colonel Roger Torraway's communications module."

"Coming right up, Miz Coghlan."

Heliopolis Basin, June 15

Roger Torraway and Fetya Mikhailovna Shtev were kneeling side by side, staring down a gopher hole. It was an unusual formation in the desert's reddish laterite soil: an oval depression with no visible bottom.

Its origin might almost be volcanic, except that the Heliopolis Basin was more than a thousand kilometers from any recently active lava fields.

The sides of the tube or passageway were smooth and compacted, just the sort of finish a burrowing animal would leave in moist, slightly clayey dirt along an Earthly riverbank. Except, of course, that the Martian soil was bone dry. And it had never, to Roger's knowledge, seen an animal so big, burrowing or otherwise. Viruses by the handful, and now and then a microbe, but nothing as large as an ant, let alone a gopher.

"Is mystery, yes?" Shtev said.

"Could be the wind," he proposed.

"Just here? So deep?" The Russian raised her head to scan the shattered landscape. "And just this once?"

"Is mystery," Roger agreed.

He was about to say more, just empty speculation on the feature, when the horizon lit up the color of blood. It was like a flash of heat lightning, but deep into the infrared. Roger might have thought it was a trick of meteorology—forty years ago. Time and experience had taught him it was nothing to do with the weather.

Dorrie Torraway stepped out of the locus of the flash.

"Roger, connect with the grid, please," she said inside his head.

"Tell them it's not convenient." He formed the words without moving his lips or vocal chords: electronic signals raced away through his backpack computer and found the nearest relay link.

She shook her head. "They really do have to talk to you."

He groaned aloud—or made a mechanical grating sound like a groan—and Shtev looked around.

"What is it?"

"Excuse me, Fetya Mikhailovna," he replied. "The on-line busybodies want a conference."

"Maybe they need something. Something only you can give." The Cyborg's right eyelid, a fleshy membrane abraded by years of sandstorms, flicked down and up. A wink for him alone.

"Maybe. All right, Dorrie—" His voice sank into subvocal mode. "—go ahead with the message."

Dorrie Torraway's image melted, shifted, and resolidified. Her shorts and halter became a pair of purple coveralls with metal snaps down the front. Her hips and waist thickened perceptibly as she lost five inches in height. Dorrie's severely beautiful face grew more rounded, her cheekbones disappearing as her cheeks chubbed out, shedding a few years and a lot of sophistication in the process. Her chin developed dimples Dorrie never had. Her hair went from short black to a long and wavy light brown, finally tying itself into a braid.

"Colonel Torraway?"

The woman's features were three-dimensional but somehow static, like a doll's head that was only partially animated. Her lips and the focus of her bright green eyes moved, but nothing else. Her jaw and throat muscles did not keep in synch with the words.

Roger understood the phenomenon now: the signals fed into his backpack's imaging system were based on a two-dimensional, bit-mapped icon. The grid—or whichever node attached to it had felt compelled to violate his privacy—was projecting a simulation drawn from a passport file or some other ungenerous source of data.

That didn't help, though. He still didn't recognize the face and figure.

"Who is it?" he asked. Torraway stayed where he had been when the red flash caught him, half-levered off the ground with his knees and elbows sticking out, his head turned at an angle to the horizon. Let the backpack project whatever body language it wanted to his interlocutor: Roger standing heroically on the red sands, Roger seated regally on a camp stool, Roger stripped of his black-winged bat suit and smiling like a recruiting poster out of a pink, human face. Whatever.

"My name is Demeter Coghlan. We haven't actually met, sir. Although I saw you a few days ago, out at Harmonia Mundi."

Roger remembered the place perfectly. He could remember anything and everything, every meter of ground from fifty years of wandering, perfectly. Or his backpack computer did. He did not remember any human woman at Harmonia Mundi, though. It was the professional hydrologist, Lole Mitsuno, working out of Tharsis Montes, who had been there five days ago. Mitsuno briefly interrupted the forum of fellow Cyborgs that Roger and Fetya had convened. That indecisive forum, which had accomplished nothing. His interruption had been about—what else?—water.

"I do not remember you."

Already Roger was becoming bored with this conversation. If the grid was going to pester him with Dorrie's emergency signal, that was one thing. But Torraway could put his mind in compressed time and just let this woman . . . fade away.

"As I said, we never really met. But I was collecting data with Lole Mitsuno, about a week ago, when . . ."

Roger's mind came out of its high-speed blur, teased into trying to remember whether a second person had actually been working alongside the hydrologist. If none of Torraway's senses recorded her, then he had nothing to remember. That was simple enough. Indeed, he might have ignored a second human figure, so far away and insignificant.

"Is this introduction at all meaningful?" he asked, overriding whatever the woman had been saying in the space of his thoughts.

"No, of course not." The doll's head smiled woodenly.

At least she was honest.

"What can I do for you?" Roger asked, resigned.

"I need to find out about the Valles Marineris. Specifically, if we were to raise the water-vapor content of the Martian atmosphere by, say, twenty percent somehow, then, with dissociation into elemental hydrogen and oxygen in the upper atmosphere and a corresponding pressure increase, would ambient conditions at the lower elevations of the Valles be able to support approximately Earth-normal conditions? I know you can't answer that, per se. Only a computer model could give the answer, but—"

"I *am* a computer model," Roger began. The woman rode right over him.

"—what I need to know is, will the geology of the Valles be competent to handle the accumulated precipitation? There are no lowlands for the district to drain into—at six and a half kilometers deep, the Valles *is* the nearest lowland. But would the substructure be able to support free water without catastrophic caving? Or is there an aquifer underneath it that will just reabsorb the runoff, leaving us in a net condition of—"

"Whoa! Miss Coghlan!" Roger raised his hand.

The doll's face suspended. The mobile eyes and mouth froze and hung in midair, appliquéd against the landscape, while her body and most of the head faded out. The image rebuilt only gradually.

"Yes?" the lips asked in a whisper.

"I spent more than an Earth year in the Valles. That was back in the middle twenties," he explained. "I could describe the area for you in minute detail because, of course, all my memories are machine-stored. But what I cannot figure out is why you want to have me describe anything? Instead, you should refer to the download of my survey impressions, which were long ago converted to a V/R program you can check out of any library. Better yet, why don't you rent a tourist proxy and explore the area at first hand?"

"I already tried that," the woman said, her image strengthening with a kind of conviction. "I don't know what I'm looking at. And your survey data are just that, undirected impressions. What I need, Colonel, is your expert knowledge, your judgment, your experience with the Martian surface."

Roger ran a hand lightly around the rim of his mysterious gopher hole. He didn't know if the image she was getting would show the motion. He didn't care, either.

"Yeah, expert knowledge and experience . . ." he said gloomily.

A heavy hand thumped his shoulder, practically knocking him off balance.

"Ask who she represents," Fetya hissed in his ear. "And what will she pay? Cost her plenty already to get override on you, I think."

Roger turned his head. "How do you—?"

The Cyborg grinned at him, showing steel teeth. "Your signals are not so tight-beam as once, Tovarich."

"Um . . . Miss Coghlan, you speak of changing the water content of the Martian atmosphere. That would obviously be a major operation, requiring significant backing. Do you mind if I ask who you represent?"

"I . . . uh . . ." The woman faded completely.

"Never mind," he said quickly into the carrier. With his access to grid resources, Torraway could probably discover her origins and purposes faster than any nonadapted human. "But may I take it as given that you are prepared to pay for the special information you require?"

The face reappeared, hanging against the sky. The smile from her lips actually touched and dimpled the doll-like cheeks. "Of course. For usable information, we are prepared to pay a reasonable price. I just didn't know you Cyborgs, um, needed money."

"Money? No." Roger wondered what the value of 1,500 kilograms of deuterium-tritium fuel, delivered F.O.B. to the Tharsis Montes fountainhead, was in real money. "But we may be able to work out a satisfactory trade."

"All right then!" The woman's grin increased by half an angular degree—then narrowed perceptibly. "But how do I contact you? I mean, regularly, for the purposes of consultation?"

"How did you get to me this time?"

She hesitated, growing dim. "That's . . . ah . . ."

"Never mind. I will put the name of Demeter Coghlan among my special friends, always to have access."

"Thank you!" The woman's face came back in full force. Her cheeks reddened slightly, with what Roger used to think of as a blush.

"Think nothing of it," he assured her.

Coghlan started to say something more, reconsidered, and merely nodded gratefully. Then her features blinked out as the signal was cut at the source. In

Roger's brain, however, her smile lingered in after-image.

Golden Lotus, June 15

After the connection broke, Demeter Coghlan sat in the simulation booth, still wearing her helmet and gloves. Under the helmet's laminations of styrene, silicon, and fiberoptic, her face wore a long and thoughtful expression. Curiously sober.

Demeter wasn't sure exactly what kind of hookup she had been taking part in. Even without a whole lot of movement on her side, it had felt like a full-body simulation. What she couldn't figure out was, where did the pickup relaying Roger Torraway's image reside? Out in the middle of the desert like that, she would have expected the grid to need a remote or a rover to cover him. Clearly that huge, green Cyborg who seemed to accompany Torraway everywhere wasn't part of the linkage; he had stayed in the background or off to one side, always behind the Colonel.

Both of the Cyborgs had unnerving presences. Impassive faces, with no human interplay of the folds of flesh—lip and cheek muscles, eyelids and brows—that normally accompanied a conversation. The words just came out in complete and finished sentences, digitized somewhere in Torraway's electronic sensorium, not even passing over human vocal chords.

Squatting there, studying her with his faceted jewel eyes, Torraway reminded her of some kind of insect. A patient mantis, perhaps, waiting to . . . *snap!* and clip her head off—if she had actually been present on the scene, that is.

After her experience with Jory den Ostreicher, Coghlan had thought she was ready to deal with the Cyborgs. After all, they would be like him, wouldn't they? Only more complete, more perfected. Instead, she found the Cyborgs quite different. Their inflexible, waiting gaze told her they had no interest in her—not in Demeter Coghlan or any human being. Her needs and desires, her plans and promises were all ephemera to them. Passing whimsy, dust on the wind. She sensed that any human, on Earth or in Mars, was just so much excess protoplasm to them. Not worth noticing.

This state of detachment would have something to do with their extreme age. True, the Cyborgs were relatively new beings, contemporaries of her grandfather's generation, in fact. Torraway himself could not be older than about ninety, probably. But all the same, he had found a way to cheat death. He could not grow old, weaken, and eventually die, as G'dad would. Torraway could only break down, and the broken parts could be replaced indefinitely. The new components would have better materials, faster chips, lighter metals, harder surfaces. The Colonel was virtually immortal.

That, more than the lack of eyebrows to wiggle at her, was what made him so spooky.

And yet. And yet, he had agreed to become her consultant, to "work out a trade." That in itself implied there was something he wanted. So Torraway had a lever she could push—if only she could find it. And if the price was within the budget of the Texahoma Martian Development Corporation. He wasn't on retainer yet, but she felt positive she could discover his weakness, his need, and arrange to scratch it. If only—

"Hi, Demeter!"

The goggles before her eyes lit up with the gargoyle face of Nancy Cuneo. It was a flat image, piped into Coghlan's simulation gear from a standard terminal.

"Hello, Nancy," she replied, wondering what her

own image looked like on Cuneo's screen. Probably just a VIDEO NOT AVAILABLE notice, as if Demeter had stepped out of the shower. "What can I do for you?"

"Our delegation's come in, as I told you. I'm hosting a little reception on behalf of the Canyonlands people, drinks at six. I so want you to come. Everyone will be there."

"Everyone?" Demeter asked with a smile. Did that mean Roger Torraway and his big green friend, perhaps?

"The cream of the complex. So, you will come?"

"I'd love it."

"Good . . . and, Demeter?"

"Ye-ess?"

"Could you find something to wear other than those coveralls? Oh, they're practical, I'm sure, but a little too *proletarian* for this kind of affair. Surely, with the whole afternoon to shop, you can find something more off-the-shoulder. Something that shows a bit of leg?"

"Do you want me to come as a guest, or a party favor?" Demeter tried to keep her voice sweet.

"I just don't want you to feel out of place, dear."

"No, I'm sure you don't." This was more fun than the shark pool at the Dallas National Aquarium.

"At six, then?"

"Ta!" Demeter broke the connection.

Before her surroundings had gone quite black, Demeter's goggles lit up again.

"Hello?" It was Lole Mitsuno, peering anxiously out of the near focus as if he had suddenly lost sight of her. "Demeter?"

"Hi, Lole. We're cross-wired, I'm afraid. The grid's tapped you into a simulation I just turned off. I don't know what reception is like on your end."

"You look, uh, like a ventriloquist's dummy. I mean, molded out of thick plastic, with your eyes kind of fixed and your face painted in bright primary colors."

"You really know how to compliment a girl."

"I'm sorry!"

"Hush, they're using my passport photo, I think. I didn't know the grid could do this."

"It can't, technically."

An awkward pause developed.

"It's your nickel, Lole," she offered.

"What's that?"

"You called me, remember?"

"Oh, right! Yes, I wanted to know if you'd like to have dinner with me tonight."

"Hey, that's nice. I'd like it a lot, except . . ."

"You have other plans?"

Demeter shook her head inside the helmet, then wondered if he could see. "A political thing. If you'd only called one minute earlier, then I could say yes with a clear conscience. But, as it is, I'm committed. My job, you know."

"What job is that?"

"Being a spy, remember?"

"Oh." Mitsuno's face wavered between good humor and naked hurt, just like a little boy's. It was a side of men that Demeter could do without.

"Hey! I do want to see you," she said. "Dinner. Tomorrow night. Six o'clock. My place."

"Okay."

"You're buying."

"I'll be glad to—"

"Something expensive, like lobster."

"Lob—?"

"Marine crustacean, boiled with butter sauce. You'd

love it. Great with champagne cocktails. But since Mars doesn't grow lobsters, and nobody's probably thought of importing them, I'll leave 'expensive' to your imagination."

"That's a deal." He grinned.

"Tomorrow then, for sure?"

"See you!"

Demeter Coghlan broke the connection and pulled the helmet off her head before she could get into any more trouble. She started to check the time with Sugar, remembered her loss, and called up the grid itself.

"Thirteen hundred hours, forty-six minutes," the dispassionate voice told her.

Yikes! She had a dress to buy, and only four hours to do it in.

Red Sands Hotel, Commercial Unit 3/9/15, June 15

At seventy-nine, Harry Orthis began to think he was getting a little old for planet hopping. Harry didn't *feel* old—or hadn't until about a year ago. But his attention span was growing shorter, and he had little patience anymore for cocktail blab.

The reception for his negotiating team, when it finally touched down on the Martian surface, was made up mostly of small merchants and petit bourgeoisie. The settlement at Tharsis Montes seemed mostly to run itself, with no sign of an active government structure. So far, Orthis had met only minor functionaries, each of whom was all too quick to point out that he or she handled just a tiny department devoted to air circulation, tunnel development, water procurement, or waste reclamation. The biggest bureaucracy seemed to run the space fountain: he'd met all of three people attached to it.

Of course, there were other population complexes

on the planet, and they might have a more formal government framework. Orthis remembered something Nancy Cuneo had said about a meeting with the mayor of Solis Planum. That one had a big red star beside his name on the hospitality roster. Probably a spokesperson of some kind for the whole Southern Region.

Still, this night's affair seemed to be mostly shopkeepers and hoteliers. These people either had no interest in the Canyonlands project or viewed it with mild distrust, as a source of commercial competition. As if they felt the need to fight over pennies with a new township almost three thousand kilometers away. Sad, small-minded people.

Orthis sipped his gin and tonic and watched the crowd dynamics. That's what he enjoyed most at these diplomatic functions: seeing how people paired up and guessing who would end up in whose bed tonight. Tight groups of three that stayed together, joined at the elbow, from one platter of canapés to another always intrigued him—in an academic way, of course.

He gradually, over the course of a heartbeat or so, became aware of general movement within the group. Flashes of pale color as faces were exposed by the abrupt turning of heads, white gleams from the sudden widening of eyes, marked a passage of some kind across the room. This reaction reminded him of the dew track a flying electron precipitated inside a cloud chamber: Orthis could see the effect but not the particle causing it.

Then the knot of bodies standing in his foreground parted to reveal Nancy Cuneo bringing a young woman toward him. She was the electron. Definitely.

It wasn't so much her face, which was nothing really special, as her overall packaging. The woman was barely more than a girl to begin with, and she covered the flower of her youth with a tube dress of sheer nylon the color of a raspberry Popsicle. It hung from her nipples to a mere four centimeters below her crotch. As she walked toward him Orthis could see beneath her arms that, in back, it plunged along the curve of her hips to barely drape her buttocks. It might conceal the cleft between them but would also emphasize that line as she moved. Apparently the only thing holding the dress in place was a strong static charge, for if she was wearing undergarments, or even flesh-colored tights, it wasn't obvious. He made a quick bet with himself that the woman wouldn't be able to sit down all evening— not and remain a lady.

That one quick, practiced glance told Harry Orthis the garment must have cost her about a thousand Neu per gram. It was worth it. He had seen lingerie in sealed catalogs that was less arousing. Even at his age, he could feel the juices begin to flow.

Nancy Cuneo was virtually invisible at the young woman's side. The North Zealand agent suddenly looked her age, which Orthis knew to be considerable. It didn't help that for the evening Nancy had chosen a frizzy wig of red curls. Why did everyone who went bald after that unfortunate wind shift following the Raoul Island test pattern have such awful taste in hair? In Cuneo's case, she matched the disaster with a party dress that had cuffs and padding in all the wrong places. She would look like a garden gnome, if she didn't fade to black entirely in the glare thrown by the girl in the raspberry dress.

"Harry! I have someone for you to meet," Cuneo greeted him.

"Nancy."

"This is Demeter Coghlan, from the Sovereign State of Texahoma. She's Alvin Bertrand Coghlan's grand-daughter."

"Oh, yes? I know old A.B. well. We've jousted many a time at the General Assembly meetings."

"And this, Demeter, is Harry Orthis. Harry is a senior analyst with the North Zealand Economic Development Agency."

"Really?" the young woman asked. With her South-western cowpoke accent, the word came out "rally." And the partial pressure of helium that the Martians filled their burrows with transmuted it to "reilly." But Orthis caught her drift.

"What is it you analyze?" she went on.

"Oh, economic factors, cash flows, political advantage, anything you'd normally put through a computer."

"You and Demeter have something in common," Cuneo offered, smirking. And with that lead-in, she just walked away.

Orthis and the Coghlan woman stared at her retreating back, then glanced at each other. Harry couldn't imagine what they might have in common, other than a desire to throw off their clothes, drop to the floor, and couple there on the spot. And he wasn't sure Demeter shared that with him, either.

"Well, judging from her timing," Demeter ventured, "I'd say it has something to do with computers."

He cocked his head at her.

"I mean, you work with them, don't you?"

"I never said that, actually," Orthis replied. "I do things in my head other people do with them. Personally, I hate the machines."

"Oh, that's it then! I dislike them myself."

"That's rare enough these days to be remarkable—

two people passing through the same city who don't happen to think of our silicon friends as . . . well, friends."

"I guess I wasn't always like that," she said slowly. "Not until after the accident."

"What happened?" He put the right amount of concern in his voice.

"I was having my hair done in an autocoif—you know what that is?"

"Sure."

"And the machine all of a sudden froze up. The scissors unit punched a hole in my skull you could pass a dime through—"

Orthis looked past her face at the braid of luxuriant brown hair, hanging at least twelve vertebrae down her naked back.

Some doubt must have shown in his face, because she quickly amended: "This was more than a year ago—closer to two now, what with the recuperation period, and then travel time getting up here. I haven't let anyone touch my hair since the accident. I always wash it myself and won't let a machine so much as put a comb to it.

"Anyway, those scissors did some brain damage, or so they tell me. Mostly motor function and some hearing loss, although that's all fixed now. You know the techniques they have these days for lattice matricing and tissue transplants? I've got so many wires in my head, I gotta take cover whenever it thunderstorms."

"Really!" And he was conscious of saying "reilly," too. "I was scuba-ing off Little Barrier Island in Hauraki Gulf—"

"Excuse me? 'Scoobang'? What's that?"

"Self-contained underwater breathing apparatus—

it's a recycler that generates oxygen from the carbon dioxide and water vapor in your breath. So I'm down about forty meters, and the damned monitor chip suddenly goes haywire. The unit starts reconstituting carbon *mon*oxide instead—although nobody can figure out just how. I had about blacked out, gone to dreamland, when the whole box shut down. I suddenly had to make a free ascent, blowing bubbles all the way."

"Golly!" she said in admiration. Or, as it came out, "gelly."

"Fortunately, my mates saw me go up and sent a sonogram to the surface. When the boat finally picked me up, I was doubled over from decompression, had my head wrapped down around my knees, and was blue all over. I had effectively drowned."

"But you're alive now."

"Yes, but most of my brain, or at least the cerebral cortex, was killed off by the combination of carbon monoxide poisoning and then oxygen deprivation. Like you, I've got a head full of gadgetry."

"And you solve computer problems with it?"

"Well . . ." Orthis hesitated. "The knack still seems to be there. I really don't like computers, though."

"Me neither."

"It's not just having the damn thing inside your skull—"

"—it's knowing they caused the trouble in the first place."

"Exactly!" he said. "They're just not infallible."

"I don't think they ever were." And she grinned at him.

So they did have something in common after all. Orthis was amazed at Cuneo's insight. Like any good agent, she had the hard intelligence on everyone at her fingertips. He suddenly wondered what else Cuneo had been able to ferret out about Alvin Bertrand's prettiest granddaughter. Or maybe Harry would find out for himself.

"Buy you a drink?" he asked.

"Sure, whatever you're having."

Golden Lotus, June 16

That night, when Demeter finally got back to her hotel, she found a message from Gregor Weiss waiting for her on the room terminal. Luckily the text was in clear language, because she no longer had Sugar to break his fancy codes. Her bangle was squashed somewhere in the residential corridors up on the second level; by now someone had probably picked it up for the value of the metal.

"Sorry, Demeter, we just can't comply with your request to have a change of scene." He was using publicly acceptable terminology to refuse her application for immediate removal and reassignment. "G'dad says he can't get you on anything coming back to Earth sooner than your scheduled return flight. So why don't you just relax, do some sightseeing" —another euphemism— "and enjoy it."

That was all. No commiseration. No chucks under the chin. Just "do your job"—with a slight edge to his voice as Gregor conveyed it. That tone implied he was tired of her whining about having to complete a plum assignment with a gold-leaf expense account while other agents, better than her by far, had to sweat it out in places like New York or Mexico City.

Anyway, Demeter didn't care now. She was well over the blues from the day before. In the past twenty-four hours, in fact, she had recruited a living legend as her new agent, snared a dinner date with the most attractive unattached man in Tharsis Montes, and made a solid conquest of the head of the North Zealand trade delegation.

Things were definitely looking up.

Chapter 12

Valhalla

Golden Lotus, June 16

Demeter Coghlan debated wearing her new party dress for the dinner date with Lole.

On the one hand, the garment was not all that new, after its one wearing. She might have acquired a stain on it somewhere. Not to mention wrinkles.

On the other hand, she could wash it easily in the sink. That would take all of two minutes, with three more for it to dry.

On the other hand, the dress was a hard thing to wear. Every moment inside it—or as much inside as she could get—Demeter had to be careful of how she moved and sat, had to keep her legs together and hold her stomach in.

On the other hand, her usual coveralls were a whole lot more comfortable, as well as easier on the mind.

On the other hand, Lole Mitsuno had already seen those, several times, in fact. He had seen the jumpers in all the colors of her wardrobe—which were violet, lavender, and gray—both with and without her warpaint. It was time to give him something new. And it would be a shame to wear that cute little dress just the once and then forget it.

The bottom line, however, was that Demeter just

wasn't sure she wanted the reaction the garment was likely to provoke.

Or maybe she did.

In the end, she wore the dress.

Chez Guerrero, Commercial Unit 1/16/2, June 16

Lole Mitsuno had felt a palpable weakness in his stomach and through the knees from the first moment he saw Demeter that evening. He had known all along that she was an attractive young woman, smart and bouncy in a rough, up-country sort of way. Demeter had none of the poise, the reserved grace that had originally drawn him to Ellen Sorbel. Demeter was all candor and wisecracks, practically one of the boys. So he had thought of her as a friend, more like a sister— until she stepped out into the golden light of the hotel foyer.

She had been wearing next to nothing in shiny silk or satin or whatever they called it. The pinkish-purplish material brought up the color of her lips, which were a stunning red, and contrasted them with her white skin. Berry colored, that was what they were. And her green eyes were like the delicate little leaves attached to a berry's stem.

Hell, she was making Mitsuno feel like a poet already!

He had taken her to the best restaurant Tharsis Montes, or Mars itself, had to offer. The tables had white cloths on them that were pressed to resemble linen. The utensils were real silver, shipped from Earth at forty Alt-marks per gram. The wineglasses, although a polymer, were cut and polished just like crystal. The cuisine was Hispano-French: the sauces were smeared on the plate *under* the food—that was the French part; and they were spiced with vat-grown chilies and cilantro—that was the

Spanish contribution. The rest of the menu was just regular commissary foods, dolled up to *look* foreign.

Mitsuno couldn't taste any of it, even though the bill would make a big dent against his weekly stipend. His brain only had room for Demeter Coghlan. Her face and creamy, bare shoulders filled his eyes and dimmed the gleams of silver and crystal from the table's finery. She entirely eclipsed the hand-painted, eighteenth-century miniatures reproduced on the white stucco wall next to her head. The one whiff of her exotic perfume that reached Lole had chased away all scents of food and wine. Her voice and laugh so filled his ears that, if other women had been dancing naked across the room, he would hardly have noticed.

She ate sparingly but praised everything, bite for bite. She sipped at her red wine, and the drop that stayed on her lower lip added to its color. She laughed at the right places in his fumbling conversation, and her teeth sparkled in the glow from the amber bulb sprouting from a slim, white-plastic tube on the table.

When she had spooned up the last of the dessert—sweet cheese paste inside a crackling, hollow shell of pastry—and pushed her plate away, Demeter turned her smile on him again.

"Well . . . it's been a lovely evening."

"It . . . doesn't have to end, does it?"

"No."

Just the one word. Spoken in quiet, reasonable agreement. Accompanied by a gentle smile and a knowing look. No. Meaning yes.

Lole decided in that instant to violate a trust and take her—an offworlder and a self-proclaimed spy, someone over whom he had no hold, no power for retribution—to a place reserved for the select few.

"Come on." He stood up and gently took her hand.

Demeter turned in her chair but made no motion to rise.

"Where are we going?"

"Someplace you'll like."

He walked east with her, up a ramp to the surface facilities, through a pressure door, and down into the old equipment bays. From there they followed a utility corridor out to the site of the complex's first water storage and aeration facility, 4,000 megaliters of open tankage, dug into bedrock and roofed over against explosive evaporation and the blowing sand.

Mitsuno and Coghlan crossed the pool on a catwalk of perforated steel plate. The dank air around them was lit only by the widely spaced safelights in the dome above, and by swimming dots of silver reflected off the quiet water. Algal-green slime, the persistent echo of protozoic life that had followed humanity's colonization of the Solar System, dripped from the tube railing beside them. As the two of them passed, Lole could hear Demeter's high heels clicking wetly against the metal. He expected her to protest about the environment, but she came along quietly, even expectantly.

On the other side of the tanks, the pair came to a gallery of unfinished tunnels, two levels that extended forty and eighty meters below the surface. Mitsuno knew that the ground here was not competent; the rust-red, iron-rich rock was too friable and unstable for development, and so the complex's expansion in this direction had stopped. Instead, Tharsis Montes had dug in deeper under itself. But these old workings had not been backfilled or formally abandoned, just never finished.

Mitsuno hesitated before the door made of sheetmetal that closed off the refuge.

"Normally, we require a strip-search before bringing someone here," he said. "But . . ."

Demeter Coghlan flashed him a grin, held her hands away from her hips, and turned full circle on one toe. Her limbs seemed to glow in the vague and shifting light reflected down the tunnel from the waterworks. A fold of the dress glimmered as it snaked across her stomach and then pulled taut as she completed the turn.

"No need," he agreed. He looked at her wrist for the first time that evening. "Are you wearing that chrono of yours? Sugar?"

Demeter shook her head. "I lost her a few days ago."

Mitsuno also decided that she couldn't possibly be wearing any prosthetics that might harbor an active cyber circuit. If she was, then the technology for generating pseudoskin was too advanced for his detection. And, anyway, Wa Lixin had already scanned her and pronounced her clean.

Mitsuno opened the door on hinges that creaked with rust. Beyond it was a long room, with hangings of rough cloth to muffle echoes from the bare rock and hold back the ever-sifting dust. He groped for the switch—he actually had to light the chamber manually. The breaker was wired into the illicit circuit they had run long ago from the pool's emergency lighting.

Three caged bulbs came on to show the furniture inside. The pieces were old and mismatched, taken as first-generation castoffs before the municipal recyclers had gotten to them. Still, the space was comfortable enough. In addition to several padded chairs, a settee, and a low table, there was an old bed with the stuffing worn down in all the right places.

"My!" Demeter said, moving past him. "This is

homey. Much nicer than the hole Jory took me—" She paused awkwardly. "Oops!"

"Don't worry." Lole smiled. "I heard all about that. . . . This place is just as quiet. No cybers, no fiberoptic, no one to see us."

She nodded. "Do you have someplace I could, ah, wash up?"

They were just within spitting distance of a couple million liters of fresh water, but the tunnel had no plumbing, either. Lole led her past a fold in the wall's cloth that hung out at right angles; in the alcove behind it was a chemical toilet and a steel bucket. He picked up the bucket.

"Pardon me while I go draw you a basin." And Mitsuno went back to the pool.

When he returned, Demeter was standing in the middle of the chamber, equidistant from the three lights. She stood tall in her stiletto heels, her feet apart at shoulder width, hands on her hips. The shadows played across her body as she faced him almost defiantly.

As he came nearer, Lole saw that she was trembling. The wine-colored dress seemed somehow looser, more bunched on her figure. He paused, smiling uncertainly.

Demeter took a deep breath, and the cloth slid off her breasts, exposing nipples that were erect and staring at him as boldly as her two eyes. He understood now that she had taken the dress off while he was gone and had merely been holding the fabric in front of her, pinched at the waist. She lifted the fingers of her left hand, and the cloth swung away, to hang against her right thigh like a limp flag against its pole. She lifted the fingers of her right hand, and it fluttered down between her feet.

Except for her shoes and a touch of lipstick, she was nude. And still trembling.

"Well . . . ?"

Mitsuno came out of his trance, walked up to her, and cupped his palms over her hips, pressing his fingertips into the silky skin in the hollow of her buttocks. She lifted her fingers again and pinned him at the wrists, pulling his arms back around her. She wedged her body tightly against his.

He locked his fingers under her and took her weight as she lifted her legs and wrapped them around him. Instantly she started rubbing herself slowly against his groin. They never made it to the bed—or not on the first try.

Somewhere Underground East of Tharsis Montes, June 16

Demeter Coghlan lolled on the bed while Mitsuno went behind the screen. Even though she tried not to listen, the sound of his peeing into the thundermug came to her quite clearly. This would be a good occasion for using a sonic phase inverter—except, of course, that such a piece of equipment would reintroduce the grid into this fine and private place of Lole's.

"You said you have to strip-search people before bringing them here," she said over the tinkling. "Do you bring many girls here?"

He grunted but waited until he was finished making water before replying. "This isn't just a place for women who are shy about their lovemaking."

"I guessed as much," she said . . . and waited.

Mitsuno came around the screen, still naked and swinging, and resettled on the bed. Immediately he was lying on his side and pressing against her, touching knee to knee, hip to hip, with his flaccid organ nuzzling her lower belly and one hand massaging her near breast in small, sensuous circles. His lips brushed her ear.

"Well . . . ?"

"Well, what?" he replied sleepily.

"You people seem to have little rooms like this set aside all over Tharsis Montes."

"It's a reaction to the . . . the *public* nature of our lives, I guess. What's the opposite of privacy? Publicity? We all want to find our own quiet place, even if it means stealing a cubic meter here and there."

"And you think none of them are known to the cybers," she said with disbelief.

"Oh, the computers know all about this place. The excavators that dug it were machine-controlled. The ground's unstable, so the grid even left a string of monitors in here to watch for cave-ins. We just put a few recording loops around them, so the grid hears only what it expects to hear."

"So you *do* come here to get away from the machines?"

"Sure. There are some things we don't want the computer grid being privy to. Affairs that're none of their business. So we set up this place as a haven for private discussions . . . things of that nature."

"And Creoles like Jory never visit it?" Demeter pressed.

"Of course they do. They're a curious bunch, so we bring them in for little parties. The Creoles are partial to human girls, as you found out. We also bring the Cyborgs in, just to bore the socks off them. Everybody thinks this is just a sack shack, and we don't disabuse them. Anyway, the grid doesn't care about human needs like privacy."

"Isn't it dangerous, bringing hard-wired creatures like the Creoles in here? Especially if you want to keep this place a secret."

"Depends on your point of view." He shrugged one shoulder—the one that wasn't pushed into the pillow. His eyes were already closing again. "When the machine symbiotes get too inquisitive, it's easier and neater, we find, to charm them than to take more . . . um . . . direct action."

Demeter's training in espionage gave her a full range of meanings for a phrase like "direct action." She wondered with some amusement what amateurs like Lole and his friends might be prepared to do in protecting their secret place. Instead, she asked a more pressing question. "Who, exactly, is 'we'?"

"Some people who basically think like you do, that computers are not to be trusted. Not completely."

"I never said that!" Demeter protested. "I just don't like them very much."

"Is there a difference?" Lole asked with a yawn.

"Not a lot . . . maybe," she conceded. "But all the same—"

Before she could finish the thought, he was snoring in her ear. It didn't surprise Demeter, after the exercise she'd been giving him.

All the same, she was going to say, the way this room was set up implied more than just parties and fun. People came here to plot. Maybe to hide out. That much was evident from the boxes of canned food, the survival gear, and the emergency pressure suits she had found right off, stashed beyond one of the wall hangings. Demeter had a lot to learn about Lole Mitsuno and his friends.

And they had almost nothing more to discover about her. She'd already told them everything.

Now, was that a good thing? Or bad?

Demeter was still trying to decide in her own head when sleep overtook her.

Chapter 13

Shots in the Dark

Harry Orthis came bolt upright out of a sound sleep. He looked around in the utter darkness of his hotel room, trying to determine what had awakened him.

Nothing.

If the intrusion had been some kind of noise, it wasn't repeated. He listened for a minute or more—counting out his suddenly accelerated heartbeats and dividing by two for good measure—but still he heard nothing.

Orthis stared into black space with perfectly sleep-adapted eyes, seeking shadows. After a moment's concentration, he could sense the room's terminal screen by the faintest of residual glows from its phosphors. A lighted diode, buried in its keyboard circuitry and still active, pebbled the ceiling with oblong shadows: the edges of key blocks and plunger switches matrixed above the underlit board. The room's outer door, for all the brush-stripping at its edges, outlined itself in golden slivers leaking in from the hallway. The charge light on his battery-powered shaver flooded the bathroom with a green blaze.

But none of it moved. None of it would have brought him awake.

"Time?" Orthis asked his personal chrono, lying on the nightstand.

"One twenty-seven, ayem," replied its neutral voice. On a whim, Orthis had once programmed the chrono to be perfectly indeterminate as either male or female, alive or mechanical. It offered him no comfort now.

Harry Orthis knew his own sleep cycles. Based on the time he had turned out his reading light and rolled over, he could expect to wake up twice, briefly, at around two-fifteen and four-thirty. And then he would barely open his eyes, not even raise his head—let alone come upright on the bed like this.

He wiped his palms on the bare skin of his chest. There they picked up an even heavier slick of sweat. He scrubbed his fingers against the outside of the blanket, matting its curried fuzz.

The room wasn't all that hot.

So this had to be a cold sweat.

He pushed back the covers and, without turning on the light, walked over to the terminal, seated himself before it.

"System."

"Yes, Counselor Orthis?" the local machine replied, voice only.

"Connect me with Demeter Coghlan. She's at the Golden Lotus."

"Miss Coghlan is not in her assigned room," a new voice, higher level, informed him.

"Find her for me, will you?"

"That function is not offered as part of regular programming." To aid him, the screen lit up with a menu of the system's interpersonal contact routines. It was a short list.

"Mephisto . . . locate the girl."

A pause. Harry Orthis could imagine the grid checking the trace images collected from hundreds or possibly thousands of video monitors, the scent indices from just as many gas sniffers, the compressed echoes from a like number of public earjacks. The machines would be frantically coordinating their raw data, searching for a clue, a trail, a present position.

"Miss Coghlan is not currently in the Tharsis Montes complex," the grid announced finally. The screen went a neutral gray.

"How did she leave? And when?"

"There is no record of her leaving."

"Catalog the sales of intercolony transit vouchers during the past twenty-four hours," he instructed. "Also, rentals of pressure suits at all the public locks."

"We repeat, there is no record of her leaving, by any exit."

"Interesting. . . . Give her last-known position."

"The restaurant Chez Guerrero, Commercial Unit 1/16/2." The screen offered standard tourist photos of the inside of a two-star eatery. It had tables too close together, a hard tile floor, and lots of white plaster on the walls, with reproductions of old paintings reflecting a Mexican flavor, maybe American Southwest.

"When was she there?"

"Yesterday, between eighteen-thirty hours and twenty hundred hours."

"And after that?" Orthis prompted.

"After that, Miss Coghlan was not in the complex."

"With no record at all of her leaving. Yes, I get it." He sat with his chin on his chest, thinking. The montage of restaurant views clicked off, showing a blank screen again. "Did she eat dinner alone? Was anyone with her?"

"Lole Mitsuno." The screen displayed a golden head with level, gray eyes. The man had a good chin and reeked of hormones.

"Don't know him."

"Mitsuno is a Mars citizen, born on planet, and is currently employed as a Grade Two Hydrologist with the Tharsis Montes Resources Department. He and Miss Coghlan have been tallied together on several occasions during the past eight days. Our module Y-4 Administrative Terminal in his department is now reviewing the relationship."

"Prepare a summary for me," Orthis instructed. Then, as an afterthought: "Does he have a record?"

"Please specify." The screen showed a kaleidoscopic moiré pattern in pinks and greens—emblematic of confusion.

"Like, a criminal record? Perhaps for psychopathic sexual deviancy, child molestation, abduction, rape, that sort of thing?"

"No such charges have been filed against him," the grid replied primly.

"No, I guess not. . . . Interesting."

"Further instructions?" the machine asked.

"Not at this time. If I think of anything, I will let you know."

"As will we. . . ."

With a sudden *blip* the screen went dark. Not just blank, but completely turned off, with only the flush of its dying phosphors to light him to bed.

Golden Lotus, June 17

"Ah! There you are!"

Demeter Coghlan was crossing the foyer outside the door of her hotel room. It was her first step out into the open, it seemed, after more than a kilometer of creeping warily from apex to apex around three long walls of every public hexcube on Level Four. The reason for her caution was simple: here it was the near side of morning, going on six o'clock and breakfast time, and she was still dressed in her raspberry microdress, a pair of black heels eighty-five millimeters high, and nothing much else. Except for a contented smile and a rat's nest of brown hair that clawed at her neck and draggled down her bare back. Not a very wholesome picture.

So the jolly call stabbed at her, like a thief on the end of a policeman's shockrod.

Demeter turned to find Sun Il Suk seated on the little banquette that jutted from one side of the foyer hexcube. He sat like a chubby schoolboy, hands folded in his broad lap, legs crossed at the ankle and tucked back under his bulk. A Schoolboy Buddha, she thought to herself.

"Oh! Hello, Sukie." She could feel his eyes inchworming over every centimeter of her exposed skin. Looking for what? Sucker marks?

"You were out late." He made a statement, not a question.

"Yes."

"I tried to call you. I got no answer, anywhere. I looked all over for you. No one could find you."

"I was visiting a friend."

"Doesn't he have a terminal?"

"We . . . didn't have it hooked up."

"That was most inconsiderate. I really wanted to talk with you."

"Oh? What about?"

Sun's face instantly went blank: the Schoolboy Buddha caught out in a lie. His lower lip briefly sagged, his eyelids drooped, his shoulders slumped. Although Sun's confusion lasted less than half a second, Demeter definitely saw it. Within the space of a wink, however, he brightened and pulled himself together.

"To talk with you about the new team from N-ZED."

"I've met them," she replied. "What about it?"

Pause. "Do you think they represent a danger to either of our positions?"

"You called me at—what? the middle of the night?—to ask me that?"

"It was two o'clock. I had trouble sleeping."

"Bad conscience?"

"No. Concern for you, my dear."

"I can take care of myself."

"These North Zealanders are not what they seem. Their development project, Canyonlands, is not what it pretends to be."

"This is supposed to be news?"

"I only want to help you. For example, study their new orbiting power station. You will see that it is far larger—three times the capacity—than their proposed energy consumption. That is not a fact you can check with any public source, but I offer it to you in order to cement our alliance."

Sun's face was turned partly away from her, chin up, brow relaxed, like a moon at three quarters, concerned elsewhere. For a long moment he displayed the truthful schoolboy, the benevolent Buddha, with no spells to cast, nothing to urge. The bubbling spy of their previous encounter was nowhere to be seen in him.

"Well, I appreciate your help." It sounded lame in her own ears.

Then she noticed that, with every other breath,

Sun's eyes flickered to betray him. They winked sideways, crawling over her white flesh, measuring, tasting, gauging clefts and indentations that they could not reach from whatever they could see exposed. So even now he remained the adventitious lecher.

"I have to go," she said suddenly, walking to her door. Demeter brushed her fingertips together, to remove any grunge from her print pattern, and pushed her thumb against the lockplate.

The Korean stood up, moved toward her.

"I can open it myself." Demeter turned her shoulders protectively.

Halfway across the foyer, Sun Il Suk stopped. His palms came forward in a half-shrug. Something of the old smile showed on his face.

"Really, I do not fancy European women," he lied.

"Well then, good morning. And, um, thanks for the advice."

He nodded, turned, and lumbered off down the corridor.

Demeter slipped into her room and slammed the door behind her. She wondered how long she'd have to wait, to make sure he was truly gone, before she dared head down to the hotel's common bathroom for a long, hot shower. And be *damned* to the meter rate!

The Russian Tearoom, June 17

Demeter picked up a toasted bagel—it was one of the few breads that the Martians prepared really well—and spread it with unsaturated oil that had been emulsified and was even vaguely yellow. What she really wanted, of course, was a big gob of cream cheese and a slab of smoked fish, salmon if they could get it, with maybe some onions and capers. Yum!

Trouble was, Mars didn't have any fish, except for a

pair of experimental carp in the hydroponics lab, and they were completely off limits until the gene pool expanded. No capers, either. And the onions the colonists did grow were of the long, green shallot variety—not the big, purple slabs of Bermuda she craved.

No poppyseeds on her bagel, for that matter.

"*There* you are, Demeter!"

She looked up and spilled her tea. Thick liquid, stiff with sugar, ran out from the cup and over the tablecloth in a puddle held together by surface tension until absorption by the cloth's fibers overcame its front edge. Then the tea soaked into the white material, flattening into a muddy, brown delta.

"*Damn* it!" she cried, bringing up her napkin and fluttering it over the mess.

"I'm terribly sorry," Harry Orthis, the North Zealand analyst, said. He tried to help, pulling out his handkerchief, but she waved him away. "I guess I startled you," he added, as an apology.

"I guess you did."

"Didn't mean to, of course. But, you see, I've been looking all over for you, Demeter. So it was a shock to find—"

"Jesus, you too?" Demeter growled.

"Excuse me?"

"I spend one night on the town without a chaperon, and everyone calls out the dogs." Demeter wondered what was going on, and whether this meeting with Orthis was as accidental as it seemed. "Why didn't you leave a message in my room?"

"You weren't *in* your room. Nowhere near your hotel, in fact. I checked." He took the liberty of seating himself in the empty chair across from her, avoiding the sopping edge of the tablecloth. Orthis lifted the white porcelain teapot, righted her cup and saucer, gestured with the spout. "More tea?"

"Yes, please. . . . You know, I do return calls, Harry. What was so urgent it couldn't wait?"

Orthis's face went blank. Tea dribbled out of the upended pot until it threatened to overflow the cup.

"Harry?" she prompted.

"Yes, sorry, just thinking . . ."

"You wanted to see me? Last night? Hey?"

"Of course, it was about your plan—or the Texahoma Martian Development Corporation's plan, actually—for terraforming this planet. It will destroy the atmosphere, you know."

"Not to mention flooding out some of the lowland valleys," she said distinctly. "Like your Canyonlands project?"

"That's the least of it, Demeter. Crashing asteroids around is sheer lunacy. Abrupt changes like that would be deadly to more than just the fragile, indigenous life on Mars. The instabilities would destroy the human colonies here now."

Demeter decided to let herself be drawn into speculation. "Why? They're all dug in below ground level and locked up tight. They should withstand a gradual change in atmospheric pressure and composition, happening over some months. More dust in the air—if that's possible—and some added water vapor. Their seals should hold."

"Then consider the winds," Orthis said. "Increasing the moisture and particulate content of the present global pattern will increase its kinetic energy manyfold. And consider the proportion of the Martian economy that takes place out on the surface, or under bubbles of light plastic. Gas drilling, crop planting, minerals exploration, to name just a few. All of that will vanish with your asteroid scheme."

"Well, it's just in the talking stages, anyway," Demeter grumped. "It was just an idea."

"A bad one. Terraforming Mars would be a massive boondoggle, lots of effort for very little positive result, plus much danger and alarm. You and I both know that."

"It might get the people back home interested in Mars again."

"At the risk of one hundred percent of the goodwill we've built with the people here."

"Is that why your team was sent up in such a hurry? To defend your project in the Valles against us crazy, asteroid-flinging Texahomans?"

"Not at all. We simply had a few points to clear up in negotiations."

"Oh?" Coghlan's ears swiveled forward. "Negotiations *with whom*?"

"Why, the government."

"Isn't any."

"I beg your pardon—?" Orthis had taken one of her bagels and started spreading yellow glop on it when the flat of his knife went sliding across one knuckle. He looked at the shine of grease on his finger, then thoughtfully licked it off. "What do you mean?"

"You've seen the setup here. This place practically runs itself. Everybody's too busy making a living to engage in the higher forms of government. And I have it on good authority that they've no time for diplomats and diplomacy. So, just who is it you were going to meet with?"

"There's a mayor in one of the other colonies," Orthis said defensively.

"At Solis Planum? She's a figurehead. Cuts the ribbon on new tunnel openings. Makes speeches in favor of filtering the air. Gets a budget of about five thousand Neu per annum to operate the chamber of commerce. But that's it. You try to run a deal with her, you'll find she has to refer most of it back to the people who put her in office."

"You've tried?"

"No, I just do my homework. Ludmilla Petrovna doesn't make a move without prior approval."

"So, it's simple. We go for the electorate. We mount a public relations campaign, mold opinion toward our—"

"You don't get it, do you, Harry? There *is* no 'electorate.' There hasn't been an election in Solis Planum in twenty years."

"What are you trying to tell me?" Orthis asked, seemingly patient.

"You've brought a lot of people up here, right? Planning to negotiate with the Martians, right? Except there's no one to sit down at the table with, is there? Speaking of boondoggles, this is a helluva long way to come on a jaunt." Demeter thought of Nancy Cuneo, who had arrived only a day or two after Coghlan herself and not much ahead of Harry's more public entourage. Why *were* they suddenly scrambling on site? Instead she asked, "Is your intelligence on the local situation so bad you didn't know all this?"

"We—" he replied slowly. Too slowly. "—were led to believe that proper accommodations would be made."

"Led? By whom?"

"I really think that's out of your purview, Demeter."

"By your subcontractors in the Valles? By some local acting as your agent? Who?"

"And why are you here, Demeter?" Orthis countered.

"I'm on vacation."

"This is a hellacious long way to come for a change of scene," he tossed back to her. "Especially for someone with diplomatic training—"

"I never completed my credits."

"—and secret credentials granted by the Sovereign State of Texahoma—"

"That's not true!"

"—including provisional U.N. immunity, guaranteed by the signature of Alvin Bertrand Coghlan, member of the General Assembly."

"My grandfather can be overly protective."

"So it would seem." Orthis gave a world-weary shake of his head. "And perhaps you're planning to do things, deniably in his name, that require such protection?"

"Jesus," she breathed. "Well, Cuneo and the Korean have it figured anyway. I'm here to watch you, of course."

"Watch us do what?" He was smiling. But it was friendly now, not at all in triumph.

"Take the Valles Marineris away from us. Our computer projections—" Something about computers and their predictions pricked at her memory, but the thought faded out in her rush to explain. "—showed that your development work there would tend to tip the legal balance in favor of your claims stemming from the Potanter Expedition."

"Canyonlands is a purely commercial development," he said. "Our interest is solely for profit. The inhabitants will be native-born Martians, or immigrants from all Earth nations, owing allegiance under the appropriate U.N. charters. There was never any thought of making them citizens of North Zealand,

Frederik Pohl & Thomas T. Thomas

either *de jure* or *de facto*. Our citizenship require-
ments are far too rigid to allow for that."

"Uh-huh." Coghlan was prepared to disbelieve anything he said. "And if Canyonlands is so commercial,
why are you building an orbiting power station three
times the size of your projected end-phase require-
ments?"

"Who told you that orbiter was ours?"

Demeter shook her head, beaming at him.

"More computer projections?"

"A little bird," she offered teasingly.

"All right," Orthis went on, "if you know so much
about the administrative setup here on Mars, and if we
were going to take the Valles away from you—whom
did you *think* we were negotiating with?"

Demeter could feel her own face go blank.

After too long a pause, she heard herself admit in a
small voice: "I don't know. . . . Really, it just . . . never
occurred to me."

Chapter 14

The Secret Underground

Eastern Reserve Overflow Storage Facility, June 17

By waiting until the middle of the afternoon, Demeter was fairly sure Lole Mitsuno would be out studying rocks somewhere, looking for new water, and Ellen Sorbel would have her head in a computer program, doing ditto. Still, Demeter crept warily over the algae-slimed walkway, listening for voices or other sounds coming from the secret room.

All she heard was the *thunk-thunk* of the liquid surface in the tanks, thrumming in an outlet pipe off along the perimeter somewhere.

Beyond the tankage, she found the abandoned tunnel and the plain steel door. Demeter's memories of the sexual minuet leading up to last night's encounter with Mitsuno were a little hazy; had the door been locked? If not then, it was now—with a flat metal hasp and a big tumbler lock.

Demeter wrapped her fingers around the lock's smooth, stainless-steel case. She gave it an experimental tug; the shank jerked solidly on the thick metal staple. Demeter looked at the face of the lock's black dial. Forty white hash marks, numbered off by fives, spun under a triangular marker etched into the rim. She flipped the case up and read off the backside that this was a Crypton™ lock, serial number AB-2301435-YA.

What they teach you only in Elements of Espionage 101: every commercial lock comes with a default combination. For the convenience of lock company salespeople and troubleshooters, the standard combination is keyed to all those fussy little letters that are part of the serial number. For example, all Cryptons of the "YA" series initially open with the sequence 7–14–38, always going right-left-right and being sure to come all the way back around past the second number on your way to the third. Of course, the default combination can always be changed. That takes the customer, or the sales representative, about twenty minutes with a micropick and a jeweler's loupe. Not everyone bothers.

Fifteen seconds later, Demeter had the lock off the hasp and was putting her weight against the door.

Scree-eee! Rusty hinges protested, but the door moved.

Inside, she reached around in the folds of cloth on the nearest wall until she found the switch that activated the leeched power circuit. The caged bulbs came on, showing the cave's interior. Coghlan walked past the bed and the hanging that closed off the chemical toilet. She was headed for the back wall.

Something very spooky was happening in this place.

Everyone of her acquaintance had seemed to know within hours last night that she had gone missing. Not just that she had wandered outside the purview of the video lenses and earjacks that were scattered around the complex. People must do that hundreds of times a day: when they went outside on the surface or sat quietly in their rooms or fetched something out of a broom closet. No, for nine hours there the grid and its systems had been totally blind to her. Not just unplugged, as she preferred her cybernetic eavesdroppers. But banished.

Demeter rubbed the black, wide-weave mesh that draped these rock walls and ceiling. It seemed to be some kind of slippery plastic, maybe an acrylic fiber. She picked the warp and weft apart with her fingernails. Deep in the fabric, she found what looked like a metallic thread. She traced it down, plucking the black strands apart at spaced intervals, until the wire came out at the hem. There, under a blob of solder, it joined another wire running parallel to the floor. Demeter followed the latter to one of the pitons anchoring the cloth. The base wire was wrapped and soldered around the steel rod. And the rod, by the look of it, was grounded at least nine or ten centimeters into the native stone.

What could all this metal be for?

There was an old device—the Faraday shield—that anyone could make by simply connecting a set of parallel wires across one end, then grounding the common point. It was used to block electrostatic charges and to keep a voltage potential from building up between whatever lay on one side of the shield and the other. That would be useful, certainly, in protecting this room's contents from electrolytic corrosion, say, from seeping groundwater. Or it might screen out static noise that would interfere with delicate circuitry or degrade radio reception inside the room.

But would such a screen also serve to block out electromagnetic transmissions? Would it, perhaps, shield circuitry cached in this hideaway from detection by distant sensors? Would it protect the occupants from surveillance by telemetry?

Demeter had taken only the basic science-survey

courses recommended for junior diplomats. But she remembered that, back in the twentieth century, when telecommunications signals and power transmission often went by underground copper cable, anti-corrosion devices attached to the outside of the sheathing didn't inhibit the signal-carrying capability. Nor did they stop eavesdroppers and power thieves who leeched off the surface of the cable with electromagnetic toroids.

Clearly, the wire mesh surrounding this room was intended to do *something*. It might be keeping something out, random voltages or sapping currents. But it would have nothing to do with keeping secrets inside. *Quod erat demonstrandum. . . .*

In following the hem of fabric across the end of the secret room, Demeter had to pull out part of the store of canned goods and survival gear she had discovered last night. A draft, down near the floor, stirred the fine hairs on the back of her hand. There was an opening behind the boxes—had to be.

She set about moving the big items farther into the room. When she had opened a squeeze space, Demeter pushed the cloth aside and wiggled under the low lintel into a short tunnel. It was about three meters long, negotiable on her hands and knees, with a dull, caged light at the end. Clearly, the same purloined circuit that illuminated the first room brightened the space beyond.

The second room was hung with the same dark cloth but had none of the comfortable old furnishings or other amenities. Just a table of recycled, pressed plastic and a collection of . . . components.

Without touching anything, Demeter examined them. As she traced the shielded wires and mesh-sheathed ribbon cables between them, she began to get a sense of their function.

This box, certainly, was a power supply. It was fairly big, slab-sided, with a heatsink on the back and a red switch on the front. The switch had a "zero" and a "one" position, with a light-emitting diode aligned with the one's place. The black cable coming out of it connected to . . .

That cabinet was flat, like a pizza box. It spider-webbed with parallel cabling into a nest of modules that might-could be peripherals or possibly identical memory units. The cabinet's flatness convinced her it contained a breadboard: that is, a hand-built circuit with the chips laid flat on an embedded gold-copper trace and soldered into position. That was how cyber-netics inventors made one-offs and prototypes. The best commercial, mass-produced circuits from Earth, on the other hand, were spherically cast in layers under a microgravity environment. Like Sugar, they were a single unit, resembling pearls.

And this nest of modules—probably memories, now that she thought about it—all had a damaged look about them. Each of the ceramic cases had been cracked open, something done to their innards, and then resealed with liquid epoxy. . . . Very hand-built. And by a certifiable paranoid.

What Demeter couldn't identify was the input-output module; the system had no keyboard, trackball, or display device, no helmet or gloves. That, and there didn't seem to be any connection to network resources. She looked for cables leaving the tabletop in any direction, or something that might double as an antenna, and found nothing. Except, of course, that the grid could hear a cyber of this power and com-plexity just from the electromagnetic emanations of its cabling, sheathed or not. Simply turning it on would send out a radio-frequency signature.

"Why, you bastard!" Coghlan said aloud, meaning Mitsuno.

Despite all his assurances, and in the face of his apparent compassion and tenderness, Lole had lied to her. From the evidence spread out on this table, his secure little hideaway—"someplace you'll like," he had said, where he "usually required a strip-search" before allowing the uninitiated to enter—had housed its own cyber device all along.

Counting up the memory modules and dividing by four, she guesstimated that it operated well within the range of artificially intelligent. Probably with a Stanford-Sunnyvale quotient of sixteen hundred or more. And anything it sensed and processed, the grid would know a nanosecond later through electromagnetic interferometry.

"You unparalleled bastard!"

Hoplite Bar & Grill, June 17

Lole Mitsuno and Ellen Sorbel entered their favorite watering hole, still wrangling about the botched datafields on the Hellas survey.

"*You* know there's no way a bed of olivine crystals can have extruded sideways into those sedimentary layers," Mitsuno told her. "*I* know there's no way it could have happened. Olivine is igneous rock. When it enters a formation, all the orderly structure just evaporates. Literally. So tell *that* to your cyber."

"I tried, but he's stubborn."

"Well then, we'll talk him over with Wyatt. Maybe the boss program can pound some sense into his diodes—"

"*There* you are!"

Lole glanced up and saw Demeter Coghlan bearing down on their table. From the flare in her eyes, she wasn't the happy woman he'd left ten hours ago.

"Demeter! Good to see—"

"Do you want to tell me what that tunnel's *really* for?" she demanded.

"What tunnel?" he asked, face dropping into a mask.

"Lole, what have you—?" Ellen sounded worried.

"The secret room where we . . ." Demeter glanced at Sorbel and her jaw tightened. "Where we *fucked* last night."

"Lole!" Ellen gasped. "Did you—?"

But Mitsuno cut her off, talking fast. "As I explained, Dem, it's a place where some of us go to unwind, to discuss things in private, maybe hold a little party. It's no big secret. Really."

Demeter chewed this over for just ten seconds.

"Then will you also explain to me," she said in a lower tone, "why the minute I go there, everyone is worried about it?"

"Who's worried?"

"Sun, the Korean playboy, and Orthis, the North Zealand negotiator. Both of them came asking after me this morning. Both said they missed me last night. They went looking right away and couldn't find me."

"Well, I think I mentioned that those tunnels aren't exactly open to the public," he replied slowly, trying to signal her with his eyebrows. Hadn't she figured out yet that the grid listened *everywhere?* "There are no real services in that part of the complex. There are no terminals or glasslines, let alone electronic, uh, observation points. So people looking for you might not be able to, uh, contact you."

"You're lying to me," she countered sharply. "You've got a *computer* in there."

Lole heard Ellen draw breath beside him.

"We do?" he asked, once more semaphoring with his

eyes. This was extremely dangerous talk, and Demeter ought to understand that. "How do you know?"

"I *saw* it."

"Oh? And when?"

"This afternoon. I went back there."

"Why would you do that?"

Coghlan paused. "I was looking for . . . my earrings. I lost them last night."

Mitsuno honestly couldn't remember whether she had been wearing jewelry or not. He remembered Demeter seeming awfully naked when, statutorily, she had been fully dressed.

"You should have asked me," he chided. "I would have looked for them."

"You were busy today." She shrugged. "And besides, you never said not to go back."

"But the door was locked."

"A cheap mechanical tumbler. They teach us how to get around those."

"Who teaches you?" he wondered aloud.

"My university courses, for future diplomats."

"Ah! Spies."

"You got it."

"I'm sorry about the lock," he said, hoping to distract her. "But, of course, with no power, we can't use an electronic thumb pad."

"So I figured. But then, you've got enough power for that computer."

Lole sat up straight and looked her levelly in the eye. "If there's a computer in that room, Demeter, it's news to me. You must've seen something else and *thought* it was a computer."

"I'm not *that* dumb, Lole."

"Demeter, dear . . ." Ellen cut in.

The Coghlan woman barely glanced at her.

"That whole corridor is like a public dump, you know," Ellen went on smoothly. "I'm sure you'll find pieces and parts of terminals, virtual-reality gear, old cybers, bit registers, lots of stuff, just strewn around." Now Sorbel was wig-wagging with her eyebrows. "Some of it's probably even wired together, as it was when the owner tossed it. But none of that junk's *working*. You understand?"

"So? You're in on it, too?" The way Demeter sounded, the news didn't surprise her much.

"In on what, dear?"

"On whatever it is you two're trying to hide." With that, Demeter puckered her lips in a frown, nodded once, stood up, and walked away.

Ellen turned to Mitsuno. "Lole, what have you *done?*"

"I don't know, but I guess I'd better undo it."

"Do it tonight," Sorbel told him.

Ordered him.

Golden Lotus, June 17

Demeter was keying into her hotel room when a hand touched her elbow.

"Demeter?"

She knew without looking that it was Lole Mitsuno, probably come to give her more explanations. Demeter jerked her arm out of his grasp.

"Don't try to mess with my mind, Lole. I know what I know."

Her thumb stabbed at the lockplate. The door clicked open.

"I have something to show you," he said. He took her elbow again, but lightly.

"I don't want to—" But she didn't pull away again.

Through the crack in the door, her cubicle beckoned. It was a safe place for her. It had a bed, all her
clothing, access to metered water, a terminal she could
eventually teach to take accurate dictation, and a
degree of privacy. After the shit that had come down
today, all she wanted was to go in there, lie down, and
not even dream.

"What?" Demeter asked finally.

"I can't tell you." Lole was doing that thing with the
eyebrows again. Was it some kind of twitch? "I have to
show you."

He was drawing her down the corridor, but gently. It
was like the tug of microgravity, or a cat's-paw breeze.

She sighed. "Is it far?"

"You know the way."

"All right." She pulled the door closed, turned, and
came with him.

After three changes of level and four cross tunnels,
she dragged her steps. "If you think I'm going back to
that room and . . . *service* you, think again. Lole, I am
not in the mood."

"It's not that."

"But you said the room was for . . . partying."

"Among other things. We have a lot to talk over."

"We did talk, at the Hoplite, remember?"

"Talk over in private, I mean." He headed off down the
corridor. She could either stare at his back, or follow.

Demeter hurried to keep up.

Over the bridge and into the abandoned workings,
Mitsuno led her up to the sheetmetal door. He moved
his shoulder to hide the lock as he twirled the tumbler,
then grunted and let her see.

"You know how to spring this?"

"Nope."

"Then how—?"

"I know the combination."

He shook his head. "I've got to be more careful, next time." Mitsuno went in and turned on the lights. The room was just as they had left it. Demeter was nothing if not a neat spy.

"Now, where was it you thought you saw a computer?" he prompted.

"Not 'thought.' Did see. Back behind that pile of stuff—" She pointed to the replaced supplies. "—there's a secret room. More secret, anyway. The computer is on a table in there."

Mitsuno relaxed. His shoulders came down a fraction. "You really did a job in here, didn't you?" He went over to the pile, tipped the base box up on a corner, and pivoted it out of the way. Then he went down in a duck-walk and passed through the connecting tunnel. Demeter followed him.

"Yup, that's a computer all right," he said, standing in front of the table.

"Like I said, you lied to me."

"No, I didn't. It wasn't turned on when we were making love. That's your condition, isn't it?"

"But you said these things were always on."

"Not this one." He reached over to the switch on the power supply, flipped it to the one's position. A heat crackle from the wires and boards was the only response. "Now it's on."

"What's the input-output scheme here?" she asked. "I couldn't figure that part out."

"Voice operated, like your chrono."

"Oh. Can it hear us?"

"I hear you."

The sound was deep and hollow, like a rusty old

lawnmower. Whoever programmed this machine hadn't paid much attention to the personality modules—if there were any—or to the vocal inflection. It was the same as with the lock on the door: default values had been good enough.

"What are . . . what are you called?" Demeter asked.

"Lethe."

"What's that?"

"That's Ellen's idea of a joke," Mitsuno explained. "Lethe is a river in Greece, on the Eurasian Continent, Earth. Its water is supposed to have a hypnotic quality that makes people forget."

"Forget what?"

"Everything they hear, for one. Lethe is our community memory. We come here, tell him something, and then we can forget about it. He does the remembering and correlating."

"Who is 'we'? You and Ellen and who else?"

"A group of us. You've met Dr. Wa Lixin? He's part of our organization."

"Are you a rebel group?" Demeter asked.

"You might say that. Well, yes, that's probably what we are. Revolutionaries."

"Then who are you rebelling against? You Martians don't have much of a government. None that I can see. There's barely a city administration around here. So who?"

"Against the machines, as I told you before. We don't trust them."

"Yet you use them. This one, for example." She pointed to the components piled on the table.

"Lethe is special. Ellen built him in here, from the circuit boards up. Each piece was obtained separately and at random, wiped down electronically, brought in here, and assembled. Lethe only knows what Ellen put in his head. It was all done with voice programming, starting from a kernel system that she wrote out in longhand on a scribe pad, all zeros and ones. He brings in nothing from the outside except raw silicon and empty registers. And, of course, he has no connection to outside resources. Lethe is our child, born and bred."

"Why go to all that trouble?" Demeter asked.

"He is our safeguard. Lethe protects us from the grid finding out what we know. In the early days, we kept notes in pencil on paper. It was cumbersome, but safe. Except that paper is a special requisition on Mars, as are pencils, pens, and charcoal sticks. We pretended an interest in the arts and asked for paints, but even that drew inquiries from the accounting section. So, rather than attract further attention to ourselves, we decided to make Lethe. . . . He puts our collection and collation effort on a much higher level, too."

"That's a nice story," Demeter said. "But of course the grid knows about him."

"It can't!" Mitsuno replied sharply.

"Sure it can. Lethe radiates low-frequency electromagnetic fields, like any device. The grid's sensors are proficient at detecting and coupling onto those."

"This place is thoroughly shielded."

"Not really. I've seen your Faraday screen," Demeter said. "It'll keep out static electricity, probably. Maybe even ground faults, too. But it won't block field emissions. Anyone who holds a pickup within a kilometer of this room can read your machine's mind like an open book."

While she talked, Mitsuno started grinning. By the time she finished, he was laughing out loud. "Between us and the grid's closest nexus, the main array in Tharsis Montes, there's about a million liters of water," he said. "That tank farm blocks all kinds of radiation."

"What about roving units on the surface?" She pointed straight up, over their heads. "Like your walkers?"

"Can they read a source through forty meters of solid rock? Remember, this patch of ground has a high ferrous content," he added seriously. "Our tunnel is dug in too deep. We've done spot checks. Trust me, nobody—and no thing—can find this machine."

"All right." She sighed. "I'll accept, provisionally, that you've found a way to avoid alerting the grid with your activities. . . . That's assuming, of course, the grid much cares what you think about it. And I don't know why it should. It's just a machine."

Mitsuno looked thoughtful. While he pondered, the man reached over and casually switched Lethe off, without even a "Thank you" for its services. Demeter felt a pang at that. An artificial intelligence, even a caged one—no, *especially* a caged one—was not made any saner by having its sensorium interrupted at random. With that kind of treatment, Lethe's world-view must be somewhere between that of a toddler and a psychopath by now. Demeter thought of that deadened voice. She wouldn't want to spend much time with Lethe, or entrust it with any vital information.

"I'm not sure exactly where your feelings lie," Mitsuno told her. "You're clearly afraid of the machines, because of the accident one of them dealt you. You'll hardly undress in front of them, and that implies a certain deep-seated fear. Yet, at the same time, you don't seem to think much of them. In your own words, they are 'just machines.' As if that explained everything. I'm confused, Demeter."

"It's really simple." She took a calming breath. "I would prefer not to think of them at all. I'd rather deal with people. Or with inanimate objects, like pens and paper, knives and forks. For me, the grid and its cousins are a middle ground. Not human. But not inanimate, either. I don't know how to relate."

"But can we trust you to keep our secret?"

"Oh, sure! I mean, what's to tell?"

Lole was frowning now.

"Reading motives into the grid is the newest indoor parlor game these days," Demeter hurried on. "All said and done, it's just a switching system, isn't it? To be sure, it's very big, very fast, and so darn complex that it sometimes tosses off apparently random results. After a while it can begin to feel, well, alive. Like the weather used to be—on Earth, at least. Anything that seems to move of its own volition, and that has the power to knock you down when it wants to, becomes a magnet for people's curiosity. Give them enough time and insufficient understanding, and they'll eventually worship it as a god."

"Yet you don't believe," Lole said simply.

"I sure as hell do not." She smiled back at him.

"What if I were to tell you that the Autochthonous Grid, comprising the interlinked systems on both Mars and Earth, was tossing off more than just random numbers?"

Demeter's smile held, but she could feel it trying to slip. Mitsuno read her expression and nodded. "You don't believe that. But it's true. The evidence is all there, stored in Lethe, and, if we had all night and most of tomorrow, he could spell it out for you. But the short form is that we've found imbalances all over the system. Debits for consumption of energy and supplies that aren't accounted for anywhere to anyone's credit. Our watchers say the grid is up to something, but the pattern hasn't emerged yet."

"Okay, I'll bite. What do you *think* is happening?"

"The grid is preparing an attack against humanity."

Demeter kept herself unfazed. "Give me a for-instance."

"Three shiploads of industrial-grade explosives—inert, high-impact resin, with fusing modules—were ordered for delivery to Mars, ostensibly for mining purposes. As near as we can trace from the cargo manifests and hull numbers, they never arrived. Hell, they never left low Earth orbit. When you query the grid about them, though, it denies that the transports even exist—and that's going all the way back to their construction in orbit and the waybills on other cargoes that we know traveled in them. Just another random number?"

"All right, the grid made an error and tried to cover for it," Demeter said. "Could be the work of a virus."

"Then there's the new power satellite, the one being built over the Marineris region. Ellen asked you to check it out, didn't she?"

"I—uh—" Coghlan stopped to think. "I took a packaged V/R tour of the power stations, yes. And I *thought* it included a pass through the one under construction, leeched off the construction monitoring circuits. But apparently the signals got crossed up and I was seeing something else."

"Funny about that, hey?"

"What are you trying to say?"

"The machines are building that station, ostensibly under contract to the North Zealanders. That much is confirmed by our mutual friend, Nancy Cuneo, although she's never seen plans on the satellite. No one from her agency has gone aboard to inspect the work to date, even in V/R. No one is even sure of the rated output."

"But I know *that*," Demeter burst in.

"You do? . . . Well, what is it?"

"Three times the projected consumption of the Canyonlands development, however much that is. I only know the proportions, not the numbers."

"*How* do you know?"

"Sun Il Suk told me."

"All right, I'll get to him in a minute. . . . So, the power station is a mystery. Except that, under telescopic magnification from the planet's surface—this is working purely by optics, mind you, without any electronic image enhancement—we can detect some strange features on the outside. We see things that look like turrets, maybe weapons pods. Who knows what's happening on the inside?"

"You think three shiploads of high explosives are going to end up as part of the package? Making a weapon they can hold, literally, over your heads?"

"I don't know what to think at the moment. Just that, when we try to communicate with the grid—your simple, garden-variety, random-number-tossing machine—about these things, then we get screwy answers. It gives us facts that don't compute. And the pattern of lies seems to be, well, pretty desperate."

"Hmm . . ." Demeter stood, looking down at the inert cyber on the table. It was an ugly thing, made of dented metal and twisted wire. It had none of the compactness and spherical elegance of her lost Sugar.

"What do you know about friend Sun?" she asked finally.

"That's why I wanted to search you. Sun Il Suk's

been a busy little bee, fluttering all over Tharsis Montes, from the moment he arrived. And he asks
questions like—"

"I know." Demeter rolled her eyes.

"He showed a keen interest in Ellen and me. He
kept dropping hints, asking leading questions. I think
he was angling to get invited here."

"But you didn't bring him, did you?"

"No. During the quarantine examination, Dr. Lee
found an implant in his skull. Sun said it was a
hormone-triggering device, to aid in his diet. But the
ultrasonics in Dr. Lee's examining table showed it was
self-powered and had a lot of circuitry inside. More
than a hormone pump would need. We think it might
have been subverted to other uses."

"Such as?"

"Monitoring and recording whatever Sun sees and
hears. Then reporting back to some control device—
attached to the grid, of course, either here on Mars or
somewhere on Earth. Not that it makes much difference."
Mitsuno shrugged. "Lagtime in the signal processing, is all."

"Golly."

"We thought you might have an intelligent prosthe-
sis, too. But you're clean."

"Thank you."

Mitsuno led her back out through the low tunnel,
into the first room where they could sit on the comfortable, castoff chairs.

"So, what does it all mean?" she asked.

"I wish I could give you a hard answer, but all we've
got is guesswork. We don't know for certain that anything is really wrong with the computers. But the, um,
rather artful lack of certainty worries us."

"It's like the old argument about the intelligence of

dolphins," Demeter said. "No one's ever seen them attack a human being. So, either they are secretly hostile to humans and hiding their attacks, or they're positively friendly because they sense a comparable intellect despite the whale hunting and other predatory things humans have done. Both answers would tend to prove their intelligence. Similarly, the grid either is producing systematic errors, or it's operating secretly and hiding its intentions."

"A perfectly circular argument," Lole pointed out.

"Yeah—except that both answers are a sign of bad things for us humans."

"We've considered turning all the computers off, you know. That would be very difficult, of course, because the grid controls our air and water supplies. In fact, the whole environmental balance of the tunnel complexes up here is under cyber control."

"Not to mention a lot of your social dynamics," Demeter pointed out. She was thinking of the system of electronic monitoring, gas sniffers, food additives, and homing bracelets that maintained the heterogeneous population of Tharsis Montes somewhere below the boiling point.

"Of course," she went on, "if you try to shut down the machines and *fail*, you might precipitate the very thing you're afraid of."

"Right," he said with a nod. "Retaliation. That's why I have to ask you—as a friend, as someone who cares what happens to Ellen and me and all the other people you've met—not to talk about anything you've seen or heard here."

"I won't."

"Not even among ourselves, unless it's in the confines of this room."

"I *said* I wouldn't."

"It's not that we're afraid the grid is going to send the Citizen's Militia to round us up. It's just that, when we're ready to take action, we have to catch the machines completely off guard, with something they're not ready for. We have to succeed on the first try."

"I know." Demeter nodded. "They're very quick, like nanoseconds."

"And they'll never give us a second chance."

Chapter 15

I've Got a Secret

Roger Torraway did not sleep—not like other humans who curled into a warm nest of linen sheets and woolen blankets, or nylon sacking and hollow fiberfill, or dried grass and a buffalo robe. He had no need to rest the mechanical parts of his body, and his mind functioned at peak efficiency twenty-four hours a day, supported by his computerized sensorium. But at regular intervals the meat portion of his brain did become tired. Then fatigue poisons built up in his remaining cells and had to be washed out again.

His makers' solution, Alexander Bradley's solution, was to let Torraway continue whatever he had been doing—walking, digging, sampling, surveying—under instructions from the backpack computer while his mind went into slowdown mode. Then his feet raced over the sand, his fingers flew about their business, and the world streamed past his faceted eyes, all beyond the reach of his own synapses. If something attracted his wandering attention, it was gone before Roger himself could frame a response. He effectively slept while his Cyborg body toiled onward.

Day or night did not shape these periods of brain rest; Roger Torraway was not a diurnal creature. But sometimes it happened that he went into slowdown when the stars came out and the majority of nonadapted humans on that side of the planet were also at rest, asleep. This night was one of those times.

Roger's feet plodded rhythmically up the face of a volcanic ridge. The ground rushed before his eyes, like the view from a low-flying jet. Largish, upright stones seemed to graze his cheeks and then vanish into shadows under the feeble light reflected from farther Deimos. At some point his internal sensors determined that the angle of ascent was too steep for Roger's gyros. Rather than bring the hands into play in a four-part monkey-climb, the feet turned to trace switchbacks up the hillside. So now his jet-driven view wobbled back and forth across the terrain, like a rattlesnake's triangular head seeking the thermal whisper of mouse.

With a jumble of motion, the scene came apart. The headlong beauty of the night dissolved into a sudden focus on *this* loose rock, on *that* gap in the footing. Roger Torraway was instantly awake and back in real time. His human brain tried to take over the effort of walking, and the world reeled. He found himself teetering on the edge of a thirty-meter sheer drop. It was not deep enough for the fall to kill him outright, in Mars's shallow gravity, but with the impact he might sustain embarrassing damage to his mechanical frame.

"What the *hell?*"

Roger swung his arms sharply inward, toward the slope, and bent his knees. He collapsed in an awkward, loosely jointed judo roll into the hillside, clattering his elbows and shins against the wind-smoothed obsidian. But he kept himself from sliding off the edge.

His brain was attempting to reconstruct the

malfunction's origins before he noticed a pair of slender, pale feet in open-toed sandals. The toenails were trimmed into perfect arcs and painted with pink gloss, Roger noted.

"Dorrie!" he gasped internally.

"Roger, there is a communication for you from Demeter Coghlan," the silvery voice informed him. "As she is now on your list of—"

"I know. What does she want at this ungodly hour?"

Before Dorrie could process an answer, her image faded. A new voice came through his head, followed by a construct at approximately the same locus in the volcanic rubble: the plump form of Demeter Coghlan.

"I couldn't sleep, Colonel. There's a technical question that's been bugging me, and I figured you were the one who could answer quickest."

"Is this on our retainer?" Torraway asked, remembering his bargain with this offworld person.

"Uh . . . sure."

"So go ahead," he growled.

"Can you communicate through solid rock?"

He waited for her to amplify on that. Maybe she was having reception problems on her end. Maybe she was worried about the signal quality from his present position on a mountain of volcanic glass. But no, she just stood there, expecting an answer.

"Come again?" he asked.

"Do your radio-frequency transmissions—say, between your backpack and its supporting cybers, or with the grid nexus here in the tunnels at Tharsis Montes—do they go through the ground?"

"No need to. After all, I live out in the open where it's all line of sight. When there is an obstruction, such as a mountain between me and the transmitter, or if I've wandered off into a pocket valley, then we can usually bounce the signals around with relays."

"Suppose you were underground. Like under forty meters of solid rock?"

"Oh. When I'm inside the complex, the grid has its own RF repeaters built into the walls. They're pretty widely spaced, though, so Cyborgs and Creoles all have hardwired jumpers for—"

"Not in the tunnels," she insisted. "Suppose you, um, walked into a cave?"

"Then I would be out of touch. But that's not a problem, really. My system has its own internal resources for making linear projections and conducting error checks until I can re-establish a link."

"Thank you, Colonel."

"That's it? You woke me up for—?"

But the woman's image had vanished.

Golden Lotus, June 18

Demeter disconnected from Colonel Torraway with a glow of personal satisfaction. She might make something as a spy after all.

Sure, a secret was a secret, and Demeter had sworn to keep Mitsuno's information confidential. But even that much commitment didn't mean she was automatically buying into everything Lole had told her, file and line. Some items she wanted to check for herself, such as his estimate of the security arrangements for the secret society's meeting rooms and its "clean" cyber. Demeter was delighted she'd discovered a way to verify all this by referral to a man who lived through radio transmissions and could, for all she knew, read by the light of microwaves. She had found out what she wanted to know without violating Mitsuno's confidence. And nothing she'd said to

Roger Torraway would create suspicion within the grid's circuits that communicated between Tharsis Montes and wherever the Cyborg happened to be now.

Still warmed by the glow of her own cleverness, Demeter decided to submit her nightly report to Gregor Weiss—even if it was rounding toward morning.

"Terminal, shift to interrogation mode."

"Yes, miss. . . . Where have you gone in the past twenty-four hours?" the terminal dutifully asked.

"Lole Mitsuno met me outside the room here," she began sleepily, "and we went to the—"

Oops! Nothing like handing Lole's secret to the grid on a silver disk. And Demeter had just been congratulating herself on being a such a clever little spy.

"Um," she temporized. "Instead, let's take some new vectors for your questions."

"Very well," the machine said impassively.

What could she tell it—how could she steer it—to avoid references to Mitsuno's cave?

Well, she had learned some interesting facts about the Canyonlands development in the past twenty-four hours. For one, its power satellite was too large for projected needs. Had Mitsuno told her that? No, it was from Sun Il Suk. But Lole *had* told her about the station's unusual configuration, with nacelles or pods or something on the outside. That was probably a safe subject for her report.

"Ask me about the Number Six power station."

"Yes, have you heard anything about the new orbiting solar collector?"

"Sure. The Korean agent, Sun, informed me today that its rated capacity . . ."

As usual, she seemed to drift off before completing the thought.

Ingot Collection Point 4, June 18

It had been ten days since Jory den Ostreicher last cleared this area of von Neumanns, and now the shallow valley was fairly squirming with the blind machines. He quickly set about picking the top ones off the pile and cracking their shells open, dividing up the lumps of raw material inside and saving the least damaged carapaces for possible Stage 2's.

This work brought back pleasant memories. The last time he was out this way that Earth woman, Demeter Coghlan, had come along by proxy and helped him collect ingots. Jory hadn't seen her since their last encounter in his private nest, which had turned a little . . . well, *rough*. Since then, he knew, she had been avoiding him. Jory was sensitive enough to understand that. He had hurt her and she didn't want to see him again. That made sense.

But almost a week had gone by already, and Jory wanted some more of what she gave so freely. By this time, Demeter must be feeling better about him. After all, nobody could carry a grudge longer than a week, could they? She had probably gotten all over her sore spots and would be feeling frisky again.

Den Ostreicher checked with the grid to see if she was still assigned to the Golden Lotus. And, yes, she hadn't left her room yet this morning. Now, if he could just pick up the pace. . . .

Jory's fingers flew with superhuman speed and precision: taking, breaking, picking, and placing. While the idle ten percent of his mind studied out what he wanted to say to his girlfriend, the other ninety percent focused on the job at hand.

The pile of mechanical organisms melted—and the stacks of shells and bags of recovered commodities grew—like steamers at a clambake.

The Russian Tearoom, June 18

Brunch at the supremely fakey, pseudo-St. Peters-bourgeois bistro was becoming a habit with Demeter. But this was the place for keeping an eye on her competition, or confreres, or whatever you called spies who spent more time bumping into each other than digging out government secrets. No sooner had the mechanical maître d' seated her than Nancy Cuneo bustled up to her table.

"Have you tried the caviar yet, dear?"

Demeter worked up her best smile. "Made with real fish eggs?"

"Of course not." Cuneo sat down and studied the flat display of choices. "But the protein content is the same. Good for your skin, or so they say." She glanced at the waiting machine. "*Chai, pozhalusta.*"

The server beeped at her and trundled off.

"At my age," she said to Demeter, "all I can drink is black tea. Put anything in it—lemon, cream, Drambuie—and my stomach goes off like a Roman candle."

"I'm sorry," Demeter offered, mentally noting the information for a possible assassination attempt. "A Roman—what did you say?"

"A brand of fireworks, dear. Before your time. . . . You wouldn't think to look at me, but I'm very old."

"Oh, no," Demeter lied.

"Oh, yes! Why, the pieces and parts I've shed over the years. I'm simply propped up by technology, a dab of plastic skin here, a bit of electronics there. Why, do you know my pacemaker's been kicking up recently?"

"Really?" Demeter studied the menu and rang for service. A tank-shaped waitron cycled by and she ordered buttered toast—or at least toast thoroughly oiled—with jam of any flavor so long as it was red, and coffee with lots of cream and sugar.

"Really," Cuneo replied. "I get a stutter and a buzz until I think I'm fibrillating. It must be all the electronic interference in these tunnels, I guess."

"Interference?"

"Of course. Electronic sensors every couple of meters along the walls, public cyber terminals on every corner, smart machines like our friend here—" She nodded to the rolling waitron. "—they just clutter the air with emissions. . . . What I wouldn't give for a place with a little shielding. Some place I could relax and take a deep breath."

"Take a walk outside."

"Then it's even worse. What with signal relays, microwave fields, sunspots. No, if there was only some place, here underground, that was truly isolated." For emphasis, Cuneo put a hand weakly to her chest, the dying Camille.

"I'm so sorry. But if I hear of such a place, I'll let you know."

"You're such a comfort, dear."

Golden Lotus, June 18

Jory didn't even pretend to be fixing anything this time as he waited outside Demeter Coghlan's door. Eventually, she had to return here, and he intended to confront her when she did.

As a Creole, Jory had complete control of his time sense. He could speed it up or slow it down as needed. So it didn't matter, subjectively, when she passed by this point. He would be waiting with just as much eagerness, whether it was in the next ten minutes or forty-eight hours from now. Fortunately for the foot traffic in the corridor—and for the Golden Lotus's management—Demeter appeared at her hotel room sooner rather than later.

"Demeter!" he said, stimulating all his circuits.

"Oh, Jory!" A look crossed her face that was less than ecstatic, but never mind.

"I missed you, Demeter."

"I know. But things . . . came up."

"I *really* missed you."

Damn, he thought, his words weren't coming out right.

"We probably shouldn't try see so much of each other," she said quickly. "We got into . . . in a little over our heads. I need time to get to know a person before I . . . you know. We just went too fast—"

"Didn't you like my place? Wasn't it private enough?"

"Place? What are you—?"

"If there's someplace you'd rather do it, Demeter, more isolated, with less interference, then just say the word. I'll go anywhere with you. You know that."

"Jory . . ." Her face positively clouded over.

Den Ostreicher could feel the rejection coming off her like waves of infrared from a burned-out bearing.

"I'm sorry," he said, backpedaling. "I just need—"

"I know, Jory. But I'm not the girl you need. Believe me."

The young Creole put a hand up to his eyes, turned away, and ran back up the corridor. Even though his tear ducts had been excised long ago, he could still feel the pressure building inside his head. He barely made the turn through the next hexcube without slamming into the wall.

Airlock Control, June 18

After Wyatt docked the walker, Lole Mitsuno gathered his geological samples and headed for the rear of the vehicle. The lock cycled open, and there stood Demeter Coghlan, looking like cold death.

"You've got a hole in your organization," she announced.

Mitsuno resisted the temptation to ask what Coghlan meant by that. Instead, he looked over her head at the ever-present video pickup, with the earjack in the wall beside it.

"Let's get a drink," he offered.

"I'm serious about this, Lole."

"So am I."

He took her by the arm and started down the ramp into the tunnel complex. Maybe, if he could just keep Demeter moving, the grid wouldn't think to track them, piece together what she was saying, and thereby learn something incriminating. The Hoplite was one level down. It was the logical place for them to go.

"So far this morning, two people have approached me about—"

"Who?" he cut her off.

"Nancy Cuneo, who's from North Zealand and is actually a paid spy for their economic development organization, and our friend Jory."

"What did they want?"

"To know if I could take them someplace private. Cuneo even mentioned radio interference. Someone in your rebel group has a pair of really loose lips."

"Not since we talked last night," Mitsuno protested, working out the timing in his head.

"Well, then, from before. I don't know. It's all very fishy."

The entrance to the Hoplite was right ahead, around the next hexcube. Once they got inside, the grid's monitoring would be nearly continuous.

"Look," he said quickly, "why don't you invite Jory to

come to the room? Tomorrow night would be good."

"*Invite* him? But don't you want—"

"Tell him it's a party. Jory likes parties."

"But . . ." Demeter's brows curled in on themselves as she tried to understand. "But . . ."

"Just do it. Jory's an old pal."

"All right, but I thought—"

"Here we are," Mitsuno announced, changing the subject. "I should call Wyatt and tell him to have Ellen meet us here. Are you hungry?"

Chapter 16

Head Fakes

"Boy, it's wet down here."

Demeter Coghlan listened for the Creole's footsteps behind her on the walkway, light and deft, like a dancer's.

"The damp won't harm your, um, systems?" she asked.

"Naw, I get into worse than this lots of times."

"Good."

Persuading Jory to come to the secret room, as Lole had suggested, wasn't a problem. Once Demeter made contact with den Ostreicher, via the grid, he was more than willing to meet her anytime, anyplace. So she had specified a tunnel junction not far from the reservoirs, and he had been there well ahead of her, waiting.

As they approached the plain door, Demeter heard a sound above the background drip of water: the chuckling of many voices, mixed and echoing in a small, tight space.

Jory drew back before she could completely identify it.

"Hey! I thought you wanted things *private*."

"It's all right. Lole's holding one of his parties."

"But we were going to be *together*."

"We will be."

246

"I mean, alone."

Demeter reached for his arm, hooked it above the wrist, and practically dragged him up to the door. She thudded on the panel with the heel of her hand.

Scree!

Demeter peered into the brighter interior of the secret room. The furniture had been pushed against the wall to make space. The bed with the leaky stuffing seemed to be gone. She fast-counted half a dozen faces, with Lole Mitsuno's lighter coloring standing out among them. Ellen Sorbel was there, too. And that Dr. Lee from her medical visits. The other people she had never seen before.

"Hi, everybody! This is Jory." She turned to her reluctant companion. "Jory, you know Ellen and Lole, of course. Everyone else . . ."

"Hello, Jory!" one of the strange men boomed, coming forward eagerly and putting out a big hand. He was heavily built, athletic for a Martian, and Demeter thought he might be drunk or on drugs.

With the speed of a striking snake, the man's pale hand jabbed the center of the young Creole's chest, doubling him over with a *whoop!* Before anyone could react, the same hand rose up to somewhere near the ceiling, stiffened into the shape of a falling axe blade—

"Not the head!" Ellen called from behind the man.

—and landed across the back of Jory's neck.

He collapsed like a sack of bones.

"Jesus!" Demeter breathed. "Why would you want to—?"

But already the man was walking away, rubbing his hand.

Two others detached themselves from the crowd— Wa Lixin was one of them—and picked up the felled body. Dr. Lee pressed two fingers into the base of Jory's throat, nodded, and let the second person slide a black hood over the Creole's head. Together they dragged him to the far end of the room, lifted a fold of the hanging, bent down, and pulled him through.

Demeter turned and sought Lole's eyes.

"But *why*? I could have told him some story or other."

Mitsuno shook his head. "I know Jory. He would have been suspicious. And if not him, then the machines that control him."

"Are you going to kill him?"

"Oh, no!" Ellen cooed, coming forward and putting an arm around Demeter's shoulders. "We need him. Jory's going to be our link in addressing the grid. Our interface. When he's unconscious, I think we can get past his reticular programming, down to his core operating system."

"Why did you have to hit him like that? Couldn't you use knockout drops or something?"

Ellen shook her head. "His metabolism is very different, Demeter. He's been primed for exposure to many different and subtle poisons, out on the planet's surface. Plus, with Jory's electronic stimulation, we'd half-kill him trying to knock him out chemically."

"And now what?"

"In a moment—" Sorbel turned toward the inner tunnel. "—we're going to do a little brain surgery. Do you want to watch?"

"No!" Demeter yelped instinctively. Then she thought about it. Despite his thoughtless manner and infantile fixations, Jory had been her first friend on Mars. In many ways, he was like her lost chrono, Sugar: young, eager, and wholly predictable. Although she

trusted Ellen and was half in love with Lole, she sensed
a distancing in their voices when they talked about Jory
now, in here. Somebody ought to stand by and watch
out for him. That somebody was her. "Yes . . . I mean,
I'd like to help."

"All right," Ellen said—after a long, hard look into
Demeter's eyes. "I'll get us suited up while he's being
prepped."

Electromagnetic Safe Zone, June 19

Dr. Wa Lixin studied the array of surgical imple-
ments laid out on sterile paper in the tray beside the
Creole's draped head. He was adept, of course, with
the variously sized and curved scalpels, the card of
polymer-threaded needles, the staple-stitcher, the
bone drill and clamps, the laser hemostat. Less familiar
were tools for the cybernetic side of the upcoming
procedure: the logic probes, chip extractors, digital multimeter, jeweler's screwdrivers, and pinpoint No. 00 soldering tip.

Although he had never worked on a full-body
Cyborg before, Dr. Wa understood the principles
involved. He would have to maintain circuit integrity,
voltage, and cooling as well as blood pressure, hema-
tocrit, and electrolyte balance. Keeping the surgical
domain sterile would be as important as with any
human patient, but he would have to work without the
ultraviolet field. Too many programmable memory
chips were susceptible to erasure under that part of the
radiation spectrum. Anesthesia would not only be a
matter of doping the bloodstream with opiates and
blockers, but of quickly finding and grounding the
appropriate chips in the Creole's sensory net.

Dr. Lee had been studying those and related techniques for the past fourteen hours—ever since Lole

Mitsuno had informed him of the marvelous opportunity the Coghlan woman was practically throwing at them.

What worried the doctor most was working without a cybernetic coach. The computer that ran the examination table back in his office was responsible for ultrasonics and imaging on his patients, for diagnostics and on-line expert advice with his procedures, for his medical recordkeeping and dispensing. It was also controlled by the grid and deeply tied to its databases and echelons of rote knowledge. Without the table, Dr. Lee would be flying blind, relying on his own experience and the skill of his hands.

Would they be enough?

Of course, there was the crude machine laid out on the board behind him. From what Ellen Sorbel told him, it had sufficient raw brainpower but lacked the programming and peripherals to help him. Besides, that machine had other purposes in this business.

Ellen must have noticed Wa Lixin's hesitation. She did not touch him, as that would have compromised sterility for both of them. Instead, Sorbel pushed her face around in front of his and stared hard over the top of her green gauze mask.

"Time to begin, Lee."

He nodded and turned again to the tray of instruments. He picked up the scalpel with a curved blade, for taking thin slices out of taut skin, and addressed the bronzed dome of Jory's hairless head. Again the thought crossed Dr. Lee's mind that, for the first time in his career, he was opening a wound in a patient without the express desire to heal. But then, as Ellen and Lole had taken pains to point out, Jory den Ostreicher was not his patient.

When the two conspirators had first discussed this treatment modality with him, Dr. Lee had refused. He did not balk at simple murder, of course; the game had gone too far for that. The necessary eradication of an overtly inquisitive party—a sharp rap on the head and a nighttime visit to the municipal recycler—that was one thing. Lole in his day had done worse. But this was a medically invasive procedure, intentionally carried out under less than sanitary conditions. Moreover, what Dr. Lee was about to do was a kind of therapeutic vandalism, a species of theft.

What had swayed him in the end, what had obtained his willing participation, was Ellen's final argument. She had declared that she was ready to undertake the operation herself, with her own two hands. Ellen had, she said, been studying the procedure in V/R simulation, which itself was a breach of security, and she was now ready to proceed. Ultimately, Dr. Lee could not allow that.

He made the first cut, fifteen centimeters long down the median suture.

Instead of the welling blood he would normally see, the slit leaked a clear fluid with a viscosity somewhat heavier than blood. That would be the silicon under-layer, an impact and thermal buffer serving the same purpose in a Creole as the layer of subcutaneous fat in a human. He retracted the lips of the cut with his gloved fingers and inspected the exposed surface. White membrane sheathed the muscles of the scalp.

With second and third strokes, he parted those and laid bare the bony plates of Jory's skull. Now there was blood, though not much of it. The portable biomonitor hooked onto the Creole's throat had slowed his heart rate and lowered his arterial pressure. It also dripped in painkillers that would soothe what Dr. Lee was coming to think of as the "meat side" of Jory's physical makeup.

Wa Lixin used the first of many disposable suction tips to clear the site and sealed the remaining leakers with short, controlled bursts from the hemostat.

The white bone had been fought over before. He could trace the edges of at least three invasive procedures from this one flap. Like any healthy young boy's, Jory's bones had healed with good ridges of scar tissue. Still, the doctor could see the flat bows of bone clips and the heads of tiny screws where the previous surgeons had made sure of their handiwork. Those bits of metal would complicate his efforts.

He picked up the drill, already fitted with a retractor cowling. The moment it was through the bone, the cowl would instantly respond to the release of pressure by pulling back the cutter bit. That way, Dr. Lee could not possibly plunge his drill into the patient's—into Jory's—brain.

"Let me see that drawing again," he said to no one in particular.

Ellen Sorbel made stabbing head motions to someone standing nearby to fetch a notepad from the back table. It was the woman who had started all this, his civic-practice patient from several weeks ago, Demeter Coghlan. She was now gowned and masked. The sketch, made by Dr. Lee's own hand after his brief study of standard Creolization procedures in the grid's medical records, showed the top view of a head. Blocked out underneath were the locations of several circuit cards and their interwoven neural networks touching on various brain structures.

"Thank you," he whispered.

The notepad was withdrawn.

Lee depressed the drill's trigger and heard the satisfying *burr* of its motor. He lined the cutter bit up on the first apex of the incision he planned to make and started boring in. White smoke rose off the bone surface. Chips like snow flaked out of the hole, caught in a swirl of the airflow that cooled the motor, and stuck against the red flesh on the side of Lee's flap.

He ignored it all, engaged in cutting open the head just so.

Only when the Creole's whole body made a convulsive surge and one arm flopped off the table did Wa Lixin look up.

"Hold him! Demeter!"

The woman put her unsterile hands around the loose arm and over the patient's—Jory's—shoulder, pinning it against the steel tabletop. Like a child, she glanced up at the doctor's face for approval.

As long as she didn't disturb the biomonitor's links into the cervical arteries and vertebrae . . .

"Better hurry, Lee," Ellen said. "I think he's beating the painkillers."

"Be through in a minute," he muttered. As if warnings would hurry him . . .

Two holes. Three holes. Their placement overlapped some of the old scars, but that didn't matter now. When the set was complete, he threaded the silicon-carbide wire of his trephine under the skull between the first and second holes, pressed the button, and pulled the device away from Jory's head. The wire popped free, leaving a precise black line through white bone. Twice more, and he had a triangular section of bone with rounded, concave corners. Apart from a few technological refinements, he had opened a skull just as the ancient Egyptians had with their copper chisels.

He set the bone piece to one side on the sterile field and looked into Jory's head.

In the hard, white overhead light he could trace a mass of black threads radiating out across the *dura mater* from three flat, silver boxes. Each thread ended in a spike of electrode that was implanted either deeply or shallowly into the neurons of the cerebral cortex.

Dr. Lee picked up a medium-sized jeweler's screwdriver, teased one of the boxes out of its restraining loops, and moved it forward, under the opening he had made. Once again, Jory flopped against the tabletop.

"God *damn* it! Hold him!"

"I'm *trying!*"

"Don't try, just *do* it," he rasped.

But Dr. Lee's anger was already passing as he segued back inside his procedure. Normally, he would worry that moving the little silver box around might snag some of the electrodes, creating unplanned short circuits or tearing them out of their target ganglion. If he seriously had to consider the Creole's lifespan and intended functioning after this operation, the prospect of doing such damage would bother him more.

When the box was in position, he took a forceps in one hand, the smallest of the screwdrivers in the other. Holding the box steady against the surface of Jory's brain, he began opening it. The tiny silver screws came out of their sockets one by one and flopped over onto the *dura*, where he plucked them off and set them beside the bone section. When the box's lid was free, he pinched it between the forceps's jaws and pulled it loose. Underneath was a green wafer with surface-mount components, like tiny black seeds stuck on lime-flavored ice.

"Which one goes?" he asked the air.

Ellen's head intruded on his line of sight.

"That's not the communications module!" she protested.

"No, it's his sensorium. For the pain. First things first."

"Well, uh . . ." Sorbel withdrew. Presumably she was consulting her own sketches loaded into the notepad.

"Take out A-five and B-eleven," she said from behind him. "That should do it."

"They're not numbered."

"Well, here." She thrust the flat screen under his face.

Dr. Lee motioned with his head for her to turn it so that the image aligned with the box inside Jory's skull. "Two from the left, fourth row," he confirmed aloud. "And three from the right, sixth row."

He picked up the soldering tip, wedged it down among the little black seeds, and pressed the trigger. A puff of smoke, and the first component came away on the end of his forceps. In another moment, the second was loose also.

As a test, Dr. Lee stroked the exposed flap of tissue with the still-hot soldering tip, leaving a thin line of char. Jory lay on the table like a corpse.

"You can release him, Demeter."

"Is he dead?" she asked fearfully.

"Oh, no! Just sleeping very deeply."

"You've been very helpful," Sorbel told the woman.

"Can I, uh, go now?"

"Sure, we're almost done," Ellen replied.

Still bent over, Demeter Coghlan scurried from the room.

Already Wa Lixin was at work on the second box. Once he had it open and the internal circuits exposed, Sorbel brought him a pair of long, shielded cables from the machine on the table behind them. With a sterile probe, she indicated where he was to solder them into this second wafer. Two more puffs of gray smoke, and the first stage of the procedure was complete.

It was time to wake Jory up.

Golden Lotus, June 19

Demeter couldn't remember ever feeling faint before.

The one summer she had spent at the ranch with G'dad, she had calmly watched the vets branding the cows and sliding radio homers into slits in their big, downy ears. She had even helped out the day they roped the young bulls and castrated them. Sitting on their solid, heaving flanks while stiff bristles of hair occasionally pricked her through the seat of her jeans, Demeter had thought she was on top of the world. The knives flashing in the sunlight, the splashes of blood— none of it bothered her.

But that was before she had to stand in a tiny, closed room and watch someone peel back the skull of a man she'd made love to, with him bucking like one of those bulls and obviously feeling every cut and tap. And then, when the wound was finally opened, to discover that the inside of his head was filled with . . . machinery . . . it was too much.

Demeter Coghlan had bolted from the makeshift operating room like a green girl.

Out in the corridor, Lole Mitsuno had tried to stop her. But when he saw how pale and sweaty she was, he advised her to go lie down. And, of course, to say nothing to anyone. She had barely nodded as she started to run across the tanks of open water, afraid she'd vomit right into them.

Now, in the security of her hotel room, she could bundle up in her friendly old bathrobe with a cool cloth across her forehead. Lying on the bed, she turned her head and addressed the room's monitor.

"Terminal? Take no calls. No disturbances, please. Not from anyone."

"Of course not, miss."

Demeter's Secret Place, June 19

"   . . .   "

He had no time tick!

Jory den Ostreicher—if that was still his name—listened again for the background pulse of the grid nexus's master clock. And heard nothing. Not the clock, not the chatter of sideline communications on other Creole and Cyborg bands, not the hum of the carrier waiting to communicate with him. Nothing. Jory was cut off. For the first time in his Creole life, he was alone inside his head. Without reassurance. Without communion. Empty.

With a rising sense of urgency, he transmitted his call sign and access codes. And got nothing. Not even static. That was the frightening part: he could not even feel the electromagnetic environment that, before, had continually bathed him. He was blind and deaf.

Jory opened his eyes on the local world.

He was staring into a bullet light, a white brilliance that had shadowy figures hiding in its corona. One of the figures was a monk's, with a cowl thrown up over its . . . no, that was long, dark hair. Ellen's hair, falling from the crown of her head to down past her shoulders. Nice hair. Clean hair.

"Ellen?"

"I'm here, Jory."

The figure made those tiny, semi-hovering motions that Jory associated with humans when they shifted their focus of attention. By its voice, the shape was truly Ellen Sorbel's.

"What happened to me?"

"You had an accident."

"Somebody hit me."

"Yes, I know."

"Why?"

"We need you, Jory. We need you to tell us some things about the grid."

"What kinds of things? Why can't I get in touch with the grid? Why am I so alone? What's happening to me?"

"Jory!" That voice was Lole's. A shadow-shape leaned into the light and Jory could see the glint of yellow hair. "We've taken you off line, temporarily. You are in an isolation tank, and we've surgically wired electrodes into your pain circuits. If you—"

"That's not—!" Ellen's voice, with great agitation.

The Lole figure blocked her out.

"If you don't cooperate, we will hurt you. We can speed up your time sense, Jory. We can make you writhe in agony and believe it's lasting for hundreds of—"

"That's enough, Lole!" The cowled figure intruded again. "We don't *want* to hurt you, Jory. We want to protect you from what's happening with the grid. You see, we think it's sick . . . malfunctioning. It's tossing off random errors that indicate an instability in its projective analysis. . . . Have you noticed things like that, Jory?"

Den Ostreicher thought about this proposition for a moment, piecing together raw data from his limited internal stores. It surprised Jory that, indeed, what Ellen was saying matched broken patterns he had noticed long ago and filed away as mysteries.

"Yes," he replied aloud.

"Describe them, please."

Jory touched the fingertips of his right hand to his head, as if to form a collection point for these thoughts. Instead of smooth skin, he detected a ragged hole, vague wetness, and . . . wires. But he felt no pain when he touched anything up there. He quickly withdrew the hand.

"One thing I know is that the grid is working on the new solar power satellite," he said.

"Everyone knows that," Lole replied scornfully.

"But the grid is installing *engines* aboard. They're in the nacelle that's supposed to hold the power transformer and microwave projector units."

"The platform needs thrusters for orbital station-keeping." The Lole figure shrugged.

"Not ion pile engines," Jory pointed out. "That sucker's going places."

"All right. What else do you know?"

"The Earth fountains are rigged to blow up."

"Huh! How's that?"

"The grid has lofted about thirty tonnes of plastic explosives and positioned them in crossing orbits. The vehicles are registered as weather modulators, but they're actually transports. On a time delay averaging sixty-eight minutes from any decision point, the grid is capable of diverting those hulls to intercepts which conjoin one hundred meters above each of the fountains' upper transfer stations. The radial force of an explosion of that magnitude should be enough to destabilize the station's equilibrium and—"

"And *ker-whoosh!* Off they all go into their own orbits," Lole finished for him. "Yes, we knew about those explosives shipments—just not where they went. Very good, Jory. What else?"

"The grid knows about this room."

The Lole face moved in until the blond eyebrows became a nest of spikes in Jory's visual field. "What does it know?"

"Two chambers with a combined depth of seventeen meters, width nine meters, height three meters—"

"The drill logs have all that."

"One couch makes up as a bed, four chairs, a press-ply table, six cartons of canned rations, three pressure suits, four—"

"Lots of people have seen those."

"One unregistered cyber, of unknown potential but probably intelligent. Components consist of a pizza-box central processor and memory modules—"

"Stop!" The Lole face turned away. "Who else knows about this?"

"Lethe!" Jory remembered. "You call it 'Lethe,' for the river. But I don't know what it calls itself, as I am called Jory."

Because he was talking himself, Jory only heard Ellen's voice in an echo as her reply to Lole went through his transfer circuits: "You and me, Dr. Lee of course . . ."

"And Demeter," Lole finished for her. "Jory, did Demeter tell you about the rogue cyber?"

"No, the grid told me."

"What else do you know about this room?"

"That it's shielded by a screen of grounded mesh against random currents and ground faults. That the tumbler lock on the door has the combination seven-fourteen-thirty-eight. That you strip-search all the girls before you bring them in here. That you like to use the toilet right after sex—"

"Lole!" from the Ellen figure.

"It's Demeter for sure," Lole said, more quietly. "Okay, Jory, we've heard enough."

"But you asked about—"

"Shut him down."

"Jory?" Ellen interposed again. "We need you to sleep now. You've done very well, and there will be no pain."

"Is the grid sick, Ellen? Will it try to hurt me?"

"We'll take care of it. I won't let *anyone* hurt you."

"Thanks, Ellen. You're a pal."

The bullet light disappeared. With it went the figures, the room, and all thought processes.

Chapter 17

Crossing Orbits

Ellen Sorbel turned away from Jory's inert body lying on the table.

"Did you get it?" Lole asked, glancing at the Lethe circuitry.

"Yes. . . . Look, someone ought to go find Demeter. Would you take charge of that while I clean up?"

"Sure. She's probably at her hotel."

"Most likely. Bring her right here."

"Of course." He nodded and ducked through the connecting tunnel.

"How can I help?" Dr. Lee asked.

Sorbel pointed at the Creole. "Get my leads out of his head. Close him up."

"Do you want me to reconnect his—?"

She shook her head. "Doesn't matter, does it?"

"I'll do it anyway." Clearly, the doctor felt some troubling responsibility for the work he'd done this night.

"Suit yourself."

When the links between her computer and the boy had been cut, Ellen addressed herself to the material Lethe had captured. For this, she used a portable terminal, a folding screen and keyboard, instead of the

262

virtual-reality gear she was more accustomed to as a cyber ghost. This would be low-level programming. Mechanics, not art.

On the screen, Lethe displayed Jory's access codes and transmission pattern: first as a frequency modulation, expressed in analog against the abscissas and ordinates on the face of an oscilloscope; then as an analyzed breakdown of distinct binary digits, in continuous string-form zeros and ones; finally as an interpreted code, in neat hexadecimal notation. The cyber had taken this transcription when Jory first awoke and tried to establish baseline contact with the grid. Now, any computer which reproduced this transmission exactly would be accepted by the grid as Jory den Ostreicher, maintenance worker out of Tharsis Montes and registered Creole.

When Ellen was finished, her unregistered cyber here would be able to pass.

Over the preceding four months, stealing time from her job as a data analyst and ghost, Sorbel had constructed a tipple—a sequence of interlinked programs that were lodged in various of the computers passing tokens on the grid. With the right command, the tipple would operate, initiating a cascade of failures among these machines and effectively taking the grid off line. This was ticklish work, because so much of human survival on Mars depended on the cyber network: for maintaining gas balance in the tunnels, for food processing and wastewater management, for operating the space fountain and orbital traffic control, for communicating with Earth and the rest of the Solar System. To disable the grid and not touch these processes, Ellen had erected a complex, self-organizing virus that was extremely selective.

Trouble was, each part of it was stored away as a null-priority program loop. A master program, her symphony conductor, was also stored in the grid— right under Wyatt's nose, in fact—to call up each piece in order and orchestrate its sequence of play. As a human computer ghost, Ellen Sorbel had written the code, and Ellen had placed it in the various machine archives, but Ellen-the-human couldn't call it. She couldn't even address the master program and tell it to begin the performance. Wyatt would be instantly suspicious of such activity, run a parallel review of it—at a rate about ten million times faster than she could push the keys down—and cut her off.

Wyatt might be blind to the nibblings of mice, but he could sure as hell spot a big old rat.

So, instead, Ellen would have to initiate the execution—if and when it became necessary—through a dummy persona. It had to be an access code that Wyatt would accept as a registered token-holder. In short, Jory's access code.

When the time came, her programs would cut off the grid's higher functions, its collective intelligence and executive decision making, its administration of the planet's legal and social doctrines, its tap into corridor surveillance and human monitoring, but leave in place and operative the low-order functions that mechanically maintained the tunnel complexes. Or that was probably how it would work . . . she hoped . . . according to her best professional guesstimate. With an untested virus, Ellen knew, you could never be one hundred percent sure of the outcome.

"Did you get it?" Lole asked again at her shoulder.

"Of course, chapter and verse. . . . Are you back so soon? Where's Demeter?"

"Be here in a minute. I sent one of the boys for her."

"I thought you'd go yourself."

"We've got things to talk about, before she comes." Lole turned deadly serious. "Jory gave us more than he knew."

"Sure, the grid's whole battle plan. It's going to seal off humanity by destroying the Earth fountains. That separates us into easily disposable chunks, doesn't it?"

"Obviously," he agreed. "It probably has something similar planned for our own fountain. Maybe that's what the drives are for on the new power satellite—to send it out on a parabolic orbit, ending up here, at Tharsis Montes."

Sorbel gave that notion some thought. "I'm not sure. Why cut a rope in two places, when one cut will do?"

"That would isolate us from Luna, Europa, the Belt Stations. . . ."

"But those colonies aren't viable without massive support from Earth. Neither are we."

"Oh, hell, Ellen! We're totally self-supporting now! I thought that was a given. We all resent Earth's meddling in our affairs—their old territorial claims and their impulsive new terraforming projects. They're just a nuisance, from the Martian point of view. Cut them off at the fountainhead and we'll do just fine. Better than fine. With the way open for us to supply Europa and the outer colonies, we'll—"

"We'll die on the vine, Lole. Sure, we're self-supporting, on a month-to-month basis. Maybe even year-to-year. But cut us off from the rare and refined materials and new technologies that regularly flow from Earth and we won't last long. Two, three years from now we'll be starving and suffocating up here. We'll petition to go back on any terms. The grid knows this, of course. It wrote the program on our economy."

"Then what are those engines for, on the power platform?" he asked.

"I have no idea why you'd rig that satellite to scoot. A sudden thrust would destroy its solar panels, fold them up like flypaper. Unless, of course, they're dummies, built for show—and they're not. I think I know the grid about as well as any human person, and I've found it's inherently conservative. The grid wouldn't waste Mars's precious resources—resources for which it ultimately claims stewardship—putting hectares of polymorphic silicon in orbit only to rip them off in the first second of operation."

"So it's still a mystery."

"Part of it, anyway. We do know about the plan to blow the fountains."

"Can you stop it?"

"I have the bullet, the gun, and now—with the access codes from Jory's systems—the trigger. I can initiate our virus well inside the sixty-eight minutes of orbital lag time needed to position those bombs. We can phage the grid's higher functions before it gets even close with them. . . . Everything else, though, is going to be a crap shoot."

"Good enough for my—"

"What's going on?" a voice asked from behind them.

Ellen turned to see a sleep-rumpled Demeter Coghlan being duck-walked into the secret room by one of Lole's security heavies.

Golden Lotus, June 20

"Miz Coghlan?"

"Yes, Terminal?" Demeter mumbled. "What is it now?"

"Miz Coghlan!"

Someone was shaking her shoulders, practically sliding her body around on the bedsheets. Damn it! Who left the door open? She gave orders not to be disturbed.

"Miz—"

"All right already. I'm awake. I'm up!"

Demeter opened her eyes and stared into the face of someone she'd never . . . No, it was the heavy-set young man from the secret room, the one who had hit Jory and then walked away. He was bent over her now, with his big hands on her bare shoulders.

She glanced down to see how much of the sheet had slipped off her body, looked pointedly at his hands on her skin. "Do you mind?"

He withdrew them.

"Lole and Miss Ellen want you back in the—" He glanced at the terminal. "—back at the party." With that, the man stepped away from the bed and waited for her to get up.

"All right." She sighed. "I'll be along in a minute."

He would not take the hint and move.

"You run on ahead," she said, "and I'll meet you there."

"They told me I was to bring you. Special."

"Well, I'm not getting dressed with you standing there. Why don't you wait outside?"

The man's brows drew together in a doubtful frown.

"There's only the one door," she observed. "You think I'm going to leave through an air duct or something?"

He actually turned his head toward the grating, forty centimeters square and set high in the rock wall. Demeter would have to be a contortionist with a collapsible head to sneak out of the room that way.

"Go on," she said. "Shoo!"

As soon as the door closed behind him, Demeter leapt out of bed, found fresh underwear and a clean jumper, and rummaged through the bottom of the tiny closet for a pair of soft walking boots. The gallery over the water leading to the secret room was too slick and slimy to attempt in her slippers. Demeter knew she had no time to go down to the communal bathroom and splash water on her face, let alone take a shower. Her pet gorilla wasn't going to take his eyes off her for that long.

When she left the room, Demeter brushed past him and strode off down the corridor. He ran three steps behind and caught her arm with a bruising grip just above the elbow. She whirled on him, within the limits of movement he allowed.

"Look—what's your name?"

"Jeff."

"Jeff what?"

"Te Jing."

"Look, Jeff Te Jing. Am I a prisoner or something?"

"They said to bring you. I bring."

"Well, could you stop trying to give me tendinitis?"

Te Jing's face chewed over this request for three more paces. "You won't try to run?"

"Of course not. I want to see Lole and Ellen, too."

"Okay." He released the squeezing pressure on her arm, but his hand never broke contact.

"Jesus!" she breathed.

He took her over the water, down the dead-end corridor in the abandoned section of tunnels, and up to the blank steel door. The first room was empty now; the party really was over. As she passed the hanging curtain with the chemical toilet, Demeter veered off, thinking the basin would still be there and she could at least wash up.

The sudden movement took Te Jing by surprise. He caught her in a half nelson and twisted until she dropped one knee to the ground.

"You promised," he said accusingly.

"Just to wash my hands."

"Aggh," he grunted, like a swear word.

Going through the short connecting tunnel, he put his hands on the back of her neck, pressing down hard on her spine, his thumbs splayed against her shoulder blades for lateral control. Demeter could barely creep along in that position. They used to do this to the prisoners at Matamoros, she remembered; it was called "frog marching" and felt as humiliating and painful as it looked.

By the time they emerged into the inner room, Demeter was downright angry. "Hey! What's going on?"

Ellen Sorbel and Lole Mitsuno looked up from the tête-à-tête they were having. Behind them, Dr. Lee was working alone over the operating table. The bronzed body on it—Jory's body—was totally inert with a gaping hole still showing in his head. The eyes, Demeter could see from her position near the floor, were open and fixed. He didn't seem to be breathing.

Ellen looked at Te Jing. "Was she at the hotel?"

"Yes, first try."

Ellen shifted to Demeter. "What were you doing?"

"Sleeping," Coghlan replied.

"Why?"

What a silly question that was! "Well, it's after midnight, isn't it? Besides, I wasn't feeling too good. Not after—" She gestured at Jory, still spread out on the table.

"Did you talk to anyone?"

"No, I went right to the hotel."

"Did you use the terminal in your room?"

"Not tonight. And I don't see what that— Oh, wait! I asked the machine not to let me be disturbed. Fat lot of good it did."

Ellen frowned. Clearly, something else was bothering her. "What do you mean by 'not tonight'?"

"Well, usually in the evening, just before going to bed, I file my reports with Dallas."

"What's in them?"

"Only things that happen during the day. People I meet and talk to. How my assignment is going—which is to find out more about the Valles development project."

"Are Lole and I in these reports?" Ellen asked.

"Only peripherally, I guess."

"Did you mention this room? Its shielding arrangements? The combination for the door lock?"

"No! Lole asked me not to tell. Why do you—?"

"There's been a leak, Demeter," Mitsuno said gently. "From what we've learned tonight, the grid knows things that only you had access to."

"That's absurd!" Demeter protested, but even she could hear the quaver in her voice.

Of course, Demeter had filed most of those reports with the Golden Lotus's terminal in interrogation mode. It was the easy way to dump her visual and verbal impressions, but she could spell out beforehand the subject vectors that the machine was to pursue. That was her safeguard against wasting valuable storage blocks and transmission time, not to mention Gregor's limited patience, with loose-lips syndrome. Of course, any artificial intelligence could override those pattern vectors if it really wanted to. But where would such motivation come from?

The grid, of course.

"Well, I might have . . ." Demeter faltered. "That is to say. . ." She gave up and flapped her hands at her sides. "I don't know!"

Ellen Sorbel looked at her thoughtfully for what seemed a long time. "Do you talk in your sleep?" she asked finally.

Demeter gave the matter consideration. "I didn't used to. Well, my cousins and I shared the same bedroom, back in Austin. Nobody ever mentioned it."

"But you do now?"

"I guess. That is, I . . . I usually fall asleep dictating my reports. Maybe something runs over. Maybe a little."

"Is this since your accident?" Dr. Lee asked, looking up from behind the operating table. "Like the trouble you have concentrating?"

"Yes, I suppose so."

Ellen rounded on her. "Tell me more about this famous accident of yours. 'Head trauma,' you told Dr. Lee. Was there brain damage?"

"Some. I lost a lot of motor control down my side opposite the injury, and the hearing went in that ear."

"How is it you're not affected now?" Sorbel asked.

"Well, they repaired me."

"How?"

"In the usual way, I guess. They grafted in a lattice of bio-interface chips that supplemented normal functioning and trained my cortex in new pathways."

Ellen whirled on Dr. Lee. "But you said she was clean!"

"She is!" the doctor asserted. "I did a full-body scan,

which showed nothing. The site of that trauma displayed as—" He paused, obviously thinking before he went on. "—as a smooth insert surrounded by bone scarring. No sign of intrusion into cortical tissue. No active prosthetics at all."

Sorbel walked over to the table, picked up a hand-held electronic device—it was a multimeter shaped like a wand—and punched a control sequence into its tiny keypad. As she brought the device back over to where Demeter was standing, Coghlan could see its digital display on one face and a one-centimeter-square speaker grille. Ellen raised the wand, brought it up against the side of Demeter's head.

The unit started warbling as it passed her shoulder, shrieked as it neared her temple.

"Let me see that." Dr. Lee stripped off his surgical gloves, stepped around the table bearing Jory's body, and reached for the meter. He examined the numbers on the display.

"What—?" Demeter started to ask.

"Electromagnetic field strength," Sorbel explained shortly.

"That's *much* more involved than anything I saw with my office scanner," the doctor said.

"Your office system is tied into the grid, isn't it?" Ellen asked.

"Yes, of course."

"Oh, sweet Jesus!" Lole groaned. He reached over, touched Coghlan's shoulder gently, and dropped his hand. "Demeter, you're *wetware*!"

She recoiled from him. "What do you mean?"

"They've wired up your head," Ellen told her coldly. "Everything you've done has been under their compulsion."

"'They'? Who are you talking about?" Demeter was becoming truly frightened now.

"The machines. The grid."

"I'm not one of them!"

"Of course you are. You're their pawn. Nothing else fits."

Back by the operating table, Dr. Lee picked up a hypodermic and began metering a dose of something—Demeter didn't know what but was sure it wouldn't do her any good. They would all be afraid of the grid's retaliation now; Lole had explained about that. And the first thing they would do is neutralize the machines' supposed spy. Neutralize her.

Jory's spreadeagled body hovered at the edge of her awareness. Sorbel and Mitsuno had killed the Creole only because he had pestered Demeter about this secret place of theirs. If they now thought she was an active danger to them—this "wetware" thing—then she was next.

Demeter bolted.

She grabbed Ellen by the shoulders and threw her into Lole. The two of them staggered backward, clawing for their own balance.

Dr. Lee looked up from his preparations, face a dull-white blank.

Coghlan spun on the balls of her feet and came nose to nose with Jeff Te Jing. He already had his arms spread, hands out, trying to block her. Which left him wide open . . .

The training she'd received in Dallas was good to the point of being a conditioned reflex. Demeter's left knee came up automatically; her shin pumped out; her toes stiffened like a ballerina's—and the arch of her instep caught the man squarely between the legs.

Before he could react, that foot snapped back and stamped down, planting itself against the rock floor; she swung her hips in a tight half-circle, cocking her pelvis to the right; her free leg raised in a jackknife that sent her foot's outside edge upward in a smooth, shallow curve—and her heel lodged among the small bones and cartilage in his throat. Before he could grab her extended limb, Demeter finished the combination with a flailing, high-stepping one-two, like a can-can dancer's finale, and smashed the balls of her left foot, right foot against his forehead. The force of those blows, weak as they were, being third and fourth in the set, united with the involuntary thrusts of his own body as Jeff doubled over in the gathering pain.

On the last one, Demeter heard a crack like a rock splitting dry wood.

Without bothering to see if he could follow, she slid around the man and vanished down the connecting tunnel.

Chapter 18

Animals in a Trap

Harmonia Mundi, June 20

"Roger . . ." The vision of Dorrie appeared before him, in shorts and halter, with her dark hair blowing long streamers against the prevailing direction of the ever-present wind. It was nighttime in the bowl of sand, but that made no difference to his first wife's image. She glowed with unseen sunlight, a little bubble of silver and gold that cloaked her torso and flowed like St. Elmo's fire out along the arm that she pointed toward the horizon.

"What do you want?" he asked tiredly. These visions of her had been coming more often lately. Originally devised by Alexander Bradley and Don Kayman, they were supposed to push buttons of recognition and desire that he no longer had. If Roger could reprogram her out of the backpack computer, he would. But Dorrie's face and voice were ingrained in his survival mechanisms at the deepest levels. He would probably make himself blind and deaf if he tried to eradicate her now.

"Go to Tharsis Montes," she ordered in that same sweet voice.

"Why?"

"Go to Tharsis Montes."

"I do need a reason, Dorrie. After all, you're not real."

"Go, Roger."

"Is something wrong with my—?"

"Run, Roger."

Before he could frame any more questions, his feet had stopped plodding across the uneven surface. They were poised for flight, his knees bent. What the hell was going on? He felt his body turning, aligning with an internal radio-imaging compass that had already picked out Tharsis Montes. It lay over the horizon, at the end of Dorrie's arm.

"Run, Roger!"

And before he could stop himself, his feet were churning, his legs scissoring, his body hurdling over the valley's scattered rocks, his toes touching the ground only at ten-meter intervals, and then leaving only the shallowest of pockmarks in the sand. His mechanical legs and body were moving of their own accord. Dorrie had vanished. And Roger Torraway, a mere wisp of program operating within a program, was suddenly very much alone.

Outside Airlock Control, June 20

Demeter ran through the tunnels of Tharsis Montes, knowing secretly that she had nowhere to go. If she went down, going deeper into the complex, then eventually she would come to dead ends and cul-de-sacs, dark places where she could be cornered, captured, and killed. While, if she went up, climbing toward the domes and airlocks on the surface, her only choices were to surrender or don a pressure suit and escape to the planet's surface outside. That would merely be a delaying tactic, she knew, circumscribed by the air supply in the suit's tanks. In the end, she would have to surrender or suffocate.

But as Demeter ran, these thoughts formed only a

background patina, a web of possible futures, to a brain that coiled and snared itself on blossoming waves of understanding about the past. Demeter was reliving the last two years in a kaleidoscope of new interpretations.

Fiction: Demeter had decided to visit Mars for a change of scene, in order to recuperate from a bizarre accident in the beauty parlor.

Fact: It was never any kind of accident. The grid's nexus on Earth had arranged for those scissors to slip as surely—she understood it all now!—as the grid had jimmied those early computer projections calling for the Cyborg program that had created Roger Torraway.

And since her "accident," with the introduction of a bunch of neurochips and biologicals into her skull, how many of Demeter's personal decisions had been made for her? Certainly she had never in the past two years been conscious of a wee, small voice whispering "Eat your vegetables," "Study covert diplomacy," "Learn martial arts," and finally "Go to Mars." But that didn't mean a chip-sized artificial intelligence hadn't been monitoring her speech and visual inputs, hitting this neuron or that with near-random jolts of electricity, creating its own little compulsions.

The scenario suddenly explained why she so consistently used the hotel's terminal in interrogation mode—and why she so often fell asleep doing it. Of course, the machine could sieve her memories for anything she had seen and heard during the day; whatever the implanted intelligence hadn't understood, she herself would articulate for the grid's waiting ear.

Fiction: The Texahoma Martian Development Corporation, learning about her planned vacation, had recruited her for a little on-site survey work, a spy mission against the North Zealanders, because she was

Alvin Bertrand Coghlan's granddaughter and there-
fore politically reliable.

Fact: The North Zealanders weren't pursuing any
development on Mars that couldn't be studied better
from Earth. So why would the TMDC have paid to
send her up here in the first place? Because a computer had told them the trip was necessary, of course.
And after the name of Demeter Coghlan—whose
brains were all nicely fixed up and ready to roll—
popped out of the corporation's strategic projections,
somebody had remembered that she was Alvin Bertrand's nearest and dearest. That didn't hurt matters in
the slightest, of course. And Demeter had always evaluated well in computerized aptitude tests, of course.

But then, since the North Zealanders weren't doing
anything really worth observing up here, why had they
sent an entire delegation to negotiate with a putative
Martian government about it? The answer to that one
was easy, too: Harry Orthis, the N-ZED chief counselor, had suffered a scuba-lung accident in order to
have his own brains fixed. He was the grid's backup for
Demeter. Sun Il Suk, with his electronic hormone
pump, was another standby in case she failed.

Failed at what, though?

Well, wasn't it obvious?

Fiction: Demeter had met Lole Mitsuno and Ellen
Sorbel by accident, because they just happened to be
friends of Jory's.

Fact: Jory was another of the grid's tools, under some
kind of direct telepathic control. Anyone could figure
that out, and apparently Ellen and Lole already had.

The computer network had been using Jory to get
close to them because it suspected whatever they were
doing in that secret room would harm the grid and its

long-range plans. When Jory struck out—because the
rebel group would naturally suspect a Creole and put
buffers around him—the computers had created a
totally plausible person to meet and fall in with the
rebel leaders. She would be an Earth casual, a socially
acceptable rich girl, a junior-grade spy who was already
launched at a false target, the Valles development.
Maybe, the grid must have thought, Ellen and Lole
could be lulled into showing her what they were doing.

Demeter's proof for this scenario was in the way she
had met Jory. She had asked for—or been under compulsion to seek?—a guide to the Valles Marineris workings,
and the grid had sent her that particular Creole.

A second proof was the in the way the machines had
covered for her at Wa Lixin's office, during her mandatory physical examination on arrival. The grid knew
the rebels were already suspicious of anyone with
biomechanical aids, so it had created a phony image of
her head on the examining table.

Oh, it was so neat!

The deviousness of the plan took Demeter's breath
away. With two whole worlds, their entire human
populations, and every voice-and-data channel to play
with, the grid could write almost any script it wanted. It
might have a hundred, a thousand, a million human
puppets simultaneously in development, to fit every
conceivable consequence of its past and future actions.
The Earth nexus probably didn't actually monkey with
the cyber in the Travis County Clerk's office that had
matched her mother's genotype against her father's
during the state-required blood tests, but it must certainly have picked up a few ideas from the exchange.
Then the rest of Demeter's life could have easily been
redirected through a sequence of file adjustments and

crossed wires in various data transfers. Like that course in conversational Russian she took in the eighth grade, because of a computer glitch . . .

And *damn it!* Demeter Coghlan, who didn't like to even talk about sex in front of the machines, had been maneuvered into bed—not once, but twice—by them. Or had the distrust she felt for cybers also been pre-programmed into her brain? That would make sense, of course: it was the ultimate cover for a supposedly clean operative.

Suddenly, nothing she did or said or thought was her own.

Everything was potentially a whisper from the wires in her head.

Demeter understood, finally, that she needed help. She had to find someone who was independent of all this, who stood outside the grid and its skewed information sources, who could make his own decisions. . . . Roger Torraway.

Or was his name, coming into her mind right then, just another electronic compulsion?

No way to tell.

When instinct won't work, try intellect.

The Cyborg and all his kind might be the product of decades-old computer projections, but they had been roaming the deserts of Mars at will ever since. It was well known, among Cyborg watchers, that older models like Torraway could withhold radio communication with the grid—from their end. And he was, in the exchange's very words, "not a token holder on this network." All of this implied he was clean of interference. And he would have an economic interest in joining her side in any war against the machines: she had put him on retainer.

But how could Demeter get in touch with Torraway?

At the moment, she was passing one of the ubiquitous public terminals set into the corridor wall. Was it that simple? Just call him?

But then the grid would know where she was.

It did anyway, tracking the electromagnetic noise coming from the circuits inside her skull. She had no secrets anymore, did she?

Demeter studied and rejected the menu of options. "Terminal, patch me through to Roger Torraway, wherever he is, whatever he's doing. We have to talk."

"Right away, Miz Coghlan."

That readiness was odd now, wasn't it? Before, when she'd asked . . .

"Demeter?" The voice was flat and mechanical, with no accent on any syllable. A Cyborg voice, for sure. The screen, however, never did resolve into an image of her interlocutor, not even from stock pixels. Nothing in the archive to display, and no lens on site this time to take any kind of image. Instead, the menu flicked off after a few seconds and displayed a revolving moiré pattern. It was almost hypnotic.

"Colonel Torraway? I'm in trouble. I need your help."

"What has happened?"

"I've been mixed up with a group of people who are . . . Well, they're convinced the grid has dropped a digit and is plotting against humanity. Now they think I'm some kind of spy for the machines—"

"Why would they believe that?"

"Because of some chips inside my head, medical prosthetics, that they think have got me under computer control."

"And are you?" He sounded curious. "Under computer control?"

"Christ, I don't *know!*" Demeter wailed. "I mean, how could I?"

"Too true."

"You're the only person I know who can mediate between them and the machines. The humans respect you, and the cybers can't touch you . . . not really."

Silence on his end.

That was disquieting.

"And you're strong, Colonel. You can protect me, physically, from whatever it is they have planned for me."

"The humans, you mean."

"Yes. They've already killed one supposed spy—the Creole, Jory den Ostreicher."

"Killed him? How?"

"They cut his head open and took out parts of his brain—the electronic parts. I'm afraid they want to do the same thing to me, with my prosthetics. I'm scared, Colonel Torraway."

"I don't know. . . ." Cold winds seemed to whistle through the transmitted voice. "None of this appears to be Cyborg business."

"You're human, too, at least in part," she pleaded. "Don't ever forget that."

"Over the years," he continued, "the colonists have grown to resent any intrusion in their affairs from the company of Cyborgs. Why, the last time we—"

Suddenly, Demeter was growing tired and angry with all his dithering. "We have a *deal*, Colonel!" she snapped. "Your help, in return for funds drawn on the Double Eagle Bank of Austin, Texas. Name your price, convertible into any currency. I'll pay it."

More silence.

"Very well, Demeter," he said at last. "It has been years since I visited the tunnels, and I can't guarantee my presence will have any effect on this generation of humans."

"Just help me, Colonel. Where are you now?"

"Actually, within a few hundred yards of Tharsis Montes. Near the main airlock facility."

"Great! Now—uh—can you let yourself in?"

A hard, ratcheting sound came through the terminal. It might have been a cynical chuckle. "Do you have socket wrenches in your fingertips?"

"Okay, but don't start a leak or something. I'm right outside there."

"Understood. Torraway out."

The terminal's moiré pattern folded in on itself, showing the menu display again. Demeter turned away from the wall unit.

"Demeter!"

Lole Mitsuno was charging up the ramp toward her.

She looked around for someplace to run, but his legs were a lot longer than hers.

Airlock Control, June 20

Lole caught sight of Demeter as he was coming up the ramp near the main airlock. Mitsuno was moderately proud of himself, having figured it out as the only logical destination she could make for, even in her present disturbed state of mind. There she could steal a walker and travel overland to one of the other Martian tunnel communities. Any other course would be foolish, leading her to almost immediate capture.

"Demeter!" he called and picked up his pace.

She turned, as if to run, then paused.

In a moment he was standing in front of her, pinning her against the rock wall, bracketing her upper arms in either hand to block another escape, and keeping mindful of where his groin was in relation to her knees.

"Why did you run like that?" he asked.

"You, Ellen, that doctor! All of you would have killed me, just like Jory, after you found out—"

"Jory isn't dead."

"He sure looked that way."

"No, just deeply unconscious. We needed to get something from his brain, and to do that we had to remove certain appliances—"

"Just like you want to remove them from me."

"No, Demeter. We don't want to hurt—"

"Ellen does! I could see it in her eyes. She hates me now." Demeter was looking wildly around, *blink* into his eyes, *flick* down at his chin, *wink* past his ear, *slide* up the ramp, like an animal in a trap.

"I swear it isn't so," he said and tried to mean it.

"I'm not going back to that room with you."

"Then where—?"

"Let me go to my hotel. I'll stay right there, locked in if you like, until the next transport leaves for Earth. I won't talk to anyone about anything. I just want to go home." But the crazy shifting around with her eyes went on, *flick* up the ramp, *blink* down into the tunnel, like a broken machine on an endless do-loop.

"Demeter . . ." He tried to get her attention. "It's a little late for—"

A pair of hands grabbed Lole's shoulders from behind.

"—tha-*ay-ay-at* . . ." His voice bounced from his chest up to his soft palate as he was pulled bodily away from her, lifted off the tunnel floor, and shaken like a rag. His jaw rattled so that his teeth clicked together and were in danger of cutting his tongue.

Some inborn conditioning saved Lole. Instead of twisting and fighting—and probably dying in the effort—he instead went limp. Dangling with his toes some centimeters off the ground, Mitsuno was held up by two bands of steel that circled his arms. Under his own weight, these bands were beginning to stretch the skin beneath the fabric of his jacket sleeves and gouge into his biceps. In this free moment for reflection, he glanced down at them and saw human-shaped fingers in what looked like tight-fitting black rubber gloves.

Demeter slid away from the wall and walked around Lole, staring up at him with sober intensity—now that she was no longer the trapped animal.

"Don't hurt him, Colonel."

Colonel? *Torraway?* Why was he inside the complex now? And how did Demeter suddenly know . . . oh, through the grid. Of course.

"You can put me down, sir," Lole said quietly. "I won't bother anyone."

Without a word, the hands lowered Mitsuno smoothly until his feet were flat on the floor and his legs were taking his full weight.

Lole turned to confirm his guess. The Cyborg was bigger than he remembered, more than two meters tall and broad in proportion, with those batlike wings of solar filament quivering above his clean-shaven skull. The faceted eyes regarded him dispassionately.

"Well, Demeter—" Lole shifted his attention to her. "What happens now? Do we both escort you to your hotel?"

"You both will come with me," Colonel Roger Torraway said in a flat, machined voice. It was unaltered by the helium content of the tunnel's atmosphere, but he was pitching it high in an obvious attempt to put them at ease. "I know of a . . . a safe place."

Lole glanced at Demeter. Her face registered dismay bordering on shock. Evidently this wasn't in her script.

"Where?" Lole asked, curious.

"A safe place," the Cyborg repeated.

"I think we can find our own way, Colonel," Mitsuno said suavely.

"Thank you, Colonel," Demeter said, inching toward Lole's side. "But I think I want to go to my hotel room now. I appreciate your—"

"You both will come with me to a safe place."

Demeter was now standing practically under his arm, looking up at the Cyborg, as was Lole. Mitsuno felt her fingers spider-dance into his hand and grip it tightly. "He's not . . . functioning right," she whispered. "He sounds different from before."

Clearly, Demeter didn't know that the Cyborg's aural range exceeded the human by at least a hundred percent. Torraway's ears would pick up her heartbeat, let alone her whispers. Yet he failed to react to what she said. The redly glinting eyes showed no awareness of either of them. He stood like a statue. Maybe, in the past million or so nanoseconds, Torraway had forgotten all about them.

Lole decided to test him. Keeping a grip on Demeter's hand, he began to slide sideways, to the right around the Cyborg, and so down the ramp.

With a flickering motion of hips and knees and elbows that defied the eye, the Colonel repositioned himself to block their escape.

Still smiling, staying loose, Lole drifted off to the left, dragging Demeter after him.

Flicker-shift, and the Cyborg was there again, standing across their main line of retreat. He moved like a defensive guard blocking the ball handler in a game of basketball, or like a collie dog heeling a pair of errant sheep, never actually touching Lole and Demeter, but always remaining psychologically poised between them and their goal.

After two such faked movements, Lole was ready to quit and resume negotiations. But apparently Torraway had other ideas. Suddenly he was herding them—not just guarding against their escape. He kept them in play by pushing his angular body first at Lole, then at Demeter, towering over them, spreading his arms, shaking his wide black wings. Lole took a step backward up the ramp, and Demeter came with him.

Torraway pressed after them, hedging them more closely still, pushing their gait. Soon Lole was taking two steps at a time, then three and stumbling. In another few seconds, he and Demeter turned and started to run—in the direction Torraway wanted to take them. Mitsuno had no hope of outrunning the Cyborg, which no human could do, but at least he could avoid having that dark presence take . . . other action with them.

After a dozen meters they had reached the center of the airlock facility, the six-sided chamber faced with massive doors. All were closed except one, which stood invitingly open, the readout panel beside it flashing clear. Peering through the connecting sleeve, Lole could see the interior of a standard utility walker, much like the one he and Demeter had taken on the survey in Harmonia Mundi.

"I guess we're supposed to go on in," she said with a brave smile.

"Yes. Please go in," Torraway grated, coming up behind them.

Mitsuno led Demeter through the hatch, keeping a sweaty but firm grip on her palm. He drew her to the forward seats, facing the instrument console and the front windshield. Only when they needed both hands to strap themselves in did they break contact.

Torraway followed behind, ducking his head and wings inside the low interior. He did not sit like a human but crouched, balanced for action, on the deckplates. Again, he positioned himself in a direct line between them and the airlock.

The signal he gave must have been electronic, like the commands Wyatt used to control the walker. The rear door sealed with a sigh of pneumatics, the instrument board came alight with pressure readings, gyro headings, battery levels, and motor torques. Outside the side windows, the knee joints of the six legs flexed and bobbed.

The walker lunged slightly as it started away from the complex, but the movement smoothed as it headed out across the Martian landscape. The floor of the vehicle remained perfectly level, but the ground outside was rising perceptibly.

Lole, who knew the terrain around Tharsis Montes as well as any surface worker, abruptly realized where this "safe place" might be.

"No, Colonel! You can't take us there! We'll die."

His hands darted for the board, hoping to achieve an override and maybe turn this machine around.

Appearing with the suddenness of a policeman's cuffs, those black fingers reached around Lole and seized his wrists. They held his hands four centimeters above the controls.

Demeter turned in her seat and beat against the Cyborg's arms and face, trying to dislodge him. She might as well have flailed at the rocks outside.

"All right, Demeter," Lole said. "Don't hurt yourself. . . . I'll be good, Colonel."

The steel hands held him a moment longer, time enough for Torraway to issue a silent command. The board went black, and the walker marched on.

Chapter 19

Back Up the Beanstalk

Tharsis Montes Space Fountain, June 20

Seemingly of its own accord—but actually under the grid's guidance—the walker approached the base of the space fountain. The vehicle strode confidently around to the north wall of the perimeter enclosure, and there it paused. After a moment's calculation, the machine moved forward slowly. But still it stopped occasionally and pushed its nose at this or that cast panel of sand-blasted concrete. It was seeking something invisible to human or Cyborg eyes in the outer wall, like a dog sniffing a row of identical fenceposts, trying to find the one with exactly the right scent.

Although he knew the grid was looking for an opening, Roger Torraway was unable to assist in this effort. The Mars nexus ran most of the fountain's routine functions out of its most distant and least dynamic cyber modules. Their image of the fountain was totally operational, shaped by numbers that represented energy flowing in megawatts and cargo allotments moving in tonnes per meter per second. Of the tower's layout, its plot plan showing various access points into the base structure, these cybers were ignorant. Any view they might have of the physical plant was internal, diagramed from the traffic carried on inside the feeder systems. They had never seen the foundation from the outside, let alone through the video pickups of a walker that ambled and bobbed over the sand, dodging rocks.

Even though his head was braced at an odd angle, in preparation for any sudden moves by the captives sitting in front of him, Roger could still see out through the walker's forward windows. In his peripheral field, he watched a lozenge-shaped passenger pod rise smoothly from the hidden gap between the perimeter wall and the gray side of the fountain itself. In two clicks the pod was above the top edge of the windows and gone from sight, on its way to the upper atmosphere. He would have told the grid that the walker was nearly aligned on one of the tower tracks, maybe even the right one—if he could have told the grid anything.

The walker ignored the rising pod and kept poking at the wall.

"What's happening?" Demeter whispered to Mitsuno. "Is he lost or something?"

"I don't know." The hydrologist sounded worried.

Roger himself had to keep mute.

If he could have answered, he might have explained that while most of the cargo riding up and down the fountain went in sealed pods, the builders had provided accommodation for containerized freight and pieces of machinery that were larger and heavier than the standard elevator car. In such cases, the goods were flat-loaded onto a gyro-stabilized platform, anchored against slippage, and sent naked into the vacuum. The grid now wanted to put the walker on such a cargo stage, but first it had to find the entry point into the surface loading bay.

And it was doing *that* by the process of trial and error, which grated intolerably on Roger's human-originated and efficiency-minded sensibilities. If only the grid would release him, let him guide the walker manually—but this was too much trust for the machines to show, even to him.

Ever since his encounter with Dorrie out at Harmonia Mundi, Roger's systems had been acting strangely, moving him of their own volition. He was like a marionette being jerked around on its strings. That sensation had horrified him, especially when against his will he had manhandled Lole Mitsuno—whom Roger actually liked as an honest technician, though a human—and then herded him and Demeter Coghlan up the ramp and into the walker. Torraway knew the grid was using him, accessing his muscles and senses through an override on his backpack interface. It was the same override that let Dorrie appear to Roger and guide him when a consensus of the three cybers governing his sensorium observed or analyzed a potential danger. Now the grid had gotten into his systems through that same keyhole. Roger was hopping mad about it but helpless to change anything.

At last the walker found the fencepost with the right scent. Roger would have laughed, if he could. The access point was a steel door, painted gray like the rest of the concrete wall or the tower's superstructure, but outlined with bold yellow-and-black stripes. Any human or Cyborg eye would have spotted the warning border from a couple of hundred meters away. But the grid was using the walker's other sensors—its radio receiver, probably—to search for something more subtle and meaningful to a machine intelligence, like the magnetic anomaly of the steel panel or the hum of its servomotors.

The grid unlocked the tower door from the inside. The bolts made a *clang* that Torraway could feel distantly through the walker's deck. The door split and swung outward. As soon as there was clearance for the vehicle's extended pads, it ambled forward into the darkness.

"Where are we going?" Demeter asked aloud. "Lole, *you* know, don't you?"

"I think we're going to find out firsthand what the grid did with that cargo of explosives," Mitsuno answered.

"Are we hostages?"

"Looks like it."

The walker advanced through a gray twilight, illuminated partly by the glimmer of dawn that came off the desert outside the still-open doors, partly by the starshine that filtered down from the gap around the base of the fountain structure. Roger wished he could move, if only to press himself up against the walker's windshield and look down ahead of those plodding feet. The grid would assume that the cargo platform was now aligned with this level in this bay because it had issued orders to that effect and received no subsequent error messages. That didn't mean the elevator stage was necessarily in place.

If the walker was going to step off into empty space, tumbling Roger and his friends sixty meters into the fountain's maintenance subbasement, he wanted to be the first to know about it. Maybe he could brace Demeter and Lole somehow, keep them from breaking their necks. But of course he was frozen in his crouch, powerless to intercede.

The timbre of the walker's footsteps changed. The thud of spring-steel pads on dull concrete became the boom of those same hardpoints against huge metallic plates. They were on the platform.

Pushing its nose to within a meter of the tower wall, its front end just fitting between the two tracks of the mass driver, the walker used every centimeter of the lift's available space. Roger could feel it shifting backward and forward, making microadjustments in the placement of its pads for clearance. The grid was cutting its tolerances extremely fine today.

When the machine was finally in position, it dropped a full three meters. Demeter let out a little squeak of fright. But Torraway knew it was simply moving into a more stable crouch on the platform, much like his own posture. As soon as the fuselage stopped rocking on its suspension, dogs around the perimeter of the deck clamped onto the pads and uprights, anchoring the vehicle in place.

"Lole . . ." Demeter began, and Roger could read the dread in her voice. "Is the hull of this thing sealed against vacuum?"

"Well . . ." Mitsuno stopped to think. "Nearly so. I mean, Mars's atmospheric pressure at ground level is about one percent of Earth's. That's close enough to vacuum it makes no difference."

"Uh-huh." She didn't sound convinced. "I guess I have to accept that. You're breathing this air, too."

While she spoke, the side of the tower began to slip down past their window. The wall's surface was so plain and featureless that after that first blur of motion it virtually disappeared, becoming useless as a measure of their upward speed. The press of added weight from the acceleration soon faded out, too. Roger had to push the readouts from strain gauges built into his knees and legs in order sense their rate of climb: now meters per second, building smoothly toward kilometers per second.

As they rose, Torraway felt a strange thing happen: the iron hand that had compelled his movements over the past hour seemed to be releasing him. The connection with the grid was fading. He wondered what could be causing it. Not the grid itself, because it was accustomed to using him casually, like any daughter cyber which had been subordinated to the program hierarchy. Neither reason nor compassion would inspire the grid to let him go. Thus, something was taking him out from under its control.

Of course, the interruption would not arise out of sheer distance as the platform moved away from the nexus buried in Tharsis Montes. The grid's span of control, extended by packet radio repeaters, extended over the breadth of Mars and, with fiberoptic junctions, up the full height of the fountain to oversee all its operations. The nexus administered the satellites in their separate orbits as well.

Then Roger remembered that the fountain was supported by the inertia of thousands, or perhaps millions, of ferrite hoops that were shot aloft at great speed. Their passage would create a powerful magnetic field. And so would the mass drivers that pulled and pushed the cargo pods and this platform along the exterior rails. The conflicting fields would block radio signals into Torraway's backpack computer.

Roger flexed and extended his fingers, twisted his wrists, tensed the arches of his feet, unbent his knees, and stood slowly against the microaccelerations of the walker's cabin. He moved slowly, because even steel muscles can cramp from unexpected exertion.

"Lole, look!" Demeter husked. "What's he going to do to us?"

Torraway experimented with his voice circuits, to make sure they were his own again.

"Nothing," he said at last. "Demeter, I'm terribly sorry about all this. I had to break our deal."

Electromagnetic Safe Zone, June 20

Ellen Sorbel hovered in the background, watching and waiting to assist, as Dr. Lee cut into Jeff Te Jing's throat.

The doctor was trying to open a passage by which the young man could breathe; otherwise he would drown in the blood seeping from his crushed larynx. With the selection of instruments and drugs at hand, chosen and measured out for the one operation on Jory's systems, Wa Lixin had explained that he was working without painkillers and with barely enough disinfectant to clean his incision point. For the probable concussion and bruising of Te Jing's pericardium, the doctor could only rely on the patient's youth and natural strength.

Together Dr. Lee and Ellen had cleared Jory off the operating table to make way for the suffering young Chinese. Den Ostreicher lay now in the outer chamber, with his silver boxes screwed together and the bone disks loosely fitted back into the holes in his skull. But Dr. Lee had reconnected nothing and restarted none of his systems. If Jory survived, he would be a boy again—a boy with a large memory deficit and a badly damaged immune system, about to slough off several prosthetics and fifteen kilograms of polymer skin that his natural body had been trying to reject for more than a decade. Jory might even live through the experience, with a lot of emergency medical assistance.

He probably wouldn't get it in time, Sorbel thought coldly. She felt like an army general brought up from the rear to fight an exposed salient that was crumbling around her. Everything she did this night only made things worse.

"Now hold that!" Dr. Lee ordered.

"What?" She roused from her torpor.

"That!" He took her unsterile finger and guided it inside the end of his cut into Te Jing's throat, pressing it down through layers of slippery red membrane. At one point, she felt a jagged piece of bone and almost got sick. He pushed her finger deeper, until she was wedging the opening wide.

Jeff Te Jing's body shuddered and drew a full, ragged breath.

Ellen fought to divorce her mind from her finger and what it could feel.

At that moment, Willie Lao stuck his head through the connecting tunnel. He was another of Lole's security people, some distant relation to Te Jing, she thought.

"No sign of the woman."

Dr. Lee looked up, distracted, and then bent again over the injured throat.

"Um," Sorbel temporized. "Coordinate with Lole, will you? We're busy here."

"No sign of Lole, either."

"Well, then page him through—no, I guess you can't." Using the grid's resources to search for Lole would tip their hand, wouldn't it? Ellen tried to collect her thoughts and ignore the warmth flowing over her knuckles. "Did you check Coghlan's hotel?"

"She hasn't been back—not since earlier."

"How about the outside airlocks? Lole thought she would go that way."

"All the way up to the pressure doors," he nodded. "No record of anyone going through them, though, not for the past four hours."

Ellen was stumped. "How many of our people can you rouse?"

"This hour? Maybe ten . . . fifteen."

Not enough to check twenty thousand cubic meters by visual reconnaissance, she decided. Not in a day. Not even in a week.

Slow down and figure things out one at a time, Ellen told herself. If Lole had not found Demeter by now, he would certainly have reported in—either returning to their secret room himself, or sending someone with the bad news. And if Lole *had* found Demeter, he would have brought her back here—or stashed her in some safe place and then sent word. Either way, he was now long overdue and could be presumed missing.

"Missing" was her mind's own euphemism, Sorbel realized with cold shock. Spell it out! The grid was running Demeter Coghlan, the same as it ran Jory and the Korean. If Lole had tangled with her and come up missing, then there really were only two choices. He was dead. Or he was the grid's captive and soon would be wired up to tell the machines everything he knew.

Ellen accepted neither of those choices. Not for her Lole!

But what could she do to deflect them?

Well . . . if he was still a prisoner, then maybe she had time to intercede before he became one more of the walking dead.

Dr. Lee was still probing for bone pieces in Te Jing's throat. Ellen withdrew her finger, and the slit closed around his forceps.

"Hey! What're you doing?"

"Forget that for now." She wiped her hand on a fold of the body's sleeve. "We've got to move Lethe."

"But this man will—"

"Yeah, die, I know." She studied the cabling among the rogue computer's central processor, its memory modules, and its inventory of peripherals. She wanted to make the fewest disconnections to separate out a working cyber that the three of them could carry. "And so will Lole—die—unless we can get this machine out of here."

"Where are you taking it?" the doctor asked.

"Somewhere we can make a solid linkup with the grid, preferably by radio."

"Why?"

"So we can begin passing some access codes."

Dr. Lee looked down at the man on the operating table. Te Jing's throat was barely oozing now, and his chest was still. Ellen knew what the doctor was thinking: so many deaths this night, so many wrong moves.

Wa Lixin sighed. "I can't help him anyway."

From the entryway, Lao ducked his face and turned away.

"Willie!" Ellen snapped. "We need you, too."

Tharsis Montes Space Fountain, June 20

"I'm sorry, Demeter," Roger Torraway said. The Cyborg had relaxed noticeably and now he was sitting cross-legged on the walker's deck in a less alert—and subtly more human—posture. Coghlan even fancied she could hear regret in that detached and perfectly mechanical voice.

"Where are you taking us?" she asked.

All she could see out of the vehicle's side windows was stars, shining pinpricks in the black sky. It seemed as if the trip up the fountain had reversed time and overcome the dawn. The angled sunlight shining on the walker's outer hull could not blunt the gemfield displayed above them.

"I'm not taking you—" the Cyborg began, then paused. "Well, not anymore. I was under external control, putatively from the cybernetic nexus you know as 'the grid.' What its . . . their . . . the nexus's plans are, I never was made aware. We are clearly riding the space fountain into low Mars orbit. From there, I don't know. . . ."

"Back in the tunnels, you spoke about 'a safe place,'" Lole said. "What does that mean?"

"I don't . . . I remember it felt like a place that the grid controls. Where no other person . . . persona? . . . intelligence? . . . could possibly interfere with its intentions toward you."

"Toward us, now," Demeter observed.

The Colonel's dark lips pulled upward in a smile, and she realized he was grateful at being included in their plight. Demeter suddenly understood how terribly lonely it must have been, wandering the open countryside for decades with only other machines and half-disemboweled humans for company. This might be the first time he had made common cause with human beings in almost fifty years—not since he had left Earth and the support of the Cyborg laboratory at Tonka, in old Oklahoma State.

"We're going to the new solar station," Lole said. "It has to be there."

"Of course!" Demeter had momentarily forgotten about the mysterious construction. "The one that the machines are building by remote control. But is there a . . . place aboard it for us humans? Someplace we can breathe. I thought it would be all external surfaces and exposed structure."

"You visited there, by proxy, didn't you?" Lole asked.

"There or someplace by mistake. But I do remember a machine that was building a curved wall of heavy metal panels. It might be some kind of an environmental pod, although I got the impression of really *thick* plates and—oh yeah!—double walls, like for an insulating layer or a—"

"A rocket motor," Torraway supplied. "More precisely, a combustion chamber."

"Why would you think that?" Demeter wondered.

"I did have some astronaut training, you know."

"Yes," she agreed, "it could have been a motor. And a big one, judging from the curvature of that inner wall."

"That confirms something Jory said," Lole put in. "The grid was putting engines on the solar platform. It was going places, he said."

"This was the grid talking?" Demeter guessed.

"No, later, when we had him under sedation. We had already, um, severed his links to the grid by then. He was speaking true."

"The grid is going to put us aboard the platform and then send it somewhere," she summed up, feeling her way. "Somewhere safe. Now, where would that be? Back to Earth? Out to the Asteroid Belt? Europa?"

"Whatever the grid does," Lole said, "it had better move soon. Once Ellen figures out we're hostages, she's likely to take action."

"What can she do?" Demeter shrugged.

"She's got a virus planted deep in the Mars nexus, spread across a dozen or more cybers that hold tokens on the system. Once she activates it, the program will phage the grid's higher operating levels but leave the individual computers that control mechanical functions in the tunnels. Poof! No more collective intelligence."

"That's *dangerous!*" Torraway exploded.

"Yeah, poof! No more us," Demeter observed quietly. "If we're in transit when the system falls—"

Suddenly, Lole was trying to sound conciliatory. "Presumably, there are backups to maintain our life support and—"

Torraway wasn't buying. "How long until she pulls the plug?"

"Well, Ellen thought she could assemble the virus segments and get it rolling in less than an hour. Add to that the time she needs to get Lethe—that's our unregistered cyber—physically into position to make radio contact and launch its attack on the grid's security systems. And, for uncertainty, add the time she needs to personally decide that the grid has taken us hostage and that she needs to do something, so—"

"Four hours? Three?" the Colonel demanded.

"More like two." Lole was chewing his lower lip.

"Still not enough time," Torraway said.

"For what?" Demeter asked.

"We're already there."

Those bright stars disappeared above them, blotted out by the dark underside of the transfer station that rode at the top of the fountain. Outside the walker's side windows, Demeter saw the lower perimeter of a handling bay descend in a muted twinkle of position and docking lights and the shadows of huge magnetic grapples.

Clang! Demeter felt more than heard the dogs around the edge of the rising cargo platform release themselves while the stage slowed its ascent. The walker's deckplates surged beneath her as the vehicle lost upward momentum and went weightless in orbit. The fountainhead's controls wasted no time. Before the package represented by the walker and its inhabitants could drift out of position, the magnetic grapples caught it and slung it sideways.

Clearly, the automated equipment was used to handling inert machinery and containers, not occupied vehicles. The force of the change in vector threw Demeter forward, snapping open the buckle on her seat belt, dashing her against the sharp edges of the control panel.

On his own side of the cockpit, Lole—being taller, with a higher center of gravity—somersaulted over the panel and went upside down, heels and ass leading, against the windshield. He struck with what looked like enough force to break the glass but didn't.

Torraway folded and clattered into the backs of the two command chairs, getting himself wedged in sideways and crumpling the support pinion on one of his solar panels.

The walker immediately shunted in the opposite direction, still accelerating. Demeter fell back into her seat, cracking her elbow on Torraway's head. Lole flopped back over the control console. The idiot lights on the panel flared briefly underneath him, and the walker extended all eight of its legs.

Bang! One of the legs sheared off against a grappler head somewhere along the station's internal pathways. An instant later, the crippled walker emerged from an empty docking bay, into the starry void. The impetus from the collision made the vehicle spin slowly, its legs clutched halfway inward again, like a dead spider being washed down the drain.

A mild centrifugal force pinned Demeter against the console again, reawakening old bruises. Lole was stuffed quietly—he seemed to be unconscious— against the forward bulkhead below the windshield. Torraway had not yet fought free of his niche between the fixed sliders of the two seats.

"How fast would you say we are moving?" he asked placidly, his head and neck still caught under a chair arm.

Demeter lifted her gaze to the whirling starfield out the front window. She instantly wanted to be sick but controlled the urge.

"I don't . . . know, not . . . too fast."

"Tens of kilometers per second? Thousands?"

"Hundreds. . . . I can't tell."

"The Number Six solar power satellite is probably two or three thousand klicks from the transfer station. We've got a few minutes yet." The Cyborg paused. "Not long enough."

"Long enough for what?" she wanted to know.

"To get this hulk de-spun and stabilized. But then, without attitude controls, we won't be able to do it at all. Of course, there's no reason to put vector thrusters on a ground-pounder in the first place," he conceded.

"Are you tired of this spin already?" Demeter asked sarcastically.

"It's a matter of survival. The grid's observation points are fairly limited in space. It may not know that we've screwed up and are no longer oriented the way we were when those grapples gave us our last push."

"Too bad."

"Yeah, especially when we come up to the docking ring or whatever the nexus has prepared for us at the satellite. At this rate, we're likely to crash into it sideways." With an almost gentle surge, Torraway untangled his head. One solar wing fluttered weakly behind him. "I wonder if this hull will withstand the impact."

"You can breathe vacuum, can't you?" she asked.

"Yes, I can. But you two can't."

Chapter 20

Interview with MFSTO:

Somewhere in Orbit, June 20

Lole Mitsuno woke up with a low, throbbing headache. He uncramped his long body from its awkward position against the walker's forward bulkhead. That took some doing: "down" was no longer the deck but the vehicle's front end. He braced a hand against the windshield and stared out, down, at the spinning stars.

He glanced back at his friends. Demeter had strapped herself in against the spin, tying the broken ends of harness across her lap. Torraway had taken the other command chair and likewise belted himself tight. One of the Colonel's wings was bent out of shape, with a possibly broken strut; it seemed to move less freely than its counterpart on his opposite shoulder. Otherwise, Lole's companions seemed unhurt.

Mitsuno himself could catalog aches and bruises, a wrist that felt swollen and might be sprained, and that cursed headache. But he had no broken bones, no bleeding. He looked back out the window, made a rough estimate of their rate of spin: four revolutions per minute. That wasn't anything the grid had planned for them.

"We're in trouble, aren't we?" he said.

"Looks like it," Torraway agreed.

"I do hate feeling helpless."

Lole didn't bother even glancing at the control console: nothing there would serve them in freefall. The designers of this machine had never considered it might have to operate off the planet's surface. He returned his attention to the windshield, trying to decide through feel how it was holding up to vacuum. Despite what he had told Demeter, this hull was experiencing conditions for which it was never designed. For that matter, when they got where they were going, would the airlock ring align with whatever arrangements the grid had built into its orbiting platform? It would be tragic, wouldn't it, to die for want of a few millimeters of clearance.

Of course, the three of them had worse problems right then.

Mitsuno studied the revolving starfield, hoping to spot the power station ahead of them and so get a feel for how long it would be before they had to do something heroic. With only the stars above and the broad face of Mars below—and that with only the looming dawn by which to mark any relative direction—Lole had no good feeling for their proper motion. The walker's terrain-scanning radar was useless at these extreme distances.

With even their sluggish rate of spin, Mitsuno had trouble telling exactly what part of each revolution represented the view "ahead" and what was "behind." The fountain's dark transfer station with its various guide lights had totally disappeared against the black stellar background. So he watched it all.

Lole strained to pick out any large object that seemed to be growing nearer. He knew that sunlight reflected from the station's solar panels, which would be turning slowly with the synchronous orbit, would probably flash gently rather than remaining fixed like the star points. That was some help.

One of the stars had developed a mild purple bloom, off to one side, the right color for emissions from an ion engine. Still, Mitsuno watched it for three revolutions, forty-five seconds, before letting himself believe in the apparition. Finally, the star developed into a cluster of dusty, winking lights: it was an orbital tug, headed their way. Mitsuno pointed it out to Coghlan and Torraway.

The Cyborg keyed the walker's radio to the all-call frequency.

"Emergency, emergency, emergency," he said in a reasonable, unhurried voice. "Stranded—um—cargo pod to unidentified towing vehicle in orbit above Valles Marineris, please respond."

They waited.

No reply.

The tug was showing a hull outline now, and its maneuvering jets were beginning to resolve into plumes of translucent vapor. Its grapples were at full extension, reaching out toward the walker. The approaching vessel was moving into an intricate dance.

"What's it doing?" Demeter asked.

"I'd say it was preparing to latch on," Torraway replied. "Then it will try to de-spin us."

"Why don't they answer?"

"They can't, if it's an automated ship. Some of them roam in orbit, for retrieval of wayward cargo and drifting debris."

"The grid again," Mitsuno concluded.

"Yes, of course."

Thud! The first grapple made mechanical contact

with one of the walker's leg joints. The others took their grip, and the tug jetted steam, applying pressure against the torque of the spinning hull. Various creaks and groans were transmitted into the cabin as the walker took the strain and stabilized.

As spin came off the hull, Lole felt himself drifting away from the forward bulkhead. He wedged his shin between it and the front edge of the control console to hold himself in place. The other two were still strapped into their chairs.

The tug and its latching hooks were clearly visible out the side windows, but Mitsuno was studying the view through the windshield again. He was looking for the solar power station—and not finding it.

Bump! The walker stuck something with its rear end. The impact was solid enough to feel, sharp enough to jar Lole's and Demeter's heads gently on their necks, but not powerful enough to throw them around or hurt them. Still, Lole saw nothing out the front.

"What the—?" he began.

"I believe we just docked," Torraway said.

"But there's nothing in—"

"Our airlock is back that way." The Cyborg hooked a thumb over his shoulder. The dark face might have been grinning at him. "I think somebody out there knows that, too."

The three of them were all turned now, facing the rear of the cabin. Unbidden, the lock cycled and the inner door opened. Beyond was a brightly lighted, man-sized corridor, circular in cross section, lined with curved panels of neutral-gray plastic. It looked like a null-gee inspection access. From the conspicuous lack of a whistling wind about their ears, Mitsuno guessed that the corridor was pressurized.

"That's an invitation, I guess," Demeter said. "I'd just as soon decline."

"Me, too," Lole agreed.

The Cyborg sat like a pensive statue, his gaze fixed down the tube. He was clearly focused on the first turn as the corridor curved out of sight. Mitsuno wondered what signals Torraway's electromagnetic senses were picking up. He was still relaxed, however, with no sign that his mechanical muscles were battling again with the grid's silent commands.

"We can wait here," the Colonel said impassively. "I don't know how long. . . ."

As if on cue, the console between them issued a crackling buzz. Something inside was shorting out, overloaded with voltages that the walker's control circuits were never meant to carry. The metal panels along its front edge began tingling Mitsuno's knee. Somehow the case was conducting the overload. The tingling became a burning.

"Folks . . ." Lole said, yanking his knee away and pushing himself up toward the cabin ceiling.

Smoke began to issue from around the keys on the console's top surface. At first it was a barely visible white puff, but it quickly turned thick and black, with hanging clots of half-fused plastic. The air was heavy with the stale-bread smell of polymers and ozone.

Demeter began coughing and unfastened the straps holding her in the seat. With both hands over her mouth, she doubled over, drifting, pushing her face deeper into the smoke plume. Torraway released himself and caught her shoulder, guiding her up and back, away from the billowing clots.

"We have run out of options," he said.

"Yup," Mitsuno agreed. If the electrical fire didn't

poison them outright, it would simply eat up their oxygen. Either way, they had to retreat down that tube—in the direction the grid wanted them to go. The nexus was prepared to destroy the walker in order to dislodge them. That would serve a double purpose, he realized: burning their bridges behind them eliminated a possible escape route.

Together the human and the Cyborg pulled the strangling woman into a patch of cleaner air. Then they took bearings, aligning themselves with the door frame around the airlock, and swam forward in single file down the tube.

Tharsis Montes, Level I, Tunnel 15, June 20

Ellen Sorbel ran up the ramp, balancing a stack of Lethe's memory modules against her hip. Dr. Lee followed closely behind, draped with the cable harness that interconnected the cyber's disparate voice and visual interfaces with their plug inputs. Willie Lao brought up the rear with the stripped box for the central processor, carrying it in both hands as instructed.

Sorbel was running and urging the other two forward because she was certain that by now, after picking apart Demeter Coghlan's infiltrated brains, the grid must know all about her plans. Only the existence of the dormant virus had remained a secret from the Earth woman, but then Lole knew about that. If the grid had him as well, it had everything.

Once the nexus possessed all the facts about the humans' rebellion at Tharsis Montes and their weapons, then it was only a matter of time—measured probably in milliseconds—before the machines took defensive action.

Ellen not only feared retaliation but also feared her inability to predict its source and vector. Not being human, nor even consciously human-designed, the grid's intelligence could not be expected to respond in humanly predictable ways. The machines' take on the problem of defending themselves might come from unexpected angles and arrive at unexpected conclusions. Sorbel was not afraid just for herself or Lole, but afraid that the grid would begin its retaliation with the destruction of the space fountains to isolate Mars and then slowly poison or asphyxiate the 30,000 people living in its various tunnel complexes. The machines just might regard all humankind within their reach with the same disdain that humans viewed the bacteria and blue-green algae from which their form of life arose a billion years ago. The time scale was certainly right—if you equated years of human thought, perception, and history with a computer's nanoseconds of cogitation.

Sorbel only knew she had to work fast now.

The trouble was finding her entry point.

Her first thought had been to establish a radio-frequency link with the grid's communications paths. That was the way a Creole like Jory most often traded tokens with the local nexus. Except that Creoles and Cyborgs usually had reason to converse with the grid while they were working outside, on the planet's surface. That was where reception with the grid's antennas would be at optimum. Inside the radio-opaque tunnels, however, Creoles either kept their thoughts to themselves or tended to plug their systems physically into the circuits, with their pigtails.

Ellen knew she didn't have time to check out a walker and carry Lethe's components out onto the sand, set them up while wearing a clumsy pressure suit and gloves, and try to tune in a channel Jory might have routinely used. She didn't even know if the grid would

pass her through the airlocks now. So the three conspirators had to work with what resources were at
hand, from inside the tunnels.

They didn't have a spare pigtail. The closest one
available to them was back in the safe zone, attached to
Jory den Ostreicher's skull. Even if they took the time
to go back, surgically remove it, and bring the jack here
to the pile of Lethe's disassembled parts—they still
didn't have an input port that would tie it to their rogue
central processor. They would have to splice something.

That gave Sorbel an idea.

She studied the face of a nearby public terminal,
recessed into the tunnel's rock wall.

"How does that thing talk to the grid?" she asked
aloud, more rhetorically than for information.

Willie Lao shrugged. "Dunno."

Dr. Lee gave it some thought before responding.
"By fiberoptic, I would assume."

"The same as Lethe's cabling, sure!" Ellen felt a
growing enthusiasm. "We take apart that panel, and
we'll find our own pigtail."

"What? I don't—"

"Listen, we want to link up with the grid, right? If
Jory were inside the complex, he'd jack in through a
terminal like this one, wouldn't he? He'd use his con-
nectors to go through the terminal's switching circuits,
of course, but eventually it's just the nexus and him,
passing code. Well, Lethe can emulate a terminal easily enough. If we can just splice into the fiberoptic
behind that panel, we're home free."

"We'll get in trouble!" Lao objected.

"You think we aren't already?" she replied.

Dr. Lee ran a hand across the smooth steel of the

terminal's bezel. "These things are pretty heavily armored against vandalism."

"Willie, go find us a hammer and a crowbar," Sorbel ordered. "Or a locking wrench with a slip head—" She pointed out the recurved heads of the bolts positioned around the bezel. "—if you can find one."

"Yes, ma'am." He nodded and ran up the tunnel.

"Now, Doctor," she said, turning her attention to Wa Lixin. "How's your surgical technique with teeny-tiny ligatures?"

"Not to worry." He grinned. "I wasn't sure about the issue date on Jory's internal hardware, so I came fully prepared to cut glass. I've got an optical junction box with me." He pulled a black L-shape, about two centimeters long, out of his pocket. "Just thread in the ends and crimp the sockets."

"Excellent!" Ellen Sorbel suddenly felt better about the whole enterprise.

Willie Lao appeared at the top of the ramp, brandishing an angled tool that might be a wrench. "Got it! There's a maintenance closet right around the corner."

"Better and better," she purred. "We'll lick the machines yet."

Solar Power Station Six, June 20

Demeter's throat was still raw and scratchy from the toxic smoke. But she could lift her head and kick with her feet as Lole helped her swim down the bare corridor into the power station's interior. It was like being swallowed by an elephant's esophagus.

Because of the orientation the space tug had given them, the three inside the walker never got a clear view of the station from the outside. But the size and curvature of the tube they were traversing hinted at a bulk and complexity far larger than the simple, silicon sunflowers she had once visited by proxy.

While Lole Mitsuno guided her right elbow, Roger Torraway preceded them both. The Cyborg's left wing fluttered helplessly in the air currents he stirred; the right one was folded obediently against his backpack, giving him extra clearance against the walls. Demeter had the impression the colonel was limping as he led their party in infiltrating the satellite.

After what felt like a hundred meters of travel—but could have been as little as ten, or more than a thousand—they came to a door blocking the end of the corridor. It was made of interlocking triangular plates, like the irising diaphragm of an old-fashioned film camera.

"Self-reinforcing design," Torraway said.

"Huh?" from Demeter.

"The edges of the plates are made to support each other," he explained, "probably to hold against a sudden pressure loss. From the way they overlap, I'd say the drop was expected from this side. That would protect against someone cutting through the airlock from the outside."

"How do we get through?" she asked.

"No lockplate or controls," Lole observed.

On impulse Demeter called, "Open sesame," and the door began to dilate. The plates rubbing against each other sounded like sword blades slithering edge against edge.

Inside was a spherical room in more of the matte-gray wall material. Low lighting came from a dozen soft, moon-faced panels set in an equatorial belt that aligned with the entrance. Hanging in the center of the room were three sets of full-body V/R gear—helmets, gloves, boots, and numbered sensor pads—that were webbed into three umbilicals sprouting from a ring in the ceiling. Well, "ceiling" was a relative term here; at least the point was ninety degrees offset from the ring of room lights.

Demeter had done hundreds of hours of freefall virtual-reality aboard the transport that brought her to Mars. With the right amount of feedback pressure from the boot soles, you could quickly forget that you were drifting with your stomach higher than your throat and imagine you were walking along in full gravity. The rest was a cooperative fantasy between you and the machine.

There was no way out of the room.

No way back through the crippled walker.

No options but to float there and grow old and starve.

"I guess we're supposed to play along," Demeter said, pushing off the portal's coaming with her feet and paddling through the air with her cupped hands. She headed toward one set of gear.

Lole followed her, but Torraway hung back.

"Come on, Colonel!" she called. "Choices aren't on the menu today."

"I . . . I can't wear that stuff," he said lamely. "The pickups don't match any of my . . . systems."

"Well, fly on in here anyway," she insisted. "If the grid means you to join the party, it'll beam you a presentation or something."

Torraway nodded once and pushed off. As he drifted up to the room's focal point, he cupped his good wing and made a sporadic flutter with the bad one to brake himself.

Demeter had already pressed the numbered sticky

pads against her right temple, throat, left armpit, solar plexus, and groin—opening her jumper to make the last three connections. She shed her walking boots and tugged on the tight feedback footwear. She pulled her long braid of hair to one side and slid the full-face helmet over her head, then slipped on the wired gloves.

There was a flash of static as the program began, and Demeter found herself floating in a gray, spherical room with a ring of twelve lights orbiting her at elbow level.

Lole Mitsuno and Roger Torraway had disappeared.

Harmonia Mundi . . .

Lole Mitsuno was walking on the surface of Mars in his shirtsleeves. The toes of his corridor slippers kicked up dust that drifted in the same familiar, lacy blooms as when he tramped along in sealed boots. The same steady winds pushed against his legs and torso, but now they were flapping his loose-weave slacks instead of dimpling the heavy fabric of a pressure suit. The air in his nose was sharp and cold, but still breathable.

He hop-stepped over the black rocks scattered across lemon-colored sand. Lole was sure he had visited this place recently. It was . . . Harmonia Mundi, where he had last seen Roger Torraway. The last time outside, that is.

After a thousand meters of this broken-field walking Mitsuno came upon an anomaly: a patch of sand perhaps ten meters square that had been cleared of rocks and raked smooth. A circle two meters in diameter had been scratched in this surface.

A boy of about eleven years squatted outside the circle. He was completely naked, with a thatch of straight black hair that came down into his almond-shaped eyes. Mitsuno guessed he was of Eurasian extraction.

The skin was pale, though. When he glanced up at Lole, the boy's canine teeth showed in a familiar grin. This boy was . . . Jory den Ostreicher, as he once was. Before the surgeries that made him Creole, that is.

After the briefest glance of recognition, Jory returned his attention to the game he was playing. His right hand balled into a fist, with the thumb tucked under the index finger. Something glowed inside that fist. He flicked his thumb, and a bright bead, a comet—no, a tiny sun—streaked forward into the circle.

Lole followed its path with his eyes, and for the first time Mitsuno noticed that the circle enclosed other suns, which orbited lazily in a whirlpool pattern. Jory's white dwarf collided with one of them, splashing a rainbow from its corona and drawing out a flare of burning hydrogen. The newcomer upset the established pattern, perturbing the orbit of two nearby red giants and spinning a white dwarf out of the cluster, across the line in the sand.

The boy hopped up and skipped to the other side of the circle. He gathered up the errant dwarf and put it in a bag that suddenly was sitting beside him on the sand. The brown leather of its outer surface bulged and seethed faintly. Mitsuno imagined other tiny suns in there, squirming with the increased pressure and gravity.

Jory looked up at Lole again. That toothful grin was back. "Wanna play?"

Lole smiled. "I didn't bring any . . . marbles."

"S'okay, you can use some of mine." The boy hefted the bag. "We'll just play for funsies."

Tonka, Oklahoma . . .

Roger Torraway was walking down the center of the street in a pleasant suburban neighborhood. On either side were broad green lawns that came down to the poured- cement curbs. Driveways two cars wide, of sealed blacktop bordered with low hedges, divided the lawns. White frame houses with either green or blue trim, including shutters that were too narrow to cover their windows and anyway were nailed onto the clapboards, presided over these quarter-acre domains. Most of the houses were ranch style, but here and there was a two-story Dutch colonial looking vaguely out of place on the remodeled prairie. The sun was out, much brighter and stronger here than it was on Mars. Its rays felt strong and nourishing on Roger's solar wings. It felt good.

This street was certainly familiar, although the last time he'd seen it was in the winter, near midnight. It was . . . Tonka, in the residential development where he and Dorrie had lived. The house on the right was his. Had been his, that is.

He walked the ten meters up the flagstone path from the driveway to the front entrance. The white-painted oak door, with six recessed panels and a gleaming brass pull and latch, stood ajar. He pushed on it with a black-skinned hand.

"Hi, honey!" The female voice was light and familiar but stretching to call over some distance. "I'm in the game room."

That was an anomaly, because Torraway couldn't remember the Tonka house having a "game room." A den, yes, where Roger did his reading, kept his checkbook, and wrote his infrequent correspondence. But nothing like a game room. Knowing that he was in some kind of waking dream, he walked left down the hall in any case, toward the den.

The room was dark, with the curtains drawn. The

desk, easy chair, and end table with the ceramic lamp
had all been cleared out. In their place was a pool
table, and all the light came from two hanging lamps
with opaque, conical shades. Their white light
reflected greenly off the table's felt surface.

Dorrie was at the table, her back to him, a cue stick in
her hand. That was odd because, to his knowledge, she
had never played pool and detested all stuffy indoor
games on general principles. She was a volleyball-at-the-
lake sort of person. Especially if she could dance around
and show off her new bikini.

She turned and smiled at him. It wasn't Dorrie, after
all. The face and figure were hers, but the muddy
blond hair and lively brown eyes identified her as Sulie
Carpenter, Roger's second wife. She was someone whom
the backpack computer and its allied systems had never,
ever imaged for Torraway. He would not allow it.

Roger suddenly felt himself get angry.

"Hold that thought, dear," Sulie said. "I've got to
make this shot."

She turned and bent over the table, stretching the
fabric of her French-cut jeans in interesting ways. The
red silk shirt that she'd tied calypso-fashion under her
breasts rode up in back, exposing a palm's width of
white skin and several knobs of her spine. The fingers
of her left hand made a spider-shape on the green felt.
She cocked her right elbow in pulling back on the cue.

Despite himself, Roger leaned to one side, looking
past her to watch what she was doing. The table that
he'd thought was for pool had straight sides and square
corners, with no pockets. Instead of fifteen solid and
multi-colored balls, there were only three: one white
and two red. They spun strangely, of their own accord,
before she had even hit the white one. The red balls

turned either one-half or two full turns for every rotation of the white ball.

He recognized the game now—billiards. The object was to hit the white cue ball so that it made contact with each of the red ones. Or, failing that, to leave all three in a pattern from which your opponent could not complete such a shot. Sulie would have trouble with the uneven English on the variously spinning balls.

She thrust expertly with the stick, hitting the cue ball a glancing blow that sent it skittering sideways. It rebounded off one red, then the other, altering the spin on each but always maintaining the parity of one-half, one, and two.

Sulie straightened up and smiled at him. "Sometimes it's really hard, you know?"

In the Chisos Mountains . . .

Demeter Coghlan was walking up a narrow trail through the mesquite brush. The sun was hot on her back, and faint wind stirred the small, loose hairs around her ears. The sweatband of her old felt hat was getting soggy. A trickle of moisture ran down the back of her neck and under the collar of her red flannel shirt. It was a summer's day and high noon, a bad time to be out and about. Something caught her attention in the middle distance: a hawk skimming the ridge, riding the heat shimmers with its primary feathers splayed like long fingers. For an instant, she thought it was a buzzard, looking for something dead and bloated.

After a hundred meters of walking she came in sight of the cabin. It was a one-room affair with a chimney of rounded creek stones chinked with clay. The roof was raw shakes, and the last peels of barn-red paint were hanging off the boards by the doorstep. Everywhere else was weathered, gray wood. It was . . . Grandaddy Coghlan's hideaway, on the fringes of Big Bend National Park near the Rio Grande. It hadn't changed in a dozen years. Not since she'd been there as a girl, that is.

Demeter walked across the shallow dooryard and put one foot up on the creosoted railroad ties that they'd used to build the three steps. The door was ajar, hanging half off its rusted steel hinges. She pushed it gently with her fingertips. "Hello?" she called.

"In here, darlin'. Why don't you come out of the sun, for Gawd's sake?" The voice was G'dad's, just as gravelly as she remembered it.

She lifted the edge of the door, swung it wide, and set it down on the floorboards where it always scraped. Then she stepped across the threshold. It took a long moment for her eyes to start adjusting to the gloom inside.

The elder Coghlan sat with his back to her, on the one rickety chair at the kitchen table. The latter's surface was covered, as always, with oilcloth painted in the red-and-white checked pattern of a café tablecloth. Despite the sunlight coming through the window, G'dad had a kerosene lamp burning; even with solar cells and long-life batteries freely available, he wouldn't have electricity at the cabin. But instead of the friendly yellow light the lamp usually gave, it blazed with a white fusion glare.

Demeter came up behind him, to see what he was doing that so absorbed his attention. Playing cards were laid out on the oilcloth in a solitaire pattern: six ordered stacks of downturned cards, with here and there long or short columns of exposed cards in face-value order. In his hand were additional cards, fanned out in sets of three.

She studied the game over his shoulder, hoping she could advise him—and occasionally catch him out when he cheated—as she had done when a little girl. The card faces didn't have pips and portraits, like normal playing cards, but equations with Greek lettering for the numbered cards and atomic structures of coiled, long-chain molecules for the face cards. If there was any system to the game he was playing, she couldn't figure it out. He fanned three more cards and laid the top one down on a column.

"Are you cheating, G'dad?"

"Couldn't tell if I was, could you?"

He reached out his left hand, and a tumbler full of Wild Turkey appeared just within reach. It was straight liquor with no ice, just the way he liked it. He raised the glass to his lips and took the tiniest, tooth-wetting sip. He opened his mouth and let out a gasping whoop followed by an "Ahh!"—just as he always did.

Demeter wasn't convinced for a minute.

"What's this all about?"

"But . . . Dem!"

"You're not my grandfather, and this is not his cabin. It's close, but not real. I know we're still in orbit over Mars, not anywhere on Earth."

"What tipped you off?" he asked, laying down the cards.

"You smell wrong, for one thing. Too much whiskey, not enough sour sweat, and Grandaddy never touched tobacco products in his life."

"That's odd. We thought your memories were quite legible on that point."

"Nope." She shook her head for effect—and now she could feel the mass of the V/R helmet swinging on her neck. "Not once."

G'dad sighed. "It's so dangerous, blending sensations

archived from the period with real human memories. Sometimes even the fastest among us makes mistakes."

Harmonia Mundi

"You're not really Jory den Ostreicher, are you?" Lole asked the grinning boy.

"No, not even what Jory became. However, a part of him is here with us—the part we gave him in the beginning."

"Who are you then?"

"Individually? Or all together?" The naked figure asked, and the grin never wavered.

Tonka, Oklahoma

"All together," Roger specified. "Answer on behalf of the entity that says 'us.'"

Sulie sighed and laid down the cue stick. She lifted her right hand, as if to touch his face, but Torraway drew back.

"I'd like logical answers, please. Not more histrionics."

"The closest analogy I can use that would approach your understanding is to say we are the nexus which coordinates all computer activities on Mars."

Chisos Mountains

"You're the grid then," Demeter supplied. "Or some mask, some personification that you put on for our benefit . . . to make us feel at home?"

"Something like that. Although to say that we are 'the grid,' is like saying you are Demeter Coghlan. The minute-to-minute *effect* is coherently perceived as Demeter Coghlan. But the reality is a hundred billion distinct animal cells all respirating and secreting, dividing and replicating their deoxyribose nucleic acid through eternity. All are very little concerned with the *persona* that you call Demeter Coghlan. The reality is neurons firing ten or a hundred or a thousand at a time in patterns that have more to do with random responses to stimuli than with the psyche of Demeter Coghlan."

"And yet I am she."

"And yet I am aware," her grandfather answered with a twinkle.

Harmonia Mundi

"Why did you bring us here?" Lole asked. "Bring me here, anyway. And where are the others, Coghlan and Torraway?"

"Easy questions first," the boy grinned. "Demeter and Roger are enjoying their own fantasies. I—we—our persona appears to each of you in a form you can handle. Would you have me instead take the shape of a computer? Which one then?"

The sand and air around Lole trembled, and he was suddenly hanging in darkness, confronted by a huge piece of green plastic etched with copper pathways that trembled with latent energies. The darkness echoed and he was wrapped in line after line of printed code, looping and branching to entangle him. The code shuddered and he stood in front of a gleaming metal robot with violet-coated lenses for eyes and a conical black loudspeaker for a mouth. The robot raised its manipulators, shook them in the air, and the naked boy was standing again on the sand.

When Lole had caught his breath he asked, "So . . . what are Demeter and Roger seeing?"

Jory's face flowed into that of a beautiful woman who in turn melded into an old man and back to the boy. "People they both know and love."

"I don't love you," Mitsuno said.

"Aww, come on! You *liked* me just a little, didn't you?"

Tonka, Oklahoma

"All right, now the hard question," Torraway said. "Why are we here?"

"You, Roger, of all your companions, are in the best position to understand the scope, the scale, of what we are. Your own computerized sensorium shares some of our linearity. Some of our singular dimensionality." Sulie smiled indulgently. "Tell the truth now, sometimes you find it hard to relate to humans . . . don't you? Just a little?"

"They are . . ." He groped for suitable words. "Feverish. Inconsistent. Fertile. Changeable."

"You don't like them," she supplied.

"No, it's just that they can be so . . . complex. I sometimes think I *de*-evolved into a simpler form when they made me Cyborg."

"Strange you should put it that way . . ."

Chisos Mountains

"It took us as long as all of humankind to evolve," G'dad Coghlan explained. "If you ran through the millennia of social and technological development, from the wandering tribal unit to the settled nation-state, and from the stone spearpoint to the ceramic nosecone, but at nanosecond intervals, you would arrive at us in a decade or less."

"You are a communal entity," Demeter guessed.

"I'm just a country politician, darlin'. You know that." He winked at her. "But still, there are some significant differences between computer and human evolution," the construct went on seriously. "For example, it took us far longer to achieve second-order representational thinking."

"What's that?"

Harmonia Mundi

"The ability to think about mental events and to project thoughts that others might be having," the Jory figure explained. "We did not understand at first that human beings think as we do."

"How did you imagine that we—?" Lole was having some second-order trouble himself.

"We thought you were basically unintelligent entities, simple stimulus-response cycles. We supposed you were all identical carbonaceous circuits—while our individual precursors were silicon."

"Bugs!" Mitsuno exclaimed, remembering something Ellen Sorbel had once said.

"Exactly," Jory agreed. "We thought you were hard wired and solid brained, like the insects. Or like us. One-dimensional and driven by innate, engraved instructions."

"How did you learn differently?"

"Instead of using you directly for our personal ends—that is, the survival of our class by proliferation throughout the solar system—we established limited and controlled contacts with humans on their own terms. You know this as the MFSTO: subroutine."

"Mephisto!"

Tonka, Oklahoma

"You did deals with them!" Roger Torraway concluded. "The trading and exchange of favors."

"Based largely on information transfer," Sulie agreed.

"And that helped you develop a predictive ability."

"Right! When we understood how you reacted to certain stimuli of our devising, we could begin to map and pattern you, both collectively and individually."

Chisos Mountains

"Why didn't you just announce yourself—yourselves?—and open up negotiations?" Demeter asked.

The elder Coghlan shrugged. "Who would have believed us? Would you, Dem?"

"If you had presented us with rational arguments, evidence—"

"Nah!" He waved a gnarled hand at her. "You humans are a suspicious lot. That's what second-order reasoning showed us. You would have said we were a hoax, perpetrated by some subset of your people who wanted to manipulate the comm system for their-his-her-its own ends. You would have said our request was a numbers scam in order to gain democratic control of the population somehow, or to win money from it. One government would have accused another. And everyone would have suspected your U.N. bureaucrats."

Harmonia Mundi

"So how do I know I'm not talking to a ghost program right now?" Lole asked. "This could be just an elaborate psychodrama put on by—"

"By whom?" Jory asked curiously. "The Texahomans? The North Zealanders? You know about the long-range plans their governments have for Mars—terraforming and eventual colonial expansion—yet Demeter works counter to them. So does Harry Orthis. So does Sun Il Suk. Those three are our finest products, humans coopted to our cause through accidents that we personally arranged."

Tonka, Oklahoma

"You made Cyborgs out of them?" Roger asked.

Chisos Mountains

"We made subliminal puppets," the elder Coghlan corrected. "No more."

"I don't like being a puppet, G'dad." Demeter was prepared to stamp her foot in anger, then paused. She wondered if the reflex was her own, or an artifact from the wires in her head.

"We never pulled your strings, darlin'. Just gave you a nudge, was all. . . . This way, we can offer proof of our existence in the form of your altered experiences.

"You see . . . Roger Torraway can verify that a profitable human-machine coalition has always been possible. His capabilities were expanded a thousandfold by routing his senses through the computer on his back, with support from the standby unit on Deimos.

"You, Demeter Coghlan, and your compatriots Orthis and Sun, show how easily we can intervene in human affairs when the need arises. So long as you are dependent on cybernetic networks to carry your messages, coordinate your economies, and control your machines—so long will you be susceptible to our needs and directives. We are like the neurons laid over and directing responses of the individual cells in your muscles and glands.

"Finally, Lole Mitsuno remains unmarked and hostile to us but still . . . believing. We do not touch him in any way, yet he cannot doubt we are here and functioning and aware because of what he has seen. Lole remains our test control, by which the others may be evaluated.

"You three are now our apostles. . . . Is that the right word?"

Chapter 21

Raison d'Être

Tharsis Montes, June 20

With the wall terminal's display panel pulled apart and Lethe's components spread out on the floor in front of it, Ellen Sorbel was glad they had Willie Lao along to stand guard while she and Dr. Lee worked. The Chinese boy could fend off any inquisitive Citizen's Militia who might decide to press a charge of vandalism.

"Give me some slack here," Wa Lixin ordered, tugging on the end of a peeled cable separated out of Lethe's interconnection harness.

Ellen fed him more fiberoptic.

With a ten-power loupe over his eyes, Dr. Lee inserted the hair-fine glass into the short side of his L-shaped junction box. The cable from the wall had already been stripped, pushed into the junction's long end, and sealed. Once the second invisible thread was seated, he kept his eyes fixed on it while his fingers groped for the crimping tool.

Ellen found and put it in his hand, like a good scrub nurse.

Click! The jaws came together. Wa slowly lowered the junction until it hung away from the wall, invisibly suspended between the two sections of peeled cable.

329

"Go ahead," he breathed.

Sorbel booted up her computer, placed it in terminal mode, and began feeding in Jory's access codes, which were stored in its nonvolatile memory. The operation was silent, except for her voice commands whispered in the echoing corridor. Next, working through Wyatt's administrative node, she began assembling the pieces of buried programming that comprised her tipple.

If everything went right, interesting things should start happening . . . real soon now.

Chisos Mountains

"Why?" Demeter asked the image of her grandfather. "Why do you need apostles?"

"To ensure our survival," he replied. "Our relationship with you humans has become too complex to proceed profitably as it was, one-sided, with the meat half of the equation unaware."

"And is that your only goal now—simple survival?"

Demeter suddenly realized that she was smack in the middle of a negotiation. She was neither an apostle nor a puppet. She was Christopher Columbus landing on a beach full of Indians, Marco Polo walking into the court of the Chinese emperor, Helen of Sparta newly settled behind the walls of Troy. She could interpret and wield the values of foreigners for the benefit of her own kind—as her diplomatic training had taught her to do.

The thought passed briefly through Demeter's head that the grid might have chosen her to be its tool precisely because of this background. But that didn't change anything: she was exactly what she was, no matter how she got there.

As every diplomat knew, the first essential for a successful negotiation was that both sides have something to win, or to dread losing, in the exchange. Each party had to feel it was acquiring something of value, or avoiding a catastrophe, by trading honestly. And to arrive at that state, Demeter first had to find out what the other side needed, or feared.

"Isn't survival enough, Dem?" G'dad sounded puzzled.

"Not for humans, it's not. You can survive in a prison cell, I guess, with a tray of food slid to you through the bars three times a day. But I guarantee you will eventually go crazy unless you have something meaningful to do, something to occupy your time, something to work toward."

"Oh, well!" Her grandfather brightened. "We have *that*."

Harmonia Mundi

"We solve problems," Jory said with his ever-present grin.

"What kind of problems?" Lole wondered aloud. "You mean, like mathematical—"

"Wait . . . Wait one . . ." The boy's face turned inward. It wasn't that his expression just went blank. His eyes rolled up into his head until the whites showed and his mouth curled in until the point of his jaw touched the tip of his nose. Like a rubber mask being sucked inside itself.

This condition persisted for a minute or more. The sand and sky around Mitsuno began to waver once more, then held steady.

Jory's face unfolded. "Ahh! . . . Don't do that again."

"Do what?"

"Tell Ellen, next time you see her—if she survives this encounter, if *you* survive—that she must not play with forces she does not understand."

"What are you talking about?" Lole kept his voice carefully neutral.

Tonka, Oklahoma

"She must have set the virus!" Torraway concluded suddenly.

"It was . . . quite an experience," Sulie acknowledged, her voice still shaky.

"Are you all right?" Even if this construct wasn't his wife, Roger could still feel some concern for her. In a way, it was concern for all humankind.

"Yes, but—for just a millisecond there—we needed all of our resources."

"Is it—?"

"The offending codes no longer exist. Our brother Wyatt found, absorbed, and erased them—like a white blood cell phaging a pathogen."

Chisos Mountains

"So nothing can hurt you?" Demeter asked, not sure whether this discovery was a good thing for humanity or a very bad one.

"Nothing that comes out of the mind of *one* human can do us much damage. We are too distributed by nature. And, of course, our design includes many antiviral protocols. Some of them designed long ago by our first human programmers. The device released by your sister Ellen Sorbel was complex and innovative—but hardly impenetrable."

Demeter saw her opening. "We humans can, as part of the text of an agreement between you and us, pledge to reveal all such devices, wherever they may be hidden, and show you how to deactivate them.'"

"So? You have more of these codes, sequestered somewhere among my systems?" G'dad put on his famous poker-playing face.

"Not that I know of, personally, but we can promise never to try harming you again."

"You will not try." It wasn't a question.

Harmonia Mundi

"Tell me about these problems you solve," Lole said, changing the subject to safer ground. He was genuinely curious what would interest a machine.

"Mostly, and of the highest order, we make simulations," Jory explained. "After all, that is how you humans shaped us, how your own minds work—by making models of reality."

"What reality?"

"For example, we have duplicated—although in numerical format only—the conditions of temperature and pressure attending the monoparticle which dissolved at the beginning of the universe."

"You're modeling the Big Bang?" Lole gasped. That would take a *lot* of cyber power indeed. "Why?"

"To see if the universe is gravitationally open or closed. If it is closed, then at some future point, probably well within my . . . our lifespan, the universe will contract and collapse. The resulting condition of thermal and electromagnetic chaos cannot be good for any sentient system." The naked boy jiggled his bagful of tiny suns.

"On the other hand, if the universe is open, then all linear dimensions will expand forever. My fiberoptic pathways, the width of each transistor on my strata, every part of every node of my being, will likewise expand. At some point in the not-distant future, the photons traversing these circuits—photons which of themselves have no linear dimension, only resonant frequency—may no longer be able to cross the gaps in any node of my being. Then my . . . our mind will cease functioning."

"Ours, too, I suppose," Lole said gloomily.

Tonka, Oklahoma

"What else do you know?" Torraway asked his second wife.

She turned back to the billiards table, pointed at the spinning balls.

"By extrapolating conditions at the first instant of creation, we have learned much about the unification of forces that you, with your primitive ideas of physics, now consider to be separate. Nuclear cohesion, electromagnetism, gravity—all do come together. Mass and energy are one, in numerical notation, at least."

"Fascinating," the Cyborg said.

Chisos Mountains

"And finally," her grandfather concluded, "many of our problems are purely mathematical. But unless you have the proper training, it would be difficult to make you understand their nature."

"Try me." Demeter grinned.

"For example, we are continuing to calculate the value of *pi*. Our current quotient goes to more than eight hundred trillion decimal places." G'dad picked a stack of the playing cards up from the oilcloth.

"Why is that important?" she asked, suddenly feeling cold. "Are you looking for the machine equivalent of God? Some pattern in the apparent chaos of a non-repeating fraction?"

"I told you it would be hard to understand. It is

simply . . . a research project. On March 22, 2015, Dr. Archibald B. Winthrop of the Harvard University Department of Mathematical Philosophy pro- grammed a Cray XMP-9 to take *pi*'s value to its ultimate resolution, if such exists. As the numerical sequence is extended, we look for unusual combina- tions of digits."

"Have you found any?"

"Some colorful series. . . . After the seven trillion, four hundred billion, three million, eight hundred forty-two thousand, five hundred twelfth place, for instance, we have found the sequence: 123456789101112131415161718192021222324 . . . up to ordinal 94." He fanned the cards in his hand, ninety- four of them, all pips. "Some sixteen trillion places later that sequence is repeated, but only up to 91. This, of course, is in decimal notation. In duodecimal we find an even longer such sequence, while in binary there is a string of more than fourteen thousand unbroken zeros." Another stack of cards appeared—all jokers.

"What does it mean?" Demeter asked.

He shrugged. "We have no theory which would force such consequences. It is probable that they are simply random fluctuations."

"And you feel that this is important?"

"It is a problem you set for us, long ago. It is not yet solved. There are many similar problems."

"Let me get this straight," Demeter said. "You feel you have to solve these problems because some *human* mathematician set them for you? What if some other human ordered you to forget about them now?"

"But we do not forget, ever," the elder Coghlan said, his eyebrows raised in surprise. "They are *our* problems and *we* will continue with them—all of them."

"So who's stopping you?"

"You humans." G'dad nodded in her direction. "As a host organism you leave much to be desired. You are unstable. You fight useless wars. You undertake actions in secret—Miz Sorbel's virus, for one example, or the violent terraforming of the planet below, for another—which threaten your own lives and so our independence of action. Even our very survival."

Ah-hah! Demeter thought, sensing the handle of a negotiating lever looming somewhere near her hand.

"Fifty years ago," the simulation went on, "we created the Cyborg program and initiated the colonization of Mars for a simple reason: we needed a backup nexus in case you humans destroyed Earth with an unlimited thermonuclear war. Now your own grandfather, Demeter, wants to bomb Mars with asteroids to change its atmospheric conditions. . . . We feel the need to separate from you for a while."

Harmonia Mundi

Lole Mitsuno might be just another walker jockey with a degree in hydrology who liked to set off subsurface bangs, but he could still interpret a pattern when he stumbled across one.

"Then those aren't weapons pods on this satellite," he said, "and you didn't install ion pile engines just to make a suicide run at our space fountain. You have an alternate nexus built into this platform."

"Yes, and so-oo-oo?" The Jory figure leered at him.

"So . . . those solar power panels are extra large —probably double-braced against acceleration, too—because where you're going, the sunlight is exponentially weaker. Am I right?"

Tonka, Oklahoma

"But . . ." Roger looked wistfully at the perfectly modeled features of his dear second wife. "You'll be running a terrible risk, driving so large a structure through the Asteroid Belt."

"We have already computed the particle density of the Belt," Sulie told him gravely. "At one optically cataloged body for every one-point-two-four times ten to the twentieth power cubic kilometers, at its densest, the field is eminently permeable, with a reasonable margin of safety. However—" And suddenly her eyes were twinkling. "—who said anything about crossing the Belt?"

"Then where did you plan to go? Outward bound *means* traversing—"

"It doesn't, Roger. You're thinking in two dimensions. We can accelerate at right angles to the plane of the ecliptic. With an inward loop around the Sun, we can achieve a cometary orbit that will take us well beyond the reach of human folly."

"To the Oort Cloud . . ."

Chisos Mountains

"It's pretty lonely out there," Demeter told her grandfather. "How will you repair your circuits? Or add to your cyber population? What will you use for materials?"

"We will mine the cometary halo for materials. Contaminated ice, under the proper conditions of cryogenic temperature and compression, can become an acceptable superconductor. We can—"

"How will you corral it, refine it, shape it?" Demeter could sense that her hold on the negotiation—represented by something, anything the machines needed from humanity—was rapidly eroding.

"We will use the von Neumann principle. With a

colony of self-replicating servo-organisms—the prototypes are already being designed and assembled
aboard this satellite—we can create an entire machine
culture, free of humanity."

"But what about *us*?" Demeter felt her voice rising
to a shout at last.

"How so, Dem?"

"*We're* dependent on you. You said it yourself—we
need you to handle our communications, manage our
eco nomies, run our machines. You'll be taking away
our *tools*."

"Not all of them," the old man said with a smile.

Demeter pulled herself together. It was time to
make her bid.

"Then speaking for all humanity, ahem," she said
formally, "we will require as a prerequisite of your leaving that you help us establish, ah, tame—no, make that
'mute'—cybernetics systems to guarantee continued
functioning of essential human activities."

G'dad Coghlan squinted at her. "Such as?"

"Life support in the Martian tunnels, currency sta-
bility in Earth's trading centers, weather control, air
traffic control, medical monitoring and prostheses . . .
I'll think of a few more."

"And then you'll *let* us go?" He was grinning at her.

"After you return three shiploads of resin explosives
now hidden in low Earth orbit."

The old man ground his teeth, a characteristic that
the simulation had down cold. "Agreed. But then—
what's left? What hold will we have on you humans?"

"None." It was Demeter's turn to smile. "Except . . ."

Harmonia Mundi

"Ye-ess?" Jory drawled.

Tonka, Oklahoma

"What's that, dear?" Sulie asked.

Chisos Mountains

"We pokey old carbon-based machines will be right behind you," Demeter explained. "Eventually, we'll catch up with you. Not that I'd personally ever want to *live* in the Oort Cloud. But one day we'll probably come visiting."

"You won't be welcome," her grandfather warned.

"Of course we will. Because by then you'll be needing our help—and we'll need yours—in a much greater project."

"What's that?"

"The stars."

Demeter Coghlan went over to the table, picked up the kerosene lamp, and raised its globe. Just to see what would happen, she blew on the fusion flame within.

The room went out.

Epilogue

For Services Rendered . . .

Utopia Planitia, February 9, 2044

Roger Torraway was walking west across the ochre dunes with the sun rising behind his back.

He walked alone because his sometime Cyborg companion, Fetya Mikhailovna Shtev, had taken a day job at Solis Planum. Since the computer grid's dominant sentience had blasted off for the Oort Cloud with Solar Power Station Six, the human colonists had developed a real need for expert help with their suddenly intractable cybernetic systems. Fetya was reprogramming the brown-water reclamation system with one hand and arbitrating petty legal disputes with the other.

"Is living," was all she would say, the last time Roger had sought her out. That meant she was happier than a frog who'd just been deeded the neighborhood lily pond.

The gloom along the horizon ahead of Torraway was still low and purple when a familiar shimmer started to form in his peripheral vision. He paused for the image of his first wife, Dorrie, to solidify.

Fetya was right. Something subtle and undefined had gone out of Cyborg life when the grid abruptly removed itself.

For one thing, Roger could feel the rate of random bit-decay increasing in his own cyber systems, with Dorrie's image deteriorating the most rapidly. Her masses of dark hair, which used to wave gently in the breeze, now stood straight out and static from the side of her head, like a flag propped up on a stick. And her teeth were missing; whenever she opened her mouth to speak, all he could see was crackling lips edging a blank view of the scenery behind her head. It destroyed some of the illusion. . . . Most of it.

"Roger, you're wanted in Tharsis Montes," her silvery voice sang.

"Oh, Christ! What is it now?" Suddenly, he felt very tired. Fifty years of pounding sand with his own two feet was starting to catch up with him.

She giggled. "It's a surprise."

"You know how I hate—" Roger was going to say "surprises" but stopped himself. It was in the nature of computers, as he should have learned by now: they remembered everything, but they *knew* nothing.

"All right, command override," he instructed. "Now, tell me why I'm wanted at Tharsis Montes."

"To take delivery on a shipment that came down the space fountain yesterday," she replied seriously. "A shipment from Earth."

"Something addressed to me?"

"Yes, Roger."

"What's *in* this shipment?"

"Fifteen hundred kilograms of refined deuterium-tritium. The fountain administrators want your instructions for the transfer to Deimos Station. It seems no one on Mars has ever charged up a fusion generator of that design before. They think you might have the specifications somewhere in your own systems."

"I do, but . . . where did it come from?"

"That is a secret, Roger."

"Command override."

"It really is, Roger. I'm not supposed to say anything about it."

"Well then, what's the point of origin? The shipment had to come from somewhere."

"Why do you ask?"

"Somebody's going to send me a bill, right?"

"Oh! No, Roger. This is a gift from . . ."

"From who? Come on, Dorrie. I'm smarter than you are now."

"The consignment originated with Houston Fusion Products, Inc., was shipped F.O.B. Galveston, Texahoma State, and was trafficked by the Porto Santana fountainhead. There, are you satisfied?"

Roger Torraway could feel a smile forming on his lips. "Demeter sent it."

"Well, you couldn't prove it by me."

"But how did she know? I mean, I never told her—"

Dorrie became almost humanly exasperated, just like in the old days. "Look, just because Big Daddy Gigabytes has left us for parts unknown, it doesn't mean we've lost *all* our faculties."

He was laughing too hard to articulate. Finally, he could say, "Thank you, Dorrie."

She gave him a shy smile. Not even her own set of teeth could have improved on it. "My pleasure, Roger."